BETWEEN
THEIR WORLDS

BETWEEN THEIR WORLDS

A NOVEL OF THE NOBLE DEAD

BARB & J. C. HENDEE

A ROC BOOK

ROC

Published by New American Library, a division of
Penguin Group (USA) Inc., 375 Hudson Street,
New York, New York 10014, USA
Penguin Group (Canada), 90 Eglinton Avenue East, Suite 700, Toronto,
Ontario M4P 2Y3, Canada (a division of Pearson Penguin Canada Inc.)
Penguin Books Ltd., 80 Strand, London WC2R 0RL, England
Penguin Ireland, 25 St. Stephen's Green, Dublin 2,
Ireland (a division of Penguin Books Ltd.)
Penguin Group (Australia), 250 Camberwell Road, Camberwell, Victoria 3124,
Australia (a division of Pearson Australia Group Pty. Ltd.)
Penguin Books India Pvt. Ltd., 11 Community Centre, Panchsheel Park,
New Delhi - 110 017, India
Penguin Group (NZ), 67 Apollo Drive, Rosedale, Auckland 0632,
New Zealand (a division of Pearson New Zealand Ltd.)
Penguin Books (South Africa) (Pty.) Ltd., 24 Sturdee Avenue,
Rosebank, Johannesburg 2196, South Africa

Penguin Books Ltd., Registered Offices:
80 Strand, London WC2R 0RL, England

First published by Roc, an imprint of New American Library,
a division of Penguin Group (USA) Inc.

First Printing, January 2012
10 9 8 7 6 5 4 3 2 1

Copyright © Barb and J. C. Hendee, 2012
All rights reserved

 REGISTERED TRADEMARK—MARCA REGISTRADA

LIBRARY OF CONGRESS CATALOGING-IN-PUBLICATION DATA:
Hendee, Barb.
Between their worlds: a novel of the noble dead/Barb & J. C. Hendee.
p.   cm.
ISBN 978-0-451-46435-4
I. Hendee, J. C. II. Title.
PS3608.E525B48   2012
813'.6—dc23   2011031880

Set in Adobe Garamond
Designed by Alissa Amell

Printed in the United States of America

BETWEEN
THEIR WORLDS

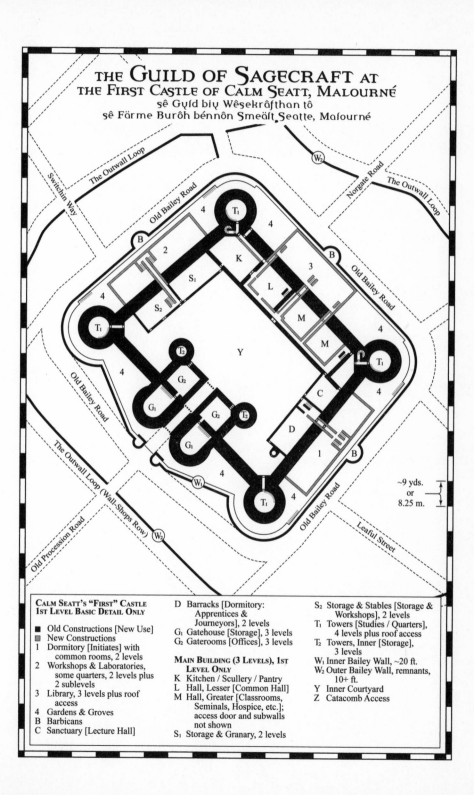

THE GUILD OF SAGECRAFT AT
THE FIRST CASTLE OF CALM SEATT, MALOURNÉ
sê Gŭld biŷ Wêşekrấfthan tô
sê Färme Burôh bénnôn Smeält Seatte, Maſourné

~9 yds.
or
8.25 m.

**CALM SEATT'S "FIRST" CASTLE
1ST LEVEL BASIC DETAIL ONLY**

- ■ Old Constructions [New Use]
- ▨ New Constructions
- 1 Dormitory [Initiates] with common rooms, 2 levels
- 2 Workshops & Laboratories, some quarters, 2 levels plus 2 sublevels
- 3 Library, 3 levels plus roof access
- 4 Gardens & Groves
- B Barbicans
- C Sanctuary [Lecture Hall]

D Barracks [Dormitory: Apprentices & Journeyors], 2 levels
G₁ Gatehouse [Storage], 3 levels
G₂ Gaterooms [Offices], 3 levels

MAIN BUILDING (3 LEVELS), 1ST LEVEL ONLY
K Kitchen / Scullery / Pantry
L Hall, Lesser [Common Hall]
M Hall, Greater [Classrooms, Seminals, Hospice, etc.]; access door and subwalls not shown
S₁ Storage & Granary, 2 levels

S₂ Storage & Stables [Storage & Workshops], 2 levels
T₁ Towers [Studies / Quarters], 4 levels plus roof access
T₂ Towers, Inner [Storage], 3 levels
W₁ Inner Bailey Wall, ~20 ft.
W₂ Outer Bailey Wall, remnants, 10+ ft.
Y Inner Courtyard
Z Catacomb Access

PROLOGUE

Night had settled over the city of Calm Seatt, where a silent figure lay flat atop a darkened, closed shop. Hidden beneath a voluminous, dusky wool cloak with a full hood, his attention was fixed on the mist-hazed, erratic shapes of the city's rooftops. The watcher raised his head and stiffened at a sight in the distance.

A black silhouette dashed down the sharp slope of a shake roof. Upon reaching the eaves, where the lamplight below showed its tunic as forest gray, it leaped, seeming to hang in the air for an instant. It arced across the gap of a narrow street and landed without a sound upon another building's top. As it raced onward, it was not alone.

The watcher spotted other figures here and there across the night landscape of city rooftops. One and then another appeared below on the only street visible from his vantage point. They darted out of cutways and alleys, only to vanish from sight on the street's far side. The watcher's sagging hood turned in the direction where all those figures raced.

Amid a gap in the cityscape sat a bulky and squat four-towered castle shaped like a block with a hollow center for its inner courtyard. When he looked again for those other figures in the night, all were gone but for one. It dashed up an alley parallel to that one visible street. As with the others, the last figure turned out of sight toward the castle.

The watcher rose, towering over the clay and tile chimney behind him.

He would have been nearly a head taller than an average male, should he have been seen among such. When a soft whistle came from somewhere below, it did not startle him. He walked to the roof's edge, crouched, and looked down.

Below, in the alley behind the shop, two cloaked figures raised their hooded heads to him, but the mist's shroud and the alley's shadows hid their faces. Even so, he knew their clothing, which had been chosen to blend in with the local population.

One was clearly male, though not quite as overly tall as the watcher, and wore a tawny brown, hooded cloak, its wool turned fuzzy by age and wear. He carried a long and narrow canvas bundle on his back, lashed over his right shoulder and across his chocolate-colored felt vestment by a length of the bundle's binding cord. A quiver protruded above his right shoulder, its arrows' fletchings made from crow feathers, and in his right hand he carried a strung and readied bow with subtle curves.

The second figure was shorter, less than average in height, and female. A soiled wool skirt of dark green showed below the hem of a faded burgundy cloak. She carried nothing but a shuttered lantern, and the narrow fingers of her gloved hand clutched its handle too tightly. Perhaps she shivered, though there was little chill in the air, and she tried to close her cloak more tightly with her other hand.

The watcher, prepared to drop over the roof's edge, paused and looked up, as if sensing something nearby. He looked back in the direction opposite from where those flitting silhouettes had gone. At first he saw nothing he could pinpoint.

What had seemed a crudely shaped, overly tall smokestack in the distance suddenly shifted position. Another figure moved across that other roof two blocks away, barely visible in the night mist.

It was a puzzle, for this could not be one of the others who had gone ahead. And what had at first looked like a broad tin rain shield atop the false smokestack now appeared to be a wide-brimmed hat, dark in color to match the lone figure's midlength cloak. The figure drifted in the mist and then suddenly dropped, plummeting from sight between the buildings.

The watcher hesitated, uncertain.

Looking back to where the first silhouettes had vanished, he saw no sign of them anymore. They were the ones he had been waiting for, and his attention could not be divided. He dropped over the roof's edge, landing lightly in the alley with no more sound than a boot's toe tapped upon the damp cobble.

"They have found her for us," he whispered, passing his companions without pause. "She has finally reappeared."

Barely glancing both ways as he stepped out of the alley's mouth, he moved quickly across the mainway with his followers close behind. Not a sound rose from his footfalls, though not so for the other two. Though the tall male moved with care, the smaller female's feet clapped carelessly on the street stones in her rush to keep up.

The watcher never paused at their noise. There was no one near enough to hear them, nor to see his face when a street lantern's light briefly touched him.

Dressed in a dark dun cloak, he wore a jerkin that was common and weatherworn. A black wrap of cloth hid the lower half of his face. What skin was visible was darkly tanned, and the lantern's light sparked in his large amber eyes, framed with the creases of age.

The right eye stood out the most.

Four ridges of straight, pale scars streaked at an angle through a feathery eyebrow, then skipped that eye and continued down across his cheekbone. The scars finally disappeared beneath the black face wrap. His right amber eye peered through those scars, like a furnace coal burning through caged bars, and out into the night.

He paused before entering the alley across the way, ushering his companions ahead, and the other male made too much noise in clambering up the back eaves of a shop. The watcher held out a hand to stay the female, who uttered a frustrated sigh as she halted. Then he stared down the mainway called Old Procession Road to where it met the gate of an inner bailey—all that was left after the city had grown in around the old, small castle.

The watcher crossed his arms and slipped his hands up opposing sleeves. When he withdrew them, each hand gripped the hilt of a long, silvery stiletto, pulled from their hidden sheaths.

Brot'ân'duivé—the Dog in the Dark—Greimasg'äh, a Shadow-Gripper and master among the Anmaglâhk, glared intently toward the Guild of Sage-craft. He then slipped into an alley with both blade hilts settled in his hands—but lightly, always softly, for a kill.

CHAPTER 1

Magiere tried to remain expressionless. She sat on a stool, amid her friends and loved ones, in an alcove within a catacomb below Wynn's home—this Guild of Sagecraft in a land far from her own.

The alcove was sparsely furnished, with only a faded oak table and a few stools, but broad archways nearly filled all four of its narrow walls. In one corner stood a tall staff with a leather sheath covering its top.

Magiere barely glanced at her surroundings.

She didn't think of wanting to go home, to her own home, left behind for so long. She wasn't even thinking of Wynn in her long gray sage's robe, still crouched in one alcove archway, or whether Chap—a silver-gray dog like an oversized wolf—had answered the little sage's last question.

"What happened to you . . . all of you . . . in the Wastes?"

Hopefully, Chap hadn't yet answered her. Not that he could've in the brief moment that had just passed. Even using the mental "voice" by which he could speak only to Wynn wouldn't have been enough. Too much had happened for a quick or easy response. But Wynn couldn't know this. She'd simply asked what anyone might after being apart from her friends for a whole year and seeing the changes in them. Now that they were all reunited, it was just like Wynn to blurt out the first thing that popped into her head.

But even this wasn't what plagued Magiere. For as soon as Wynn asked her question, Leesil, Magiere's husband, turned away from everyone and stared blankly into an empty corner of the alcove.

Magiere watched him by the dim light of Wynn's cold lamp upon the little table, its glowing crystal illuminating the books and papers strewn around it. With Leesil's back turned and shoulders hunched, his head sagged forward. The tail of his white-blond hair and the ends of a tattered green scarf tied over the top of his head barely reached past the collar of his hauberk, which was covered with worn and scarred iron rings. He stood there with his back to her, his arms folded across his chest.

Magiere couldn't see his beautiful, half-elven amber eyes. She couldn't see the old scars upon his wrist, from one frightening moment long ago when he had made her feed on him to save her life. And she couldn't see the more recent scars that were now all along his forearms.

Leesil wouldn't look at her.

Right then, Magiere almost did want to go home, to their little Sea Lion Tavern. Given time, he—she—might forget everything. She could have him, just him, and he could have her as he wanted her . . . as his partner and wife, with nothing else between them.

Was that even possible?

Almost one year ago, Magiere, along with Leesil and Chap, had parted from Wynn, leaving her here in the safety of the guild. They'd had to travel north to hide the first orb they'd found half a world away. It was an artifact, a dangerous device of some kind that had served an unknown purpose to the Ancient Enemy in a war waged upon the world a thousand years ago. But in Magiere's time, numerous portents were now hinting that this Enemy would return. She'd been determined to place the orb she'd procured far, far from any harmful hands that might try to use it. But this attempt had brought her more than she'd bargained for . . . including her discovery of a second orb.

Magiere wasn't ready to talk or even think about the horrors that happened on that journey. But after all that occurred, she'd come looking for Wynn. Not just to tell the sage about the second orb, but in the hope that

Wynn might have learned something more about these artifacts, about what was coming. There had to be something in all those old books and scrolls Wynn had forced them to carry off when they'd seized the first orb in a lost castle in the highest peaks of Magiere's own continent.

Chap had safely hidden the two orbs that Magiere had recovered—and only he knew their locations. Yet even this wasn't enough for Magiere. What did the very existence of the orbs mean to the past and the future? Perhaps in all those dusty old books, taken from that icy castle, Wynn might have uncovered something more.

Magiere knew she couldn't go home until she was free of her burdens: to hinder the Ancient Enemy and avert another war, to never allow her dhampir heritage to turn her into a pawn, and to follow her own path. But the path she was on now seemed never ending, and it continued to drag her forward.

The silence in the alcove—Leesil's silence—grew more and more unbearable.

Tonight, Wynn had just told them that in the year they'd been separated, she too had found an orb in some lost dwarven stronghold . . . and then she'd revealed that there were two more still to be found. This news had hit Magiere like a wall falling down. There were five altogether—*five* times the burden Magiere had thought she could be rid of when she'd left her home, again, to hide the first one.

Magiere knew she could not walk away from this, that she and her companions had to find the last two before anyone else. But she closed her eyes in near despair. It was too much to take in—too much for Leesil—and now, after Wynn's question, he wouldn't look at anyone, even his wife.

"Magiere?"

She raised her head, though it wasn't Leesil who'd whispered her name, and she looked to the alcove's nearest archway.

Wynn stood there, one small hand clutching the opening's frame stones. Her cowl was tossed back, exposing soft brown hair hanging to her shoulders around an oval, olive-toned face. Those rich brown eyes of hers were too wide and fixed. Worry strained her features as she looked to Magiere, or maybe it was confusion.

Wynn glanced once toward Leesil.

Magiere didn't follow that gaze. Instead, she noticed Chap watching her. He sat on his haunches beyond Wynn, where the outer passage's deeper shadows made his fur look almost leaden instead of its true silvery blue-gray. The effect made him appear old and worn, but his crystal blue eyes caught the light of the cold lamp's glowing crystal. Chap's eyes burned with twin white sparks, too fierce as he watched Magiere.

Did he want *her* to answer Wynn's question?

"What happened to you . . . all of you . . . in the Wastes?"

No memories rose in Magiere's mind. Over their journey north, that had become Chap's most common way to express his intentions. When there wasn't time for more cumbersome ways for him to communicate, he'd slip into her mind and call up her own memories to try to show her what he wanted to say . . . or command.

Magiere suddenly couldn't take her companions' scrutiny anymore. Perhaps Wynn expected her to say something, and Chap wished her to stay silent. But she couldn't tolerate Leesil ignoring everything, everyone . . . including her. She had to do something to end this lingering moment.

Magiere reached beneath her cloak, toward the small of her back. She gripped something cold and metallic hooked onto her belt, jerked it out, and slammed it on the small table.

Leesil flinched and spun around, but he looked at *it*, not her. Wynn stepped farther into the alcove, her gaze fixed on the object as her large brown eyes filled with more confusion.

Magiere had heard Wynn once call such a thing a *thôrhk*, a word having something to do with the dwarves. It was shaped like a circlet of thick metal—about a fourth of the object was missing—but it had been made that way. Its open ends had knobs or studs that pointed directly across at each other rather than in line with the circlet's curve.

Wynn reached for it, hesitated, and raised her eyes to Magiere.

"What happened to it?" she began. "It looks so . . . "

"It's not mine," Magiere said quietly.

Indeed, the one on the table was made of a ruddy metal, and the one Wynn referred to was something else. Magiere tugged open her hauberk's collar, exposing another open-ended heavy circlet around her neck. But this one was made of a metal so silvery it was almost white.

Wynn's eyes widened, and her mouth hung open as she looked down at the second *thôrhk* on the table.

A flurry of questions filled Wynn's head so fast that the next blotted out the last. She'd always thought Magiere's *thôrhk*, her orb "key" or handle, was the only one. In a deep cavern of severe heat, that object had been given to Magiere by the Chein'âs—the Burning Ones—one of the Úirishg, or five mythical races of the Elements. Yet here was another so different from the first. So worn with age it looked almost ancient, and it wasn't made from the Chein'âs's white metal.

Where had it come from? What did it mean? Did each orb need its own key? If so, why had Magiere's been able to open the orb of Water, if her *thôrhk* wasn't designed specifically for that one?

Or was Magiere's *thôrhk* something special?

In lost Bäalâle Seatt, two of Wynn's other companions, Chane and Ore-Locks, had found the orb—the anchor—of Earth. Somehow they'd beaten a wraith named Sau'ilahk to it, which had seemed impossible, for that spirit form of an undead, a Noble Dead, had gotten ahead of all of them. Ore-Locks and Chane hadn't come back with a *thôrhk*, a key for that orb. If one had been there, perhaps it had been overlooked. Or maybe . . .

Wynn turned chill inside.

Sau'ilahk had gone ahead after the orb. What if he'd found it first? But if its key was missing, was that why he hadn't taken the orb—because he couldn't have used it? Or had Sau'ilahk, that black-robed monster without a face, taken only the key? And if so, why?

Who is this figure in the black robe with cloth-wrapped hands?

Wynn's breath caught as Chap's words erupted in her head in every language she knew. She twisted about, staring at him, and he was on his feet, inching toward her.

"What's wrong?" Leesil asked.

Wynn swallowed hard when she met his hard, worried eyes. Even Magiere sat upright, her old scowl of suspicion returning. Even so, Magiere's pale face was lovely. Her long, black hair with its bloodred tints was tucked back behind her ears. Leesil, however, was still studying Wynn, and he frowned.

"I see," he said. "It's been so long, I forgot that Chap can jabber right into *your* head."

Wynn didn't relax one bit, annoyed at herself for not being more careful. Indeed, she was the only one with whom Chap could truly "talk." She couldn't even begin to wonder how these three had fared without her to give Chap a convenient voice. She eyed Chap sidelong, for his question still hadn't been answered.

Instead, Wynn quickly stilled her thoughts, banishing all images of Sau'ilahk from her mind, for memories of him could lead to those of someone else. . . .

Her more recent traveling companion, Chane, might already be back from escorting Ore-Locks to Dhredze Seatt—back from hiding the orb of Earth in the last great stronghold of the dwarves. Wynn didn't need these three old friends learning of Chane's presence right now. Chane was a physical Noble Dead, a vampire, and Magiere, Leesil, and Chap all hated him, perhaps more than any other undead they'd already finished off.

Wynn needed time to think of a way to explain a great deal, and without Chap overrunning her with questions based on whatever he caught in her errant, rising memories. There were larger issues at stake that needed—

"Journeyer Hygeorht! Why is this *animal* wandering unattended about my archives?"

Wynn shuddered at the sound of Domin Tärpodious's aged and crackling voice echoing through the archives. He must have stumbled upon her dog, Shade, somewhere near his chambers. As she stepped toward the alcove's near archway, Chap's voice rose again in her head.

We cannot be seen down here.

"But why? When——"

"Uh-oh," Leesil whispered.

Wynn's eyes widened. "What did you do?"

Not now. We will discuss our . . . hastened entry later.

Before Wynn could ask Chap what he meant, Magiere snatched up the darker *thôrhk* and tossed Leesil his cloak. She got up too quickly and had to grab the stool before it toppled. Chap hurried by her toward the alcove's far arch, rumbling at Leesil as he passed.

"It was nothing, honestly," Leesil whispered, in his usual feigned innocence. "And completely necessary."

After that, he glanced at Wynn and put a finger across his lips in warning just before Magiere jerked him out the alcove's far side.

"Wynn?" Tärpodious called out, much closer now. "Get this beast under control! And why was the archive door left unlocked?"

Wynn's eyes narrowed, but Leesil was already out of sight when she hissed under her breath, "Leesil, I'll shove those lockpicks where you won't get them until you . . ."

She quickly calmed herself, turning back to the archway.

"Yes, Domin. I'm here," she called out. "I was just busy in the books and didn't notice Shade had wandered off. I'll be right there."

"Well, be quick about it. Premin Sykion is waiting in her office to speak with you."

Wynn slumped against the archway's side. *"Valhachkasej'â!"*

Sykion was the last person she wanted to deal with tonight, but at least she'd stopped old Domin Tärpodious from coming all the way to the alcove. Now . . . she just had to get her friends out of here.

One thing at a time.

Hiding in the back passage, Leesil raised an eyebrow as Wynn uttered his own commonly used elven curse.

"You're a bad influence, as usual," Magiere whispered.

This time, he did look at her.

"Me?" he returned. "You think I'm the influence of concern here?"

There was no humor in his voice this time. After everything that had happened to them, she was the influence that worried him most of all. Since finding that second orb, she'd changed. Yet even after that, they—he—had been so close to putting an end to all this and going home.

It would have taken only Wynn's assuring Magiere that nothing more had been learned—nothing more *could* be learned—about the orbs. Never mind that they'd found another and that Chap had hidden away the pair. Those cursed lumps of stone could stay wherever they lay, forever. But no . . .

Wynn just couldn't shut up, even once, when it mattered most. The sage had nosed her way into something more, something worse, that Magiere would never let go. There would be no dragging Magiere away now.

Without another word, Leesil stepped back into the alcove.

"I don't believe this!" Wynn whispered at him as she gathered up her belongings and the strange staff. "You're here less than a quarter bell in the night, and I'm already in more trouble—and I don't need your help with that."

"Trouble?" Leesil returned. "When did you *ever* need help with that? What have you gotten yourself into this time?"

Wynn straightened, and her mouth gaped.

Leesil immediately regretted his words. Wynn was like a little sister to him. It just wasn't in her nature to sit still for long—or to stay out of anything that caught her attention. If it were, she'd never have joined him, Magiere, and Chap in the first place. Tonight, she'd been so glad, so relieved to see him, and he'd just taken out his long-pent-up frustrations on her.

Moving toward her, he began, "Wynn, I didn't mean to—"

But before he could finish, she suddenly jumped a little, her expression aghast, and she turned on Chap.

"What?" She exhaled at him, and then her voice rose above a whisper. "Don't you take his side. You have no idea what I've—"

"Quiet, all of you," Magiere insisted. "Save it . . . at least until we're out of here."

Everyone went silent at that, even Leesil, though he wondered exactly what Chap had said to the little sage.

Magiere started to glance about, and Leesil followed her attention in puzzlement. She looked around the alcove, through its archways, at the books on the table, and then fixed on Wynn.

"I know you must've been working on those texts," Magiere began quietly. "The ones we hauled out of the Pock Peaks along with the first orb. I need to know anything else you might have learned about the orb—I mean orbs. Or even about these servants of the Ancient Enemy that you mentioned."

Leesil sighed, long and heavy. The last thing he wanted was Wynn pushing Magiere onward in this obsession. Yet on the journey north, even he'd imagined Wynn finally having the chance to live as the scholar that she was, spending her days digging through all those texts. He'd tried to tell himself that they'd done her a favor by leaving her behind.

But Wynn fell strangely still and mute, perhaps growing a little pale as Magiere went on.

"Before we leave," Magiere went on, "grab anything you've uncovered, or any of the texts themselves. I—we were hoping you could help figure out what these orbs are, what they do, especially now that you've told us there are five of them."

Wynn flinched, and to Leesil's surprise, she looked stricken.

"Oh . . . oh, Magiere," she faltered. "No, I don't . . . I was never allowed . . . The texts aren't here. They were taken from me as soon as I arrived."

It was an instant before Leesil realized his mouth had dropped open, and he shut it. It was another instant after hope flooded him that Magiere might at least be slowed down, if not stopped, before he heard Magiere's sharp whisper.

"What?!"

Wynn became frantic in trying to calm Magiere. "I've learned much that you need to know, just the same. Things that might not even be in those texts. I'll tell you everything, though there's more I have to figure out, but right now, we have to get you out of here."

Magiere's expression went dark at the prospect of another delay. Then Chap huffed once in agreement and padded toward the far archway. Wynn sagged a little and turned to follow him, but Leesil didn't move.

He watched Magiere heft her pack a little too roughly and follow the sage and the dog. She was tall for a woman, slender but strong, and wore a scarred and weathered studded-leather hauberk under her cloak and a sheathed falchion on her left hip.

Leesil couldn't take his eyes off her dark hair swinging when she walked. He watched her leave, and he remembered all of the times *she* had tried to stop *him* in some scheme or ploy. He was helpless now in stopping her.

He hefted his own pack and stepped out to follow Wynn's lamp. Its crystal's white light in the dark seemed as cold as those icy wastes he'd left behind.

Chap padded along beside Wynn as the young sage led the way, scurrying along the dark passages. The way was tight and narrow, for every wall was lined with dusty stone and wooden shelves and casements, all filled with books, cases, and other texts.

But even in this silent rush to get out of the archives, Chap could not stop pondering something he had seen inside Wynn.

In the alcove, the barest, fleeting memories had risen into Wynn's conscious thoughts. Foremost was one of a tall, black-robed figure, its face hidden in a deep, sagging black cowl. The image vanished before he could catch more. But since that moment, not a single memory had risen in Wynn's mind.

What was she hiding from him? And how had she learned to do this so well?

Wynn suddenly halted before an overloaded casement along the passage's right wall. She cast a quick, accusing glance at Leesil, who stood back behind Magiere. Then she frowned, dropping her head to look down at Chap.

"Aside from *him* breaking in here," she whispered, cocking her head toward Leesil, "how did all of you manage to get inside to sneak about?"

Chap was lost for words. This was what she now wanted to know?

"It wasn't hard," Leesil whispered.

Wynn balled her free hand into a fist, but Chap cut in before she went at Leesil again.

You are right in that we need to leave. Then he added more pointedly, *But we all have questions . . . and expect answers.*

Wynn took a deep breath, let it out slowly, and nodded. When she turned onward, Chap lapped her small fingers with his tongue. In spite of their being caught in a tense moment, he knew she was relieved to see them all.

Chap felt Wynn's hand drag up over his snout and between his ears, until it came to rest upon his neck. Her little fingers nestled into his fur as he walked beside her. This familiar sensation was something he had not felt in a long, long time, and it did not seem right that the one person in the world he could speak with directly should rejoin him under these circumstances.

Yes, there were questions to be answered. They included whatever foolish notions had gotten into Wynn to make her go roaming about the land after the difficult choice he'd made to secure her here. She should have remained among her own kind, wrapped in the safe haven of humanity.

Then Chap found himself facing an entirely different kind of "meeting." Beyond the passage's end ahead, his daughter stood watching him, without blinking.

He kept on at Wynn's side, halting at the entrance into the cavernous main chamber of the archives. Wooden shelves lined the walls, filled with matching, bound volumes of dark leather among a few cedar-plank sheaves of loose pages. Several tables filled the space, lit by cold lamps hung at the chamber's four corners.

Shade, as Wynn called her, waited before the far stairs that led back upstairs—away from this scholar's maze beneath the guild. At the sight of his daughter, it was Chap who lost all control of his memories.

He had never forgotten, never would forget, what he had done to her.

Several years ago, he'd been spending what he knew would be his last night among the an'Cróan—the elven people of the eastern continent—and he had fled from their one true city, racing back into the forest. At the next dawn, he would have to leave on an elven ship to watch over Magiere and Leesil on their journey to find the first orb.

Because of this, sacrifices were necessary.

His mate, Lily, had waited for him beyond the forest's edge.

She stood among the ferns below the long branches of a redwood . . . a white majay-hì like no other. Her blue, crystalline eyes held flecks of yellow, and from a distance, sunlight blended her irises to a green almost as verdant as new leaves. He ran his muzzle along hers, inhaled her scent laced with fragrances of the wild Elven Territories, and she sent memories . . . visions . . . of the children she would bear. It was the most painful joy of his unnatural life, for he would not be there to see them born. And to one child he would do far worse than that.

Chap had already known that he had to leave; that Magiere and Leesil needed him. But after what he had done when his kin, the Fay, learned that Wynn could hear them, he knew he had to protect her from them, as well. As much as Magiere and Leesil needed him, he had to see to Wynn's safety. Not only as cherished companion, but because even then she was an integral part of what was to come.

He did not spend that last night with Lily trying to forget that he would leave his mate. He tried to remember for her to see all that must be done. Someone else had to be sent to watch over Wynn, for he knew eventually she might be left behind. He gave Lily every memory he held, and in his faltering memory-speak, he begged her for something far worse.

One of their children would be condemned to banishment, or at least that was how a child would think of it.

Only someone akin to himself would have a chance to stand between Wynn and the Fay. A child of his would have to cross a world alone to protect a human. Once Chap had finished making his request, he and Lily lay there through the night. When he left her before dawn, her eyes were still closed, but she could not have been asleep.

But it wasn't until tonight, when Chap came to find Wynn in this place, this old castle somehow given over to the guild, that he truly knew his request had come true.

Any brief relief drowned instantly in the deepest depths of guilt. The charcoal black majay-hì stood before the far stairwell leading out of the catacombs, watching him. And then his daughter turned away without a sound.

"Everyone wait here," Wynn whispered. "When I signal, stay low and hurry across to the stairs."

As she stepped out, passing in front of Chap, he lost sight of Shade. When his sightline cleared, all he saw was the tip of a black tail disappearing into the dark up those darkened, rising steps. Chap stood numbed by pain and regret, barely hearing Wynn's voice coming from somewhere out of sight.

"Um, Domin, I had to leave some stuff on the table in the seventh alcove, so—"

"Yes, yes, I will see to it. Now run along," an aged, cracking voice answered. "But leave the key I gave you. When I retire, I will be certain the archives are properly closed . . . this time."

Chap inched forward, and he peeked around the corner.

Wynn stood off to the right, directly in front of a small archway, with her back to the open chamber. In her left hand she held the staff with its leather-sheathed top tilted slightly out. Her other hand was braced on the opening's right, and the spread of her robe and sleeves somewhat blocked the entrance— so that whoever was inside might not see out.

Her free hand suddenly dropped and swung behind her, repeatedly waving off toward the far stairs.

"I'm sorry," she said to the person in the chamber. "I thought I locked the door behind me when I came down."

A humph rose sharply from beyond Wynn as Chap padded softly across the chamber between its four long tables. He heard Magiere and Leesil creeping along behind him.

"Do you know what the premin wanted to see me about?" Wynn asked.

Chap reached the stairwell and ducked in, but he did not climb up. He waited as Magiere and Leesil slipped past him and up the stairs.

"No," the other voice answered. "I would imagine it has something to do with your latest excursion."

"All right," Wynn answered. "And again, I'm sorry about Shade . . . and the mess."

It was only a breath or two before Wynn appeared around the corner to the upward-curving stairwell. Chap waited for her to lead onward, but she paused, looking up the stairs.

The barest flash of two images passed through Wynn's thoughts. Just as quickly, those surfacing memories vanished. This time Chap caught the second, as well. The first was again that of a tall figure in a black robe and cowl, its cloak appearing to waft under the pull of a night breeze. The second was even more bizarre.

A man in a long cloak with a full hood, wielding a longsword of mottled steel in one hand and a shorter, true sword blade in the other, turned his head. Within his hood, where there should have been a face, Chap saw only a leather mask and black-lensed spectacles with heavy pewter frames where there should have been eyes.

That was all Chap caught before Wynn's memory vanished, and she hurried up the stairs, brushing one hand over his head as she passed. He hesitated a little longer, watching her disappear around the turn in the steps. All notions of memories slipped away as he thought of a young charcoal majay-hì, someone he should have known before yet had only met but moments ago.

That someone would be waiting at the door above when the others arrived.

Chap slunk up the stairs, his head down, thinking of the daughter who had turned away from him. He could not raise his eyes, even when he reached the top and the others were waiting for him in the keep's back passage.

Wynn crept around another corner, always peeking ahead before she led the others onward. Shade remained silent at her side the whole way. Wynn looked back once or twice, checking that everyone was still with her. Now Chap remained at the rear.

Shade never looked back once.

Much as Wynn wished there was something she could do for Chap concerning Shade, a much bigger problem clouded her thoughts and filled her with fear.

It wasn't that she was worried about running into other sages along the way. True enough: visitors shouldn't be found wandering the halls at this time of night. And she, of all people, being their escort, wouldn't count for much. No, even encountering Domin High-Tower or High Premin Sykion didn't worry her.

The only place Wynn could take Chap, Magiere, and Leesil at this time of night might be the last place they should go: her room. And that would also be the first place Chane would wait if he found she and Shade weren't there.

Wynn fervently hoped that Chane hadn't returned yet. Or perhaps had come back early and after waiting all this time, he might have gone on to his own guest quarters.

She led her companions all the way to the keep's front and stopped in the main entryway, holding everyone back again. Her eyes lowered to an unexpected object sitting to one side of the entryway: a small travel chest. Leesil hefted it up and over his left shoulder.

"You left your chest up here?" Wynn asked softly.

He shrugged. "Why not? It was getting heavy. I figured it would be safe among sages. Now, you'll be finding us rooms here, I'd guess."

"Well . . ." Wynn began to answer. "Yes, of course."

Normally, the sages welcomed visitors, especially ones from far off that might offer useful information about the world at large. But how could she explain to Leesil, standing here in the entryway, that she was practically a renegade among her own kind, and anyone with her would be treated with equal suspicion by her superiors. The mood of the whole guild had changed over the past six moons, partly because of her.

There wasn't time to explain it all, let alone all the other questions everyone had.

Wynn glanced left and then right down the long passage running along the front of the keep. Then she stepped forward and cracked open one of the great double doors and peeked out into the courtyard.

It was empty, but this didn't reassure her. She looked left toward the barracks and up to its last window slit at the far end of the top floor. No light shone there, but that didn't mean anything; Chane never minded the dark. At that thought, Wynn grew frantic, looking about the courtyard for anywhere else to go.

There simply wasn't any place to take strangers at this time of night. She couldn't possibly just tell them to leave and come back tomorrow. Could she? The high premin was already waiting for her, and who knew what trouble she was in now. If it was as bad as the last time, she might not get to speak with her long-lost friends for days, and there was far too much catching up to do.

"What's the problem?" Magiere whispered.

Wynn turned her head quickly, straining her tense neck. Magiere was flattened against the passage's nearer side, with Leesil just behind. Chap lingered farther back beyond them. Magiere scowled and settled a hand on the hilt of her falchion. That certainly didn't help Wynn's state of mind.

"It's . . . nothing. Nothing's wrong," she whispered.

Before Wynn could say more, Shade thrust her head through the cracked door and forced it open as she wriggled out. There was nothing Wynn could do but wave the others on as she stepped out, as well. She only hoped she could make them all wait downstairs from the barracks, on whatever pretense, until she checked her room. And if Chane was there . . . then what?

Wynn hurried onward, waving her companions along, though Shade led the way.

"Journeyor Hygeorht."

Wynn was barely halfway to the barracks door when she spun about at the sharp call of her name.

CHAPTER 2

If Wynn thought her panic couldn't get any worse, she was wrong. From out of the northwest building that housed storage, guest quarters, and sublevels of laboratories came five sages, and High Premin Sykion was in the lead. Right behind the tall, willowy, and stern elder of Wynn's order of cathologers came Premin Hawes of Metaology in her midnight blue robe, and Domin High-Tower, Wynn's most direct superior, in gray. Last came two other metaologers that she couldn't place at the moment. The entire group walked straight at her with tense determination on their faces.

Wynn briefly wondered what Sykion had been doing in the northwest building, since she'd been told to go to the high premin's office in the main keep's upper floors.

Shade wheeled and rounded in front of Wynn as Magiere and Chap halted at the approaching entourage of sages. Leesil watched them, as well, as he stepped closer to Wynn.

"What's going on?" he asked in a hushed voice.

"Shush!" she answered, glancing anxiously at Magiere. "Let me do the talking."

High Premin Sykion stopped four paces off, not even looking at the night visitors with Wynn.

"What were these people doing in the catacombs?" she demanded. "And why did you violate another rule by letting outsiders into our archives?"

Wynn blinked, thrown by the sudden question, and a hollow formed in the pit of her stomach. How had the premin learned so quickly about trespassers? Even Domin Tärpodious hadn't known and only chastised her for leaving the archive unlocked—which she hadn't. That was Leesil's doing. Wynn almost blurted out that she hadn't let them in, but the truth would do no good for her friends.

Lady Tärtgyth Sykion, once a minor noble of nearby Faunier, was aging and slender but tall and straight. A single braid of her long, silver-gray hair hung out the side of her cowl and down the front of her pristine gray cathologer's robe. She always maintained a temperate and motherly veneer to obscure whatever she truly thought, but she'd long since given up that maternal pretense in dealing with Wynn.

"And you can skip your usual denials," Domin High-Tower added to Sykion's demand.

As the only dwarf in any branch of the guild, he stood out. Tall enough to look Wynn in the eyes, he was an intimidating hulk, stout and double-wide under his gray cathologer's robe. Coarse, gray-laced reddish hair hung barely past his shoulders, the color matching his thick beard with its small end braid. His broad, rough features made his people's black-pupiled eyes look like iron pellets embedded in pale, flesh-colored granite.

Considering how good-natured dwarves generally tended to be, an angry or resentful one was something to worry about. High-Tower's warning troubled Wynn even more. How much did her superiors know about what was happening here? And *how* did they know?

Shade backed toward Wynn but remained between her and Sykion. That, too, wasn't a good sign. Worse again, Wynn heard Magiere's slow, hissing breath and took a furtive glance.

Magiere eyed only High-Tower. Chap let out a brief rumble, but his gaze wandered over the entire entourage, one by one. Suddenly, Leesil stepped out with a lighthearted smile.

Wynn tried to grab him, but she stumbled over Shade's rump before she could get a grip. Leesil, balancing the travel chest on his shoulder with his left hand, held out his right hand to Sykion and spoke in Belaskian.

"Forgive our rudeness. I don't think we've met."

He probably assumed most sages would understand him, which they wouldn't. That language was almost unknown on this side of the world, and only those sages traveling to the Farlands would work to learn it.

Wynn's stomach knotted, for she knew what Leesil was doing. More than likely, he didn't care about the actual words. He was just using disarming charm in playing the ignorant foreigner.

It wasn't going to work, and Sykion ignored his extended hand.

Wynn knew something was very wrong here. Outsiders weren't allowed in the archives without special prior arrangements, but visitors were never treated with this kind of open hostility.

All five sages looked Leesil up and down, from his slightly slanted amber eyes, white-blond hair, and tan face, to his battered leather hauberk with some of its rings badly scarred, the strange winged punching blades strapped to his thighs, and his cracked and worn calf-high boots.

Wynn could only guess what he looked like to them—some outcast elven mercenary, if they didn't catch that he was only half-elven. As the sages assessed him, Wynn took stock of the two others flanking Premin Hawes.

Both were metaologers, and both men in their early twenties, so likely journeyors. Positioning and demeanor made them look more like bodyguards. Wynn knew firsthand that the premin of metaology didn't need protection, but then she recognized one of the journeyors.

The one on the left . . . what was his name? Dorian?

He was wide shouldered, with dark, straight hair, and Wynn hadn't seen him around the keep since before she'd first left for the Farlands with Domin Tilswith. He'd been a third-year apprentice back then, and likely he'd been off on his first journeyor's assignment while she was away. But when journeyors returned, it was either for a new assignment or to attempt the arduous petition process to achieve master status. Later, should an official position open up, one might achieve the official rank of domin.

Here were two journeyor metaologers at the same time, neither one tucked away preparing for petition and examinations or a new assignment. It didn't make sense, and Wynn turned her eyes on Premin Hawes.

Frideswida Hawes was late middle–aged, judging by her short-cropped hair, which was as fully grayed as dull silver. But her narrow features were smooth, from her cold hazel eyes down to the clean, tapered jaw that ended in a slightly pointed chin. Her expression rarely betrayed mood or thought, only calculating awareness.

Right now, Wynn definitely thought Premin Hawes looked . . . tense.

She pushed all of this aside. She needed to get her friends out of the courtyard to someplace where they could speak alone. And then she'd have to face whatever Sykion wanted from her.

"Premin," Wynn began, as deferentially as she could. "These are friends of mine from the Farlands. They don't know our ways or—"

"Go to your room immediately," Sykion cut in, and she turned to Leesil, though her words were still for Wynn. "Tell them to leave. Now."

Wynn's mouth fell open.

"Then Wynn leaves with us," Magiere said, her voice barely shy of a growl.

At that, Leesil's head swiveled toward Magiere with worry plain on his face.

Magiere's foreign accent was heavy, but her Numanese was good enough to catch all five sages' attention.

"Out!" High-Tower barked at her, taking a pounding step and pointing toward the gatehouse tunnel. "You do not tell us how things will be!"

And the realization hit Wynn that Sykion and High-Tower must know exactly who these visitors were. Wynn had written extensively of Magiere, Leesil, and Chap in her journals, which Sykion and High-Tower had once taken from her. This was all escalating too quickly, and by Magiere's reaction, it was going to turn ugly.

Sykion dropped a slender hand to her side and snapped her narrow fingers, and Dorian quick-stepped straight toward Wynn.

Shade growled at him, but he ignored the dog. The instant the journeyor raised a hand toward Wynn's shoulder, Shade clacked her teeth at him. Still, Dorian's hand came down on Wynn's shoulder.

Chap lunged three quick steps, baring his teeth.

Magiere gripped her falchion's hilt. "Get your hand off her!"

Leesil rushed into Magiere's way, but she pressed forward against him, almost driving him off his feet as he struggled with the chest.

"No!" Wynn shouted, and shifted in front of Dorian to block Shade. "It's all right."

Even with her friends in such trouble, Wynn couldn't risk being thrown out of the guild. The archives were her only resource for information regarding the remaining two orbs. If her friends were driven out, at least they would be nearby somewhere.

Wynn looked to Chap and slowly shook her head.

He was silent, as opposed to Shade's continued growls, but his voice didn't rise in Wynn's head. He kept eyeing Dorian, his jowls quivering, but his gaze flicked more than once toward Sykion . . . and then fixed on Hawes.

Leesil appeared even more hesitant, still holding Magiere back, but even his expression had gone flat as he scanned the courtyard and all within it. Magiere's state was always plain to read, but there was no telling what scheme Leesil was concocting even now.

"Chap!" Wynn whispered in desperation, turning all of her attention upon him.

She tried to pull a memory to the forefront of her mind, hoping he would catch it. She pictured all of those shelves of old texts she had searched through in the guild's archives. She pictured the open books, bound sheaves, papers, and her journals as she sat in alcoves late into the night amid her search. And lastly, she pictured the first orb they had all found together, not knowing what it truly was as they prepared to leave the ice-bound castle hidden in the heights of the Pock Peaks.

Chap's tall ears pricked up.

Hopefully, he understood she had to stay where she was. But as Wynn dropped her eyes to look at Shade, she realized the dog had gone silent.

Shade looked up, and another memory rose in Wynn's mind.

Wynn saw in her mind Chane's blacked-out scroll unrolled before her. It was from a memory of when she had once sat upon the cold stone floor of her room, trying to figure out what had been blotted out on that restored parchment.

Blind fear swept through Wynn.

She squelched the memory before it led to one of Chane, and when she looked at Chap again, he was still watching her. Had he seen the scroll in the memory Shade had recalled? Shade fully understood what was necessary. But had Chap caught anything more that Wynn had let slip into her thoughts?

All that mattered was that Wynn remained here. The archives were her only hope for figuring out whatever was left to find in that scroll. After all, no matter what happened here, she was in no danger from her own superiors.

But where was Chane?

Chane Andraso stood in the darkness of Wynn's room, watching the courtyard below through the one narrow window. He had only just returned from Dhredze Seatt, the stronghold of the dwarves on the peninsula across the bay. The orb that he and Wynn had found was now safe with Ore-Locks, taken into the depths of the dwarven underworld in the care of Stonewalkers. Having found Wynn's room empty, Chane knew Shade must be with her. With that little comfort, he had decided to await their return.

It was getting late now, and as his patience waned, his worry grew. Then, standing at the window, he spotted Wynn and Shade suddenly emerge from the keep doors. At the sight of them, his worry drained, replaced by relief.

But then he clutched the window's deep ledge; his hardening fingernails grated upon its stone.

Following Wynn out the doors were Magiere, Leesil, and Chap.

His initial shock faded, replaced by hate-fueled hunger, all of it fixed upon Magiere. Wynn's true companions were back. Where did that leave him?

He dropped a hand to his sword's hilt. Back on his home continent, these three had hunted him like an animal—like a monster. They viewed any undead as an enemy without question. This had culminated one night in which he had hesitated in killing Magiere, at Wynn's pleading.

In turn, Magiere had not hesitated. In one swipe of her falchion, she had taken his head.

Although Chane had managed to come back from that second death, his hatred for Magiere now almost overrode his love for Wynn. If Magiere started anything, he would not hesitate again. He would be the one to finish it this time. But all his rage wavered as five sages came out of the far building, with Premin Sykion in the lead.

Chane's gaze paused at the sight of Premin Hawes, and he grew even more lost as to what was happening down there.

Should he go down? No, that would only make things worse . . . for Wynn.

Chane did not believe Wynn could ever be in physical danger from her own people, so for the moment, he stood there and watched.

Leesil grew more alarmed and uncertain with each breath. As soon as the dark-haired sage in the dark blue robe went at Wynn, he realized he'd lost control here. Magiere, Chap, and Shade had reacted instantly, not that Leesil blamed any of them. There had to be a way to get Wynn out of here. But when Wynn shouted for all of them to stop, she'd focused on Chap, and both dogs had gone suddenly quiet.

Leesil watched the dogs, waiting for some memory to rise at Chap's urging that might tell him what was happening. What did Wynn want them to do?

"Remove her," ordered the tall, aged woman with the long braid.

The dark-haired sage took hold of Wynn's upper arm and started pulling her toward the building where Wynn had first been heading. Before Leesil could even look back, he teetered as Magiere's pressure vanished. Dropping the chest quickly, he tried to grab for her, but she slapped away his hand and went straight at the dark-haired sage.

Chap snarled in warning, rushing in on the outside of Magiere, but he spun to face away from her. As Leesil bolted in, he saw what Chap faced.

Only one sage, the woman with bristling steely hair, had stepped out beyond the others. She stood poised three strides beyond Chap. With one hand outstretched, palm down with her narrow fingers relaxed in an arch, it looked as if she might gently lay that hand upon Chap's head if she drew closer. But the eyes in that passive, stern face were fixed on Magiere as Leesil caught up.

Wynn twisted in her escort's grip and shoved a hand straight into Magiere's sternum.

"No!"

Both Leesil and Wynn's voices came in the same instant as Leesil grabbed the shoulder of Magiere's cloak.

"I'm not leaving you!" Magiere growled, the words slurred too much.

Leesil grew more anxious. If Magiere lost control here, everything would go straight to all seven hells at once.

Wynn grabbed the collar of Magiere's hauberk and jerked hard, forcing Magiere to look down at her.

"Not this way," she warned, and looked to Leesil, shaking her head again. "Not now, but soon. Go."

Wynn clearly wanted to avoid any confrontation here, as did Leesil and likely Chap. Leesil pulled Magiere away, though she wouldn't take her eyes off Wynn. All this time, Shade just sat at the door Wynn was dragged toward, as if waiting and knowing how it all had to end.

Wynn, Shade, and the escort sage vanished from sight. As the door thumped shut, Magiere jerked free of Leesil's grip, turning toward the other sages in the courtyard. The one beyond Chap had lowered her hand, though Leesil couldn't figure what that had been about.

Before Magiere took another step, Chap wheeled on her and huffed twice for "No."

"Wynn wants it this way," Leesil whispered in Belaskian.

Something in his voice or his words must have gotten through to Magiere. She stood rigid, eyeing all who had cut them off from Wynn.

"What do you think you are doing?" she nearly spat. "Get her back out here."

The remaining four sages, especially the one with hair like a gray porcupine, just stood there looking back, but mostly eyeing Leesil and ignoring Magiere. The woman with the long gray braid struck Leesil as . . . imperious. He didn't like her.

"This is an internal affair and no concern of yours," she said coldly. "Leave or I will summon the Shyldfälches to remove all of you. You can ponder and learn our customs and laws from inside a garrison cell."

None of this was playing out at all as Leesil had expected. He, Magiere, and Chap had only arrived in the city tonight. They'd come straight here, anxious to find Wynn and the hospitality of the guild. Through Wynn, Leesil had known the ways of the sages for several years, or thought he did. The few things he hadn't worried about upon arriving were an open welcome, warm food, and a decent bed.

This was nothing like what he knew of sages. What was going on?

Chap huffed once and started toward the gatehouse tunnel. Confused and uncertain, Leesil made the choice to follow his companion since his youth. He snatched up the travel chest and hoped that Wynn had somehow told Chap something to make sense out of all of this.

"We have to go now," he whispered to Magiere. "We can't help her if we're locked up."

Magiere's head swung toward him, and thankfully her irises hadn't flooded black. At least she still controlled her inner nature.

Then she turned her ire on the stiffly standing sages again. "We will be back."

Leesil almost groaned. Threats weren't going to help. He pulled Magiere along after Chap, though she resisted before giving in. He didn't know whether to feel relief or anger at himself. He didn't want to abandon Wynn any more than the others, but something had passed between Wynn and Chap.

After all they'd been through since leaving Wynn behind nearly a year ago, Leesil trusted Chap's instincts—and reasoning—far more than Magiere's. Once they passed out of the gatehouse tunnel and approached the bailey gate, which emptied out into the city, he heard the clank of gears and a rumbling.

"What are they doing now?" Magiere asked angrily.

Of course, he'd heard that sound many times in his youth, when he was enslaved with his parents as a spy and assassin to a warlord in his homeland.

Leesil turned around and watched the tunnel's outer portcullis rumble downward. The wedged ends of its vertical beams slammed into the stone pockets of the tunnel opening's floor.

Magiere again turned her eyes on him, her mouth tightened in bitten-back fury.

Leesil hoped more than ever that Chap had some answers from Wynn.

Still looking down from the window of Wynn's room, Chane went cold when the dark-haired metaologer grabbed her arm. He shifted back a half step before stopping himself from making a blind rush for the door.

He would never willingly hurt a sage, but Wynn came before all others. Even so, he forced himself to remain, still not believing she could be in physical danger from her peers.

Returning to the window, Chane watched the metaologer dragging her toward the barracks door. He had only an instant to see Magiere, Leesil, and Chap being expelled, but he could not care less. All that mattered was what happened to Wynn, and it appeared that the dark-haired metaologer was bringing her up to her room.

That washed everything else from Chane's thoughts. No one in the guild knew he had returned, but if the Premin Council had turned its eyes on Wynn again, what would they think of finding him in her room?

Looking down again, he did not see Wynn or her escort—meaning they were already inside this barracks, which functioned as a dormitory. They would arrive at the door to this room any instant.

Rushing to the room's inner side, Chane flattened against the wall behind the door. Almost immediately the door abruptly swung inward. Wynn stumbled in with Shade at her heels, and, to Chane's relief, no one else entered. Wynn got her footing and whirled around to glare at whoever had shoved her inside, and then her eyes began to widen at the sight of him in hiding.

Chane put a finger to his lips.

Wynn quickly averted her gaze and looked out the doorway into the passage.

Magiere stood helpless outside the gatehouse, staring at the closed portcullis. Being helpless and hobbled made her angry. Confusion amplified that, and the frustrating mix left her edging again toward rage.

"Come on," Leesil said, backing toward the bailey gate. "We need to talk to Chap and find out what's going on."

Magiere turned on him as the only outlet for her anger. "What's there to figure out? We just let Wynn get dragged off . . . and we left her . . . again."

Leesil flinched, but the sight gave her no satisfaction. It seemed she couldn't seem to stop hurting him, even now.

"Those are her own people," he responded, his voice even and cold. "She didn't want an open fight . . . and neither should you."

Leesil's being right didn't make Magiere feel any better, any calmer.

Chap barked from the bailey gate, urging them to hurry.

Magiere fell into step beside Leesil, but she was far from giving up on Wynn tonight—no matter what he thought. She hadn't known what she would find when they'd come seeking Wynn's home, but if those sages in the courtyard were indeed Wynn's people, they had absolutely no regard for her.

This fortified stone castle didn't match Magiere's imagining of a sages' guild. Back in Bela, the sages lived in a decommissioned barracks given to them by the city's council. That place had been filled with warmth and kindness, cups of mint tea, faded tables, and stacks of old parchments. This place was more like the buildings of the feudal nobles and tyrants of her own homeland, or those of Leesil's youth in the Warlands. The small guild annex back in Bela had nothing in common with this Calm Seatt branch.

Wynn didn't belong in there.

Chap's barking grew insistent, and Magiere walked faster, growing as annoyed with him as she was with Leesil. Why were they both in such a hurry to abandon Wynn? As Leesil leaned forward to open the gate, Magiere's anger escaped again.

"We can't just leave Wynn in there!"

Chap snarled at her, barked twice for "no," and then raked the gate with his claws. What did he want now?

Leesil opened the gate as he answered. "We're not going to leave her. But we're also not going to blindly assault this place, let alone the sages. Not until we learn what Chap knows."

As soon as Chap had enough room to slip out the gate, he darted northwest, running along the outside of the bailey wall. Leesil quickly followed, and Magiere had no choice but to jog after them.

In the shadows of the wall's curve below the west tower, Chap slowed to a halt and turned about. Leesil dropped beside him, put down the chest, and then took off his pack to dig inside it. He pulled out a long, rolled piece of treated leather as Magiere joined them.

Talking with Chap had been a challenge since they'd left Wynn and gone off on their own. In their earlier days together, after they'd first discovered that Chap was much more than a dog, Wynn had used a "talking hide" inked with Elvish letters and a few words to help him speak. He both read and understood that language. Wynn would ask him questions, and he'd paw or nose the letters or words to answer.

Later, through Wynn's fumbling with magic, she became able to hear Chap's "sent" thoughts like a voice inside her head. That had certainly made talking easier on him, but without Wynn, he'd lost his voice. It proved a greater problem than any of them expected, since neither Leesil nor Magiere understood Elvish. Fortunately, in all his sneaky years with Leesil, Chap had picked up Belaskian, as well. Leesil had created his own version of a talking hide in that language.

When they'd first journeyed across the world from the Farlands, Wynn had tutored all of them in Numanese. Magiere was quicker than Leesil when it came to spoken tongues, but he was far better than her when it came to written words.

There was barely enough moonlight to see, and the instant Leesil had the talking hide out, Chap pawed it open on the cobblestones. He went at it with both his nose and one paw flying across letters until Leesil grabbed him by the scruff.

"Not so fast! What was that about books?"

"What's he saying?" Magiere cut in.

Leesil ignored her. "Chap, start over. What are you talking about?"

Chap began again, slower this time. Magiere was still left behind in trying to follow the indicated letters, but when Chap finally paused, Leesil looked up, shaking his head.

"I don't think Wynn could tell Chap much," he explained. "Something about the catacombs . . . and all those books, and then some special scroll or parchment. Obviously she didn't want to leave the keep . . . castle—whatever that place is. Chap thinks she's afraid of . . . losing access to the archives."

Magiere hadn't known what to expect from Chap, but she'd expected a better reason than this.

"That's all he knows?" she demanded. "And he made us leave her in there?"

Chap's paw started moving again, and this time, Magiere recognized one word that he spelled out.

"Prisoner?" she said aloud, and she immediately stood up.

Chap's furry canine face appeared just as frustrated as Magiere felt. He huffed three times for "maybe" or "uncertain," and then locked his crystal blue eyes onto hers. As well as dipping into the surfacing memories of anyone in his sightline, Chap could make any memory he'd seen before rise in the owner's mind. This was sometimes a faster, or simpler, way to communicate.

Without warning, a rush of memories flooded Magiere's thoughts.

First came a clear image of Wynn being captured by Lord Darmouth's men during their time crossing the Warlands. Those soldiers had dragged her away to lock her up. At that time, there had been nothing Magiere could do to stop it. Even the memory brought up a wave of impotent rage. That same anger had rushed upon Magiere when the dark-haired sage had grabbed Wynn.

The memory passed in a flash, and the next was of Leesil wrapping up the orb they'd found in the Pock Peaks to be carried away from the six-towered castle. Then followed a memory of Wynn trying to carry away too many books from the decaying library they'd uncovered in that same place.

Magiere didn't like it, but some of what Chap tried to convey seeped through. Wynn being locked up . . . an orb being found and recovered . . . Wynn's passion for the ancient texts she and Chap had selected for taking. All of these were somehow linked.

Leesil looked up at her from his crouched position before the talking hide.

"Wynn's mixed up in something serious, if her own people are doing this to her. It wouldn't be the first time she's gotten herself in trouble, thinking she knows what's right versus any rule or law. Our showing up in the archives must have been the final pebble to make it all cave in on her. But she still insisted that we leave her behind."

He glanced down the road, his eyes narrowing, and Magiere followed his focus to the keep's smaller gatehouse towers peeking above the high bailey wall.

"Maybe she didn't think they *would* lock her up," Leesil added. "Not if she wanted to stay to keep her access to the archives."

He looked to Chap, but Chap just huffed three times. He wasn't sure, either.

Magiere glanced away, for she'd had enough of this. "Then we get her out—tonight."

Leesil rose and anger leaked into his voice. "What do you suggest? Yell a few insults through the portcullis and hope someone opens it up? Even if they did, and they wouldn't, we can't just blunder back in there. We'll make things worse for her. We need a real plan . . . not just blind, bully tactics. We need to know what's going on . . . first."

Magiere's ire at Leesil and even Chap suddenly shifted to Wynn. What had that girl been thinking, sending off the only ones who could help her? Now they were separated, and it was up to Magiere—again—to pull Wynn's fat out of the fire.

But how in a fortress held by sages?

"First, we get the lay of this place," she insisted, "if we're going to break back in."

Ignoring Leesil's retort and Chap's warning, Magiere stalked off down the road along the bailey wall. Even from ten paces, she heard Leesil cursing under his breath and Chap rumbling.

Leesil snatched up the talking hide, rolled it tightly, and went after Magiere. He wasn't surprised when she walked right past the bailey gate, heading along the wall toward its turn around the southern tower.

She moved with a determined grace, her long, black hair barely showing its bloodred tints in moonlight as its bound tail swung across her upper back. All along the way, she peered up at the keep's heights and studied the high wall itself.

Leesil knew this wasn't over, not by far. Magiere was just getting started, and he was so tired on the inside. His love for her—his desire for her—was

as certain as ever. But during their years together, she had always been skep-
tical, reluctant, leaving him the freedom to be the impetuous, sly one. That
had changed as her obsession grew, and now he had to be ever more sly with
her. He didn't like it.

"When did I become the cautious one?" he whispered to himself.

And in one more step, a memory surged upon him and slowed him almost
to a halt.

Leesil saw a white, icy waste where nearly nothing stood for as far as he
could see through freezing mist and windblown falling snow. But he saw
something. No more than a hazy silhouette, a broken gray-white mountain
range rose far ahead in the white distance.

"Don't!" he hissed, cringing as he spun on Chap at his side. "Not now . . .
not here!"

Chap exhaled through his nose, gazing after Magiere.

Most people couldn't read an animal's face, though some might claim so.
Most hadn't grown up and roamed the world with a four-footed manipulative
Fay in the form of a too-tall, too-lanky silver-gray wolf.

Leesil saw his own old worry in Chap's crystal blue eyes as the dog
watched Magiere, but he couldn't deal with that right now.

"What happened up there has to wait," he added to Chap, forcing calm
for the sake of his new role as the sensible one. "Until we make sure she
doesn't lose herself again."

Chap let out a sigh so human that it was unsettling. After a long pause,
he huffed once in agreement. Leesil jogged a few steps back to retrieve the
rest of his gear on the ground, and then he started off after Magiere again.

Whatever she might think of him tonight, she was wrong to claim he'd
abandon Wynn. First, though, they had to get in touch with their small
friend and learn what was happening in this place.

Not by Magiere's ways and means, but by Leesil's, if he could think of
something.

CHAPTER 3

Wynn averted her gaze when she spotted Chane, so as not to alert her escort to his presence. Once Shade trotted into the room and hopped up on the bed, Wynn reached for the door. Before she touched the handle, Dorian jerked the door shut without a word.

They barely knew each other—hadn't seen each other in years—but unfamiliarity wasn't enough to explain his manner. Wynn wondered again why journeyor metaologers, who should've been preparing for new assignments, appeared to be lingering about at the beck and call of Hawes and Sykion.

Chane stepped out to her, but the instant his lips parted to speak, she reached up and clamped a hand over his mouth. At his scowl, she cocked her head toward the door. His scowl faded as his gaze narrowed, and they both listened in silence.

Wynn heard no footfalls fading down the outer passage. Her escort must still be outside, standing guard. When she looked back, Chane nodded, for they both knew he couldn't be discovered in her room, not now. Then she hesitated for a few breaths, giving herself less than a moment to feel relief that he'd returned safely from helping to hide the orb in Dhredze Seatt. He was so tall, she had to tilt her head back to see his pale, handsome face and jaggedly cut, red-brown hair. Dressed in his usual boots, breeches, white shirt, and cloak, just the familiar sight of him moved her.

That moment was all she allowed. This was no time for a reunion.

Wynn quickly retreated to her desk, flipped open a blank journal, and snatched up a paper-wrapped charcoal stick to begin writing in Belaskian.

The orb?

After all that had happened, it was still the first thing on her mind. Chane took the charcoal stick and wrote one word before handing it back.

Safe.

Now began the harder part, as Wynn wrote furiously. Soon she would be hauled before the council for questioning. Chane had to get out of her room—out of the keep—before they came for her. Only two nights had passed since she, he, and Shade had returned from their long journey south. She'd come straight to the guild, but he'd gone on for the quick trip to Dhredze Seatt and back. It would be better that the premin council didn't know he'd returned, as well.

There was something of greater concern, but Wynn had barely finished writing that Chane should leave when he took the charcoal from her hand. He again wrote one word, but he wouldn't give the charcoal back this time.

No.

Wynn gasped in frustration and grabbed for his fingers, struggling to get the charcoal. It took no effort for Chane to jerk his hand free. He lifted the charcoal up, beyond her reach, and mouthed *no* again, this time with an incensed glower. Rather than make a futile jump to snatch the charcoal, Wynn smacked him in the chest.

Chane's eyes widened as Wynn jerked her hand back with a gasp of pain. A brief snarl filled the quiet room, and both of them froze at the sudden noise.

Shade sat up on the bed with her ears flattened and her jowls pulled back. But she wasn't snarling at Chane this time. Shade's memory-words rose sharply in Wynn's head—in Wynn's own voice.

—*Wynn . . . quiet*—

The last word had probably been stolen from some memory of Wynn's in which she'd admonished the dog.

Shade glanced meaningfully at the closed door, where Dorian must be standing just outside. Even Chane paused at that, glancing the same way as his hand dropped lower.

Wynn grabbed the end of the charcoal stick and snapped it off before Chane could pull it away again. She went at the journal, scrawling rapidly, and then shoved the journal at his face.

Get the scroll out of the keep!

The scroll—Chane's scroll—held the only hope of clues to finding the two remaining orbs. Wynn had repeatedly learned the hard way that anything she recorded or acquired might be taken from her. As for her journals, burned and beyond anyone's reach, she'd read everything they had contained to Shade, until the dog had memorized their entire contents. No one could take anything from the powerful memory skills of a majay-hì like Shade.

That wasn't possible with the scroll.

Its inner writing, in an ancient Sumanese dialect, had been scribed in the black fluids of a long-gone Noble Dead, and then the scroll's entire surface had been covered in dark ink, thus hiding the poem beneath. Only by calling upon mantic, elemental sight could Wynn alone see the script beneath the coating. Until she could translate the entire poem, they couldn't lose that scroll.

It could not be discovered here.

Hurrying to her bed, she pulled the scroll case from under her mattress. Chane had left it with her for safekeeping before his trip to Dhredze Seatt. She thrust it at him. Looking down, his features flattened as he took it from her and slipped it into the back of his belt, beneath his cloak.

Wynn rushed back to her desk and began writing again. If Chane got in the council's way, he could be in actual trouble. He could be arrested by city authorities, if not dealt with directly by Sykion or even Hawes. As an undead, no one could see him fall dormant at sunrise, should they manage to put him in captivity. The only problem was that the keep's outer portcullis was now closed. She'd heard the gears creaking and clanking while Dorian dragged her up to her room.

Chane would have to sneak out through the library's upper window, the same way Wynn had snuck him in when he'd first arrived in Calm Seatt. Of course, that meant they'd have to use a ploy to get Dorian away from the door and beyond sight of the courtyard.

By the time Wynn finished writing, Chane had already drawn near and read every word over her shoulder. He straightened up as he stared out the room's one narrow window. There wasn't time to ponder his stubborn reluctance; that would only give him another chance to argue.

Wynn crouched to dig through the gear tucked in her pack from their last trip, looking for a flint. She couldn't find it, and when she rose, she tore all the pages with their written conversation out of the journal, writing one last line on the top sheet.

Take these with you and burn them.

She didn't care if he thought she was paranoid. Even a hastily written conversation held bits and pieces she didn't want found.

Chane took the torn pages with a nod, but he dropped them on the stone floor. Wynn froze in puzzlement as his eyes closed halfway, focusing on the sheets. She realized too late what he was doing. It had been a long time since she'd seen him do it.

Before Wynn could grab Chane's arm or even risk a whisper, a glow brightened beneath—through—the stack of torn pages. Almost instantly, a small flame sprang from one corner. Another sheet's corner and then another on the stack caught, as well. As the pages burned, so did Wynn's temper, until the whole stack was eaten away to black ash.

Wynn glared up at Chane.

All he did was frown, briefly raising his hands as if dumbfounded, and then Shade sneezed. The dog backed up along the bed, snorting the whole way.

Wynn swatted trails of smoke in the air. She pointed at her nose and then at the door, where a journeyor still waited within hearing—and smelling.

Chane rolled his eyes and went for his packs. When he flattened against the wall on the door's nearer side, Wynn hurried to Shade, passing memories as quickly as she could. Thankfully, Shade understood and didn't argue this time. With all of them ready, Wynn went for the door. And then she faltered, thinking of that one moment when Chane had looked out the window.

Before she'd come out of the keep's main doors, she'd peered at the last window of the barrack's upper floor—her window. No one was there and no light shone from within her room. She'd been gone so long, certainly he couldn't have been standing at the window all that time. Had Chane been simply waiting, perhaps lost in reading one of his own books, or . . .

How much had he seen?

Wynn opened the door to her room, and Dorian immediately spun into view from its left side.

"What?" he asked sharply.

"How much longer?" she demanded. "I thought Premin Sykion wanted to see me."

"However long it takes," he answered. "You'll stay put until then."

Dorian's gaze drifted beyond Wynn, perhaps to Shade. Then he squinted, wrinkling his nose. Dorian sniffed and snorted, and Wynn could've punched Chane right then.

"Very well," Wynn countered, taking a forward step. "Come on, Shade."

Dorian blocked her way. "As I said, you will wait."

This wasn't the way Wynn had wanted things. If she went with Shade, the two of them could have stalled Dorian longer together. There was nothing to be done about it, and her plan changed.

"Shade needs to go out and that can't wait," Wynn said flatly. "Unless you want her doing her *business* in the passage. If so, you can clean it up, because she's not doing it in my room."

Dorian faltered in silence.

Wynn glanced back, but Shade hadn't moved. With her back to Dorian, she glared at Shade and mouthed, *Get going.*

Shade looked at Dorian and then Wynn. With a curl of jowl, she hopped off the bed and trotted for the doorway. Dorian quickly backed up, bumping into the passage's far wall. Shade just turned down the passage toward the stairs.

"She prefers the grove in the bailey's back," Wynn instructed, "below the northern tower."

Dorian stood there, his lips barely parted, caught between a stray "wolf" wandering in the keep and his instructions. Wynn folded her arms and waited, daring him not to go after Shade. Dorian pushed Wynn back and grabbed the door's handle.

Wynn had to shift aside when he jerked the door with a slam. She exhaled in relief and scurried to the window, waiting to see Shade lead the annoying "guard" off and out of sight.

Magiere still fumed as she passed the bailey gate and kept on toward the castle's southern corner. She looked for any way to get in that wasn't in plain sight. The bailey wall was at least twenty feet high in most places. Leesil might be able to scale it and then throw down a rope to haul her and Chap up. But this wide street, comprised of the backs of shops and other buildings, not to mention the keep towers themselves, some of their windows glowing from lights within, was all too exposed.

How could they possibly get over the wall without being spotted? Late at night, later than now, perhaps, though she still hadn't seen what lay around the castle's grounds along its three other sides.

"We can't just wander about out here," Leesil warned. "This isn't some sages' barracks in Bela, tucked into a forgotten corner of that city. Look around you!"

She had, and he knew it, but her guilt wouldn't let her stop. They'd left Wynn behind again, and this time it wasn't due to Chap's insistence that the sage would be safer here.

Magiere was sick of complications inevitably falling on everyone who passed through her life. At least if she kept those who mattered close to her, she might have a chance to stand between them and whatever came, until she found a way to put an end to all of this. Leesil had to understand what that meant; they were not leaving Wynn behind again.

If she couldn't *find* a way into this keep, a way to Wynn, she'd *make* one.

Magiere stopped and turned about, abandoning her search of the castle's bailey wall and high towers.

"What now?" Leesil asked.

Chap hopped out of Magiere's way as she stalked past Leesil and back toward the bailey gate.

Leesil faltered, watching as Magiere strode back along the bailey wall. At a loss, he looked at Chap, who just stood there, as well.

"Do something, you mangy mutt!" Leesil whispered. "Aren't you supposed to be the all-knowing big guide and guardian here?"

Chap curled a jowl in reply and took off at a trot, and Leesil bit back sudden shame for his outburst. He knew he hadn't been fair, and he broke into a jog to follow. Getting Magiere to listen had become just as hard for Chap.

They caught up as Magiere grabbed the handle of one side of the bailey gate.

Chap bolted in around her as the gate cracked open, and he lunged, slamming it shut with his forepaws. Leesil dropped the travel chest without a thought and snatched Magiere's upper arm, jerking her around to face him.

"What are you doing?" he demanded.

"I'm going to get their attention," she answered coldly.

"Then what? Wait to see if any of them are stupid enough to raise the portcullis?"

He had always been the one to find them a way through whenever the path was blocked by something she couldn't get around.

"Oh, they will . . ." Magiere answered too quietly. "If just one of them gets close enough to the bars."

Leesil went cold as the chill in her voice washed over him. This wasn't his Magiere. He'd done terrible things in his youth, serving a warlord who kept him, his mother, or his father hostage while one of them was out following orders. How many had he killed in those days?

Most of his victims died quietly and quickly in the night. They never suffered, if he could help it, especially those who'd done nothing but pit themselves against the tyrant who held him and his parents captive for blood work. But they weren't the only ones he'd harmed.

As Leesil stared at Magiere, he barely heard Chap's growl begin to grow in his ears.

There had been fathers, mothers, sons and daughters, and friends of his targets left behind. The living had suffered tenfold more than the dead for what he'd done in those days.

And Magiere wanted to use whatever sage she could get her hands on . . . to get her way.

Before Leesil uttered a word, he flinched at the clack of Chap's jaws, but neither of them looked toward the dog. Magiere suddenly clenched her eyes shut and hunched as if some pain grew in her head. In less than a breath, she tried to push Leesil aside as she hissed at Chap.

"Stay out of my head!"

Chap lunged at her.

Leesil got between them and slammed Magiere back against the bailey gate. He pinned her there, his forearm barred across her upper chest.

"Look at me," he ordered.

When she did, he saw her irises had flooded completely black. He shriveled inside and could've wept at the sight of her.

Her pallid face was covered in a sheen that was not quite an open sweat. Her short, rapid breaths shuddered under the vibration of fury in her body. How many times would he have to be the only one to keep her at bay when she lost herself to her other half?

She could've thrown him off, with her dhampir nature on the edge of cutting loose. She didn't, though tears began rolling from her eyes. He couldn't tell whether they came from the strain of her change or from the night growing too bright before her eyes, or from realizing she'd almost lost control again.

How many more times before that one time when she wouldn't hear or see *him*? As always, it was just as bad to watch her come back to him.

Magiere's muscles slackened, and she went limp against the gate. The lustrous brown began returning to her eyes as her irises contracted. She clenched her eyes shut, turning her head away, as if she couldn't bear to face him. She'd stopped saying "sorry" a long while back, as if that only made the next time even worse.

Leesil leaned in, with his lips close to her ear, and whispered softly, "Look at me."

She wouldn't. He carefully took Magiere's jaw with his free hand and turned her face toward himself. She still wouldn't meet his gaze.

"We'll get to Wynn," he whispered, and leaned his forehead against hers. "But not like this. If anything, they'd expect that now. We can't make things worse for her . . . or for us."

Her breath still came in shudders, her face so close he could feel it. Then her hands slid around him, up his back, and clamped on his shoulders. Her tight grip made him stiffen, because he worried she might try to fight him. But her mouth suddenly pressed hard against his.

It wasn't the time or place for this, but it had been a while. Leesil couldn't bring himself to stop her—until he heard the grind of gears and clank of massive chains.

Chap huffed and his claws scrabbled on cobblestone as he took off. Before Magiere tried something rash, Leesil grabbed the travel chest's nearest handle and jerked his wife along the bailey wall.

"Run!"

Chap raced along the street close to the wall, looking for any quick way out of sight. But whoever might come out of the keep would easily spot them if they tried to cross the open street and dash for any alley along its far side.

Once again, events had almost gotten beyond reason because of Magiere. That had grown slowly worse along the journey back out of the northern wastes.

After what had happened to her up in that realm of ice, after what she had done to gain the second orb, she was more often losing control of her dhampir nature. How long before it controlled her? Chap could not yet face what he would have to do when that happened.

When he reached the curve around the bailey wall's southern corner, he halted and turned, hiding just around the bend. Magiere had barely raced by him, ducking around, when the bailey gate swung open. Leesil joined them, crouching down, as the first figure ran out of the gate.

In too little time, too many strange events kept happening this night.

Chap watched as that one and then a second sage, both wearing dark blue robes, ran out into the night. To his frustration, the two split up, running in separate directions. The first ran straight away from the gate along the main road, but the second turned left. That one came running down the road toward the keep's southern corner.

Chap spun with a huff and bolted around Leesil and Magiere. He ducked in against the bailey wall's base and dropped to his belly. As Magiere and Leesil crouched behind him, he heard the rapid footfalls on cobble drawing nearer.

To Chap's relief, the sage did not even glance their way and kept running, soon vanishing southward into the city. In spite of not being spotted, he realized their position was still far too open. Leesil must have been thinking the same thing, for he pointed to an alley across the street.

"We can watch the gate from there," he whispered.

Magiere did not move. "Why would the guild send two sages running off into the night?"

Chap had no idea.

Leesil shook his head, hefted the chest over one shoulder as he rose, and then reached down for Magiere.

"I don't know. Now come on."

To Chap's further relief, Magiere relented, took Leesil's hand, and stood up. At least they could all get out of sight for the moment. But, in truth, Chap had no idea what would happen after that.

CHAPTER 4

Chane stood near the door of Wynn's room, listening to the sound of fading footsteps as he waited for the metaologer to follow Shade out into the courtyard. He glanced back to find Wynn still watching out the window, her back to the room and half bent over, with her elbows braced on the deep stone sill.

Moonlight or torch braziers on the gatehouse glinted off the top of her soft brown hair. Anyone's eyes but Chane's might not have caught this. Her locks shimmered as her head tilted to one side, perhaps in trying to look down to the barracks' outer door. And not a word had passed between them concerning her three visitors to the keep.

Did she even know he had seen them?

"Not yet," Wynn whispered.

Confused, Chane quickly realized she was referring to Shade leading off the guardian sage. Then he heard a muted, rhythmic clanking from somewhere outside, beyond the window.

Wynn stiffened upright. She leaned into the window's deep recess and craned her head, looking all ways through the panes.

"Is that the portcullis?" Chane asked. The clanking ceased. "What's happening?"

She shook her head, peering toward the gatehouse. In only a moment, the heavy clanking rhythm began again.

"I think it's closing now," she said. "They must have opened it briefly, though I wonder why." Her focus suddenly pivoted down and to the right. "Finally! Shade is trotting for the main doors, and Dorian is rushing to keep up. They'll be out of sight in a moment."

Wynn began to turn.

Chane stalled again at the thought of leaving her. Of course, he was concerned about the safety of the scroll, but once he was outside these walls, the prospect of reentry was doubtful. He was reluctant to leave before the council had finished with Wynn. How could he even check on her to know what had happened?

"What?" Wynn asked, staring at him.

Perhaps too many thoughts showed on his face, so he quickly redirected her attention. "Do you remember the inn I stayed at before? Nattie's, in what people here call the Grayland's Empire?"

"Yes . . . though I avoid such labels for the poor districts."

"You can find me there. Send word when . . . as soon as you can."

Chane kept his expression passive, but he could not help rejoicing inwardly at the relief on Wynn's face. She did not want to lose contact with him, either.

"Good," she said, nodding.

And yet she had still not said a word about . . .

Chane turned, about to slip out with nothing left to say—not until she did. Then he felt her small hand grab the back of his cloak, and he half turned to look down at her, but she did not release him.

"Chane . . ." she began, faltering. "How much did you see?"

There it was.

She watched him carefully. Perhaps she had seen him glance at the window.

"You mean Magiere," he whispered—or tried to—but he could hear the malice in his own voice.

Instead of being startled, she took a quick breath, held it for an instant, and then said, "Stay away from her—away from all of them."

Anger made the beast within Chane stir. The scar that ringed his entire neck and throat began to itch and then burn. It was the only mark he bore from any kind of wound since he had first risen from death. Magiere had done this to him with her strange falchion.

"You were there," he hissed, "when she took my head!"

"Because you tried to kill her first," Wynn countered.

"And whom did you protect?"

She winced, but he did not take back his words, uttered so sharply in his nearly voiceless rasp. They both knew how his voice had been forever maimed. Wynn had thrown herself in front of him, begging him to stop when he had the upper hand and was about to kill Magiere. At Wynn's plea, he had faltered, but Magiere had not even hesitated.

Chane still did not know why he had risen again. There was only the following night, when he awoke in a shallow open grave. He was covered in bodies and blood, and Welstiel Massing looked down upon him, as if waiting for him to rise.

Wynn closed her eyes, perhaps reliving that terrible moment between him and Magiere, but her silence did not last long.

"Leave her alone, Chane."

This was not an answer to his question. "And did you give her the same warning? To leave me alone?"

Her eyes opened, and she blinked several times without a word. He understood.

"She does not know. None of them do," he accused. "You did not even tell them . . . that I have been here, while they abandoned you."

"And I'm keeping it that way," she shot back, "as long as possible. I don't want you and Magiere going at each other again—not now, not ever. And, like me, they had something critical to accomplish."

"Such as?" he asked angrily. "What happened to the first orb? What did they do with it?"

"There's no time. Put any thought of vengeance out of your head. Promise me you'll stay away from her—them. Swear it, Chane! Please."

He had no intention of going after Magiere—at present. Even if he had, he was all the more angry, even hurt, that Wynn would put this on him. He had promised her that he would never feed upon a sentient being again; he had kept that promise, by the word of it, at least.

He gazed into Wynn's face more deeply and saw only worry and fear. When she looked into his eyes, it was clear that her worry was focused upon him. But what of the fear? Whom did she fear for the most—him or Magiere?

"I swear," he whispered.

Wynn sagged slightly, loosening her hold on his cloak. "Then you'd better go. Keep the scroll safe."

Chane needed no reminder. He hoisted his two packs and turned, grasping the door's handle. Wynn grabbed the side of his cloak again.

"You'll hear from me as soon as I can—I promise," she said softly.

Her grip lingered an instant longer, and then finally released.

With one last wave of regret—the feeling that leaving her was wrong—Chane slipped out the door and down the passage.

Siweard Rodian, captain of the Shyldfälches—the "People's Shield"—worked long past supper in his office within Calm Seatt's second castle. This castle had once housed the royal family more than a century past. After construction of a newer, larger third castle nearer the sea, the nation's military had taken over the second, leaving the first castle of Malourné to be turned over to the Guild of Sagecraft.

The city guard was officially a contingent of the military, but it served autonomously for domestic defense in conjunction with civilian constabularies. It was complicated, but the system worked, for the most part.

Rodian took his duty seriously and kept meticulous records of which complaints or possible crimes needed investigation and who'd been arrested, charged, and scheduled to stand before the High Advocate in court. And who had already been sentenced or exonerated and set free. This too was complicated; more so than he'd imagined when he took his oath of service years ago.

Not all who slipped from justice were innocent. In turn, some who might have legally broken the law did not deserve to be branded criminals. He'd never wished for such complications, but service forced them upon him. In recent times, he'd grown weary of it.

Rodian set down his quill, rubbed his eyes, and realized he'd forgotten to eat again. Rising from his desk, he began unfastening his sword.

An engraved silver panel on the blade's sheath bore the royal crest and a panorama of Calm Seatt. His tabard, worn over a chain vestment and padded hauberk, marked him as military. But unlike the regulars, attired in sea greens and cyans, his tabard was red. Combined with that sheath, it clearly declared him as captain of the Shyldfälches.

Some thought the position a high honor. Others considered it a dead end in a military career. But Rodian knew neither was wholly true.

Appearances were important to him. He was as meticulous with his grooming as he was with his records. He kept his hair cropped short and his beard close-trimmed, sculpted across his jaw above a clean-shaven neck.

He'd commanded the Shyldfälches for nearly four years, yet he was not quite thirty years old. Rumors spread by the envious didn't bother him. He was ambitious, and success was more important than being liked, but that didn't mean he cared nothing for the law.

Rodian had sworn his service oath upon the Éa-bêch, the first book of law from Malourné's earliest times some four-hundred-plus years ago. The nation's laws continued to grow until they could fill a small library of their own, but this first volume was the heart of it all. On the day he'd placed his sword hand upon it, his father, a plain timber man on the eastern frontier, had beamed with pride.

"Honorable service and strong faith," his father proclaimed with an unrestrained grin. "What more could a father hope for his son?"

Rodian hadn't known how to smile back.

He now glanced at all of the stacked papers carefully arranged on his desk, but for one. A letter he'd opened lay refolded on the desk's far corner. He was too tired to think about it and needed to start remembering to eat. Heading for the office door, sheathed sword still in hand, he'd almost escaped from that letter when someone knocked.

"Sir?" a familiar voice called from outside.

Rodian opened the door to find Corporal Lúcan in the outer passage. The corporal kept himself almost as carefully groomed as his captain. However, right behind Lúcan stood a young male sage in a midnight blue robe. Rodian had to fight back a frown.

The last time a sage had come looking for him, he'd been forced into an investigation involving the guild. He looked back at Lúcan.

The previous autumn, Rodian, Lúcan, Lieutenant Garrogh, and others of the guard had hunted an unknown black-robed mage that Wynn Hygeorht had called a wraith. After the deaths of multiple young sages and several of the Shyldfälches, Garrogh had been killed in the final conflict with that figure. Lúcan, only a guardsman at the time, had been severely injured in a strange way.

Taln Lúcan looked no older than his early twenties, if not for the color of his hair. Since that night in the street, it had turned almost fully steel gray. His beard was the same if he didn't keep it cleanly shaved, and if one looked closely, faint crow's-feet framed his eyes.

Rodian had had difficulty accepting Garrogh's death, more than he'd expected, as had the men under his command. Garrogh, slovenly as he had been, was liked as well as respected. But within a moon, Rodian had been forced to select a replacement.

He'd been sorely tempted to elevate Lúcan straight to lieutenant, thus skipping him over several orders of rank. He would've willingly faced the uproar from those with seniority in rank or years, but regulations wouldn't permit it, so Lieutenant Branwell became his second-in-command. After all that had happened, Rodian still felt more comfortable with Lúcan, and promoted him from guardsman to corporal.

It had been a year of deaths, letters, and reports to write. Perhaps it was no more so than any other, but this year had wounded Rodian, even unto his faith.

Lúcan glanced sidelong at the sage and frowned as he looked at his captain. He shook his head, perhaps to express that he had no idea what the sage wanted here.

Rodian fixed on the visitor. The young man was panting from a hard run—not a good sign.

"Yes?" Rodian asked, not really wanting an answer.

The sage simply held out a folded paper—yet another letter—and Rodian was slow in taking it. Once in his grip, he broke the wax seal with its imprint from the guild's Premin Council. He snapped open the sheet and quickly scanned its content.

To Captain Siweard Rodian,

Shyldfälches Command, Calm Seatt, Malourné

Rodian took a breath and let it out slowly. The official address and the reminder of his position were another bad sign.

Your immediate assistance is required at the guild. Please bring an appropriate number of city guards to secure the grounds.

Lady Tärtgyth Sykion, High Premin

Guild of Sagecraft at Calm Seatt, Malourné

Short and to the point, if utterly vague, the message's dismissive and commanding tone was insulting. He was not some lackey at the high premin's beck and call. Rodian's gaze returned to the signature.

Did Sykion think to impress—intimidate—him with a reminder of her noble rank from her homeland of Farien?

He sighed. He entertained a good deal of respect from Malourné's royal family. But for generations, the family had always favored the guild.

"Sir?" Lúcan asked, a hint of bitterness in his tone.

Rodian didn't even look up, though he almost crushed the letter into a ball.

"Find Lieutenant Branwell and meet me at the stables," he instructed. "Bring Angus and Maolís, as well. I'll have the horses saddled."

"Yes, sir," Lúcan answered, not even asking where they were going or why.

As the corporal strode off down the corridor, Rodian studied the young sage dressed in a dark, dark blue robe—a metaologer. He didn't care for the company of sages—well, most of them—but he wouldn't send one off alone on foot at night.

"Come with me," Rodian ordered. "You can ride with us."

The sage stepped away. "I can see myself back, Captain."

Typical. Rodian frowned; sages isolated themselves from "common" folk, regardless of the guild's public works and charitable institutions. As he turned to step out and close his office door, he suddenly felt lost as his gaze lingered on the other letter, across the room on his desk.

It had come two days ago, and he still hadn't answered it.

All the burdens here kept him from doing so. His father would have understood. In part, a father's pride was why Rodian took his duty as seriously as his faith in the Blessed Trinity of Sentience. But his uncle had sent this letter.

How could Rodian say—write—that he couldn't come home now? Not even to pay last respects at the grave of his adoring father.

Rodian shut his office door.

Without a glance at the sage, he led the way down the corridor and out into the open courtyard. The sage headed off for the gatehouse tunnel, and Rodian promptly strode for the stables. Upon stepping through the large stable doors, he found Branwell already saddling his huge roan stallion.

Half a head taller than his captain, with a clean-shaven head as well as jaw, Percier Branwell looked twice as wide and at least six years older. His red tabard had been specially tailored to fit his broad shoulders.

"I passed Lúcan heading for our barracks," the lieutenant said. "He told me we were riding out. Where to?"

Rodian didn't answer. Promoting Branwell had been the correct choice; he was a competent, experienced veteran of the regulars who could read and write. Had Rodian chosen anyone else to replace Garrogh, discontent would've sprouted among his men. But Rodian didn't care for Branwell, didn't trust him, and never had.

Percier Branwell was among those whose resentment was rather open concerning Rodian's early rise in position, to the point of making speculations on how it had been achieved.

Turning away, Siweard Rodian headed for his white mare, Snowbird.

"To Old Procession Road, to the sages' guild," he finally answered, still wondering what he was about to ride into.

Chane slipped silently downstairs, peeked out the barracks door, and found the courtyard empty. Several options ran through his mind.

As Wynn had suggested, he could make his way through the keep to the new library, as its back met the bailey wall's rear. Slipping out a window and dropping over the twenty-foot wall was not a challenge for him, and he knew the path well enough. But the chance of being spotted was high if he tried going through the keep this early at night.

He had no idea what might result if he was spotted. He was only a guest here, but with Wynn under constant suspicion, the council's mistrust might also spread to him and anything he did. Not to mention, the very fact that she had been banished to her room, with a guard at the door, gave him pause.

Chane glanced toward the gatehouse tunnel, framed by its two small inner towers. Of three old portcullises along the tunnel's length, only the outer one was ever used by the sages. Its controls were likely in one of the outer gatehouse towers, but he had no notion of which side. The other side would be unmanned.

He could go there, climb to the two-story tower's top, and risk a jump down into the bailey. But if he guessed wrong about which side to enter, he might run into more sages, and his sudden appearance would cause alarm.

Another worry had nagged Chane since agreeing to flee the guild. Wynn had refused to leave with him because she feared losing her resources here. She did not know that he faced the same unfortunate prospect. There were means here that he needed, as well. Chane considered the risk of one stop before making his escape.

Across the courtyard lay the northwest building, flush with the keep's wall. A passage had been built through the wall behind it that connected to a newer building in the bailey. This was where the guest quarters, his quarters, lay. But in the sublevels below that building was something more useful to him. The guild laboratories were in the first and second subfloors there, along with the office or study of Premin Frideswida Hawes of the Order of Metaology.

Chane stepped quickly across the courtyard and through the northwest building's central door. But just as he pulled the door closed behind him, voices drifted up from below. Slipping into the first chamber on his left, he rounded its upward stairs to hover at the top of the ones that descended below. The pair of voices floating up the stairway grew slightly clearer.

Chane recognized only one: that of Premin Hawes.

"The need is critical now," she said. "Besides the archives, the passageways here, and the main corridors of the keep, where else have you managed placement?"

"Placement isn't the issue," a frustrated female voice answered. "Can't you explain to Premin Sykion how long it takes to create even one of these?"

"That isn't her concern," Hawes answered. "You will place more eyes as quickly as possible. Requisition anyone and anything you need. I will handle the cost. Do you understand?"

A long pause followed, and then, "Yes, Premin."

"I'll check in later. Prepare a detailed report on how many are still under construction and those that have been distributed."

The voices fell silent. One pair of footsteps upon stone began growing fainter.

Chane tensed, ready to run should another pair of steps come toward the stairs. When he finally heard the second pair, they were brief, followed by the ringing thud of a closing metal door. He stood there, wondering. . . .

What was meant about "eyes," "construction," and "distribution"? According to Wynn, the sage's cold-lamp crystals were made here in the lower levels. What were the metaologers making now and to what purpose?

Time pressed upon him, and he had a more urgent reason for coming here.

Descending, Chane found the first sublevel's passage empty but for the six handleless iron doors, three on each side, and a portal at the far end on the right. He stepped quickly and quietly to the last one still ajar and nudged it inward a little farther.

"Premin?"

If she was inside, there would be no mistaking his maimed voice and who had come. She would be unable to ignore him, as she might ignore someone knocking. Light footsteps sounded against stone, and the door was pulled open wider.

For an instant, Chane's gaze caught on what lay beyond the narrow inner passage that was barely three strides long. All he could see were shelves pegged in the chamber's left wall in line with the entryway. The rest of the room, which opened up to the right, was hidden. Those pegged shelves were filled with books; plank-bound sheaves; and narrow, upright cylinders of wood, brass, and unglazed ceramic.

Then he looked down into Premin Hawes's piercing hazel eyes.

They had not seen each other since the previous autumn, when Chane had left with Wynn to journey south to the Lhoin'na, this continent's elven people. With Hawes's midnight blue cowl pulled back, her cropped ash gray hair bristled across her head. Any lines of her true age were faint in her even, small features. Below her small mouth, her jawline narrowed to the soft point of her chin. She might have caught some men's attention if not for her stoic demeanor and severe, penetrating gaze.

"Master Andraso," she said with no inflection.

She was the only one who called him that. Then again, Chane rarely spoke to anyone but Wynn. Hawes's eyes watched him without wavering, and she showed no surprise at his arrival. In the brief times that Chane had interacted with her, nothing ever seemed to catch her unawares.

"Forgive the intrusion," he apologized, and then quickly wondered why, as he had never been given to apologizing, even in his mortal life. "But . . . I am leaving for a while . . . tonight. I wished to speak with you first."

A flicker of something, though it was not surprise, flashed across Hawes's face. It vanished with a brief twitch of her left eye.

"Leaving? Why?"

This question was unexpected, and Chane had no intention of telling her more.

"I am taking city lodgings, rather than burden the guild further as a guest." Before she pressed him, he went on. "I wanted to know if you have continued with one of the . . . the projects we discussed."

"The healing concoction?" she returned bluntly.

Neither subtlety nor manners would help Chane here, and he simply nodded.

Hawes shook her head slightly. "It would be pointless, as I don't have the components." She cocked her head slightly. "You'd best come in."

Chane was uncertain how much he should tell—show—the premin of metaology.

She turned down the short entryway, and he stepped inside and closed the door. When he followed her, in three strides, her study filled his view. He had been here several times, always wishing for a stolen moment to explore it.

Stout, narrow tables and squat casements were stuffed with more texts, as well as odd little contraptions of metal, crystal, glass, wood, and leather. A rickety old armchair of worn blue fabric was stuffed into the back right corner beyond the messy, dark, and aged desk that contained a dozen or more little drawers. Atop the desk's corner sat a dimming cold lamp next to an array of brass articulated arms that each held a framed magnifying lens.

"How much have you gained in this pursuit?" Hawes asked.

Again Chane wavered, but he would learn nothing if he kept his progress from her. She was the only one capable of helping him, though he had no idea why she did so.

Unshouldering one of his packs, he pulled out a book with which they were both familiar: *The Seven Leaves of Life.* It was only two leather-covered flats with one long sheet of old paper between, folded back and forth into seven panels. To this he added two small, cloth-wrapped bundles.

Hawes looked at the latter as he laid them on her desk and unwrapped the first. Its contents riveted her attention, but for only an instant. The strange gray mushrooms had gray caps that spread in branched protrusions, each branch splayed and flattened at the end in a shape a little like a leaf.

"Muhkgean," Hawes said, clearly needing no confirmation from Chane. "These dwarven mushrooms will do no good unless you've managed to . . ."

Her gaze shifted to the other small bundle.

Chane pulled open its cloth.

Tiny pearl-colored petals—or leaves, judging by their shape—shimmered like silvery white velvet in the cold lamp's light, though they were as delicate as silk. The remaining stems and leaves beneath them, though wilted, were a dark green, nearly black even in the light.

"Anamgiah . . . the Life Shield," Hawes whispered, and then looked up at him. "Where did you get these?"

"In the open plain on the way into the Lhoin'na's forest and their capital. I did not steal them. They grow wild there."

Why did he feel the need to defend himself? It was none of her concern where he had gotten them.

"Can you assist me now?" he asked. "Give me further instructions to make the concoction in the text?"

This time, he wanted something conclusive, something he could put into practice. His own body was nearly indestructible; Wynn's was not. He needed anything that might keep her whole and sound, no matter the cost.

Hawes glanced at the book in his hand, and her brow creased. "I don't . . . Healing is not one of my fields. Premin Adlam would be more able—"

"No."

Besides Wynn, he trusted no one here with this exploit other than Hawes, and he barely trusted her. He had not even told Wynn of what he was doing.

"I was not suggesting that you go to him for assistance," Hawes said, and a bit of annoyance slipped into her tone. "But he knows more of these matters than I."

She looked down at the two open bundles for a long moment, and then held out her narrow hand without even looking at him.

"Leave the book and the components with me," she instructed. "I will look into testing the process."

"No."

Hawes's head barely turned, but her nearer thin eyebrow arched, and her gaze could have struck like a winter cold snap.

"If you thought to manage this yourself," she said evenly, "you would not have come to me. I will keep your secret and provide you with the result of my efforts. In exchange, I will take a portion of these components, not more than a fifth, for my own interests."

Chane's throat tightened. He feared—no, more than feared—leaving one of his precious books, as well as these rare ingredients. There was no telling how soon he could reenter this place, but she was correct in one thing: if he did have any notion of how to attempt what was written in this text, he would not be standing here.

And strangely, Hawes's attempt to bargain made him less reluctant. She would gain something from this, as well.

"Agreed," he rasped, and laid the book in her hand, which had not lowered or moved since she had extended it.

"Where will you be staying?" she asked.

He would not go that far, and shook his head. "I will contact you in a few days."

A long pause followed, and then she nodded.

Chane wanted to thank her but did not know how. So he simply turned and left the study, closing the door behind him. Taking the stairs two at a time, he made his way out and stepped into the courtyard. His thoughts once again turned over which route he should use to get out of the guild. He had taken only six steps into the courtyard before he stopped cold.

Four sages stood before him, two wearing brown robes and the other pair in the midnight blue of metaologers. They were not gathered as a group but spread in an arc, all facing him. One brown-robed sage was a small, pretty woman. Chane had never spoken to her, but through Wynn he knew who she was. Ginjeriè was the youngest sage ever in the Order of Naturology to be appointed as a domin.

"Please stay where you are," she told him, and the two metaologers stepped forward.

They *were* waiting for him. How had they known he was coming? Had someone seen him go inside?

"Is there a problem?" Hawes's voice sounded behind him.

Chane glanced back and found her standing outside the door he had just exited.

"No, Premin," Ginjeriè said, bowing her head slightly. "Premin Sykion wishes to speak with this man. We were sent to bring him."

Chane wanted to wince. The Premin Council knew he had returned, and he was being called before them, likely to give his own account of the long journey south with Wynn. Both he and Wynn had expected them to corner her first, though not quite in the way it had been done. The situation had suddenly changed again. Perhaps in questioning him first, they thought to gain something to trip her up.

Chane glanced back at the other four sages.

Could he refuse to go? Unless he had broken a law, the council had no legal hold over him. But he guessed that the council had not been adhering to the law of late, and the fact that two of the four sages were metaologers struck him as suspicious.

He would avoid hurting a sage for almost any reason; he had self-sworn this upon returning tonight and while waiting for Wynn. Flawed as the guild might be, those who lived, worked, and studied here were still far above the common cattle of mortals.

Yet he still carried the scroll.

That meant everything to what Wynn saw for the future. He could not allow himself to be hauled before the Premin Council, or, worse, to be locked inside a room by Hawes's potent thaumaturgy. He knew firsthand what she was capable of.

Chane tensed as the two metaologers took another step, and he heard Hawes approaching from behind.

Wynn waited in her room for Dorian to return with Shade, but sitting still grew too much for her. She began taking stock of her belongings, wondering what to hide should the council decide to confiscate anything. Not that she had many places to hide something in this little room.

She'd already passed the content of all her old journals to Shade via memory-speak and then burned them. Memory-speak was as easy as talking for Shade, and she never forgot anything once it was soundly lodged in her understanding. She was the perfect vessel for secrets that no one could open, even if someone ever figured out that she held them.

Wynn's one remaining journal contained only convoluted encryptions of a few key notes to help her as needed. Even sages fluent in the Begaine syllabary would need a long time to decipher it. But there were other items here that Wynn feared losing.

In the far corner beyond the door, a long staff leaned against the wall. Its upper end was covered in a leather sheath a half foot long and bound in place by a cinched cord, making it easy to pull free in an instant. Beneath the covering was a crystal like no other, for unlike those used in cold lamps, this one produced a light like the sun.

The sun crystal was all Wynn had besides her knowledge and wits in facing the undead. But, really, where could she possibly hide a staff in this little, sparsely furnished room? Even if she did, any search would uncover it quickly enough.

"Please stay where you are."

Wynn froze as she heard those words in the courtyard outside. Surely it had nothing to do with Chane. Plenty of time had passed—enough that he could've twice over reached the library's window and the keep's back wall. She rushed to her window and peered out, and her breath caught at the sight below.

Down in the courtyard, Chane faced four sages, with Premin Hawes coming up behind him. One of the sages was Domin Ginjeriè, a gentle young woman who most often tended to the initiates. Ginjeriè said something but spoke too softly for the words to reach Wynn. What was Chane doing still inside the courtyard? And why had Ginjeriè intercepted him . . . with others present?

The two metaologers took another slow step, not toward Chane but to either side of him. Wynn's small fingers pressed against the sill's stone as she realized they were going to try to take Chane. And if he fought back . . .

Premin Hawes waved one hand in a sweep, and both metaologers halted. Ginjeriè took a half step, but Hawes cocked her head slightly, uttering something that made Chane spin around toward her. Ginjeriè appeared to hesitate and then bowed her head. Wynn couldn't hear anything that was said, but the young domin of Naturology turned away with the other sage dressed in brown. Both headed toward the keep's main doors.

Reduction in the numbers around Chane didn't relieve Wynn—quite the opposite. Premin Hawes had dismissed everyone but the metaologers. Whatever was happening, it wasn't good. Was Hawes up to something she didn't want anyone but her own order to know about? Or did she simply wish to . . .

Wynn whirled around, looking about her room for any options. Metaologers were certainly not defenseless, though they rarely displayed abilities in plain sight. Chane was facing only three, but Hawes was worth a dozen of them. The last time Wynn had been called before the council, Hawes had driven and shut out Chane with barely two gestures.

Chane could be in serious danger.

About to run for her door and try to get to the courtyard, Wynn glanced out the window again. Movement near the keep's main doors caught her eye.

Shade came trotting out as a frustrated Dorian held the door, and then he rushed after her. Both of them halted when they spotted the others in the courtyard. Wynn hesitated, as well, in watching.

Leesil crouched in an alley's mouth across the road that looped around the guild's grounds. Magiere and Chap were close behind him. From his vantage point, he studied the keep's front in wondering how they were going to help Wynn—if Wynn was in any real danger.

His stomach growled and he tried to ignore it. Chap was probably hungrier than he, as none of them had eaten since breakfast. In their haste to reach the city and Wynn, they'd pressed hard, expecting to find food, beds, and even a bath waiting for them. None of that had been forthcoming.

At present, they had no lodgings at all. In addition to the travel chest, they were still carrying their packs, and Leesil didn't care to be so weighed down amid a possible crisis. He twisted about in his crouch, but Magiere now stood above him, her gaze wandering over the keep in the dark.

"Magiere . . ." he began, lost as to how to best suggest the obvious. "Maybe we should—"

The sound of multiple hooves on cobble cut him off, and Chap quickly shoved in beside him as they both peered up the road.

Five riders appeared from out of the mainway that led directly into the city, and they were heading toward the bailey gate. All wore red tabards and swords. The leader rode a white horse. Likely they were armored, though Leesil couldn't be certain from a distance.

"Constabulary?" Magiere whispered, echoing his own silent question.

Leesil didn't think so, not by their uniforms and mounts. Those were too military for civilian constables.

"Something else," he answered.

Perhaps they were a special unit attached to the city or the rulers here. But again, why had they shown up at the sages' castle in the middle of the night? This place was filling up with too many things they didn't understand, and it was no place to go snooping about until they did.

Leesil glanced back along the cutway. He gestured to the main road, away from the bailey gate toward where the castle road's southern corner met a side street. A faded sign in dim lamp light read LEAFUL STREET. At least he'd learned enough Numanese to read it.

When he slipped out, heading toward it along the near side of the looping road, Magiere and Chap followed without a word. When they reached the meeting of that side street, Chap slipped ahead, but Magiere grabbed Leesil's arm and jerked him around.

"Wait. Where are we going?" she whispered. "I thought you were just moving us farther back."

He didn't pull away but kept his voice firm. "To find an inn. We need food, a place to store our gear, and time to figure this out."

"We're not done here. We should at least check all sides and get the lay of it."

"That wasn't just some local constabulary," he argued, and he looked back at Chap, who waited for them. "Did you pick up any memories, especially from the leader on the white horse?"

Chap studied them both, and finally huffed once. Leesil's mind instantly flashed to numerous memories. Chap could show Leesil only his own memories, so at first he wasn't certain of their meaning as an answer to his question.

First came an image of a tall young man in Voldran armor. He rushed out of a city gate with his men to defend peasants fleeing for the city across the border in the Warlands, Leesil's birthplace. The second memory, farther back in time, was more to the point.

Over a chain vestment, a tall, beefy, bulky man wore a white surcoat emblazoned with two sea hawks, the royal crest of Belaski, far across the world. Upon the table sat his helmet, which had three ridges, the center one rising from a nose guard and decorated with a plume of feathers. With a blunt nose and a mass of dark brown curls that hung from his head, he had eyed Magiere a little too affably for Leesil's taste.

It was Captain Chetnik of the city guard in Bela.

Leesil scoffed and turned to Magiere. "Chap thinks they're military, a contingent for the city's safety and law enforcement . . . like Chetnik, back in Bela."

Another memory rose in Leesil's head. He saw Wynn . . . and then the rider on the white horse. Leesil looked back to Chap.

"That one knows Wynn?" he asked in surprise. "The one on the white horse was remembering her?"

Chap huffed once again for "yes."

Magiere released Leesil and stared up the road toward the bailey gate. That was enough for Leesil, and he reached for her arm. She jerked it away at the first touch of his fingers.

"Did his memories seem threatening . . . angry?" she asked without turning.

Again, Chap hesitated, but he huffed twice for "no."

Although relieved, Leesil wondered about Chap's pause. Was Chap just saying this to keep Magiere in check? Leesil waited, but Chap raised no more memories for him. Then the loud, creaking sound of the rising portcullis carried down the street, suggesting the contingent was being allowed inside.

"This is more than we can deal with," Leesil said, and stepped in close at Magiere's side. "We won't figure it out by skulking here in the dark." He carefully gripped her hand. "We need to find lodgings, stow our gear, eat something . . . and talk in private."

Magiere still gazed up the road toward the gatehouse, but then dropped her head with an exhalation. She didn't argue again.

Leesil looked to Chap for support. "Agreed?

Chap immediately huffed once and wheeled to head off down Leaful Street.

When Leesil pulled on Magiere's hand, she resisted slightly before giving in.

Chane stood flanked by two metaologers as Premin Hawes stepped wide around him.

She gestured once at her subordinates with a flip of her hand. Both halted their creeping, watchful approach and sidestepped toward each other. All three stood directly in front of Chane, but this made him more wary, not less, than when they had tried to flank him. It was more disturbing than when Hawes had dismissed those two naturologists, leaving him alone with only metaologers. And Hawes now stood in his way.

"Premin," he rasped carefully. "I have no wish to speak with the council. I am only a guest here, and as I told you, I am off to seek lodgings elsewhere."

Her hazel eyes did not blink. "If the council wishes to speak with you, it would be best for you to come with us."

Chane caught the underlying threat in her words. She had dealt with him once before and with little effort on her part. That she stood just barely beyond a weapon's reach, so poised and calm, truly unnerved him.

He gauged the distance of the sage off to her left. If this came down to violence, he would have to put all three of them down very fast. Of the three, he would have to disable Hawes first. The other two might be dangerous enough, but not like her. And his own skills in conjury, mostly by ritual, were paltry and slow compared to what he had seen of her thaumaturgy by spellcraft.

A movement off to the left caught Chane's eye.

Shade trotted out of the keep's main doors and stopped at the sight of him. The guardian sage behind her did the same. That was all Chane needed—another unknown metaologer. Shade's head shifted suddenly, and she stared in turn at the two sages flanking Hawes. Her jowls pulled back once in a quick, silent snarl.

Chane did not know what worried him more: that Shade might assault a sage or that she had a reason to do so beyond what he could speculate. Had she seen something surface from the sages' memories? He must be in greater danger than he realized.

Shade's hackles began to rise as she turned her full attention on Premin Hawes, but the other sage behind the dog crept closer and raised a hand in the air.

"Premin!" that one called out in warning.

Chane's hand dropped to his sword hilt.

"Open up!" someone else shouted.

The sharp command echoed out of the gatehouse tunnel and was followed by the clanking of the chains and gears for the outer portcullis. Both Chane and Hawes quickly glanced down the tunnel.

This was Chane's only chance. He tried to think of a way to signal Shade, to tell her what he would do, and hopefully she would do nothing to make things worse.

Without warning, Shade shot forward, leaving her escort behind as she rushed the sage on Hawes's right.

Chane bolted for the gatehouse tunnel, pulling his dwarven longsword. He focused all his effort on speed as he breached the tunnel's mouth, his eyes on the rising portcullis.

"Captain!" Hawes shouted from behind him. "Watch out!"

In the instant it took for those words to sink in, Chane saw something between the portcullis's upright beams. He caught a glimpse of men in red tabards on horseback, and the lead horse was pure white.

There were mounted Shyldfälches, city guards, on the other side of the rising portcullis.

Wynn gasped, her feet seemingly stuck, as Shade charged a metaologer and Dorian lunged after the dog. Premin Hawes turned toward the disturbance, and then Chane broke away, racing into the gatehouse tunnel. Wynn heard the premin's sharp shout of warning.

Captain Rodian had come, and Wynn came to her senses. She ran out her door, down the passage to its end stairs, pushing herself to reach the courtyard before anyone went after Chane.

Chane was almost to the portcullis when he spotted the boots of three guards hitting the ground as they slid off their horses. There was no choice but to fight, and there were too many in his way to be careful about it.

Shade suddenly bolted past him, barking and snarling.

Chane almost stalled as she charged under the rising portcullis, snapping savagely at the white horse's legs as she passed. There was no time for him to consider how she had gotten away from those sages or why she had not stayed behind for Wynn.

He ducked his head, lunged under the rising portcullis beams, and found himself face-to-face with the white horse. It was stomping and sidestepping after Shade's passing, and atop the mare sat Captain Rodian.

"You!" Rodian shouted at the sight of Chane.

Shade's snarls and the shouting of the other guards seemed to come from all around. Behind Rodian was a bald city guard, still mounted. All that Chane could think of was to put the captain off before the others overwhelmed Shade.

Chane lashed out and punched the captain's horse in the face.

Wynn flew out the barracks door into the courtyard, and the eyes of all four metaologers turned to her. She made a dash for the gatehouse tunnel, but barely halfway there, something jerked hard on the back of her downed cowl. The cowl's base cinched against her throat, choking her as she flailed to a stop.

Even as she gagged, struggling to pull free, the grip on her cowl was released as someone tried to grab her more solidly from behind. Light-headed and panicked, Wynn reacted without thinking.

She stomped back, trying to hit her assailant's foot, and missed. Her sudden rearward shift backed her up against someone tall. She twisted hard as the grip latched onto her cowl again.

Wynn wildly lashed back and upward with her little fist. It collided with someone's face, and her hand went numb in a shock of pain.

"Enough!"

At Premin Hawes's command, the air blew upward around Wynn like a storm.

A harsh crack sounded as the horse whipped its head aside from Chane's fist. The animal reared, and all the captain could do was clench his reins.

Chane ducked around the horse and saw Shade throw herself at one dismounted guard with a young face and steel gray hair. When the man raised his sword, Chane veered toward him, but Shade instantly changed course.

She clipped the guard's knee with her shoulder. The man staggered, about to topple, as she bolted for the open bailey gate. Without bothering to make sure the man went down, Chane followed.

Another guard charged into his path. Before the man's blade cleared its sheath, Chane brought his sword down, aiming with the flat of his blade.

It struck the man's head and glanced off to hammer into the hollow of his collarbone. The guard tilted under the force and dropped to his knees.

"Angus!" another guard shouted in alarm, running to help.

Chane barreled into him. Something sharp sliced across his upper arm as he threw the man off. Hunger rose to eat the pain, and Chane ran out the bailey gate. But he was at a loss when he spotted Shade.

The dog was halfway up the road to the north at a full run. All Chane could do was chase after Shade along the bailey wall.

*   *   *

Wynn's robe thrashed about her, pulled and whipped by an impossible, sudden wind. That and her wild swing knocked her off balance. She went tumbling onto the courtyard's cobblestones. Immediately scrambling to all fours, she looked for Chane in the gatehouse tunnel but then stopped, frozen by another sight.

Beyond Dorian, who crouched holding his nose, Premin Hawes was coming closer.

The open fury on the premin's face would've been daunting enough. But though her midnight blue robe thrashed, the whirling wind didn't topple her. Wynn heard the barracks' windowpanes rattling in the storm.

Hawes stepped purposefully forward, as if she were the eye of a small hurricane. Even the other two metaologers in the courtyard backed toward the keep's main doors, their wide eyes locked upon the premin as they tried to shield their faces from the wind.

Wynn did so, as well, too afraid to even scoot away as Hawes neared. She had never seen any strong emotion displayed by the premin of metaology. Those fierce hazel eyes, and even her short, bristling hair waving in the storm, were enough to freeze Wynn in place.

Hawes slowed to a halt, not quite between Wynn and Dorian. The wind died so suddenly, it made Wynn shudder.

"We do not act like common thugs," the premin said quietly, though a shout would have been less frightening. "We do not turn against our own . . . like this." Then her voice cracked like thunder, "Get up, both of you!"

Dorian obeyed instantly, as did Wynn, but she peered down the tunnel.

There was no sign of Chane or Shade. Instead, there was a somewhat chaotic group of five Shyldfälches, several trying to pick themselves up. Captain Rodian was on his feet, attempting to calm his horse as he shouted orders.

"Lúcan! Branwell! I want him alive!"

Wynn had never seen Rodian so openly angry. He normally kept his emotions in check, almost as well as Hawes. Wynn knew she was in deep now.

Premin Hawes grasped Wynn's arm and strode toward the tunnel's mouth. To Wynn's frustration, the premin's grip was like an iron shackle.

"Captain!" Hawes shouted. "Call off your guards. That man is not your concern here."

Rodian turned from Snowbird and stared up the tunnel.

Chane nearly flew down Old Bailey Road toward the west tower, not slowing until he rounded the bailey wall's curve below the tower and cleared another block deeper into the city. He had not chosen this path, following as Shade led the way. At the block's far end, beyond the buildings outside the remnants of the keep's old outer bailey wall, Shade wheeled to a stop.

Chane caught up and looked back for pursuers. He stared down the empty street, waiting for city guards to round the corner of Old Bailey Road. But they never came. Glancing down, he saw Shade peering the same way, and he slipped his sword into its sheath.

What was she doing here, and why had she run out of the gate? With Shade outside the guild, Wynn was completely alone.

"Go back," he ordered. "Find a way inside and stay with Wynn."

She huffed twice for "no."

"Shade!"

She turned on him with a growl and drew back her jowls in warning. To date, Shade had been fiercely protective of Wynn. She barely tolerated him except for the few occasions they had been forced to work for the same purpose.

"We cannot leave her alone in there," he said more calmly.

Shade ceased snarling and just looked at him with her crystalline blue eyes. She finally huffed once for "yes."

Chane did not understand. Was that "Yes, we have to leave Wynn alone"?

In frustration, he fingered the brass ring on his left hand. That small bit of metal, which he called his ring of nothing, protected him from anyone or anything detecting his presence or anything about him except by normal senses. This included masking his nature as an undead. Unfortunately, it also dulled his senses, and hid any memory from a majay-hì like Shade. He could not even call up memories to help him communicate with her while he wore it.

Even when he took it off, their communication was limited to Shade, in turn, calling up only memories she had seen within him. And because of the ring, Shade had glimpsed very few of those. It was not the same as Wynn's singular ability to communicate with Shade through memory-speak. The dog could *share* her own memories, or even the memories of others that she had glimpsed, with Wynn.

More unfortunate, with the ring off, Shade fully sensed Chane for what he was. The majay-hì were natural enemies of the undead, and somewhere in this city was another like Shade.

Along with Magiere and Leesil, Chane had to worry about Chap. He was reluctant to expose himself even for a short while. By Wynn's accounts, Chap was more potent and aware than any other majay-hì in existence. But he saw no other option.

Chane held up his hand so Shade could see what he was about to do. He always warned her before removing the ring of nothing. Her lips curled up in distaste, but she stood waiting as he slipped it off.

The world shimmered in Chane's eyes and his senses sharpened in the night. He could hear an insect crawling up the shop wall nearest to him. He could smell the life pulsing within the city, and it was a relief, like being unchained.

The beast stirred inside him, roused by the scents of life in Chane's nose.

Shade snarled softly as she looked him in the eyes, and he suddenly saw a flash of memory.

He was standing on the docks the night they had returned from their southern journey back to Calm Seatt. Before he had gone off to escort Ore-Locks in taking the orb into hiding, he had handed Wynn the scroll.

Chane heard his own voice from that night as he clearly told Wynn, "For safekeeping."

The memory faded.

He found himself further back in time, when he had crouched with Wynn in front of a city stable. She unrolled the scroll and looked at its blacked-out inner surface for the first time. This moment was from when he had first arrived in the city from halfway across the world in his search for her.

Chane had seen enough, and slipped his ring back on as he looked down at Shade in the dark. She was not protecting him, and she had not abandoned Wynn so easily. Sometimes, Shade understood Wynn far better than Chane gave her credit for.

Shade was protecting the scroll.

"All right," Chane said, knowing he would never change her mind. "Come."

Once again, he was acutely reminded that Shade was more than just an exceptionally intelligent beast. She had her own agenda, at least where Wynn was concerned. So long as they shared that, a truce between one majay-hì and an undead would continue.

CHAPTER 5

Rodian struggled to calm Snowbird as he absorbed all that had happened. His immediate focus was on regrouping his men, getting them into action, and seeing who had been injured, including his horse. Then Premin Hawes had shouted to let the man go . . . the man who'd just assaulted his men.

Hawes stood beyond the gatehouse tunnel's far end, holding Wynn Hygeorht by the forearm.

If he hadn't been called to arrest the escaping man, then why was he here? Why had Wynn's wolf attacked and then run off with the man who'd struck his horse? Rodian had seen that man with Wynn in the past, but he'd never ascertained the nature of their relationship. And Wynn had never offered much in that regard.

"Sir?" Branwell asked gruffly.

The lieutenant obviously wanted to give chase. Rodian had half a mind to let him. He again wondered what he'd just walked into.

For better or worse, Wynn Hygeorht appeared to be right in the middle of it all once again.

"Hold," Rodian ordered, handing off Snowbird's reins to Branwell. "Lúcan, go see to Angus. Make sure he's all right."

Rodian was angry and didn't bother to hide it as he strode into the gatehouse tunnel. Hawes was almost unknown to him, as he'd never directly dealt with her before. But as he neared the inner courtyard, his attention shifted to Wynn. Her oval face had come to his mind often over the winter, though he hadn't seen her since last autumn. Given events back then, he was at a loss for what to say to her.

The question became moot when Hawes frowned at his approach, half turned, and called out, "Dorian."

A dark-haired sage in a midnight blue robe appeared from beyond the left of the tunnel's inner end. He was wiping away blood dripping from his nose. Hawes whispered something to the young man and handed Wynn over to him.

"Premin, no!" Wynn cried, trying to pull from the male sage's grasp.

The dark-robed young sage, a metaologer like Hawes, began dragging Wynn toward the keep's main building. She struggled and shouted at him to let go, but to no avail.

As Rodian entered the courtyard, he had an urge to rush in and pull the bloody-nosed sage off Wynn. Then he spotted two more sages, both in dark blue robes, and the pair fell in behind Wynn. All four passed through the keep's doors and out of sight.

Rodian was alone in the courtyard with Hawes, and he turned on her.

"What is happening here?" he barked. "Where is she being taken?"

Premin Hawes was as composed and still as the keep's cold stone. "Captain, you of all people are aware that Journeyor Hygeorht is given to excesses. This is for her own safety."

"Safety from what? Don't tell me it was that man fighting his way out of here. I saw them together the night they helped put down the black mage. Remember . . . the one who'd been killing your people over old books no one was allowed to see?"

"There was trouble with other interlopers earlier this evening," she answered. "That is why the high premin called for you. We require your assistance with security."

Rodian would've preferred dealing with High-Tower. The dwarf was easier to prod into a slip of temper. Even Sykion could be shaken. But this premin was calm and unmoved. Her tone told him nothing beneath her words.

"Interlopers?" he repeated. "Not the one who just left with Wynn's wolf?"

"He is of no concern, and we managed to send away the others I mentioned. We intend that you keep them away."

Rodian tensed. Her words were too close to the tone of Sykion's "request" for his presence. "Who are these interlopers? What did they do to earn so much concern . . . and fear?"

Hawes said nothing, and Rodian chose a different tactic, putting the burden on her, if the sages wanted his help.

"I'll need complete descriptions if my men are to—"

"High Premin Sykion requests that you simply man the gate for now. Allow no one in or out without clear authorization from a member of the Premin Council."

Rodian's jaw muscles twitched. "With due respect, *Premin*, that won't—"

Hawes turned away, cutting him off. "I am certain Premin Sykion will make all clear to you soon."

He wasn't being put off that easily, and quick-stepped around to cut her off. Hawes didn't look the slightest bit intimidated.

"What does Journeyor Hygeorht have to do with this?" he demanded. "You should know that much . . . you had better, for what I just saw."

Rodian was still unsettled by the sight of Wynn being dragged off. For any trouble that had spilled beyond these walls in the past year, Wynn had usually been at the heart of it. But if they violated her legal rights, then that was all he needed to put the whole Premin Council, including Hawes, up against a wall.

She merely looked up at him, studying him dispassionately. "Journeyor Hygeorht will be returned to her room soon, but she may not leave it without the benefit of an escort."

"Without an escort?" The ramifications began to sink in. "She may be a member of the guild, but she's also a citizen. Her rights as such override *any* jurisdiction of the guild."

For the first time, the slightest flicker of emotion lit up Hawes's hazel eyes. Perhaps it was concern, but Rodian couldn't quite read it.

"Captain," she said slowly. "I believe you will find that the council has the full support of the royal family in this matter. Under the protection of the Âreskynna, we called you to provide security for the guild."

Rodian backstepped unintentionally. There it was, like some fixed game of gambling tiles. Whenever pressed, the council always played the same tile: unquestioning patronage from the royals of Malourné.

Hawes moved around Rodian and headed toward the main keep. She called out once as she opened one of the doors.

"All will be clear soon, Captain."

Once again, Rodian found himself hobbled in something murky, like everything to do with the sages. Unlike the last time, he wouldn't be fooled into accepting Wynn Hygeorht as their scapegoat. Wynn might be up to something, but she certainly was not the only one scheming within these walls. However, she appeared to be alone in whatever conflict was playing out between her and the premins.

Rodian stalked down the gatehouse tunnel to where his men still waited. Angus rubbed at his shoulder, but his armor must have protected him, as he didn't seem injured. Branwell stood there with a hard scowl, holding Snowbird's reins.

"Sir?" he asked.

His tone set Rodian's teeth further on edge. Every time Branwell used that word, it sounded like a subtle curse of disdain. Something had to be done to jerk him into line soon. For now, Rodian had larger questions and concerns.

There was only one place to seek a remedy: from the royal family, in person. He snatched Snowbird's reins from the lieutenant's hand and swung into the saddle.

"Lock this place down until I say otherwise," he commanded. Before Branwell started questioning, Rodian shouted, "Lúcan!"

The corporal was limping slightly but otherwise seemed unhurt. He'd barely drawn near when Rodian spoke loud and clear for all present.

"I have a singular duty for you, Corporal. No one is to relieve you for any reason, unless you hear it directly from me."

At that, Branwell's scowl deepened, but Lúcan's features were set in certainty. Before Rodian even explained, Lúcan nodded sharply.

"Done, Captain."

Wynn stopped struggling or trying to reason with Dorian once he'd dragged her inside the main keep. It wouldn't have mattered if she'd gotten loose; there were two more just like him right behind her.

Once through the keep's double doors, Dorian turned left and pulled Wynn down the front passage. He turned right toward the end and on to the stairway leading up, and she realized where he was taking her: to Premin Sykion's office for questioning. Without meaning to, she slowed, putting more tension on Dorian's grip.

Perhaps she had miscalculated in sending off Leesil, Magiere, and Chap, and then Chane. Now Shade was gone, as well, likely seeing what was necessary to get Chane and the scroll out of the guild. Before any of this, Wynn had thought herself at least safe here, but she began to question that assumption. She was cut off from anyone who understood anything about what she'd been trying to do in stopping another great war from coming. She was cut off from all who cared about her.

However, she'd seen Rodian's face when Dorian grabbed her, and she well knew his feelings toward the domins and premins here. She probably couldn't expect help from his quarter, but he had not looked happy with the situation. Why would Sykion call for *him* over a few unexpected guests in the archives?

"Dorian," a familiar voice called from behind.

As Wynn's procession slowed, Premin Hawes walked quickly past them. Wynn refused to even look at Hawes as the premin took the lead up the stairs. Once, Wynn had considered Hawes a potential ally, but no more—not after tonight. When they reached the landing for Sykion's office, Hawes walked right past Sykion's door and onward.

Wynn's stomach knotted as she realized she was being taken to the council chamber. Sykion wasn't the only one Wynn would have to face.

After everything she'd been through tonight, she wasn't prepared for this. Hawes walked right through the open chamber doors, and Dorian slowed to push Wynn in after the premin. All four of the other premins were already seated behind the long council table.

Hawes glanced back to Dorian. "Close the doors and wait outside."

Wynn stood there as she heard the doors shut behind her, and Hawes took her place at the council table. The premin silently settled in the smoothly crafted, high-back chair at the table's right end. All five such chairs were now filled with the members of the Premin Council, each in the robes of their own order.

Premin Adlam, in the light brown of Naturology, sat at the table's left end. Next, on High Premin Sykion's left, sat portly Premin Renäld of Sentiology in cerulean. Sykion, as head of the council, sat at the table's center, dressed in the gray of Cathology—Wynn's own order. On her right, Premin Jacque of Conamology had his elbows on the table, as was his habit.

And Hawes sat at the far right end, not even looking at Wynn.

There was one other person present, just like the last time Wynn had been hauled before the council. No real surprise there, since he'd always been present for her interrogations.

Domin High-Tower stood beyond the table, at the chamber's rear, staring out one of the narrow windows. Someone else might have thought these proceedings didn't interest him. Wynn knew he simply wouldn't look at her until he had to.

She was so bone weary as she faced her superiors that she didn't care anymore. All that mattered was how long she'd have to stand here before they'd give up.

"Journeyor Hygeorht," Sykion began, "Tell us how and why your visitors this evening entered our archives without our consent or knowledge."

With the exception of Hawes—and possibly High-Tower—the others all looked equally self-righteous. Anger—at their self-deceptions, at their ignorance and arrogance—began to feed Wynn a little strength.

"My friends came a long way to see me. They had no idea they needed permission. They've never been to a full guild branch and don't know our ways."

Sykion's brows arched. "You will verify who they are."

Had the situation been less dire, Wynn would've rolled her eyes—"verify," not "identify." She simply remained silent.

Her journals from travels in the Farlands had been confiscated upon her return, along with the ancient texts she'd brought back from where the first orb had been uncovered. Likely the entire council had read everything she'd written. But unlike with Chane, Wynn hadn't foreseen the need to hide the identities of Leesil, Magiere, or Chap in her writing.

Premin Jacque cleared his throat. "Then you admit these were the same people who accompanied you on the journey in which you recovered the ancient texts?"

Yet another obvious question that Wynn wouldn't answer. Where was all of this going?

"Why did they follow you here?" Sykion asked.

"You threw them out before I could ask," Wynn finally responded. "Is this why I've been called before the council—to account for a few visitors who didn't know our rules?"

Sykion's mouth tightened. "You've been called to account for your recent assignment to the south . . . in which you were required to complete only two tasks: to deliver one message to our guild annex in Chathburh and a second to the premin of the Lhoin'na guild branch. Apparently, you traveled much farther south, as your journey took longer than it should have."

The high premin stopped briefly, as if weighing her next words, and

Premin Renäld leaned over to murmur in her ear. She nodded, and in turn whispered softly to Premin Jacque as she shuffled through three separate papers on the table before her.

Wynn's breath caught for an instant.

Beneath that small stack of sheets was an aquamarine ribbon, the kind always used to bind royal communications from the Âreskynna family. Wynn could swear she'd seen the remnants of a broken green wax seal on one other document. If so, that one likely had come from the guild branch of the Lhoin'na, the elves of this continent.

Her anger began to fade, replaced by growing anxiety.

Premin Renäld looked out at Wynn. "Do not doubt that we know you traveled much farther than your assigned duty required."

Wynn kept silent, but her anxiety sharpened more when he glanced down at the paper stained by green sealing wax. Of course she'd used the pointless assignment they'd given her to serve her own goals, but she wasn't giving them even a clue that she'd gone in search of Bäalâle Seatt, let alone found it.

"After leaving the Lhoin'na guild," Renäld went on, "you traveled south along the Slip-Tooth Pass. That leads to few destinations, and it ends at the Rädärsherând, the Sky-Cutter Range above the Suman desert. Why did you take this route?"

Wynn felt herself being boxed in, and anxiety shifted to panic. How could the council know even this much?

Domin il'Sänke had appeared inside Bäalâle Seatt. He knew she'd made it all the way. The hinted origins of the papers before Sykion didn't suggest a connection to il'Sänke's guild branch in the Suman Empire. But what of the one with a broken green wax seal?

Wynn doubted il'Sänke would volunteer any information to Premin Sykion, let alone share it with the Lhoin'na. But upon emerging from the underground tunnel leading out of the Bäalâle, she and Chane had found three abandoned horses with their elven saddles lying nearby.

Who among the Lhoin'na might have followed her? Based on the first letter that had been bound with that aquamarine ribbon, who else might have connections to the royal family? Only one name fit both possibilities. Wynn was loath to even think it. One of the Lhoin'na had always been in the company of Duchess—Princess—Reine Faunier-Âreskynna.

Chuillyon. A white-robed elf who appeared to serve both the Lhoin'na guild and the royal family of Calm Seatt, but whom Wynn suspected mainly served himself.

"Journeyor Hygeorht!" Sykion snapped. "What were you seeking in that mountain range?"

Wynn was terrified that they already knew, and this was some ploy to see how much she would lie.

"I had no return schedule," she answered. "It was my first time in that region. I simply wished to explore and take notes that might be of use to our guild. Isn't that what a journeyor does, if without a specific assignment?"

Sykion's pale skin tinged red.

"So you were not seeking one little known Bäalâle Seatt?" Premin Jacque barked.

It was over—they knew—but Wynn blinked innocently. "And what is that?"

High-Tower turned from the window and glowered at her. "Then you deny that you traveled in the company of a stonewalker—my . . . brother?"

It was beyond a breach of decorum for a domin to speak here unless first spoken to by a member of the council. No one reproached him. The premins watched Wynn, and only Hawes showed no sign of anger, suspicion, contempt, or outrage at Wynn's evasions. Her face held no expression at all.

Wynn simply shook her head once.

"I was lucky enough to actually see the Stonewalkers," she answered High-Tower, "at a funeral during my last visit to Dhredze Seatt. Which one is your brother?"

The room fell deadly silent.

Wynn stood waiting for the next question—and the next—that she wouldn't answer.

*   *   *

Rodian passed through the royal castle's courtyard without challenge, for he was well-known here. Though the first bell of quarter night had rung before he arrived, not even the gatehouse guards had asked his business. They'd immediately raised the outer portcullis, and a stableboy had appeared to tend to Snowbird. But as Rodian stepped up the tall, broad granite steps and more guards opened the castle's main doors, he found two Weardas—"the Sentinels"—standing at attention in his path.

Both wore polished steel helms and glittering chain vestments beneath crimson tabards—which were a brighter shade of red than Rodian's Shyld-fälches. Each bore a sheathed longsword on a wide belt of engraved silver plates. Each held a short spear with a head shaped like a leaf-bladed short-sword.

Neither displayed any reaction to his presence, but he knew one of them slightly.

"Lieutenant Saln," he said with a polite nod. "I need to speak with the king or queen immediately."

Royal audiences were rarely allowed at night, but he counted on the Weardas knowing he was aware of this. His time of arrival implied urgency.

"They have retired," the lieutenant answered. "Could you return in the morning?"

Rodian stalled at this attempt to put him off. It wasn't the first time some arrangement between the family and the sages had placed him at odds with the law and his oath of duty. He was about to press for admittance when a low voice carried from an archway to his left.

"Is there a problem?"

Tristan, captain of the Weardas, stepped into view. He was a tall man with a dark tuft of beard on his chin and thick eyebrows to match. The rest of his head and face were partially hidden by his helm. Rodian had never seen him without it.

"No, sir," Saln answered.

"Tristan," Rodian said instantly. "There is more trouble at the Guild of Sagecraft . . . something to do with interlopers. The family will want to know."

He intentionally used the captain's first name, leaving off rank. They were not friends, as the Weardas had no friends, but they held the same military rank, regardless of their differing contingents. Rodian thereby made the point that he expected to be acknowledged as an equal.

"I must speak with King Leofwin tonight," he added. "Or Queen Muriel. Either would wish to guide me in anything concerning the guild."

Captain Tristan's expression changed only a little. Perhaps it was a brief flicker of worry that cinched his brows. It hadn't come at mention of the sages, but a moment after. That frown vanished as he nodded once and turned down the long hall.

Rodian followed as the captain took the long way through the main floor to the castle's back nearer the seafront. The stairs here were narrow, with regular guards all the way up. When they stepped out into an upper arched passage, there were only pairs of Weardas at either end. Halfway down the passage, Tristan opened a door to a lavish sitting room.

"Wait here," he commanded, and pulled the doors shut the instant Rodian stepped in.

Rodian paced the floor. He'd been in this room before, in almost this same situation. Walnut-legged couches were perfectly fitted in refined or raw silks or elven shéot'a cloth dyed in shimmering seafoam green and cyan. All of this was set off by walls in rich cream shades and golden yellow curtains and draperies. The entrance was carved with a large royal crest spanning both doors—an upright longsword upon a wide, square sail over a troubled sea.

He'd once admired the luxury here. Tonight it was all a distraction. He kept pacing in waiting—and waiting. After what felt like a quarter night had slipped by, the doors opened again.

Out in the passage, Captain Tristan stood aside and announced, "His Highness, Prince Leäfrich Âreskynna."

Rodian was caught off guard as the prince walked in. Leäfrich was the second born of the royal family.

Even if the first heir, Princess Âthelthryth, had appeared instead, Rodian would've still been confused. Why hadn't the king or queen come to meet him? He didn't know Leäfrich well but had seen him enough to make a few observations. For one, Rodian had never noticed any resentment between the two remaining heirs.

Leäfrich didn't appear to mind that his elder sister would one day take the throne. He often trained with the Weardas or fulfilled limited duty among the regulars, being far more interested in military arts than in ruling a nation. His elder sister, Âthelthryth, was the one who took in all aspects of politics and rulership. And their youngest brother, Freädherich, the husband of Duchess Reine Faunier-Âreskynna, had been lost in Beranklifer Bay years ago. A tragedy that Rodian himself had been called on to investigate.

Still, Rodian grew a little irritated. If neither the king nor the queen could see him, then why hadn't they sent their daughter, their heir, in their place? Where were the king and queen?

Like all Âreskynna, Leäfrich was tall and slender with wheat-gold hair and aquamarine eyes. Tonight, he was fully dressed in a tunic, breeches, and dress boots, so obviously he hadn't been roused from bed. He didn't look pleased at the intrusion.

"It's late, Captain," the prince said in place of any greeting. "What is this matter that could not wait?"

Rodian hesitated in answering, for another figure suddenly appeared in the open doorway.

The man was overly tall and slender and was dressed in elven breeches; high, soft boots; and a smock beneath an open-fronted, dun-colored robe. Rodian knew it was one of the Lhoin'na even before the man brushed back his hood. But he was a bit surprised at the change of attire when he recognized this lurker outside the sitting room.

Chuillyon had most often been in the company of Duchess—or Princess—Reine Faunier-Âreskynna, widow of the late Prince Freädherich.

The elf's golden-brown locks hung well past his overly sharp chin and were faded in age streaks. Prominent creases lined the corners of his large, slightly slanted amber eyes. His other features sometimes looked smallish, but that was only because of his long, narrow nose.

Leäfrich didn't sit nor invite Rodian to do so, and Rodian struggled to find his voice.

"Forgive the lateness, Highness," he said, bowing shallowly. "I was summoned to the guild tonight and have . . . concerns about a situation there. I thought the king or queen should be notified immediately."

Leäfrich was far too well-bred to scowl, but he did. "My father has been unwell."

King Leofwin had directly supported Rodian's candidacy to lead the Shyldfälches. "I pray nothing serious," he offered.

The prince didn't respond to this, but his tone turned dismissive. "So, you've come past quarter night to report a . . . situation . . . at the guild?"

Against Rodian's better judgment, he grew edgy and blunt. "The guild has incarcerated one of its own. Her rights as a citizen are being violated. But the Premin Council also claims that interlopers invaded their archives."

Leäfrich's expression flattened for three breaths, and then he glanced at Tristan. "Please close the doors."

Tristan stepped out and did as ordered, but not before Chuillyon stepped inside, unchallenged by either the captain or the prince. Rodian found himself alone with Leäfrich and the old elven counselor, who was no longer dressed in a white sage's robe.

"What do you mean 'incarcerated'?" the prince asked coldly. "And what interlopers?"

The prince's manner reminded Rodian of the Premin Council, and it got the better of him.

"I witnessed a male sage forcefully remove one journeyor named Wynn Hygeorht from my presence . . . at the order of a premin. I was told—without explanation—she is to be confined. Incarceration is not within the guild's authority."

Rodian hesitated for an instant before adding pointedly, "I came to inform the royal family . . . as a courtesy."

He was acutely aware of Chuillyon following his every word, though the old elf remained silent. Leäfrich shifted his weight from foot to foot in discomfort.

"What charges have been leveled against this sage?" the prince asked.

"None," Rodian returned. "No legal claim has been made against Journeyor Hygeorht. As I stated, Highness, I felt it necessary to inform the royal family before I executed my duty. The guild has no authority to—"

"Siweard," someone breathed out too sharply.

All eyes turned toward the doors, though no one had heard them open, except perhaps Chuillyon, who stood nearest to Duchess Reine Faunier-Âreskynna in the doorway.

Rodian tensed at the duchess's—the princess's—slip in using his given name, for their relationship was . . . complex. When her husband, Prince Freädherich, had been lost in the bay, she had been in the small sailing skiff with him. Unable to sail the vessel and unable to swim, she'd drifted in a frantic state until found, and then became the prime suspect in the loss of a royal heir. Rodian had convinced the High Advocate of her innocence, and no charges were made. She'd been grateful to him, as had the family itself, and tried to show it in small ways.

Duchess Reine's eyes were wide, and her smooth brow was creased in shock, anger, or both. Rodian had never seen her in such a state of undress. Normally, she wore high boots and a split skirt over breeches, so she that could ride and move with ease. And unless dressed otherwise for a formal affair, she always carried the traditional horse saber of her people, if not a horse bow, as well. She was now covered only in a silk dressing gown tied at the waist, with her thick chestnut hair hanging loose over her shoulders.

"Leäf," she said, and turned to her brother-in-law. "What is going on?"

Then she appeared to notice Chuillyon for the first time. She started slightly and stared up at him, as if both surprised and glad to see him. Before Rodian could ponder why, a white-robed elf entered.

That one stiffened at the sight of Chuillyon. Only then did Rodian wonder why Chuillyon wasn't dressed in his own white robe.

"Master Chuillyon, what are . . . ?" the newcomer sputtered, and then said more softly to the duchess, "Highness, he cannot be here."

Reine turned her confusion back to Chuillyon. "What is he talking about?"

"Shèmitrian frets too much," said the old elf, smiling at her. "He would do better to remember that I assigned him to you."

The younger elf lost his voice and appeared more than uncomfortable. Reine looked twice between the two elves, clearly confused.

"But you've returned," she went on. "Shèmitrian no longer needs to stand in for you."

Chuillyon's smile faded, and the duchess looked him over, taking in his attire.

Rodian had never understood what white robes meant among sages. He knew of no order for that color, though perhaps the colors were different among the Lhoin'na sages. But it was plain to see that the old one had lost not only his position as royal counselor; he no longer wore a sage's robe of any color.

"Chuillyon is here at my request," Leäfrich cut in, though he appeared as distressed as the duchess was about the old elf. "We were in a private conference when Captain Rodian arrived."

The prince turned slightly toward his sister-in-law. "There was no reason for you to be disturbed, sister. I can attend to this matter."

Rodian remained silent but watchful. Reine, still clinging to Chuillyon's sleeve, fixed upon Leäfrich for a long moment, and then she turned her head aside.

"Shèmitrian, wait outside," she said. "Tristan, take him out and close the doors."

"My lady, please," the young elf urged. "Master Chuillyon cannot—"

"Now!" Reine commanded.

As Tristan moved to obey, Shèmitrian backed up in shock. The captain herded him out and shut the doors, and the duchess lifted her head.

"Gentlemen . . . you had best tell me what is happening."

It was not a request, even to her to brother-in-law, the prince.

Rodian always respected her strength, though as a sister only by marriage, he wondered at the influence she had among the royal family. Before, during, and after the inquest into her husband's disappearance, the Âreskynna had stood by her as if she were beyond question or reproach. But the duchess, too, had more than once placed the whims of the guild above Rodian's authority and oath of service.

"The Premin Council has incarcerated Journeyor Hygeorht," he said before the prince could speak.

Reine's eyes widened, and she glanced at Chuillyon.

"You still have not explained what you mean by 'incarcerated,'" Prince Leäfrich cut in. "The guild long ago refurbished what was once the catacombs and prison to make their archive."

Rodian grew more suspicious. Everything Leäfrich said seemed to downplay the seriousness of the council's actions.

"She is confined to her room," he explained.

"Just her room?" Leäfrich returned. "Has such punitive action never taken place before for initiates who break rules?"

There was that calm, annoyed, dismissive tone again. Rodian felt his first wave of true dislike for the prince.

"She is a journeyor, not an initiate," he returned, "and therefore holds a rank of a kind. Illegal confinement—imprisonment—is the issue, not the setting or her standing. Unless a formal charge is made against her, it is my duty to end confinement against her will. If a charge *is* made, then only I have the authority to hold her until the High Advocate makes pretrial assessment. In either case, the guild has overstepped the law . . . again."

"Were you not asked to close the portcullis and place your men at the guild tonight?" the prince asked.

"Yes, Highness," Rodian answered, trying to regain some calm. "That is also why I came. I wished to make certain the king and queen had been informed."

"Of course we have heard," Leäfrich snapped at him. "The guild's founding branch is important to our nation. I personally approved the council's action."

Rodian grew still and cold. He'd hoped this wasn't so, for it meant the royal family once more bent the law—no, broke it this time—where the guild and Wynn Hygeorht were concerned. He found himself in a very dangerous position.

"Do you know why my men were called in?" he asked. "If any mere interlopers were expelled, the guild's castle is highly defensible unto itself."

"Premin Sykion has greater concerns," the prince returned. "I did not delve deeper, as I trust her judgment . . . as should you, Captain."

Rodian's anger rose again. He glanced at the duchess, wondering on how many sides he was now boxed in. Reine's expression betrayed no surprise at what her brother-in-law said.

She'd known everything.

"Captain . . ." she began, stepping closer. "Siweard . . . if your men stand guard at the guild, can you not watch over the journeyor yourself? Certainly her own room is more comfortable than a cell at the city guard's barracks."

Rodian tried not to swallow too hard, too visibly.

"This is not the first time Wynn Hygeorht has given the council concern," Reine went on, her voice hardening briefly before softening again. "I'm certain they would not infringe upon her rights . . . if you watch over her in her own room."

Watching over Wynn Hygeorht was not the point; assisting in her incarceration without formal charges would make him and his men complicit. Rodian saw that he would find no support here, and this left him with the worst choice.

To protect a citizen's rights and uphold the law and his oath, he would have to go against the royal family itself. They could do nothing to him openly, but his action would fulfill what most thought of a post in the Shyldfälches: the dead end of a military career.

"Both of you will agree with the captain," Chuillyon interjected for the first time. "To protect Journeyor Hygeorht, as he would any citizen, he has the only authority to oversee her confinement . . . and, should the Premin Council not file charges in reasonable time, to determine when it ends."

Both the duchess and the prince turned toward the old elf in shock.

Rodian looked Chuillyon over in suspicion, wondering at both the man's power and position here. Either the prince or duchess could have easily said otherwise, if Chuillyon was no longer the official royal counselor. But the tall, old elf had mentioned the only way out that Rodian himself could think of.

After that tense hesitation, Leäfrich answered too quickly as he turned back to Rodian.

"Of course. But I doubt that will be necessary. I assure you that my sister, Princess Âthelthryth, and my father, are as concerned with this matter as I am."

This last was a promise that Rodian would get no help from Princess Âthelthryth either, but he'd already come to that conclusion.

Reine was still studying Chuillyon, but the elf didn't smile at her. His glare was as hard as hers, and Rodian spotted her small hand slowly clenching into a fist. There was something more here concerning Wynn Hygeorht, something personal to the duchess. Chuillyon had somehow flouted her in that, and she had backed down. Rodian wasn't about to wait for an explanation he would never get, and he headed for the door.

"The guild will be protected, Highnesses," he said.

"If you find yourself stretched too thin, Captain," Leäfrich added, "you can put your Lieutenant Branwell in charge of this. I've been told he is a dependable man."

Rodian slowed, almost stopping, but he didn't turn. Was that a threat? He heard the duchess release a sharp sigh like a hiss of rebuke, and the prince said no more. Rodian cocked his head, looking sidelong at Chuillyon standing beside the doorway.

"That won't be necessary, Highness," Rodian replied to the prince.

Strangely, he thought he found some hint of kindness in the old elf's eyes. Chuillyon closed his eyes briefly in a nod of respect.

Rodian pulled the doors open and strode out past Captain Tristan.

The younger elven sage, who had lingered outside, hurried into the room as Rodian turned down the passage. For one night, he'd had enough of being the puppet of royals and sages. Worse still, the only one who'd pulled his strings in any helpful direction had been an apparent outcast elven sage.

As to seizing control of Wynn's current state, Rodian hadn't mentioned that he'd already taken this matter into hand. Lúcan, even now, would see to that by the very letter of Rodian's command. Once outside in the royal courtyard's night air, he breathed deeply and headed for the gatehouse. However, his manner in dealing with Prince Leäfrich began weighing upon him.

Rodian had always maintained the favor of Princess Âthelthryth. If the rumors were true that Leäfrich was his sister's main counselor, and the king was indeed unwell . . .

Amid collusion between the royals and the guild, everything may have changed for him. Ambition may have died here and now, and his father's words kept echoing in his thoughts.

Honorable service and strong faith—what more could a father hope for his son?

If only that were enough for Rodian.

His horse, Snowbird, had already been brought out from the stables. He swung up into the saddle and rode out into the night streets, heading for his office and barracks. He would need more men to secure the sages' keep.

Wynn had lost all sense of time. She'd been locked alone in a small side room down the passage from the council's chamber. The questioning had gone on for at least a quarter night. At a guess, it had to be near or past midnight by now.

She had no idea why she'd been brought here instead of to her room.

What more could they expect from her, since she'd given them nothing for all their interrogating? She was tired, thirsty, and longing for rest, but she refused to curl up in any of the chairs about the tiny room. If—when—Dorian returned, seeing her like that would let the council know they'd managed to exhaust her. The more undaunted they thought she was, the sooner they might give up. And yet she couldn't stop thinking about those letters on the table before Sykion.

One had to have come from the royals, likely because of something Chuillyon had told them. It seemed redundant that another letter had come straight from the Lhoin'na guild branch. And by the questions that Sykion and the others had asked, they knew everything up to the point where she'd found Bäalâle Seatt. They wanted to know anything following that, along with how to gain access to the seatt.

That told Wynn something more; whatever Chuillyon had told the royals, and whoever had followed her down the Slip-Tooth Pass, neither *seemed* to know how to get into Bäalâle. It still left the question of how anyone had known that was the place she'd gone seeking. If someone from the Lhoin'na branch had followed her, obviously the elven sages weren't sharing everything with the Numan branch here in Calm Seatt.

How far might the council go this time to silence her, if they feared she'd already uncovered too much of a distant past they wanted left hidden to all but themselves?

If only she could get word to Chane.

Wynn wondered what had made him remain on guild grounds for so long once he'd left her room. He should've left immediately and not been caught. Perhaps she should've left with him, as well. Then she wouldn't be in this mess.

No, she'd made the choice to remain, in the hope of deciphering more of the scroll's content. But now that seemed unlikely, since she'd had to send the scroll away with Chane for safekeeping.

The door's outer handle rattled briefly, and she'd barely looked up before the door itself opened. There was no time to wonder if this was all over or not as Dorian peered in, his dark hair falling forward into his eyes. The bridge of his nose—where she'd hit him—had turned a bit pink by now. He motioned her out into the passage.

"Back to face the wolves?" she challenged.

He didn't answer, but when she stepped out, a second metaologer stood partway down the passage. Dorian waved her onward, and she was escorted, front and back. It took only twenty-three steps for the lead metaologer to reach the council's chamber doors . . . and to pass it without stopping.

Wynn couldn't help glancing back at Dorian, but he didn't look at her. She wasn't being taking for more questioning. Perhaps the Premin Council had enough frustration for one night? Or they wanted to leave her wondering anxiously until someone came for her again. But where was she being taken this time?

The answer became clear when they descended the far stairs and headed for the front of the keep. Wynn finally stepped out into the courtyard between Dorian and the other metaologer, and the latter headed straight for the apprentice and journeyors' barracks on the southeast side.

They were taking her back to her room.

Relief replaced Wynn's suspicion—only for an instant. Then what? Surely she wasn't going to be left on her own.

She heard the outer portcullis begin to grind.

The sage in front of Wynn slowed to look down the gatehouse tunnel. She did so, as well, but caught only a glimpse. A team-drawn wagon entered the tunnel, the clop of heavy hoofs and iron-shod wheels on stone echoing into the courtyard.

Dorian urged Wynn onward as the lead metaologer started off again. Then she noticed there were crates and barrels sitting outside the northwest storage building, and its upper-level bay doors were open. Light spilled from the opening, but she couldn't see if anyone was in there.

As the metaologer ahead of Wynn reached the barracks door, the wagon rolled from the tunnel into the courtyard. She saw two huge draft horses hauling a bulky load hidden under a lashed-down canvas. In earlier times,

Wynn had helped with the unloading of supplies brought in several times a year. But she'd never done so in the middle of the night, nor had she seen multiple deliveries on the same night.

A driver dressed in plain breeches and a faded jacket sat on the bench beside a sage in a midnight blue robe.

Wynn blinked. Supply deliveries were scheduled well ahead of time. There was never a need to send a messenger to retrieve them.

Dorian stood watching as the wagon rolled over to the storage house, and then he looked to his companion.

"Go help unload," he said, and then cocked his head toward Wynn. "I'll handle this."

The other metaologer trotted across the courtyard as another sage— another metaologer—appeared in the far building's upper open bay and waved down at the driver.

With little choice, Wynn pulled open the barrack's door, stepping inside with Dorian tight on her heels. She shifted right, climbing the stairs paralleling the lower passage that went through the keep wall to the initiates' barracks built in the bailey. With every stair she took, she wondered exactly what Dorian was supposed to "handle." Her puzzlement grew even more as she crested the stairs and turned into the upper passage.

There was light at its typically dark far end. One of the Shyldfälches in a red tabard stood there outside her door, with a standard oil lantern at his feet. He turned his head, and his eyes locked on her without blinking, his face expressionless. Wynn walked a bit too slowly, at a loss for what this meant.

"What are you doing here?" Dorian called out.

Only the guard's eyes shifted, as if looking above—beyond—Wynn. It was hard to make out his features until she drew nearer. His sword sheath had the typical engraved plate but was not made of steel, or silver like Rodian's. It appeared to be brass. He was young, clean-shaven, and somehow familiar, but Wynn couldn't place him until she noticed . . .

His hair was gray, and yet he looked young in the passage's dim light.

This one had come with Rodian the night that she, Chane, Shade, and

Domin il'Sänke had taken on the wraith, Sau'ilahk, outside a scribe shop. The captain had called him Lúcan.

"Your men were told to watch the gate and walls," Dorian stated, as if he'd given the order himself.

Lúcan still peered over Wynn at Dorian. He turned his torso slightly, and his off hand settled on his sword hilt. Closer now, Wynn thought she saw the faintest crow's-feet around his eyes.

"I have orders to take charge of the prisoner," Lúcan said flatly, "until ordered otherwise by the captain."

"You have no authority inside the guild," Dorian answered.

Something happened in Lúcan's eyes in the following long, cold moment. Whatever it was almost made Wynn back up.

It was a change in the *feel* of him more than anything she could see, as if he'd been cast into all seven hells of the Farlands' folktales and come back. Wynn had once seen the horror in the face of a young sage who'd survived being struck down by the wraith. In place of that horror, she saw something else in Lúcan's young-old expression.

He stood there, his sharp glare never wavering, as if nothing in this world could ever make him flinch again.

"Captain Rodian is now in charge of security in this place," he said to Dorian. "You're dismissed."

Lúcan turned a little more, his off hand and sword now more toward Dorian. Though his gaze never shifted, he reached out with his sword hand and deftly opened the door to Wynn's room.

"If you please, miss," he said.

Wynn quietly stepped in, though she turned about in the opening.

Lúcan's off hand was now fully wrapped around his sword's hilt, his sword hand still holding the door open. Though Wynn couldn't see the sheathed blade behind him, Lúcan's hard grip had tilted the sword's hilt, as if readied and aimed at Dorian's head. Wynn had once seen Magiere draw her falchion off-handed and strike instantly with the hilt.

Dorian's mouth opened slightly as Wynn's mind raced.

Rodian had been placed in charge of guild security? She didn't know if she was better off in that or not, but at least she knew what to expect from a Shyldfälche under the captain's command.

"I will speak with my superiors about this," Dorian said coldly.

"You do that," Lúcan answered. "And they can speak with my captain."

Dorian swung about and headed off, but Lúcan's gaze didn't turn away until Wynn heard Dorian take the steps down at the passage's end. Lúcan looked down at Wynn with a slight lowering of his head.

"Do you need anything, miss?"

She wasn't even sure what to say, so she shook her head.

"If you do, I will be here, miss . . . at all times."

He waited until she stepped back before even trying to close the door. She suddenly felt the urge to say something.

"Guardsman Lúcan—isn't it?" she asked.

"Corporal Lúcan, miss."

Wynn faltered. "Promoted, then . . . congratulations."

"Thank you, miss." Lúcan gave a slight bow of his head and quietly closed the door.

Wynn was alone again—truly alone, without even Shade for company. A man stood outside her door, both protector and warden, who'd suffered in a way she couldn't fathom. So many had suffered in her wake.

Tension and fear broke, leaving only exhaustion. Wynn backed up until her calves hit the small bed, and she dropped onto its edge. Now she had no way even to get a message to Chane. She was stuck in this little room until the council or Rodian or both decided what to do with her. This was her whole world for now, and she was so tired she could barely open her eyes to look at it.

She did open her eyes, and then she stiffened, clenching the bed's edge. Her gaze fixed on the far corner to the right of the door. The sun-crystal staff was gone.

She looked frantically about the room. Had she moved it and forgotten? But it was nowhere in sight, and her little desk table also looked wrong. The journal with her cryptic notes, as well as the new one from which she'd ripped pages to speak with Chane, were gone. Her small travel chest was missing. Only the larger one near the bed remained.

Wynn scrambled over to flip open the chest. Her spare clothing was in complete disarray, as if someone had rifled through it. All that was left of her personal belongings were a few sheets of blank paper, her elven quill with the strange white metal tip, and her cold lamp on the desk. She looked to the room's barren corner again.

They'd taken the sun-crystal staff, her only weapon, and she didn't know whether to scream in fear, anger, or anguish. At a knock at the door, she whipped around on her knees.

At first she thought it must be Dorian. Upon hearing of Rodian's changes, the council might have even more questions for her. Then again, why bother knocking? Or had the corporal intervened?

Wynn rose, but before she grabbed the handle, the door cracked open. The gap seemed to grow too slowly, and she grabbed the edge, jerking it wide.

Lúcan looked at her in surprise—as he was still gripping the door's outer handle—but Wynn's gaze fixed on someone else. Just behind the corporal stood Nikolas Columsarn, holding a tray with a plate of food and a pot of tea.

Any harsh words died on Wynn's lips.

"Is this all right, miss?" Lúcan asked.

Nikolas was probably the only friend Wynn had left in the guild, and he also wore the gray robes of a cathologer. He wasn't much taller than she was, with a slender build, a twitchy expression, and straight brown hair that always seemed to be half hiding his face. He was also, like Lúcan, one of the few people to have survived an attack by the wraith, Sau'ilahk.

Unlike the corporal, Nikolas's brown hair was shot with streaks that were nearly pure white. Perhaps in spotting a fellow survivor, Lúcan hadn't questioned this particular visitor as he might've any other.

"I thought you might be hungry," Nikolas said, and the tray trembled slightly in his grip. "They told me I could bring you something."

Such a small kindness in the middle of the night from two victims left in Wynn's wake broke her defenses. She couldn't stop the tears.

Nikolas's constantly nervous eyes widened in alarm, and he looked up at the corporal.

"Can I go inside?" he asked.

Lúcan frowned, but he nodded. "I must leave the door open . . . a little."

Nikolas stepped in, taking the tray to the desk, and the corporal closed the door to a gap no wider than his hand. The pot of tea was steaming, and the plate held buttered bread, a bowl of soup, and a sliced apple. He'd even wrapped her utensils in a fresh cloth napkin.

"Thank you," was all Wynn could get out. In spite of the corporal's consideration, he was still a city guard standing within earshot outside her door.

Nikolas said nothing, though he glanced at the slightly open door and swallowed hard. She could tell he had something to say, but it never came.

"I'll be back in a while to pick up the tray," he finally got out.

Wynn studied his face. "All right . . . thank you again."

He turned and stepped out, closing the door, and Wynn dropped in the chair before her desk. Even those who offered her kindness couldn't do much; they all had their duties and orders. Thirsty and hungry after a grueling, tense night, she poured some tea, nearly burned her mouth taking too large a swallow, and then picked up the napkin to unroll it for her spoon.

A small piece of paper fell out as the cloth unraveled. It slipped off the desk's edge into her lap.

Wynn paused before picking it up and opening its one fold.

Let me know what I can do.

That was all that was written, but it had obviously come from Nikolas. However powerless he might be, at least Wynn had one true ally inside the guild.

CHAPTER 6

Chane paced in his small attic room at Nattie's inn as the consequences of his actions sank in, deeper and deeper. Shade lay on the bed, head on her paws, her eyes following him back and forth across the floor.

When he had agreed to leave Wynn, so she could stay within reach of the archives, neither he nor she knew the Shyldfälches would descend upon the guild. Nor had he any notion that Shade might abandon Wynn to protect the scroll. Worse still, Premin Hawes now possessed Chane's precious *muhkgean, anasgiah*, and *The Seven Leaves of Life*.

Chane cursed himself for what he had done.

As he began pacing again, Shade let out a grumbling exhale.

The room was as shabby as he remembered, with its small, sagging bed and the slant of the ceiling with the building's roof overhead. But no one would find him here except Wynn—if she were able. He suddenly remembered how Shade had stared at those metaologers in the courtyard, including Premin Hawes. Perhaps she knew more than he did.

"Did you catch any memories from those sages?"

Again, she looked at him, as if uncertain how to answer. Finally, she hopped off the bed and huffed three times.

"Not certain?" he returned. How could Shade not know if she had caught any memories from people directly in her line of sight?

Of all sagecraft orders, or anyone else, it made sense that metaologers would be highly disciplined, mentally or otherwise. Practitioners of any form or method of magic would not allow errant thoughts—especially unwanted memories—to break their focus. Perhaps Shade had seen or felt something she did not like or had not been able to grasp?

"Do you think Wynn may be in danger?"

Shade instantly huffed once for "yes."

That was enough for Chane. He had been debating one possible course of action since they had arrived here.

Digging through one of his packs, he found a quill, ink, and paper. He penned a quick note, folded it up, and shoved it into his pocket. As he donned his cloak, pulling the hood forward as much as possible to hide his face, Shade looked expectantly at the door.

"You are too unique-looking," he said, hoping she fully understood. "You would be noticed, even at night. I will be back soon."

He headed for the door, fully expecting her to argue in her own way, as always. But when he gripped the door's handle, she snarled and rushed him. He swung the pack off his shoulder to use as a shield and backed against the corner wall beside the door.

Shade did not come at him. Instead, she huffed angrily twice and growled as she clawed at the door.

Chane was not about to try to grab her and pull her away. She had bitten him more than once, and those bites had burned like nothing else, except Magiere's falchion.

"Do you want to help Wynn?" he asked.

Shade stopped growling and eyed him, her jowls twitching.

"Then let me go alone. I might pass unnoticed . . . but you cannot be spotted or you could give me away. I have an errand that might help Wynn."

He waited for his words to sink in. Shade's jowls curled back, baring teeth, but she reluctantly backed away.

Chane nodded to her, trying not to show relief, and slipped out and down the stairs to the inn's back door. Once out in the night streets, he began jogging wherever the way was clear as he headed toward Calm Seatt's great port.

Leesil worried about money as he led the way through the streets of Calm Seatt. They'd passed a few inns, but by their upscale exteriors, every one was far beyond affordable.

Years back, he'd lifted a heavily jeweled necklace from a vampire Magiere had beheaded. He sold it for less than it was worth, but its jewels had still garnered what some would call a small fortune. Certainly it was more than the hefty bounty they'd also been paid by the council of Bela back home. But in their travels across two continents, even a small fortune had its limits. The last year had eaten away nearly all of their funds.

He'd counted on the guild's hospitality; that was certainly out of the question now. Usually, he was free enough with a coin—too free for Magiere's penny-pinching, as she had once watched every groat or shil he spent. But there was a far cry between "cheap" and "short of funds."

Yet even his worrying about it marked another way in which they'd traded places after what had occurred up in the Wastes. She had become the rash and impulsive one, while he was forced into greater caution and wariness. And now, their dwindling resources rarely occurred to Magiere, unless she actually saw him take out the coin pouch.

Leesil slowed in the street, forcing Chap to circle back.

"What?" Magiere asked, and he found her studying him. "I thought you wanted a room and something to eat."

He started to bite his lower lip and then stopped.

What was wrong with him? Cunning people never let their worries show to anyone, even those they loved—especially those they loved. Wandering a foreign city was witless, as well, but he'd expected to be safely housed at the guild. It seemed he'd lost some of his edge in worrying about losing her . . .

to that *other* her, the one who had shown herself at the end of their journey into the northern Wastes.

Magiere's hand closed on his arm. "Leesil?"

He took a deep breath to clear his head. "We need directions from someone who might know of a cheap inn . . . and that someone is certainly not in this kind of neighborhood."

But where else could they look? Maybe he'd have to ask someone here, but there were so few people out at night. He turned all ways before spotting a possible prospect.

A lamplighter half a block back was unloading a ladder from a mule-drawn cart.

Leesil snorted. "Well, that one doesn't look like a local."

Magiere stepped around him. "I'll go. You still don't speak Numanese worth a wit."

Chap rushed in two steps, but Leesil grabbed Magiere's arm first—too sudden and firm. He quickly loosened his grip and faked a smile.

"I can manage," he said. And at Magiere's suspicious glare, he added, "When else am I going to get the practice?"

"This isn't the time," she argued.

"Wait with Chap. We don't need you terrorizing the locals. Save that for any ruffians invading our tavern, my dragon."

Magiere scowled over the pet name that only he called her. It was the right kind of scowl—or so he hoped—as in the old days, when he purposefully goaded her.

He passed her the travel chest and took off down the street. Keeping his hands in plain sight and feigning his lost-traveler demeanor, he approached the elderly man in a floppy canvas hat who was about to climb up and replace a lantern wick.

Again, Leesil flashed a smile. He slowly pulled out the nearly empty coin pouch, shook it gently, and then pointed to the two lavish inns within sight.

"Room?" he asked in Numanese. "Little coin?"

The old man squinted a bit at Leesil's thick accent, but his eyes brightened with a smile as he pointed northeast. Leesil nodded deeply as he touched a hand to his heart and then extended it toward the old man. The lamplighter tipped his floppy hat in return.

Leesil returned to Magiere and Chap, and they were off again. But as they headed northeast down street after street, he noticed fewer and fewer lit lampposts along the way. The streets began to change bit by bit.

Buildings became smaller, more worn, and then outright shabby. Shake and shale roofs were replaced by ones of irregular planks and sometimes even thatch. The mixture of structures grew until he couldn't be sure if any one of them was a shop, domicile, both, or something else. The only life in the street came from taverns or public houses, which weren't always marked with a sign.

A sailor stumbled out of a broad, run-down building. The noise of loud voices spilled out around him before the door swung shut.

Magiere grumbled under her breath when the man wobbled to a street side and threw up on the cobble. Chap gave the drunkard a wide berth, and if Leesil hadn't looked over, he would've been spared Magiere's sidelong glare.

"Well," he said. "I did ask the man for something cheap. He must have taken me at my word."

"Yes," she answered dryly, "he must have . . . if he understood you."

Leesil hadn't seen a single dwelling that resembled an inn. In too many places, the cobblestones were cracked, broken apart, or sunken. The remaining holes were filled with grime and rain like scattered pots of muck, all the way up the street.

This area was below even Magiere's "thrifty" standards, and Leesil didn't care for it himself. Even Chap grumbled, his head low, and he usually wanted all of them well off the mainways. Leesil had almost given up hope when he glanced into an empty side street.

Two blocks down, light leaked from the open-shutter windows of a two-story building. Two stories weren't common here, and lit lanterns actually hung under a roofed front landing. By a trail of smoke caught in the light, Leesil spotted a bear-sized man in a full cloak puffing on a long-stemmed pipe. Two people came out the front door. Though Leesil couldn't make them out as they turned away up the road, neither one was stumbling. No interior ruckus had followed them before the door swung closed, just after the pipe puffer strolled inside.

"Over there," Leesil said. He turned down that side street, but halfway along the first block, he froze and spun to his left.

"What now?" Magiere mumbled.

Leesil peered into a cutway between the buildings, but it was too dark to see where the back end might meet an alley behind the buildings. He could swear something had moved in the corner of his sight. It was only an instant's glimpse when . . .

"Leesil!" Magiere hissed. She dropped the chest, and it thudded onto the street.

Leesil spun back as Chap snarled.

A tall figure stood midstreet, short of the next crossing road. He'd barely made it out when a memory raised by Chap filled his head. That image echoed what he saw.

The light of the far porch lanterns didn't help much, but the figure wore a cloak with the corners tied up around its waist. The fabric of its leggings and sleeves was dark, but tinted to green. And in that memory he saw what his eyes couldn't make out within the shadow of its cowl.

Above a wrap of forest gray across its mouth and nose were large amber, almond-shaped eyes below high, feathery blond eyebrows in a face darkly tanned.

The figure in the street was an anmaglâhk, a member of a caste of spies and assassins among the an'Cróan, the elven people of the eastern continent. Something narrow, the length of a forearm, glinted silvery in both of the figure's hands.

Leesil heard someone land too softly down the street behind him, and he jerked free the bindings on the sheaths lashed to his thighs. As Magiere ripped her falchion from its sheath, he pulled both winged punching blades, whirling to face whoever was behind them.

Another anmaglâhk stood silent up the street.

How could they be here—now—from the other side of the world?

Chap's sudden snarl cut off in a clack of his teeth. Leesil barely looked back as Chap bolted forward, straight at the one blocking the way. Before Leesil could shout at the dog to stop, a barrage of memories flooded his head.

He saw himself and Magiere running through the elven forest in the Farlands. Then came an earlier time when they'd fled from being outnumbered by Lord Darmouth's men in Leesil's own homeland. Images came faster and faster, all of them memories of flight.

They weren't outnumbered here, but Leesil couldn't mistake Chap's intention—if they quickly overwhelmed the one ahead of them, they might be able to make a break.

"Run!" Leesil shouted to Magiere, as he dashed after Chap.

Another forest gray figure dropped from the rooftops. It landed a dozen paces ahead, between Chap and the first anmaglâhk. Smaller and slighter, it instantly charged, and Chap swerved into its path. Leesil kept his focus on the first one until . . . the second smaller one leaped.

Chap's teeth clacked on empty air as the small anmaglâhk hurdled over him.

The option to run was gone, and Leesil swerved into the small one's path. He blocked its first slash with his left blade. In that instant, he saw its—*her*—eyes. Everything around him seemed to grow still and quiet.

Leesil had faced these assassins more than once, blade for blade. He knew their cold, dispassionate, deadly calm. His mother had been one of them and trained him in their way, but this small anmaglâhk's amber eyes glistened, as if they might well with tears. They weren't filled with the calm of an assassin fixed on its target. They were overwhelmed with anguish that had built to fury.

Leesil almost faltered. He'd seen eyes like those before . . . when they recognized *him*.

They had looked upon him in youth and long after. They peered at him within his dreams, out of faces ravaged by grief. They watched him in his sleep for every life he'd taken at the order of Darmouth, who had held him and his parents as slave servants.

Those were the eyes that starved for vengeance.

But of all he'd killed in his youth, not one had been a member of this elven people, the an'Cróan—"Those of the Blood." His only an'Cróan victim had come much later, and it had been one of the anmaglâhk.

One night, when he'd stopped over in the Warlands on his way to the an'Cróan's hidden land to find his mother, two anmaglâhk had gone after the warlord Darmouth. Leesil, along with Chap and Magiere, had been forced to defend that tyrant. In the end, a master anmaglâhk named Brot'an had tricked him into murdering Darmouth. But before that, Brot'an's accomplice, Groyt, had come at him. Leesil had killed Groyt in self-defense, but that meant nothing to those left in grief.

Leesil never forgot the names of those he'd killed or those his victims left behind. And now he faced a victim of grief.

Én'nish, betrothed of Groyt, slashed a hook-bladed bone knife at Leesil's throat.

He caught the strike with his left blade, and his mind cleared. He would take the guilt heaped upon him, for he'd earned that. He could suffer that and more, as he already had, to get Magiere away from here.

Leesil drove the point of his other winged blade for Én'nish's midsection.

Chap's hope of flight vanished when the small anmaglâhk leaped over him. He did not turn back for it.

If Leesil could handle that one elven assassin, perhaps Magiere could fend off those coming from behind. But they all had to reach the next intersection, or they would be boxed in.

Chap had to take down the one that remained in their way.

He had no idea how these assassins had made it here—or how they had even picked up a trail. But there was no need to guess who they were after. Aoishenis-Ahâre—Most Aged Father, patriarch of the Anmaglâhk—had wanted Magiere dead since the day they all walked into the Elven Territories, and then left that place still alive.

When the first anmaglâhk charged wide, trying to follow its smaller comrade, it did not surprise Chap. He turned to intercept it, head-on. The elf instantly slowed, slashing down with an oversized bone knife, its silvery white blade curved into a hook.

The blade passed through air before Chap had even closed, and he saw hesitation in the male elf's eyes.

He had been uncertain if this advantage would hold. Apparently, it did. Even among anmaglâhk, all an'Cróan feared harming a sacred majay-hì. He would not be so kind in turn.

Chap leaped, snapping for the man's face, and the anmaglâhk spun out of his reach. As he landed, the elf tried to charge onward, and he wheeled around. He quickly closed from behind, jaws spread, ready to tear out the back of the elf's knee.

Magiere saw Leesil dash out in front of her and clash blades with the smaller anmaglâhk ahead of them. As the first anmaglâhk who'd appeared tried to close, Chap wheeled around it, coming at it from behind. At the snap of his jaws, that elf dove forward upon the cobble and rolled aside to its feet.

Magiere's senses widened fully, and the night lit up her sight.

Her eyes watered at the stinging points of lantern lights down the street. Hunger welled like acid rising from her stomach into her throat, and that burning flushed through every muscle and bone. Her jaw ached under the change in her teeth.

She heard and felt through the street's cobble the running footsteps behind her. She spun away to the street's side, whipping her falchion in a level arc amid her turn.

A tall anmaglâhk ducked under the blade. Before she could reverse, he charged straight at a shack's front. Her reason gone, instinct drove Magiere to turn fast. Instinct was too late.

She barely finished a direct thrust, and all her falchion did was shatter through the shack's boards. The anmaglâhk took another step upward, as if running up the wall. He pushed off, arching over her head before she could rip her sword free.

Magiere knew a blade in her back was next—but it never came.

One arm suddenly wrapped around her throat. The other shot out around her, as he gripped her wrist above her sword hand. His weight pressed on her as he wrenched her neck to the right.

Magiere began to topple under the strength of her assailant. Amid the twist, he folded her sword arm in against her stomach. He was trying to put her down and pin her.

Shock and panic cleared her mind, and her hunger receded partway. Anmaglâhk didn't fight like this. They came like ghosts in the dark, only felt by the touch of a fist, foot, or sharp, silver-white weapons.

Rage and hunger flooded back in, until it was all that was left in Magiere's mind.

She latched her free hand on to the forearm around her neck and threw her own strength into their toppling spin. She caught a glimpse of Leesil fighting the smaller anmaglâhk, and then her view filled with buildings across the street.

Magiere grounded her feet and heaved with both legs.

The shack's corner crackled as her weight and effort slammed the anmaglâhk back into it. His grip on her neck faltered, and she thrashed free, ripping her sword arm out of his grip. She slashed at him as she turned, but he ducked, and her falchion tore a hunk out of the shack's corner.

"Fhœt'as-na â, äm-an!"

Magiere barely heard that shout in the street, and then her left leg suddenly gave way. She stumbled in confusion, and only then did a searing pain cut through her heat. She looked down with wide eyes.

An arrow shaft protruded through Magiere's left thigh, and her leg buckled completely.

*   *   *

Leesil's thrust missed as Én'nish bent her midsection like a marsh reed. All he could do before her next thrust was throw himself at her. Something struck the inside of his right calf, forcing his foot to slip, but it wasn't enough. He slammed down on top of her.

Rolling off, he slashed wildly with one blade, and heard a clang of metal. He kicked out once but didn't connect as he spun away into the street.

Coming up into a crouch, he saw Én'nish do the same.

She stared at him with a hatred he'd seen cast his way more than once. Holding out her curved bone knife, she had reverse gripped it in her left hand, ready to hook one of his own blades when he came at her. Her other hand wielded a narrow stiletto of the same silver-white metal, ready to thrust in low where he'd have to drop his own second blade to catch it.

Én'nish's eyes shifted for less than a blink, but Leesil didn't catch where she'd glanced.

"Fhœt'as-na â, äm-an!" she shouted.

Leesil didn't understand the words, but he whipped his head both ways.

To the right, Chap circled the first anmaglâhk, who was on his feet but too hesitant to close on the dog. To the left, a rearward anmaglâhk struggled to regain his feet, while yet a fourth had dropped from a rooftop and was rushing toward the street side. Magiere was crumpled on one knee, struggling to get up.

An arrow shaft stuck out both sides of her left thigh.

Én'nish shifted into Leesil's path, blocking his sight as the fourth anmaglâhk closed on Magiere. Leesil couldn't hesitate any longer.

He charged, thrusting both blades at Én'nish's head as he shouted, "Chap, Magiere's hit! Archer on the roof!"

Én'nish whipped her head aside, thrusting the stiletto under at him, and he slashed downward with both hands.

His left blade pulled down her bone knife hooked in the winged blade's handle. He felt something grate along his left side, catching briefly in his hauberk's iron rings. A tearing sound came and went, but he didn't know if it came from his armor or her clothes.

Én'nish spun out of Leesil's way before his right blade could take off her hand.

Leesil didn't slow as he spotted Magiere trying to rise. Racing toward her, he slashed wildly at the fourth anmaglâhk closing in just before he rammed straight into Magiere. She toppled backward into the cutway under his force, and Leesil blindly slashed back to fend off anyone behind him.

He hated to leave Chap alone in the open, but he had no choice, and Chap could outdistance anyone here, if he had to.

Leesil kicked out at the anmaglâhk still trying to regain his feet at the shack's corner. That one ducked and somehow spun into the cutway's mouth, rising with a blade in each hand. Én'nish had to be closing by now, and Leesil had lost track of the fourth elf, but he couldn't look back. He had to keep the one in front of him from turning around and going after Magiere.

Something thin and silvery flashed downward before Leesil's face.

He had barely an instant to thrust upward with his right winged blade. A garrote caught on the tip of his blade. Then a knee rammed into his back as the wire's wielder pulled it tight. His blade jerked in against his chest, its tip and the wire cinched against his throat.

"Yield, or she dies . . . you all die!" Én'nish hissed behind him.

Her accent was thick but the words were perfect Belaskian, Leesil's native tongue, and the words stuck in his head.

Yield, or she dies . . .

They were trying to take Magiere alive.

Magiere stumbled along the shack's wall in the cutway's darkness where Leesil had shoved her, and she then crumpled. Even with piercing pain in her thigh, she struggled to gain her feet. At the sounds of clashing weapons and Chap's snarls out in the street, she clawed up the wall and looked back.

In the cutway's mouth stood the black silhouette of an anmaglâhk, and beyond him . . .

Leesil stood a few paces from the cutway's mouth with the point of one of his own winged blades at his throat. For an instant, Magiere didn't understand, and then she spotted the forest gray, cowled head over Leesil's left shoulder.

A silver-white garrote was pulled tight around his neck. Only his blade's tip kept the wire from cutting into his throat.

At that sight, fear flooded through Magiere, and hunger rose to eat her pain. She felt her eyeteeth elongate as reason died under fury, and she tried to shout at the one holding Leesil. All that came from her throat was a harsh, high-pitched screech that filled the night air.

The anmaglâhk in the cutway's mouth stiffened and backed up a half step.

Magiere shrieked as she charged.

Leesil's mouth opened, perhaps shouting to her, but she didn't hear him. She gripped the falchion's hilt with both hands. Nothing mattered but killing anyone that touched him—anything that even got near him. She didn't get far.

Magiere lurched to a halt, arching backward, as something pulled her cloak taut from behind. She tried to slash back with her falchion one-handed, but the long, heavy blade rammed against the narrow cutway's wall. She struggled to turn and grab hold of her cloak.

A sharp strike landed on Magiere's shoulder at the base of her neck. The night's brightness dimmed as everything spun in her sight. She lost her grip on the falchion as she was wrenched back down the cutway.

"Magiere!"

Leesil couldn't help crying out when she suddenly lurched backward into the cutway's deeper darkness. She vanished from his sight. In only a breath, he heard the clatter of heavy steel, as if her sword had dropped. Fear turned him cold.

How could so many anmaglâhk be coming at them from so many directions? He had just shoved Magiere into the hands of another waiting there in the dark cutway. But the one between him and the opening froze and didn't follow her. That one didn't even turn around as he whispered something sharp in Elvish.

Leesil couldn't follow the words, but he felt Én'nish fidget behind him. She barked an answer, and the only part he recognized and understood was "*bârtva'na*"—*no, do nothing.* Then he was jerked back as Én'nish shouted up the street.

"*Vorthash majay-hì—äm-an!*"

Leesil spotted Chap still ranging there. The one anmaglâhk that the dog kept at bay glanced toward Én'nish and then back down at Chap. That one raised his blades to poised positions, and then he hesitated.

Én'nish shouted again in greater anger, and Leesil took his chance. He slammed his free arm back, driving his elbow and a blade's long wing tip at Én'nish's abdomen.

It struck nothing.

The wire cinched tighter around Leesil's neck, and his pinned blade tip bit into his skin.

All that Chap had been able to do was hold one anmaglâhk at bay. He could outrun and cut off any one of them, but he could not fully outmaneuver his adversary. In his effort, he had backed farther and farther toward Leesil and Magiere. Even in his rushes at his opponent, he had not laid tooth or claw into the man. Yet his adversary still appeared unwilling to strike him. And somewhere above was an archer.

Magiere had been hit, and Chap had not even been able to turn to see what had happened to her.

"*Vorthash majay-hì— äm-an !*"

Chap understood the shout: *Kill the majay-hì—now!*

The anmaglâhk's eyes flickered above the forest gray wrap across his lower face. He raised his weapons but still did not attack. When the shout from the female came again, his eyes rose, glancing down the street.

Chap took two lunging steps and leaped.

Both of his forepaws struck the man's chest. As his weight followed, the elf began to topple. Chap struck with his rear paws, tearing at the man's thighs, snapping his teeth at the man's face. The elf jerked his head away, and his skull struck the cobble first under Chap's bulk.

Chap spun off, charging down the street, but his breath caught. The smaller anmaglâhk had a garrote around Leesil's throat, and Magiere was nowhere to be seen. Panic quickened Chap's heartbeat more than his efforts. As he was about to throw himself at Leesil's captor, he heard a breathy hiss in the night air and twisted aside.

An arrow tip struck the cobble a stride to his right.

Chap glanced up as he raced on, and he tried to gauge from where the arrow had come. He caught the soft puff of a bowstring's release, and he quickly swerved again.

No arrow struck the street. The sound of the bowstring had not come from along the first arrow's path, but a barking Elvish curse followed from that direction.

Chap had no notion what was happening up on the rooftops. There were at least two archers above, though the second had not fired at him. Two unseen archers could prove devastating with Magiere already wounded. He howled, trying to draw attention, as he closed on Leesil.

Leesil heard Chap coming, but he still couldn't spot Magiere, and the anmaglâhk in the cutway's mouth spun around. All Leesil could hope to do was scatter everyone's attention until Chap reached him. He thrust one foot back between Én'nish's legs.

He planted it hard, prepared to lurch back into her and twist, and . . .

A tall form appeared too suddenly, too silently from the cutway's darkness.

It was as if the figure had been there in the dark all along and simply materialized in the passage's opening. The one anmaglâhk standing before the cutway and now facing Leesil didn't seem to hear it. Leesil's senses sharpened as his mind took in the newcomer.

He was taller than any elf in sight and broader of shoulder. Instead of forest gray, he wore a dusky wool cloak with a full hood. His face was lost in the hood's shadows, though his jaw and mouth appeared to be covered with a black scarf or wrap. But even if he wasn't dressed like the Anmaglâhk, in his gloved hands were long, silver-white stilettos.

Leesil couldn't believe how many elves from the eastern continent had been sent so far from home to come after them—after Magiere.

It had been more than two years since they had secured the first orb and fled with it, only to have a pair of anmaglâhk come for them, demanding Magiere release what she had into their hands. The confrontation had ended in bloodshed and death on both sides.

Apparently, it had not ended at all.

Leesil tried to peer beyond the newcomer into the alley. Where was Magiere? There were too many anmaglâhk to fight, even with Chap's help, if he remained captive. In that racing instant, two things happened.

The wire around Leesil's neck slid upward along his pinned blade, as if Én'nish were trying to slip it over the blade's tip to his throat. And the newcomer shouted in Elvish.

"Fhæt'as-na dœrsa!"

The one anmaglâhk before the cutway spun about and then quickly retreated two paces at the sight of the newcomer. The fourth anmaglâhk, creeping in to join his companion, froze three paces off, raising both blades in defense. And the wire stopped sliding up Leesil's blade.

Leesil couldn't speak Elvish, and Wynn had told him never to try. He understood the few words she'd taught him, but the newcomer's command in that guttural, lilting language had come too fast for him to catch anything. He didn't know what was happening, and he didn't care. This brief hesitation was all he needed.

Leesil slipped his blade tip out from beneath the garrote. As the wire snapped tight against his neck, he twisted around on Én'nish.

Chap slowed for an instant, startled by a tall form appearing suddenly in the cutway's opening.

"*Fhœt'as-na dœrsa!*"

He understood the an'Cróan dialect perfectly: *Disable the captor!*

The captor . . . not the captive? What was happening?

Then Leesil twisted around on his captor, and the garrote pulled taut against his neck.

Chap forgot everything and leaped from a dead run. He was in the air when he heard the small anmaglâhk shriek. Then he hit her, and they both tumbled along the cobblestones. A sharp pain burned across the side of his head. He scrambled up, ready to rush her again, and then froze.

The small one rolled over, teetering as she stood up. An arrow with black feathers was stuck through her left upper arm, and her silvery stiletto lay on the street.

Leesil ripped the garrote off his throat, but Chap was still stalled, wondering what had just happened. Who had shot the small female? And the voice of the newcomer worked in his thoughts.

Chap knew that voice from somewhere.

Leesil felt the garrote drag and cut across the back of his neck as Én'nish cried out. He stumbled as Chap knocked her clear, and then he ripped the garrote off, looking for the closest opponent, and . . .

The tall newcomer went straight at the anmaglâhk between them.

Both men became almost a blur in Leesil's sight. Amid the click and screech of stiletto blades, the anmaglâhk that Chap had faced up the street came racing in. Leesil had to turn away. His slash missed as the anmaglâhk passed him, and when he looked for Chap . . .

There was Én'nish, holding her left arm, with an arrow protruding from it. She nearly screamed out in Elvish, and Leesil understood only one word—*go!*

Everything changed.

Én'nish and the one who'd gone after Chap sped back the way Leesil had first come. The one creeping toward the cutway's mouth backed up and shouted at the last, now locked in battle with the tall newcomer. That last anmaglâhk leaped backward, trying to disengage, and the newcomer matched him like a shadow in flight. One of his blades cut out and up, slashing through that last anmaglahk's shoulder.

The anmaglâhk didn't flinch or pause. He twisted away from the newcomer's next strike and came straight at Leesil, and Leesil took a step to meet him. The anmaglâhk suddenly dropped to the street in midrun.

Leesil felt a foot hook his right ankle, and he careened forward, straight toward the newcomer. Off balance, all he could do was swing on instinct.

The tall newcomer instantly inverted one stiletto and sidestepped.

Leesil's weak strike met with empty air. Something struck his right temple and the world went black. Through the ringing in his ears, he barely felt the impact as he hit the cobble street.

Everything had gone dark again in Magiere's sight as she struggled to take up her falchion and rise again. All her wild hunger was gone, and without it, the pain in her thigh nearly made her fall. Her head was ringing and her neck ached from whatever had hit her. When she found herself down the cutway again, she wasn't certain how she'd gotten there.

The first thing she spotted out of the cutway's mouth was Leesil in the street, trying to get up. She hobbled along the cutway's wall, trying to get to him, and then the silhouette of a very tall figure stepped into her view.

The cloaked and hooded man, so overly tall, suddenly turned her way, as if knowing she was there.

A distant street lantern glinted on the thin anmaglâhk stilettos in his gloved hands. The stranger stood over Leesil.

Magiere tried to raise her falchion as she lunged along the cutway's wall.

That tall, cloaked figure flipped one blade into his other hand with the second weapon. He raised his empty hand, palm out toward her. His hood shifted as if he shook his head slightly.

Leesil regained his feet, but the newcomer remained where he stood, and Magiere hesitated.

She couldn't see much inside the dark pocket of the man's hood. With the exception of the dark fabric across his lower face, he wasn't dressed like an anmaglâhk. He reached down with his free hand and unfastened his cloak's corners, which were tied up around his waist, like an anmaglâhk would do. She noticed the cloak was brown, like the jerkin beneath it. With his marred, dun-colored pants and worn, soft calf-high boots, he looked like some overly tall, overly weathered traveler.

But not so with those blades in his hand.

Leesil wobbled, blinked, and rubbed his head as if, like Magiere, he'd been struck down. Chap came racing into view from down the street as Magiere reached the cutway's mouth. His hackles were stiff as he circled Leesil and growled at the stranger. When he caught sight of her, his growl faded.

A rush of memories flooded the forefront of Magiere's mind.

She saw a grove of trees outside the glade where Leesil's mother had been imprisoned. A party of anmaglâhk had attacked all of them, and Chap had tried to drive one off, chasing him. This memory replayed several times, and Magiere understood.

The anmaglâhk had fled for some reason. Chap had given chase and then broke off to come back.

The cloaked stranger raised his head a little, just enough that Magiere thought she saw the spark of amber eyes inside the darkness of his hood. A shrill whistle rose from him as he tucked both blades up his sleeves, waved Leesil forward, and then strode straight toward the cutway's mouth.

Magiere raised her falchion, and he slowed. Somewhere behind him, Chap began to growl again. The stranger pointed beyond Magiere, down the cutway, and then just walked right past, not even looking at her.

She was exhausted and the pain in her thigh was growing. With one shoulder against the wall, she tried to turn and keep the man in her sight.

Leesil was suddenly at her side. He sheathed one blade and grabbed her arm on the side opposite her wounded leg. Just the sight of his tan face brought her a little relief. They'd survived the Anmaglâhk—again—but the manner in which this had happened left Magiere wary as she glanced along the cutway.

The stranger paused down the dark path between the buildings. Half turning, he motioned for them to follow.

Magiere looked to Leesil, about to ask who the man was. Leesil just shook his head, his eyes unblinking, narrowed, and still fixed on the tall one. He pulled her arm over the back of his neck, and they headed down the cutway with Chap close behind, growling softly.

Chap did not care for this tall, convenient "savior" who had appeared out of the darkness. Although he had chased the fleeing anmaglâhk as far as he could, they had continuously split up, forcing him into choosing a quarry. He had kept after the wounded female to the last. Even with an arrow through her arm, she'd managed to make a leaping grab at a shop's awning. She pulled herself out of his reach and was gone across the rooftops before he could see which way.

Now Chap and his two charges followed this unknown, human-garbed savior down a narrow cutway in the night. He had heard only a few words from the man, who had spoken in the an'Cróan dialect of Old Elvish, as Wynn had labeled it. He could not get this newcomer's voice out of his head. Yet try as he did, he had not heard enough to match the voice to a face. With Leesil and Magiere ahead of him, he did not have a clear enough line of sight to try to dip into any of the stranger's rising memories.

The slap of stumbling steps sounded behind Chap, and he instantly wheeled in the narrow path.

Another shadowed figure crouched in the cutway behind him, as if it had dropped from above into a poor landing. Even in the dark, Chap spotted the bow in the figure's hand. He rushed at it, snapping for its face before it could straighten up. It dropped the bow, stumbling back along the wall in a hasty retreat.

"No . . . stop . . . friend! I am friend!"

The words were Belaskian, but the light male voice was thick with an elven accent—an an'Cróan accent.

"Chap . . . what are you doing?" Leesil called from up ahead.

Chap did not take his eyes off this second newcomer. This male wore a tawny brown cloak, and he was almost as tall as their unknown savior, though slighter of build. Strangely, his sleeves were narrow, leaving no room for blades inside them, and his left forearm had an archer's sheath strapped around it.

Chap crept closer, still snarling.

The slender figure quickly reached up and pulled back his hood, exposing large, slanted eyes with amber irises in the dark-skinned face of a young an'Cróan male. Those eyes were wide in worry, as they should be in facing him.

Chap stalled as he looked closer.

Long, white-blond hair framed long features . . . the kind that Wynn had once called horselike for their slight flatness, even to his long nose.

"Yes . . . yes, me," the elf said quickly.

Chap stopped growling.

It was Osha, who had accompanied all of them, along with Sgäile, in their search for the first orb.

Indeed, Osha had been a friend, even as an anmaglâhk. He had watched over Wynn as best he could, and stood as Leesil's witness in marriage to Magiere. Osha had been very fond—possibly more than fond—of Wynn. But the sight of him brought no relief to Chap. Sgäile was dead, and if Osha was here now, then . . .

Chap whirled, a rumble growing in his chest as his hackles rose. His jowls pulled back, baring his teeth, as he raced down the cutway to get past Leesil and Magiere.

He knew who that first tall stranger must be.

Leesil stood in the cutway, holding up Magiere with one winged punching blade in his hand as he looked back. He barely made out someone else in the cutway beyond Chap. In the moment, he was functioning almost on pure instinct, but he didn't like being forced to accept help from a stranger, especially one who fought like a well-trained anmaglâhk. But Magiere was injured, they were in a foreign city without lodgings, and they'd just barely escaped a surprise attack.

"What's going on back there?" Magiere whispered, and then gasped in sudden pain. "What's Chap doing?"

Leesil shook his head and made sure he had a good grip on her. She was bad off if she couldn't see the other figure beyond Chap. Glancing the other way, he spotted their rescuer farther on, standing where the cutway intersected with a broad alley. But their rescuer was not alone.

A third figure clutching a lantern with an open shutter waited near the intersection's far left corner. This one was smaller. Though *she* was fully hooded, Leesil could see a long wool skirt of dark green below the hem of a dull burgundy cloak. Her hands were slender and fragile, and she was more than a head shorter than the tall stranger. He studied her for only an instant, and then his attention dropped to the alley floor at her feet.

Barely two steps from the female's skirt hem lay a body.

Only the torso of that dead anmaglâhk clad in dark forest gray was visible from where Leesil stood. Its head was twisted around at an impossible angle.

The tall one snapped something in Elvish, flipping one hand quickly toward the lantern. Likely he wanted the small female to close its shutter. She only flinched at his voice, and her hood turned up toward him.

Leesil stiffened as the lantern illuminated the tan face of a young elven woman. But more startling was the spark of her eyes. Not amber, but topaz, leaning almost to pure green. He knew of only one elf . . . one quarter-blood in the world with eyes like that.

"Leanâlhâm?"

Magiere shuddered in Leesil's hold. "What?"

Before he answered, she peered along his sightline.

Magiere was riveted by the sight of Leanâlhâm, and Leesil hardly knew what to think. He'd not seen the girl in several years, and that had been in the an'Cróan Elven Territories of the eastern continent. She'd been a friend to him, Magiere, and Chap, and to Wynn, as well. What was she doing here?

"Yes . . . yes, me!"

He heard that voice behind him speaking poorly in Belaskian, and looked back. Almost instantly, a snarl sounded in the alley, and Chap came at him at a dead run.

Chap's fur bristled all over. He bared his teeth as he let out a crackling growl that wouldn't stop.

Leesil pulled Magiere against the cutway's wall and out of the way, and Chap bolted straight by them.

What was happening now?

"What is Leanâlhâm doing here?" Magiere asked, her voice growing louder. "Who is that with her?"

When she tried to pull away and head down the alley, Leesil restrained her.

"Watch our backs! Watch behind!" he told her, and then he let go.

Chap hadn't raised any warning memories for Leesil; he didn't have to. Leesil suddenly knew who was inside that cloak and hidden beneath that black face wrap. It all came together around an overly tall stranger dressed—disguised—like a human, but who fought like an anmaglâhk and frightened his own kind.

Leesil took off after Chap as he drew his second winged blade.

*   *   *

Magiere braced against the wall, falchion in hand, as she looked repeatedly up and down the cutway. At the far intersection stood Leanâlhâm, but Chap had raced by in a fury, leaving someone else behind all of them.

She tried to right herself, gripping her blade, and call up the hunger to eat away her pain. It barely answered her will, and the lantern in Leanâlhâm's hand burned her eyes slightly. When she looked back the other way, someone was right on top of her.

Magiere tried to raise her falchion one-handed as she made a grab with her other hand.

"No! No fight . . . We help!"

Magiere froze, stunned, as she stared into Osha's panicked face. She quickly looked down the cutway to where it met a crossing alley.

Chap threw himself at the tall figure as Leesil grabbed Leanâlhâm and jerked the girl away. The tall man spun out of reach, and Chap bounded off a shop's back corner. The stranger ducked into where the cutway continued beyond the alley.

Leesil closed behind the dog, shouting at Chap's target, "You . . . you old butcher! What are you up to now?"

Magiere started to hobble after them, and Osha quickly grabbed her arm to help her along. She tried to shake him off, but he wouldn't let go. Ahead, Leanâlhâm rushed at Leesil, the lantern rattling in her grip, and grabbed his sleeve.

"No . . . not do this," she shouted, her words broken in a language she couldn't speak well.

Leesil jerked free and pushed Leanâlhâm back as Magiere hobbled into the intersection, with Osha still determined to help her. When Leanâlhâm saw Magiere, her eyes widened at the sight of the embedded arrow in Magiere's thigh. Her cheeks were covered in tears, and she lunged, grabbing the front of Magiere's studded hauberk.

"Make . . . them stop!" she cried.

Magiere still didn't know what was going on, but if Chap was angry and

Leesil backed him up, Chap had good reason. She pulled out of Osha's grip and shoved Leanâlhâm behind her as the tall man stepped out of the cutway's far half.

He held anmaglâhk blades again, but he brushed off his hood with the back of one hand.

"Please," Leanâlhâm whispered, as she grabbed Magiere's sword arm.

But all Magiere could do was stare.

By the jostled lantern's light, four old scars ran at a slant across the tall elf's deeply tanned forehead. They cut through his right, feathery blond eyebrow, skipped over his hard amber eye, and continued at his cheekbone to disappear beneath the black cloth over his nose and mouth. His long, coarse hair was streaked with gray a tint darker than his people's natural white blond.

Magiere didn't need to see the rest of his face to know him. His full Elvish name was too difficult to pronounce, and she'd taken to calling him by a shortened version.

The sight of Brot'an, here in this city on another continent, was too much to take in after all that had happened this night. Brot'an ignored Leesil and Chap's threats and fixed only on Magiere.

She was still at a loss, and she was weakening under Leanâlhâm's weight pulling down her sword arm. The tears on the girl's cheeks had begun to dry, but her face was stained by pure fright. Why would Brot'an bring Osha, let alone Leanâlhâm, this far across the world?

Magiere had once made a promise to an anmaglâhk who'd been their guardian. She'd sworn to Sgäile, Leanâlhâm's "uncle," that whenever possible she would protect his quarter-blood niece. Sgäile had later sacrificed himself to guard Magiere and those with her. And here was Brot'an, one of less than a handful of shadow-grippers left in the world, a master among the Anmaglâhk.

Magiere forgot about everything but Leanâlhâm; the girl would not see more bloodshed tonight.

"Chap, stop it!" she demanded, and then louder. "Leesil, you back off!"

CHAPTER 7

Even after Magiere's demand, Chap couldn't control his anger once Brot'an—Brot'ân'duivé, the Dog in the Dark—pulled down the black scarf and revealed his face. All Chap could think of was the master anmaglâhk's treachery.

Brot'an had manipulated Leesil into assassinating Lord Darmouth in order to start a war among the human provinces of that warlord's region.

Brot'an had acted as Magiere's defense counsel in her trial before the an'Cróan's council of elders, but only in his effort to discredit and undermine Most Aged Father, the ancient leader of the Anmaglâhk.

Brot'an did nothing, helped no one, unless it furthered his own agenda.

What was he doing here, half a world away from his homeland and apparently at odds with his own caste? The possibilities kept Chap's hackles raised, but try as he might, he could not dip a single rising memory in the master anmaglâhk's mind. It was as if this butcher, as Leesil had so rightly said, was not truly standing there. And the more Brot'an stared at Magiere, the more Chap wanted to add more scars to the elder elf's face.

But Chap still needed to understand what was going on, for nothing here made sense.

The group of anmaglâhk who had ambushed them had opted for a frontal attack—not their usual way. They clearly wanted Magiere alive, and Chap could only guess that they wanted to know more about what she had taken from the ice-bound castle. But only one of four anmaglâhk who had followed them to that place had escaped to return home.

Now an entire group had come after Magiere across half a world.

Brot'an waged war subtly, and since he had just "saved" Magiere again, Chap could think of no way to show her otherwise. She might not fully trust the elder anmaglâhk, but she had a blind spot when it came to him. In addition, aside from Osha, the sight of young Leanâlhâm was startling. What could have possessed Brot'an to bring a young quarter-human girl into his scheme?

Chap backed up into the crossing alley, bumping against Leesil behind him. Brot'an remained at the cutway's mouth into the crossing alley. Chap turned sideways and peered around Leesil's legs to where Leanâlhâm clung to Magiere. But when he reached for rising memories within the girl, he found nothing. Likely her conscious thoughts were too filled with the moment to let anything else rise. Osha, staring with concern from behind Magiere, offered nothing better than the girl. All Chap caught from the young man were flashes of the long journey back to Miiska after the first orb had been recovered.

And why were neither Brot'an nor Osha dressed as anmaglâhk? Even while spying on enemies, they always wore their identical garb. For that matter, where were Osha's stilettos?

"What do you want this time?" Leesil nearly spat at Brot'an. "Who dies in this city to start another of your wars?"

Chap turned his attention upon the elder elf. Brot'an did not answer, and his gaze dropped slightly, as if he finally looked at something other than Magiere's face. Chap did not turn to see what, keeping his focus on Brot'an and waiting for some memory to slip out.

Brot'an's gaze rose as he commanded in Elvish, "Get them into hiding and tend her wound. I will make certain we are not followed."

Unable to stop himself, Chap swung around, searching for the target of these orders.

Osha was looking directly at the shadow-gripper, but his eyes held no awe for the legendary elder of his caste. This, too, appeared odd. The last time Chap had seen Osha, the young elf had nearly worshipped Brot'an.

Osha took a slow breath through his nose and let it out in the same way, as if trying to calm some inner turmoil. Or was it resentment? A fleeting memory rose in the young elf's consciousness, and Chap seized it.

A dark cavern, but the air was so hot Osha fought to breathe. A far precipice glowed with red flickering from below it, and the silhouette of a small, spindly form crouched before the edge of the great depths. Between it and Osha, on the blackened stone, lay a sword without a hilt. Red light reflected off its white metal, shimmering in the dark.

The memory vanished as quickly as it had come. Osha nodded once, finally acknowledging Brot'an.

Chap grew even more wary. For the first time, he noticed an odd, long, and narrow bundle of dark cloth protruding above Osha's right shoulder, next to the young elf's quiver. It was held in place by a cord running along the same path as the quiver's strap across his chest. But such a minor curiosity had to wait.

Osha stood close behind Magiere, and when he finally looked her way, Chap saw a hint of Osha's old innocence and purity resurface. Osha's long-featured face softened as he moved in on Magiere's side and softly grasped her other arm, like Leanâlhâm.

Magiere wouldn't move and kept her eyes on the girl. When she finally did glance away, it was to Brot'an, and her gaze hardened.

"What is Leanâlhâm doing here?" Magiere demanded.

A good question, though not the first one Chap wanted answered. He did note that Leanâlhâm cringed strangely at the sound of her own name. The reaction vanished as Magiere's balance faltered, and the girl's grip tightened, the lantern jostling, as she tried to use both hands.

Magiere gently but firmly pushed the girl behind her. "Why bring her into all of . . . whatever this is?"

Leanâlhâm looked past Magiere, likely at Brot'an, but again, the old shadow-gripper did not answer.

Chap almost turned to look, as well, until he saw Leanâlhâm's tear-stained expression harden with a scowl . . . as if in blame. Suddenly, a rising memory in the girl filled Chap's awareness.

He saw through Leanâlhâm's eyes as Brot'an stepped silently out of the night between two trees. The butcher was dressed in full anmaglâhk raiment, but Chap—or, rather, Leanâlhâm—saw rips and rents in the forest gray fabric of his attire, along with several large, dark patches. When he came a few more steps, the dark spots on his clothes became visible, still glistening.

Brot'an was spattered and stained in blood, his own or someone else's—perhaps both. The steady drip down the back of his right hand and off his dangling fingers was nearly black in the dark. Chap heard himself—heard Leanâlhâm—suck a breath in that remembered moment.

She averted her eyes, and the memory sank beyond Chap's reach. The girl took hold of Magiere again.

"Come," she said softly. "We have a safe place . . . where I can tend your wound."

Chap heard a rustle of cloth behind him.

"Where do you think you're going?" Leesil snapped.

By the time Chap spun, Brot'an was halfway down the cutway to the next street. His hood was pulled back up. Before Chap could move, Leanâlhâm rushed by.

She caught up with Brot'an and grasped his arm. He turned on her, making her flinch. Leanâlhâm looked back to the dead anmaglâhk lying at the near corner where the cutway crossed the alley.

"Please," she begged Brot'an, "do not leave him like this."

Chap heard the others shifting behind him, likely looking at the body. Anmaglâhk death rites were complicated and strict, but Brot'an was unmoved.

"I will prepare him for our ancestors," he answered, "when the living are tended first."

Brot'an reached out with two fingers and snapped the shutter of Leanâl-hâm's lantern closed.

The sudden change of light caught Chap off guard. By the time he blinked, only Leanâlhâm stood in the cutway's far half. He lunged past the girl, peering ahead, but the anmaglâhk master was gone.

"Come, Léshil," Osha said in Belaskian, using Leesil's elven name. "We go quick. Safe place."

Chap did not turn back for them. He ran on until the cutway emptied into another street. There he raced up and down, peering all ways.

Brot'an was nowhere to be seen.

Chap rumbled in his throat, even as he heard the others exit the cutway behind him. A hand fell gently on the base of his shoulders, startling him.

"I know, old friend," Leesil whispered, "but he *will* answer us, soon enough."

Dänvârfij—Fated Music—stood near the window of the room at their inn. Though she had chosen an establishment for her team of anmaglâhk not far from the Guild of Sagecraft, the view simply overlooked the street below. It was safer that way.

She had sent what was left of her contingent to watch the guild's castle from all sides. Hopefully, tonight they might finally learn the whereabouts of the monster, the one called Magiere. That one would likely return to this city somehow, someday. If she could not be spotted, then perhaps her half-elven consort or the tainted majay-hì might be. One way or another, that half-undead abomination would be found.

Dänvârfij did not let her hopes rise too high. She and hers had been in Calm Seatt for more than two moons and yet seen no sign of Magiere or her companions. Only one hint—one hope—had surfaced last night.

Wynn Hygeorht had returned to the guild, seemingly from nowhere.

So long as the little sage remained here, this city was the one place where

Magiere might eventually reappear. The sage was Magiere's only other known companion besides Léshil and the majay-hì they called Chap.

Dänvârfij still pondered how to learn where the young sage had been and how to use her if necessary to locate Magiere. As yet, nothing effective had come to mind—or at least nothing that would maintain secrecy and not end with the young sage's death. For even if Wynn knew nothing of Magiere's whereabouts, the little human might still be used as bait for a trap.

Dänvârfij closed her eyes, pondering events that had brought her to this deadlock. She remembered a weathered face with sharp features and white-blond hair cut so short it bristled upon his head.

Hkuan'duv—the Blackened Sea—had been her mentor for five years.

She had traveled with him, trained with him, and slept beside him on the open ground. In the beginning, she hardly believed that one of the four remaining Greimasg'äh—shadow-grippers—agreed to be her jeóin, or "assentor." He would be the one to complete her final training, until he judged her fit to stand for herself among the caste. Always cold and remote, it was only after two years with him that she had begun to suspect his feelings for her went deeper than that of a mentor.

Dänvârfij knew she was not beautiful. Tall for her own people, she could look most males in the eyes. Her nose was a bit too long, her cheekbones a bit too wide, and then there were her scars. All anmaglâhk had scars, though some were unseen to the eye.

But Hkuan'duv had loved her, though he had never acted on it.

Anmaglâhk lived lives of service. They were not forbidden from bonding to another, but it was rarely done. They were wed to the guardianship of their people—*in silence and in shadow*—and Dänvârfij never revealed her awareness of Hkuan'duv's true heart. The day he assented and released her among the Anmaglâhk was the day she had bested him with the bow during a hunt. In the following years, they occasionally shared purpose in a mission. She found quiet contentment, simple joy for the future, knowing she might again spend such times with him.

It was enough—it had to be enough—until Most Aged Father sent them after that pale-skinned monster who had walked in and out of their land. They were to wait and watch until Magiere acquired an "artifact" of the Ancient Enemy and then take it from her by any means. More untenable was that one of the most honorable of the Anmaglâhk—Sgäilsheilleache, Willow's Shade—had sworn to protect Magiere and hers. It had all ended in horror beyond Dänvârfij's imagining.

Hkuan'duv and Sgäilsheilleache went at each other over whatever that half-dead woman had taken from the castle. That alone was unthinkable among their caste—and then they killed each other in the same instant.

Outnumbered amid failure, Dänvârfij had fled in grief for her homeland.

Telling Most Aged Father what had happened was only second in misery to her loss. He had called the death of Hkuan'duv a tragedy for the Anmaglâhk—for all an'Cróan. "Tragedy" was not a strong enough word for Dänvârfij. But it was the death of Sgäilsheilleache that struck Most Aged Father the most, almost more than the failure of Dänvârfij's purpose.

She had seen the misery beneath the rage in the ancient patriarch's eyes. Then, once word had somehow slipped out concerning what had happened, some anmaglâhk cursed Sgäilsheilleache as a traitor. Most Aged Father had suffered that in silence.

The unthinkable had happened. Anmaglâhk had killed anmaglâhk. Their collective purpose had been wounded by the death of Hkuan'duv. Repercussions spread like ripples from a drop of blood striking a pool of . . .

"Tea . . . is there any left?"

Dänvârfij opened her eyes as she turned from the window.

Fréthfâre—Watcher of the Woods—sat bent forward in a corner chair, a heavy walking rod leaning against her right thigh. As the true leader of the team, she was the only other who had remained behind with Dänvârfij. But she was not fit to lead, in body or in mind.

Once the Covârleasa—Trusted Advisor—to Most Aged Father, Fréthfâre was a fanatically loyal anmaglâhk and a sometime cunning strategist. Dänvârfij had never wanted the crippled Covârleasa included in this current mission, and her doubts grew with every passing night.

Fréthfâre's appearance was somewhat unique among the an'Cróan. Her hair was wheat gold, not the white blond of their people. It hung in waves instead of silky and straight. In her youth, she had been viewed as slender and supple. Approaching only middle age, somewhere shy of fifty years, she appeared beyond such a reckoning and almost brittle.

"Tea?" Fréthfâre repeated.

"It is likely gone," Dänvârfij answered. "I will make more."

She went to the room's small hearth, built above the one below on the inn's main floor, and set a blackened kettle in the remaining coals.

Fréthfâre nodded and then coughed, and a cough turned to a spasm as she grimaced. She buckled even more where she sat and pressed a hand against her abdomen. That hand remained there until her shudders ceased.

Dänvârfij watched this in silence. Her concern was not all for her companion's state.

Fréthfâre had aged quickly in the past two years, since the night that Magiere had run her sword through the Covârleasa's abdomen. Fréthfâre had spent long moons recovering under the constant care of healers, but she had been crippled for life . . . however long that would last. Her suffering only fed her hatred and obsession for the one who had done this to her.

Dänvârfij knew passionate emotion had no place in service to a purpose. But there had been nights since Hkuan'duv's death when she doubted even herself in this.

"Would you prefer the mint," she asked, "or savory?"

"The savory," Fréthfâre whispered with effort. She finally settled back in her chair, her breaths coming quick and shallow. A sheen had developed on her strained face.

Lately, they spoke of nothing of import, if at all. There was little to say until sound information had been gained to fulfill their purpose.

When the water began to hiss, Dänvârfij scalded leaves in a clay cup and held it out. Fréthfâre nodded and took it, and Dänvârfij prepared a cup for herself. It would be another long night of waiting.

"I know," Fréthfâre said. "I tire of this, too. But we will have our revenge."

There the truth slipped, and Dänvârfij said nothing. She returned to watching and poking at the floating leaves steeping in her own cup.

Fréthfâre seemed driven only by a need for vengeance. The crippled Covârleasa should never have been assigned to this purpose, this mission— and likely she had not. At a guess, she had demanded it of Most Aged Father.

Dänvârfij would not succumb to rage or hunger for revenge, though she had reason for both. Instead, shame and sorrow burned inside her. She had failed Most Aged Father once. She had lost a secret treasure of her own in Hkuan'duv. And her caste was tearing itself apart.

When Most Aged Father had asked her to prepare a team and sail to a foreign continent, she had not hesitated. Their purpose was direct and clear on the surface: locate Magiere or Léshil or the tainted majay-hì, learn anything possible concerning the mysterious artifact they had recovered, and then eliminate all three.

She had balked at the thought of killing a majay-hì until Most Aged Father convinced her the one the humans called Chap was an abomination, like the pale-skinned monster he guarded. She would always follow Most Aged Father's counsel—as had Hkuan'duv.

"Perhaps we could go over the city's layout again?" Fréthfâre suggested. "Has anything further been added in scouting?"

"Nothing," Dänvârfij replied, though she would take any excuse to fill the nagging silence. "I will get it just the same."

As straightforward as their purpose was, its execution had proven anything but simple. Even as the rift among her caste had grown, she could not have foreseen—

The window opened from the outside.

"Fréthfâre," a voice breathed, as someone climbed into the room.

Dänvârfij was not alarmed and calmly turned her head. She knew the sound of every member's movements, like a second voice. But when

Én'nish landed lightly on the floor, she wore a makeshift bandage around her upper left arm. Three tall forms—Rhysís, Eywodan, and Tavithê—followed after Én'nish before Dänvârfij's stomach tightened and she rose to her feet.

Rhysís was bleeding from a head wound, and Tavithê took a moment to check it. Tavithê's cloak and tunic had been slashed open across his chest, and a slow stain spread into the forest gray cloth at his shoulder.

Wy'lanvi and Owain were missing.

"What happened?" Fréthfâre demanded.

"Where are Wy'lanvi and Owain?" Dänvârfij asked.

Én'nish hesitated, as if not knowing which question to answer first. She was another team member for whom Dänvârfij held great reservations. The smallest and youngest of the team had a blemished history among the caste. She had even been cast aside by her own jeóin.

Én'nish was rash, overrun by her own emotions of hatred, born from an even deeper grief than Dänvârfij could truly imagine. All here knew that Én'nish had mated with her bóijtäna—prebetrothed—before their true betrothal and subsequent bonding. As with all an'Cróan, intimacy linked two people in a way that any ritual of bonding could never represent. It was why a period of waiting was always required before commitment or the actual pairing. Én'nish would now suffer the loss of Groyt'ashia like a sickness that could never be cured.

It had been Fréthfâre who had brought Én'nish back into the caste. All Én'nish wanted, her whole reason for hounding Fréthfâre to be included, was the blood of Léshil.

"Answer—now!" Dänvârfij commanded.

"Wy'lanvi was in position, but he never appeared." Én'nish said quickly. "Owain circled back to look for him, in case—"

"Position?" Fréthfâre cut in. "For what?"

Én'nish shook her head hard, as if to clear it. "We spotted our quarry. All three of them, leaving the guild's castle."

"Here?" Dänvârfij said, taking a step toward Én'nish. "In the city?"

Én'nish's eyes shifted several times to Fréthfâre and back before she answered.

"Yes. We decided to follow. When they headed into one of the more barren, decrepit districts, it was decided to try to take them before—"

"It was decided? You mean you decided!" Dänvârfij returned, for she knew how this had truly come about. "And when were you given lead in our purpose? You were to watch . . . and report!"

"Dänvârfij, enough," Fréthfâre said. "Continue, Én'nish."

Én'nish turned fully to Fréthfâre, ignoring Dänvârfij.

"We thought to capture one or more of them—tonight—and bring them to you," Én'nish went on. "Our position was as good as could be . . . in a narrow, nearly deserted street. Four of us blocked the street's ends, prepared to drive them into a side path, where Wy'lanvi would cut them off. Owain stayed on the rooftops to cover us, but . . ."

She trailed off, and Dänvârfij knew what she was about to say.

"Again . . . Brot'ân'duivé," Fréthfâre whispered.

Dänvârfij briefly closed her eyes; Owain would never find Wy'lanvi.

When they had left their homeland, they had been eleven in count. Dänvârfij had counseled Fréthfâre in choosing three trios of their caste. Never before had so many of the Anmaglâhk taken up the same purpose together. Their task had been that dire in the eyes of Most Aged Father, who greatly feared any device of the Ancient Enemy remaining in human hands.

Eleven had left together, but someone else had shadowed them. Even along the way, after the second death and before they knew for certain, Dänvârfij could not bring herself to believe it. Only on the night when she had seen his unmistakable, immense shadow with her own eyes did she acknowledge the truth.

Eight had reached this city, and now seven remained. The traitorous Brot'ân'duivé had been picking them off one by one, across half the world. A greimasg'äh, a master among them, was killing his own.

There had been no deaths among them since a moon before they reached

Calm Seatt. Dänvârfij had hoped they had lost Brot'ân'duivé. It had been a very desperate hope.

She glanced at Rhysís. He appeared oblivious of his head wound as he met her gaze. Of all she had selected with Fréthfâre, she knew him best and had never seen him openly angry before. He was slender and thin-lipped, always wore his hair loose; it was now matted on his forehead with his own blood. His eyes smoldered in his silence. Rhysís had liked Wy'lanvi, the youngest of their team, and had often played "elder brother" when the need arose.

Dänvârfij took a step back, but he moved closer, looking into her face as he whispered, "In silence and in shadows."

She did not need his words, the creed of their caste, to remind her of their purpose. The mission was all that mattered. Their targets were here in the city. Though only six of her remaining team were still able—as Fréthfâre was not—that would be enough.

"Let me see to your head wound," she said. "Fréthfâre, will you tend Tavithê's shoulder? Én'nish, how bad is your arm?"

Én'nish was not listening, and began pacing, exhaling hissing breaths.

"I had him," she spat. "I had my wire around his throat."

"Brot'ân'duivé?" Fréthfâre asked in surprise.

Dänvârfij almost scoffed at such a notion. "Léshil," she guessed out loud, watching Én'nish with growing concern.

Vengeance was like a disease, and Brot'ân'duivé was the carrier that kept spreading it among them. Dänvârfij looked warily upon Rhysís again.

"That is not all," he said quietly. "*He* was not alone. An archer on the rooftops hit Én'nish and then fired at Owain."

Dänvârfij grew cold and shook her head. "No . . . besides Brot'ân'duivé, who would fire on their own caste?"

No one answered her, but Rhysís would not have said it unless he was certain. Dänvârfij took a clearer look at Én'nish's arm as Fréthfâre unwrapped it.

"Are you disabled?" she asked.

"No, it was only through the skin. Eywodan broke and pulled the arrow easily."

"Did you double back to follow their escape?" Dänvârfij asked.

Rhysís glanced away, and even Én'nish remained silent. Tavithê settled in a chair to suffer Fréthfâre's ministrations and shook his head.

"We could not," he said bluntly. "With three of us injured and Wy'lanvi missing, our only course was to retreat . . . with the majay-hì harrying us. Only Owain turned back, once we lost the majay-hì."

Dänvârfij nodded. Tavithê had broad shoulders for an elf. His grasp of human languages had never been strong, but he was almost unparalleled in hand-to-hand combat. Dänvârfij could only assume he had been fighting Brot'ân'duivé to take a wound like that.

Tavithê had been correct. Better to regroup and plan rather than to counterstrike blindly in defeat.

"This will have to be sewn up," Fréthfâre said, peering at Tavithê's wound.

Tavithê grimaced. He would fight four armed opponents at once but did not care for needles. Dänvârfij decided further questions, ones that Fréthfâre had not seen fit to ask, could wait.

Pieces of the evening were still missing. She needed to learn everything as quickly as possible and reestablish a watch on the guild's castle. Then it would be time to report to Most Aged Father. All that mattered now was acquiring their targets.

Eywodan, the oldest of the team, had not spoken so far. He kept glancing out the window, perhaps watching for Owain's return. Something needed to be done, and questions were all Dänvârfij had left, regardless of the wounded.

"Tell me everything, step by step," she said to Eywodan, "beginning at the Guild of Sagecraft."

Chane stood on the docks of Beranlômr Bay, watching two sailors near a small, two-masted schooner unloading crates from a wagon. One of them stumbled getting down out of the wagon and then staggered, thumping the crate against the wagon's tailboard. Clattering and clinks of glass sounded from inside the crate.

"Easy with that!" a third, wide man ordered. "There's a score of bottles of spiced mead for a thänæ in there. Break 'em, and you'll be making up the cost for the next season!"

Both sailors flinched, taking greater care as they crept up the plank onto the schooner's deck.

The mention of a thänæ—an honored one among the dwarves—was fortunate for Chane.

"Are you the captain of this ship?" he asked, approaching the wide-chested man. "And bound for Dhredze Seatt?"

The man looked him up and down.

Chane was well aware that he no longer resembled a well-dressed young nobleman, much as he once had. His boots were too dusty and more worn than even his clothes. He spoke Numanese well, but his accent and maimed voice would always draw some attention.

"And if I am?" the man challenged.

"I am a friend of Shirvêsh Mallet at the temple of Bedzâ'kenge," Chane explained. "I need a letter to reach him as quickly as possible."

Chane pulled out his coin pouch and loosened its tie. There were few coins in it, and he was not about to show them until he heard the cost. It should not be much, considering the captain already headed for the needed destination.

The captain's expression shifted with concern. "Mallet? Is the letter important?"

"Yes."

The captain held out his hand. "I'll make sure he receives it, soon as we reach port."

Chane took a little relief as he tilted the pouch to pour out coins. "How much?"

The captain shook his head. "Mallet's done me a good turn more than once. Gained me business among the clans of his tribe."

Chane blinked in hesitation. As the son of a harsh father, a noble in his homeland during his life and later as an undead in hiding, preying on the living, he had been given little in his life that had not cost him in the end. Certainly, rarely, had it ever come from a stranger.

He did not know what to say, at first, but he had no wish to be obliged to anyone.

"I have dwarven slugs of no use to me," he offered. "Take some."

The captain shrugged with a half smile. "As you wish."

Chane counted out three copper slugs with holes in their center, not truly knowing what they were worth. The captain took them along with the folded-up paper, and he looked it over.

"No addressment?" the captain asked, for Chane had not marked the outside wrapping sheet.

"Not necessary," he answered. "Shirvêsh Mallet will understand."

"He'll get by midmorning," the captain said with a nod, and tromped off up the ramp to his ship.

Indeed, Chane had not addressed the letter, for he could not. Its ultimate destination was not the hands of Shirvêsh Mallet. He needed help, and this was his only method of sending for it, and hopefully Mallet would quickly pass it on to the true recipient.

CHAPTER 8

Pawl a'Seatt crossed the small front room of his scribe shop, the Upright Quill, and locked the door for the night. The space was neat and sparse, with only an old counter across the room's back and a few wooden display stands supporting open books with ornate examples of the shop's script work. He flipped the counter's folding section to step behind it and checked that everything beneath it had been stored away in orderly fashion. Finally, he turned to head through the right door behind the counter and into the workroom.

The rear of any scriptorium was quite different from the outer room for customers. That of the Upright Quill was filled with tall, slanted scribing tables and matching stools, along with one large desk and a chair.

Although it was halfway to night's first bell, lanterns still hung about, filling the space with saffron-colored light. Stacks and sheaves of blank, crisp paper and a few of the more expansive and traditional parchments were piled on shelves lining all the walls, except for the space where there was a heavy rear door. There were also bottles of varied inks, jars of drying talc and sand, binding materials, and other sundry tools and supplies. Everywhere lay scattered quills, blotting pads, bracing sticks to keep a scribe's hand off the page, and trimming knives.

It was rather chaotic compared to what patrons saw out front.

Most of Pawl's staff had gone home for the night, including his master scribe, Teagan. But he still awaited the return of two apprentices—Liam and young Imaret—sent off on an errand. He never sent anyone out alone after dark.

Pacing the floor of the workroom, he ran a hand through his shoulder-length black hair. Although a few strands of it appeared grayed, his face looked young. Glancing down, he noticed a smudge of chalk on his charcoal gray suede jerkin, but he didn't try to rub it off. He was too preoccupied.

Spring had edged in and the nights were growing warmer, but Pawl had been trapped in the same stalled state since last autumn. Two seasons past, his shop—along with four others—had been almost overwhelmed by work from the Guild of Sagecraft. The guild had undertaken an enormous translation project. Pages upon pages of translator's notes from a wild array of ancient tongues were sent out for transcription into more legible copies. Later came final transcription to finished pages. But the languages didn't matter, for all materials were written in the sages' Begaine syllabary, a script that few nonsages could fathom.

Though no one knew it, Pawl was one of the exceptions. A number of pieces he'd read had left him shaken.

He'd read every page that passed in and out of his shop, but there were too many gaps and disconnections. Likely the guild's premins had purposefully made sure that no one shop, no one scribe, worked on any lengthy, contiguous passages.

Though Pawl had remained stoic and self-possessed, he had grown frantic for more information, as the pieces he'd seen didn't answer his questions. His mind had churned with an urge he'd put aside so long ago. Then, two sages carrying back finished work from his shop to the guild had been murdered in an alley.

Everything changed—worsened—after that.

Before all of this, pages sent to varied shops were always mixed. Pawl had pieced together only a little of what he did read and much of it was incomplete. But after the murders, the Premin Council decided to have all transcription work completed inside their grounds, and only one scriptorium's scribes were to be brought in to continue transcription.

Pawl a'Seatt made certain his scribes were the ones chosen, but it had cost him to make it so. Unfortunately, even then, his access to the work became more limited.

While on guild grounds, his scribes were individually cloistered. None of them saw what the others worked on, and none had the gift of memory that Imaret did.

Pawl himself was cut off almost completely.

On occasion, he was allowed to check on his scribes on the pretense of reviewing the quality of their work, but he was always watched. He could never pause too long at the shoulder of one of his people or it would be obvious that his attention was on the content and not the quality of those sheets.

He closed his eyes, and unwanted memories came . . . or fragments more disjointed than those snippets of ancient writings sent out for transcription.

Had it truly been a thousand years—or was it less or more? Like so many among the fearful masses of nations long forgotten, he had gone to war, or tried to. Had he been compelled by a father, a conscription agent, or a tribal elder? Or had it been his own choice? Memories were sketchy things, like the simplistic renderings of a historian who hadn't experienced the events he recorded.

Pawl remembered hints in the lengthy shadows of time that he'd gone south along the western coast, like so many other young men. He had no memory of actual war and comrades-in-arms. He did know that he never made it that far. But he remembered a white-faced woman.

Her shiny black hair hung in wild tendrils almost to the waist of her oddly scintillating robe. That fabric, like silk or elven shéot'a, was covered in swirling patterns of flowers. It covered her small, lithe body, shifting over her diminutive curves. That full wrap robe or gown was like no attire of any people he'd ever seen. Had she come from somewhere far away, perhaps beyond the western ocean? And her eyes . . .

He would never forget her eyes.

Almond-shaped and slightly slanted, they were not those of an elf perhaps suffering under some paling illness. She was far too short for that race. Her irises, seemingly black for an instant, had changed to something akin to clear crystal. Cold and uncaring as they fixed on him, they held hungered obsession as she had stepped closer on the rocky shore.

Pawl could no longer remember if he had touched her. He remembered only awaking beneath the surf, his lungs filled with saltwater.

Even beneath the water, in the darkness, his eyes could *see*, except for the cloud of blood floating around him. He choked in panic at first, and the chill water rushed in and out of his chest as he tried to breathe while clawing for the surface. When the breaking surf tumbled his body onto the stony shore, he was still trying to breathe . . . and didn't need to. He rolled onto his hands and knees and heaved out seawater in his lungs. Air rushed in to replace water, but it did not matter.

So much could be forgotten, and the longer one existed, the more one lost. Only those memories most precious, most horrid, lasted until they alone remained, disjointed and disconnected among newer memories that replaced the ones fading again and again over centuries.

And where was this woman he had seen only once on the night he'd awakened as from drowning . . . with his throat torn open, his body cold to the core?

Pawl opened his eyes in the back room of his scriptorium. If he still existed, so must she. He had seen names in those scant sheets for transcription from the guild. Was she one of them? Could that be possible?

He ran his hands down his face. No matter the hatred and need that clung to those few, unbroken pebbles of memories, his responsibilities here came first. He had his existence, in *his* city, to attend.

The world he'd created here for himself was his best protection. He never lost sight of this, and he glanced at the unlocked back door, its stout iron bar leaning beside it. What was keeping Liam and Imaret?

Despite the guild having both slowed and altered the project, they still provided his shop with a good deal of other work. A journeyor in the order of Sentiology had recently returned from his first year's assignment. Premin Renäld had engaged Pawl's scriptorium to transcribe the young man's journals for the guild's archive. The deadline was today.

Upon arriving at the shop this evening, Pawl had found that his scribes weren't finished. He sent Imaret and Liam to assure the premin of completion by tomorrow at closing. As a matter of principle, he kept all patrons fully informed. A one-day extension should cause no concern.

Hopefully it wasn't Imaret who kept him waiting.

The first two sages murdered last autumn had been friends of hers—one of them in particular. The pair had another close companion at the guild, Nikolas Columsarn, who'd later been attacked. Naturally, shared loss had brought Imaret and Nikolas together, and the young sage had begun spending much of his free time at the shop. Imaret used any excuse possible to go visit him.

For all his quiet, nervous nature, Nikolas possessed a sharp, curious mind. More central to Pawl's curiosity was the boy's interest in history. Something about Nikolas Columsarn pulled at Pawl. It wasn't pity, but rather a driven need to . . . protect what was his.

Pawl grew more anxious and wary after each of Nikolas's visits, lingering longer each night as they pored over papers and books brought from Pawl's own home library. Attachments of any kind were a danger, and he already had enough of those in managing the shop and its staff, and especially Imaret.

And she still kept him waiting.

He stepped to the back door, reaching for his broad-brimmed hat and black cloak on a peg beside it, preparing to step out and look for the girl. But the back door flew open, and he stopped it with one hand before it struck him.

Imaret nearly fell inside, breathing hard, and cried, "Master?"

She looked about wildly, and Liam followed her in, appearing equally unsettled. Pawl startled both of them as he stepped from behind the door and closed it.

"What is it?" he asked immediately.

Small for her age, Imaret had her mother's dusky skin and mass of slightly kinky black hair. Liam stood a full head taller than her, and had reddish hair and pale blue eyes. Pawl guessed them to both to be about sixteen years old, although he'd never asked.

"The guild is locked down." Imaret panted. "It's under guard. City guard!"

Pawl froze for three of Imaret's fast breaths. "Slow down . . . and explain."

"We didn't even get to the courtyard," she rushed on. "The portcullis was down, and the Shyldfälches are walking the walls, and Nikolas is trapped inside!"

Her words left Pawl anxious, though likely not for the same reasons as her. She wasn't making sense, and he turned his hard gaze on Liam.

"We weren't able to deliver our message properly," Liam added. "We refused to leave, insisting we would stand there until a guard sent word that we were waiting . . . and we kept on waiting. We thought they'd let us in, but it wasn't Premin Renäld who finally came out. It was Domin High-Tower. He didn't care about the journeyor's work we should've completed, and he said all work on the translation project has been suspended. You're not to send any scribes until further notice . . . from him. And then he just walked off!"

Imaret was still panting, and her face was distraught. Pawl had no time to reassure her, for Nikolas was the least of his concerns. Something drastic had happened if Sykion had halted all work on the translation project. But what would cause her to call in the city guard?

Pawl was now completely cut off . . . indefinitely.

"Did High-Tower or the guards give any reason for why this has happened?" he asked.

Both apprentices shook their heads.

"Nikolas hates being locked in," Imaret said. "He hated it when he was . . . when it happened last autumn."

Nikolas had been assaulted, like several other young sages. Unlike them, he had survived, just barely. He had spent more than a moon in convalescence, and even now was not fully recovered—perhaps never would be.

Pawl could not squelch a flash of pity. Imaret was afraid for the only friend she had left, and he could not let this impede her valued skills. She was more than just a gifted scribe in training. Even at her young age, he had come to depend on her for artistic assignments.

She could reproduce anything she read from memory, character for character, whether she could read it or not.

"Liam, take Imaret directly home," Pawl instructed. "No deviations. And then do so yourself."

He looked down at Imaret and placed his wide-brimmed hat on his head. He slung his cloak over his shoulders and began to tie it. She hadn't argued, but she looked up at him, as if barely restraining an urgent plea.

"I will go to the guild myself tonight," he told her. "Tomorrow, I'll tell you what I learn."

Her dusky little face flushed with relief, and then: "Couldn't we wait here, until you—"

"Home now," he said sharply, and then calmed, looking for a rational way to dissuade her. "I already risk censure from your parents for keeping you this late. Both of your families will soon begin worrying."

Imaret blinked at him, and Pawl had a strange feeling she might argue—not with his reasoning or his instructions, but with something else he had said. She glanced back at Liam and turned away in resignation.

"You'll ask after Nikolas?" she said, reaching for the door's handle.

"I will try," he answered, not willing to make a promise.

Once Pawl had seen off both apprentices, he headed in the other direction—toward the guild's castle. He moved quickly through the dark streets, wondering if perhaps Imaret and Liam had overstated the situation. Emotion and personal concerns often narrowed the perspectives of the young. Soon he found himself heading up Old Procession Road, and the inner bailey gate lay just ahead. But as he opened the gate, he saw that Imaret's emotional outburst had been no frightened exaggeration.

The portcullis was closed, and a Shyldfälche in a red tabard peered out at him through the thick, upright beams. Pawl spotted another one heading off along the bailey wall's southern half.

He approached the portcullis, greeting the guard inside with only a nod. The man was very large, with a shaved head and an overly affected grimace.

"Can I help you, sir?" the guard asked, though his tone hardly suggested interest in doing so.

"I am Master a'Seatt from the Upright Quill," Pawl said, intentionally pitching his tone to slightly haughty and annoyed. "My scriptorium is engaged in several projects for the sages, yet two of my apprentices were sent away earlier tonight. Please tell Domin High-Tower I wish to speak with him . . . now."

The guard's expression didn't change, and he merely answered, "Domin High-Tower has given instructions that he's not to be disturbed. Come back tomorrow."

All the bald guard did was stand there, arms crossed, staring out through the portcullis beams.

Pawl stared back in a silent moment of indecision. The guild grounds indeed had been locked down. The work for his shop was the most immediate practical concern, but he had also lost the means to fulfill his own desire. Pressing the matter here and now might only prolong such loss or even make it permanent.

He finally turned back out the bailey gate and up Old Procession Road. But he kept remembering the names he had read in those mixed fragments sent for transcription at his shop.

Vespana, Ga'hetman, Jeyretan . . . Fäzabid and Memaneh . . . Uhmgadâ, Creif, and Sau'ilahk . . . Volyno and Häs'saun . . . and Li'kän.

Was *she* among them?

Patience was a benefit of a long existence, but like anything else, it could be worn thinner than the finest paper.

*　　*　　*

Magiere allowed Leanâlhâm to help hold her up as they waited in a cutway between two buildings. Chap and Leesil were flattened up against the wall nearer the street, keeping watch. Leesil had managed to retrieve their travel chest, and it rested on the ground beside him along with their packs.

The building at Magiere's back was some form of tall, three-story inn. Osha had gone around to the front to enter, make his way to the back, and let them all inside, out of sight. But in waiting, Magiere looked down and cupped Leanâlhâm's face with one hand.

"What are you doing here?" she whispered.

As the question escaped her lips, Leanâlhâm's eyes widened. She quickly put her hand over Magiere's mouth and shook her head for silence.

When Magiere had last left Leanâlhâm, the girl had been safe at home in the elven forest of the eastern continent, living with the elderly healer Gleann, Leanâlhâm's so-called "grandfather." Leesil's mother, Nein'a, had gone to stay with them as well. Magiere could only imagine the girl's grief, as well as Gleann's, upon hearing of the death of her "uncle," Sgäile. Although Sgäile had been related to the girl and the old healer by blood, Magiere had never quite understood elven familial connections. Titles like "grandfather" and "uncle" were likely a bit too simple.

What could have possessed Brot'an to take Leanâlhâm away from such a peaceful life? Magiere jerked her head away from Leanâlhâm's hand. "Why aren't you at home with your grandfather?"

Leanâlhâm didn't answer and looked away toward the cutway's back end, but Osha hadn't appeared yet.

Magiere could no longer see Leanâlhâm's face inside the girl's hood. She began to suspect something more than fear of being overheard by their enemies caused the girl's silence.

"Leanâlhâm?" she whispered, more gently.

The girl instantly cringed, almost as if the word were a blow, and then suddenly she straightened and pulled on Magiere's arm.

Osha was leaning around the inn's back corner, waving all of them to follow him.

Magiere looked back the other way. "Psst!"

Leesil glanced back, as did Chap, and she waved them into retreat. They followed as Magiere hobbled down the cutway toward Osha, with Leanâlhâm's help. Around back, Osha opened a back door that had been left cracked and ushered them inside to the nearby stairs.

The effort and agony of making the climb did little to distract Magiere, for Leanâlhâm was still too quiet.

Leesil wasn't surprised to find that Brot'an had chosen a room on the top floor. Anmaglâhk had a penchant for coming and going via rooftops. But in the moment, he didn't much care. Once he'd put down their belongings, he took hold of Magiere's arm, quickly unbelted her falchion, and then helped Leanâlhâm get her settled on the room's one narrow bed. After the madness of this night, he and Chap had finally gotten Magiere locked away in at least the illusion of safety.

"Are you in much pain?" he asked.

As Magiere leaned back, Leanâlhâm pushed a blanket-covered pack under her shoulders and head. Magiere finally shook her head in reply, but Leesil knew she was lying.

Her pale features were strained, and her jaw was clenched. He wanted to give her a few moments before they tried to remove the arrow. The pain was going to get much worse.

Leanâlhâm knelt on the floor at the bed's other side as Leesil glanced about, spotting a small pile of travel gear in the corner—water skins, another blanket, and two more packs. Besides these, there was only a small table big enough for one person's needs, two stools, and a tin pitcher and basin near the door. He couldn't tell how long Brot'an had been staying here.

Chap padded to the filthy window. He rose, and with his front feet on the sill, he huffed for attention as he pawed the open slide bolt where the window's two halves closed together. Then he growled, glancing back at Leesil.

"Lock that up," Leesil said, looking to Osha. "At least then we'll hear anyone trying to get in."

Instead, Osha unslung his quiver and then viciously pulled the slipknot of another cord across his chest. He caught the long and narrow cloth-wrapped bundle sliding down his back and tossed—nearly threw—it into the corner atop the other gear.

Osha shuddered once with a grimace, rubbing his shoulder, as if the burden were heavier than it could possibly be. Leesil wondered what was wrapped inside the cloth, but this was not the time to ask.

Chap dropped down from the sill and backed up as Osha stepped to the window. Instead of locking it, Osha opened one half partway and peered out into the night and upward toward the roof. When he closed it again, he didn't bolt it.

Chap growled softly and looked at Leesil, but they both knew what this was about: Brot'an. Osha expected the shadow-gripper to come in from above. Chap's jowls wrinkled as he stalked toward the door and lay down to watch the window and the whole room.

Leesil turned his attention back to Magiere.

Just across the bed, Leanâlhâm was already examining Magiere's wound.

"What are you doing here?" he asked her with one quick glance at Osha. "Either of you . . . why aren't you with Gleann . . . and my mother? Leanâlhâm?"

Leanâlhâm tensed but remained fixed on splitting Magiere's pant leg from around the protruding arrow. Leesil saw one of her strangely green eyes twitch.

"I must work on this," she answered.

Her Belaskian was better than Osha's. Likely, that had been through Sgäile's tutelage, though Gleann had also spoken it quite well. Wynn had worked with Osha a bit, but like Leesil himself, Osha had little talent for any language but his own.

Leanâlhâm suddenly rose and went to dig in a pack among the gear in the corner. She pulled out several pieces of white cloth and a box large enough that she needed to hold it with both hands. Returning to the far bedside, she set her items on the floor where Leesil couldn't see them. Leanâlhâm further widened the tear in Magiere's pant leg, using one of the cloths to wipe away blood so she could better inspect the wound.

"What's in the box?" Leesil asked.

"The tools of a healer," Leanâlhâm answered. "It was my . . . grandfather's."

Gleann was a renowned Shaper among his people, the an'Cróan, or rather a healer who worked on the wounded versus guiding the shaping of living things, such as trees grown into homes for their people. Perhaps like him, Leanâlhâm was gifted, and he had trained her. But had that old, owl-faced an'Cróan given up his work? Why else would he hand over his wares to his granddaughter?

"The arrow missed the bone," Leanâlhâm said. "But the shaft is lodged against it. The protruding head can be snapped off, but I will have to widen the wound a little to get the shaft out cleanly."

Magiere elbowed up from her reclining position. "Don't bother," she said, but her words sounded muffled.

Leesil's gaze flew to her face. He'd warned her earlier about letting her dhampir nature out to mask the pain.

Magiere's brown irises flooded to black, and Leesil panicked. He knew what she was about to do. As she reached under her leg and snapped off the arrow's head, he shouted at her.

"No!"

Before he could grab her wrist, she ripped the shaft out of her thigh.

A grating cry of pain or rage erupted from Magiere's widened mouth. The arrow shaft snapped in half in her clenched fist as Leesil scrambled up on the bed to pin her down. Leanâlhâm gave an involuntary cry, grabbing a piece of cloth to staunch the blood flow.

"No!" Magiere snarled and pushed the girl's hands away.

Leesil saw Magiere's eyes flood nearly black as her irises expanded. Through the pain, she clenched her teeth, and her lips parted. Her teeth had begun to shift and change. Leesil threw himself on top of her, pinning her down as he shouted, "Chap!"

Chap wasn't fast enough. By the time he latched onto the back of Leanâlhâm's cloak and pulled, the girl's eyes had gone wide. She twisted away across the floor, ducking behind Osha's legs as he rushed in.

Osha looked horrified but not surprised. He'd seen Magiere change more than once, both in the Elven Territories and while fighting beside her in the ice-bound castle when they'd gone after the orb. He had seen Magiere's dhampir half, but never like this.

All Leesil could do was hold Magiere down and hope she didn't lose control.

Every one of her muscles was rigid beneath him, and he looked to the tear in her pant leg. This ability to just call up her inner nature was new—and how she'd learned to do so in the northern Wastes wasn't something anyone else should know about. He lay atop Magiere as Chap watched them both, standing by and ready to lunge in. Leesil grew numb and couldn't even look at Magiere's face anymore. He just kept looking down at the blood-soaked rent in her pant leg.

The blood wasn't flowing anymore. He couldn't be certain amid the mess, but he knew the wound would begin closing.

Magiere whimpered and went limp beneath him. Osha and Leanâlhâm still watched as one last exhausted exhale escaped Magiere.

"What . . . what . . . ?" Leanâlhâm, now on her feet and peering around Osha's side, stammered.

"It's all right," Leesil said, his voice flat. "She'll need water and food soon."

Leanâlhâm remained there, hiding behind Osha.

Leesil swung his head back to see Magiere's face. Her eyes were closed, but her mouth was slack enough for him to see that her teeth had returned to normal. She was covered in sweat, and he reached for the scrap of cloth Leanâlhâm had dropped to wipe Magiere's face.

"It's all right," he whispered gently in her ear, not knowing what else to say.

Then Chap began growling.

Leesil looked over to find the dog staring toward the window. He felt the smallest breeze and quickly rolled over on the bed's edge and reached to his thigh for a blade.

Brot'an's head hung down in the open window. One arm followed as he grabbed the upper edge of the window's interior, squirmed through, and dropped lightly to the floor.

Leesil didn't let go of his winged blade's handle.

Brot'an rose to his feet, glancing first at the bed and then at Leanâlhâm, who still cowered behind Osha. When he took off the wrap, a frown already covered his face.

"Why does she have no bandage yet?" he demanded.

"I . . . I could not," Leanâlhâm stammered. "She is no longer—"

"I'll deal with it," Leesil shot back, suddenly angry but uncertain at whom. "Leanâlhâm, get some water."

"You find . . . them?" Osha asked in Belaskian, turning on Brot'an. "Find hiding . . . place?"

Still half focused on Magiere, Brot'an shook his head. "No."

Osha turned away, bent down, and picked up the tin pitcher. He placed it carefully in Leanâlhâm's hands. She started out of her frightened trance and turned for the door, but her wide-eyed gaze remained on Magiere until the door closed after her.

Leesil had had enough and stood up.

"Osha, what are you all doing here? Why have those other anmaglâhk come all the way here after Magiere? And don't tell me 'not now'!"

Something about Osha had changed since Leesil last saw the young elf more than a year ago. His feelings, sometimes even his thoughts, had always been so plain on his face, but not anymore.

"Protect you," Osha finally answered. "Protect you from them. Most Aged Father . . . he send—"

"I was against his strategy," Brot'an interrupted.

"Against?" Osha spit out, and wheeled on Brot'an. He cut loose with an angry stream of Elvish.

Brot'an spit out one harsh word in Elvish, and Osha fell mute. There was no awe left in the young elf's expression for the elder of his caste. In spite of their outbursts at each other, Leesil wasn't letting any of this drop.

"Protect us?" he nearly shouted. "From your own kind? What do they want?"

Nobody needed to answer.

Leesil wasn't even sure why he'd asked. Most Aged Father had sent some of his caste after them when they went to find the first orb. Sgäile died defending them and killed one of their shadow-grippers—like Brot'an. Most Aged Father wanted the orb, or at least to know what they had and where it was. None of that decrepit old elf's assassins had ever seen it.

That still didn't explain why Brot'an, or maybe Osha, had dragged Leanâlhâm along. The girl could hardly be of any use to "protect" Magiere. Worse than that, Leanâlhâm was in danger because she was with Brot'an—and now with Magiere.

Leesil glanced sidelong at Chap. He knew exactly how to get some solid answers—or, rather, how to make sure Chap got them. But the dog wasn't watching Brot'an.

Chap was staring at the long, wrapped bundle Osha had tossed in the corner. Anything that held Chap's concern more than Brot'an's presence began to worry Leesil.

"Chap," Leesil said.

Chap didn't look up.

Chap barely heard Leesil. He became vaguely aware of the others when Leanâlhâm returned with a full pitcher of water. Even as the girl crept hesitantly toward Magiere's bed, his thoughts were elsewhere. He had been trying to understand the consequences of what he had heard in Osha's Elvish rant just before Brot'an silenced the young elf.

Brot'an had tried to kill Most Aged Father.

The implications were too varied to even guess, but had Brot'an started a war, this time among his own kind, between dissidents and other anmaglâhk loyal to Most Aged Father? Had he done this on purpose? Oh, yes, even failure could be an intentional tool for that deceiver.

And as much as the Anmaglâhk had come after Magiere for the orb or its whereabouts, without actually knowing what it was, this situation was also about Brot'an. It was about them getting to Magiere before Brot'an did. That much Chap could deduce.

Now that deceitful butcher stood in the same room with her.

If only Osha had stood up to Brot'an, kept arguing, then Chap might have learned more. But he had also picked up something confusing connected to the bundle Osha had tossed in the corner.

A fleeting memory had flashed through the young elf's mind. It seemed to take place only a moment after Osha's memory of the dark, searing-hot cavern. Chap recognized that place, as he had once been there. It was where Sgäile had taken Magiere, Leesil, and him before they had headed south from the Elven Territories in search of the orb.

Osha had knelt on ragged stone somewhere still dim and dark but not quite as hot. Perhaps it had been in one of the outer passages leading into the cavern. Osha's hands shook as he held a hiltless blade, a sword made of the same white metal as anmaglâhk stilettos. The same metal as the winged punching blades Leesil now carried. The same metal as the burning dagger Magiere wore on her hip opposite her falchion.

The Chein'âs—the Burning Ones—had somehow called for Osha and given him a sword like none Chap had ever seen.

Anmaglâhk did not use swords, so what did this mean?

The last glimpse Chap saw in that memory was a flicker of Osha's face reflected in the sword's metal. Looking at the blade, his long features twisted in overwhelming grief, as if he had lost someone precious to him.

That blade was now in the cloth-wrapped bundle in the room's corner.

Chap wheeled around as he heard Brot'an take a step. As soon as Brot'an reached the bed's foot and looked down at Magiere, tension filled the room to the rafters. This close to Magiere, the tall elf once again had Chap's full attention as he crept in on the bed's near side.

Why were Brot'an and Osha dressed as traveling civilians—humans?

"Is she all right?" Brot'an asked.

Leanâlhâm was cleaning the blood from Magiere's leg. The more she removed, the more her fright grew, for there was no wound—not even a scar. She did not answer Brot'an.

"She'll be fine," Leesil cut in, just as attentive and watchful as Chap.

Osha was not the only one who seemed *different* to Chap. Back in the an'Cróan homeland, Leanâlhâm had nearly fawned over Leesil. He was the only other elf of mixed blood she had ever met—ever even heard of. Now she barely spoke to him or to anyone. Perhaps Leesil noticed this, as well.

"Leanâlhâm," Leesil said softly. "Where is Gleann?"

Chap glanced at the girl just in time to see her wince at her own name. A long pause followed before she answered quietly.

"With our ancestors . . . with Sgäilsheilleache."

For the span of a breath, everyone in the small room went still. Gleann, the kindly old healer with biting humor who had taken in three humans and a wayward majay-hì was dead.

Osha whirled angrily and rushed toward the window. He stopped and looked back, as did they all, at the sound of a whisper.

"Oh, Leanâlhâm."

The girl froze as Magiere tried to sit up and failed, and then reached for Leanâlhâm's hand on her leg. Leesil came out of his shock.

"Gleann, dead?" he breathed. "How can he be . . . where is my mother?"

"She is well and safe," Brot'an answered instantly, but even he appeared unsettled by the turn of this discussion.

Leanâlhâm's gaze drifted to Leesil, and all of her fright of Magiere had drained from her expression. Chap waited for what else the girl might say.

"We cannot tell you more for now," Brot'an said, staring hard at Leanâlhâm. "Your mother is safe with her kind, Léshil."

Chap suddenly wondered who had taken on the painful task of telling Leanâlhâm that Sgäile was dead. Had Osha been the one? She had loved Sgäile, worshipped him as a hero. He had been highly honored by their people and respected by all factions of his caste—even Most Aged Father.

Osha suddenly took a few steps at Leesil, still angry.

"You ask question," he growled. "*I* ask question. Where Wynn? Why she not here?"

That was all they needed with everything else so complicated. Osha's feelings for Wynn were no secret. Still, Chap was surprised it had taken this long for the subject of Wynn's whereabouts to come up.

"Trapped in the guild's keep," Leesil answered tiredly, perhaps reeling in relief that his mother was safe. Or perhaps hoping—as did Chap—that answering Osha's question might gain some answers in turn.

"We're not sure why," Leesil added, "but we'll get her out."

"Then perhaps we can help," Brot'an said.

Yes, Chap thought. *I'm sure you would.*

"Osha speaks the truth," Brot'an went on, and looked at Magiere. "We are here to protect you. To protect . . . what you carry."

They were not carrying the orb—orbs—anymore. Chap took some satisfaction in that, though he wondered if Brot'an knew anything more than the other anmaglâhk about what they had been carrying. Chap had insisted on hiding both orbs in a place neither Magiere nor Leesil knew of. That decision now appeared more important than ever.

None of the Anmaglâhk—not even Brot'an—would ever find those orbs or learn their whereabouts.

"Magiere should rest," Leanâlhâm said quietly, and her fear had waned, for she held Magiere's hand. "Léshil says she will need food. Can we not eat and rest for one night? Not speak of these things?"

The girl dropped her head.

Leesil's expression became shadowed for an instant. As badly as Chap wanted answers, cueing Leesil with memories to ask the right questions would not get him anywhere in this moment.

"I will take first watch on the roof," Brot'an pronounced. "Everyone else . . . eat and rest."

He pushed past Osha, and an instant later, he was gone out the window. Another awkward silence passed until Osha announced flatly that he would go in search of food. As Leesil settled on the bedside, Leanâlhâm retrieved a blanket to cover Magiere.

Chap went to lie in the corner near Osha's hidden sword. He had no intention of going to sleep. It was simply the best place from which to watch the door . . . and the window for Brot'an's return.

As Chane made his way through the dark streets toward Nattie's inn, he could not escape his numerous worries. Every time he blinked, he saw an image of Wynn on the backs of his eyelids. She must be asleep by this time, or so he hoped. But she would wake in the morning to face . . . what?

It troubled him—no, it ate at him—that he would lie dormant all day while events closed in on her. Even if she found a way to send him word, he would be beyond receiving it until dusk tomorrow night, unless . . .

Once Chane reached the inn and his room, he opened the door slowly to let Shade see that it was him. She wrinkled her nose and growled softly, but appeared more frustrated than hostile. Likely she needed to be fed and let out for her "business," as Wynn called it.

He realized he *had* to start paying more attention to Shade's needs if she was to remain his somewhat unwilling ally. His only ally, as of yet, and he would need her help. Perhaps she could even advise him on his notion.

Chane dropped his second pack from his shoulder—the one Wynn would always think of as Welstiel's pack—and set it down.

"Shade," he began, and then faltered, for though she comprehended spoken words, he was uncertain how much. "Outside, and then food. But first . . ."

He hesitated, and Shade tilted her head, watching him. There was only one thing he could do: show her. He dug into his second pack.

Chane pulled out a long velvet box and opened it to reveal the six glass vials that had carried a noxious violet concoction deadly to the living. It served another purpose for the undead, one that he had painstakingly—and painfully—unraveled for his own need. He was now running low on this concoction.

The ingredients to make more were almost impossible to acquire, but one dose, less than a third of one vile, could stave off his dormancy for several days. Still, he hesitated to use it, for the side effects were horrible. He would remain awake during the day but trapped inside by the sun unless he donned his cloak, face mask, and the eyeglasses that could block out sunlight's worst effects. Even then, he could tolerate direct sunlight for only a brief period, and he would be dressed like some abhorrent executioner. Anyone who saw him would stop and stare—and not forget the sight.

The thought of being awake, trapped by the sun, locked in this shabby room all day was a torture Chane would rather avoid.

"In here, I have a method . . ." he began, looking into Shade's watchful eyes. "A way that will let me stay awake in daylight; but I still cannot go outside. Should I use it?"

She glanced at the pack, at the door and the curtained window, and then back to him. Though she could be more expressive than any animal Chane had ever known, he could not tell what she was thinking.

Shade huffed once for "yes."

"Very well," Chane said, and he rose to open the door. "First we go out for food and 'business' . . . and be quick about it."

CHAPTER 9

The next morning, Wynn awoke to sunlight spilling through her window. Everything felt normal, and she reached over the bedside for Shade. Her hand found nothing, though she reached all the way to the braided rug on the stone floor. She sat up, looking about, and her gaze came to rest on the far corner beside the door.

Her sun-crystal staff was still gone. Shade was nowhere to be seen. She was still a prisoner inside her room.

Wynn had so often believed that almost any situation looked better in the morning. Not now, not this time, sitting there alone.

Grabbing her gray robe off the bed's end, she pulled it on over her shift and leggings and smoothed out the wrinkles. A part of her was tempted to open the door, check the passage and see if Lúcan was still outside. Of course he would be, for nothing else had changed.

A soft knock sounded at her door. It would only be Nikolas with her breakfast, but at least this made her feel less isolated. She stood up, prepared to let him in, but she had taken only a step when . . .

"Journeyor? May I come in?"

Wynn froze at the low voice coming from the other side of the door. She knew that voice, and it certainly didn't belong to Nikolas. She had to respond in some fashion, so she just went and opened the door.

There was Captain Rodian standing outside, with Lúcan at attention just left of the doorframe. The captain's red tabard looked freshly pressed. His close beard was evenly trimmed, and his neck looked as if it had been shaved early that morning. But his expression was uncertain, and just a hint of dark rings encircled his eyes, as if he hadn't slept well.

Wynn remembered a night last autumn when Rodian had locked her in a cell at the second castle. He'd come later that same night, asking permission to enter, as well. Why even bother, since she had no choice? Even here, this wasn't really her room anymore. Mild hysteria grew as she wondered what he'd do if she just told him to go away.

When she didn't speak, Rodian's brow wrinkled. He glanced at Lúcan, who said nothing, and the captain whispered something to his corporal. Lúcan nodded and turned away, and Wynn heard him heading down the passage to the stairs.

"Please," Rodian said, still waiting in the passage.

Wynn sighed, leaving the door open as she took a few steps back. He entered and then glanced back at the door, as if caught between leaving it open or not. Finally, he closed it, and they were alone.

"Journeyor," he said again, and then paused.

This did not seem like a good thing to Wynn.

Rodian had always struck her as almost comically determined to present a professional front, as if the scuffle with Chane last night and the sight of Dorian dragging her off had never occurred.

Wynn had no idea what he was doing here. With no intention of helping him or offering any encouragement, she just stood there beside the bed, waiting.

"Why has the council confined you?" he asked.

"You'd have to ask them."

"I have."

"Well, then, you know more than I do."

His gaze was intense, and Wynn wavered. He'd sounded concerned, as if worried about her. If that was true, then why had he done everything the council asked of him, aside from taking over control of her confinement? Why had he locked down the guild grounds?

Rodian shook his head and stepped closer. "You must have done something—or something must have happened connected to you—for the council to call me." His patience suddenly vanished. "Wynn, talk to me! What happened here last night?"

What could she tell him—that a dhampir, a half-elven ex-assassin, and a Fay-born majay-hì returned to her and panicked the Premin Council? And then she'd been forced to sneak out the vampire who'd been hiding in her room?

Oh, yes, that would just fix everything.

Even if Rodian believed any of it—if he didn't ask a hundred more questions in turn—she didn't believe those things had anything to do with why she'd been locked up.

"I returned from a long journey south," she finally answered. "While there, I went farther than ordered in my own exploration, without guild sanction or knowledge. I think now they know more than I realized, and they want me to admit everything . . . and I won't."

"Why not?"

"Because of dark comings they don't want to acknowledge. And the more I tell them, the more they'll be able to get in my way. You, of all people, should understand that."

"If you won't give them what they want, then why haven't they just dismissed you, thrown you out?"

Wynn smiled at him without a trace of humor. "Because they'd lose control over me."

Rodian rubbed his brow and turned a circle, as if wishing to pace but finding the small room too confining.

"Are you going to keep on doing what they want?" she asked. "Keep on serving them in this?"

She should've known better than to try turning all of this on him. He was now one of her obstacles.

"Have they mentioned any formal charges to be made against you?" he asked.

"Not to me. I wouldn't know what they've mentioned to you."

Rodian didn't respond to this. "There's more to this than your errant mission," he said. "Something happened here last night. Even if small events seem irrelevant, you need to tell me what led to—"

The door slammed open, and High Premin Sykion stood in the opening, her wide eyes instantly fixed on Rodian.

"Captain," she said with surprising calm. "May I have a word with you . . . outside?"

Rodian's carefully constructed professionalism flickered.

Wynn wondered if he might not drag Sykion into the room and demand answers here and now. But the flicker passed, and his staunch professionalism resurfaced.

He nodded politely to the premin and then turned back to Wynn. "One of *mine* will be outside your door at all times. Should you ever find that this has changed without hearing from me first . . . do your best to let me know, if I do not hear of it myself in short order."

Sykion's eyes narrowed with a twitch.

Rodian spun about, facing the premin, but he didn't move until she turned away down the passage. He followed the premin and shut the door.

The truth of the situation struck Wynn in the face. Rodian had no respect for the Premin Council, only formal politeness and ethical conduct, and he didn't care for sages in general. Their ways went against his spiritual beliefs and philosophy, yet he was faithful to his oath of service above all else.

She had seen evidence of this more than once, though she hadn't always understood it for what it was. Now he once again acquiesced to the council . . . or rather to others, as he had been pressured into two seasons ago when she had been hunting the wraith.

This was not be the first time she had seen this contradiction in Rodian's conduct—nor the first time someone else had intervened in favor of the Premin Council. That had to be the only answer.

Captain Rodian was being pressured again by the royals of Malourné, perhaps Duchess Reine Faunier-Âreskynna directly. And the royals would protect the guild's . . . protect Sykion's interests at any cost.

In spite of it all, and Rodian's likely being pressed into actions that bent his oath of office, Wynn felt strangely bereft with the captain gone. What was her world coming to if she started thinking of the captain as even a tentative ally? Was she *that* alone now?

She rushed to the door and pressed her ear against the wood, straining to hear whatever was taking place out in that passage. It seemed Sykion had moved them both too far down the passage toward the stairs. Wynn only picked up the muffled sounds of Rodian's short, clipped words and Sykion's longer, soft responses.

Rodian's voice grew suddenly sharp, and Wynn heard him bark, "As I see fit!" Silence followed that, though she remained pressed against the door in uncertainty.

The captain had obviously disliked, rejected, whatever the premin had said. She'd somehow pushed him too hard, and he'd shoved her back. But he was clearly under pressure from more than just the guild. He wouldn't bend completely to whatever Sykion had said, but neither was he willing to break loose from what the royal family expected. Until that latter part changed, Wynn could expect little help from Rodian.

She abandoned all thoughts of him as an ally and hurried to her desk. No matter how she might feel, she wasn't completely on her own, not so long as she had quill, ink, and paper. She scribbled a quick note and folded it up, but wrote no address on its outside. It wasn't long before another knock came at her door. Either it was the captain returning for some reason or the one other person she expected.

Crossing quickly, Wynn opened the door to find Nikolas standing there with her breakfast tray. There was a new city guard outside in place of Lúcan, and she didn't even try to close the door after ushering Nikolas inside.

"Anything good this morning?" she asked.

"Porridge and tea," he answered, "but I scavenged some honey, as well."

As he set the tray on the desk, she rounded him, glancing toward the open door. The angle from that side of the room was good, for the guard wouldn't be able to see them unless he leaned around the doorframe's edge.

Wynn wanted to get this done now and not wait for Nikolas to return to collect the dishes. She grabbed the front of his robe, jerking him around between her and the door.

Nikolas's eyes instantly widened.

"Thank you. The porridge still looks warm," Wynn said a little loudly, and she held up the folded paper before him and slipped it into the front split of his robe.

Nikolas stiffened, reflexively trying to glance toward the open door. Wynn jerked on his robe front again to keep him from doing so, though she did watch the doorway as she spoke.

"Oh, the next time you stop by Nattie's inn to visit that tall friend of yours, please give him my best."

Nikolas blinked in confusion.

Frustrated, Wynn raised one hand high over her head to indicate greater height, and then mouthed *my friend*.

Nikolas's expression instantly shifted to its normal but nervous state.

"I . . . I will," he stuttered.

She had to push him into motion toward the door. In the opening, he looked back once and swallowed hard.

"I'll be back . . . to pick up . . . the tray . . . later," he added, his voice shaking. Then he closed the door.

Rodian strode across the courtyard, determined not to let his frustration and fury show to his men. But Sykion's needling still stung him.

She'd politely expressed displeasure that he'd not only replaced her people with one of his guards at Wynn's door, but that he'd visited Wynn alone without guild representation present—and that he'd closed the door. She'd even dared to suggest the latter might be construed as *inappropriate*. Then

she'd reminded him that he and his men were here for reasons of guild security only.

In turn, with teeth clenched, Rodian had informed her that if Wynn was
under arrest, then she was under his jurisdiction. And none of this would last
long unless formal charges were declared.

Sykion's answer still burned in his ears. "This is an internal guild matter,
Captain, and you will only do what you are asked."

"Law enforcement is not a guild matter," he pointed out. "I safeguard
your people, and the law . . . as I see fit!"

She had gone silent at that, for she knew exactly what he meant. But he
realized he'd pushed back too hard. How soon would she go running to the
royal family again?

Lengthening his stride, Rodian headed for the gatehouse tunnel to check
in with his men. He knew Sykion had gotten to him too much when Guardsman Jonah winced at the sight of him. He didn't care anymore.

"Report!" he barked.

"All quiet, sir."

Trying to force calm, Rodian nodded, recalling Sykion's final instructions.

"Normal guild activities should resume—to a point," he relayed. "Keep
the portcullis closed, but any sages with business in the city should be allowed to enter and leave. If a wagon arrives with supplies, contact one of the
sages in the gate tower for confirmation. As long as they clear the driver, let
the wagon in. No strangers are allowed inside."

"Yes, sir."

Then light, hurried footsteps echoed down the gatehouse tunnel behind
Rodian. He looked back to see a slender, gray-robed, slightly hunched form
hurrying toward him. Recognition dawned, for he knew Nikolas Columsarn.
After the young man had been attacked by the wraith, Rodian had carried
him back here for medical attention.

Nikolas slowed, shuffling forward. He anxiously eyed the closed portcullis, perhaps purposefully to avoid the eyes of those watching him. Then

again, he always looked nervous. He was also an acquaintance of Wynn's. When he finally looked up and met Rodian's gaze, he froze like a rabbit afield that had spotted a fox.

"Yes?" Rodian asked.

Nikolas opened his mouth, closed it again, and glanced at the portcullis.

"I need to go out," he said, barely above a whisper.

"To where?"

Nikolas blinked and took on a very poorly constructed demeanor of being affronted. "To Master a'Seatt's scribe shop . . . to check on some work."

"A'Seatt?" Rodian repeated.

"At the Upright Quill," Nikolas added.

Rodian knew the shop quite well. Pawl a'Seatt had been involved in that mess last autumn regarding stolen guild transcriptions and dead sages. Garrogh had died right outside that shop, and Lúcan had been marred for life. And a'Seatt's scriptorium and scribes were regularly employed by the guild.

Still pondering what this connection meant for recent events, Rodian nodded to Jonah.

"Let him through."

"Open up!" Jonah called above, and the clanking began.

The young sage slipped under as soon as the portcullis was halfway up.

Rodian only watched and didn't follow. Whatever was happening here on the guild grounds was somehow wrapped around Wynn—again. He would not miss any chance to uncover it.

Magiere stirred and opened her eyes to find herself stretched out on the narrow bed. Leesil's legs were pressed up beside her.

He was sleeping upright, his back against the wall at the head of the bed. At her movement, his eyes opened, and he looked farther down the bed. She was covered by a blanket with no way for him to see her wound—or, rather, where it had been.

"How are you?" Leesil asked, his tone cautious.

Magiere wasn't sure how to answer. She didn't remember much—other than doing what she had to. She couldn't remain incapacitated now that they were being hunted. Pulling back the blanket, she revealed her torn and blood-stained pant leg. All of the blood had been cleaned from her pale skin. Her thigh was stiff and aching, but there was no wound, not even a scar.

Leesil bent forward, reaching over the bedside. When his hand came up, it held a bowl of biscuits and half of a roasted capon.

"Here," he said, setting the bowl on his lap.

His cautious tone hadn't changed, but Magiere felt suddenly, wildly ravenous. She grabbed a biscuit, shoving half of it into her mouth as she elbowed up to lean over the bowl.

Vague memories came to her of having tried to eat last night. She couldn't remember if she'd succeeded. The half capon looked torn off rather than cleanly cut, so perhaps she had. She knew Leesil wouldn't mention anything about last night. They never talked about any of it, about what had happened to her in the Wastes . . . about what she'd become.

Looking around, Magiere spotted Leanâlhâm sleeping on the floor at the bed's other side. Beyond the girl, Chap lay nearest the door. Osha was awake, sitting beyond the bed's foot by the window. Magiere sat up to take in the rest of the room and look for one more person.

"He's on the roof," Leesil said quietly, placing the bowl in her lap.

Magiere shoved the other half of the biscuit into her mouth, though she hadn't finished swallowing the first half. She still couldn't believe Brot'an had brought Leanâlhâm halfway across the world to a foreign land. At that thought, she remembered something more.

Last night, Leanâlhâm had told them Gleann was dead. Had he contracted a sickness from one of his patients? The thought made Magiere sad, for she'd truly liked that old healer. They all had.

With Sgäile gone, as well, perhaps Brot'an saw no choice but to take Leanâlhâm into his own care. Magiere would never say so aloud, but Nein'a, Leesil's mother, wasn't exactly the mothering kind . . . not like her son. Magiere would never trust Brot'an, but she didn't hate him as did Leesil and

Chap. No matter what Brot'an's own motives, he'd once defended her, fought for her, and risked his own life when she'd been dragged on trial before the an'Cróan elders.

Magiere briefly stopped chewing. It was so unreal that she, Leesil, and Chap should be hiding out on a foreign continent with Osha, Leanâlhâm . . . and Brot'an. After swallowing hard, she gulped from the water pitcher Leesil offered her.

"You'd better call him in," she said. "We need to talk."

"Good luck with that," Leesil muttered.

Before he could get up, Osha rose and opened the window to utter a strange birdlike chirp. Magiere downed the rest of the water pitcher, which was only half full. Leanâlhâm stirred and sat up, but after glancing at Magiere and then Leesil, she quickly dropped her gaze.

Magiere could only imagine how last night had looked to Leanâlhâm. Frightening, at least. She wished she knew what to say, but no words came.

A large, gloved hand wrapped over the window's upper edge.

Brot'an dropped into the room, landing too lightly on the floor for someone of his size. He was so large that his body seemed to fill the room, and his gaze locked immediately on Magiere's leg—with its missing wound.

She jerked the blanket over her legs again as she swung them over the bedside. Leanâlhâm shifted out of her way. The movement hurt, but Magiere tried to ignore it. She needed the spare pants out of her pack, but there was little privacy to be had at the moment.

Chap was on his feet. Though he hadn't growled, he paced over to the bed's foot, sitting between it and Brot'an.

With everyone assembled, Magiere suddenly felt lost for how to begin. They all had questions full of fear and suspicion for each other. But if a team of anmaglâhk was here in the city—sent by Most Aged Father—she wasn't about to turn down help from Brot'an or even Osha. But their first concern was Wynn.

"Is Wynn . . . prisoner?" Osha asked, breaking the silence.

It was almost a relief that he'd spoken up first. Osha's Belaskian wasn't perfect, but it was better than Leesil's bumbling Elvish. Osha always got straight to the point where anyone who mattered was concerned.

"That's what we need to find out," Magiere answered.

"Then someone has to get inside," Brot'an said.

Leesil climbed off the bed, crouching down beside Chap. "Not by breaking in . . . at least not yet. We don't even know where Wynn is, specifically."

"Then what do you suggest?" Brot'an returned.

In watching him, Magiere wasn't certain the master anmaglâhk was all that interested in the answer.

"We ask the sages," Leesil said flatly. "We simply ask to speak with her. If they refuse, we'll know she's in trouble. If not . . . then we find out what's happening."

Magiere opened her mouth and then closed it, grinding her teeth. She knew Leesil had more in mind than this.

"Watching the guild castle is most likely how your enemies picked up your trail," Brot'an responded. "They will continue to do so, with no other leads to find you. The sages have seen you. Reappearance will only raise suspicion if the little one is in trouble."

Magiere felt exhausted again. All this talk seemed pointless. She much preferred to just break in and find the "little one," as Brot'an often called Wynn. But Wynn herself was the one who'd wanted to stay, and Magiere still wasn't fully certain why.

"Asking to see her is a foolish approach," Brot'an emphasized. "Any of you *will* be recognized."

As much as this rankled Magiere, she couldn't argue.

"Not all of us," Leesil countered. "Not all of us . . . present here and now."

Magiere grew suddenly wary, for Leesil was up to something again. Just before the memories rose in her head, she saw the back of his head turn just a little, as if he'd glanced to his right. There was one person he could've looked at. And worse, apparently Chap agreed with him.

Image after image of Leanâlhâm raced through Magiere's mind as Chap continued to call up more memories. She rolled out of bed to stand protectively in front of the girl at the same instant that Osha shouted at Leesil.

"No!"

Chap did not react to either Magiere or Osha's outbursts.

"It's the only way," Leesil said, for Chap had suggested it to him just before informing Magiere.

"She's the only one who . . . looks innocent enough," Leesil went on. "And no one there has seen her."

"Leanâlhâm? That is his idea?" Magiere asked, pointing at Chap. "She doesn't know this place, these people, or anything outside her own world."

No one appeared to question how Magiere knew Chap was the one who had started this. But he could not have cared less about her anger, nor the bitter argument that followed. He merely waited as everyone vented on each other—everyone except Leanâlhâm, who kept watching the others in a worried state of bafflement.

Leesil had clearly stated the problem regarding anyone else going. Brot'an and possibly Osha were known to the other anmaglâhk and might be spotted by any such watching the guild. The only one who remained potentially unknown to all was the girl.

That Brot'an went quiet halfway through this loud debate was the only other element that gave Chap pause. But Chap had never intended to send Leanâlhâm out alone.

"Why are you talking about me?" Leanâlhâm finally asked.

Her words were so soft that perhaps only Chap heard her above the others. Of course he had expected a fight with Magiere, but it was Osha who turned the most vehement.

"Magiere right!" he shouted into Leesil's face and then bent over above Chap. "No Leanâlhâm!"

Chap ignored him, as did Leesil.

Brot'an's eyes narrowed as he looked down at Chap.

Still, Chap waited. This needed to reach a head before he would put an end to it, as what came next would only bring more for them to argue about. They needed to understand who was making the decisions here, should the girl agree.

"It's settled," Magiere stated flatly, and Osha came up, taking position behind her. "It doesn't matter who's seen. Leanâlhâm isn't going. I'll do it myself."

That was exactly what Chap had waited for—another ultimatum from Magiere.

Perhaps it was unwise to do this now, or unfair to use the girl. But Magiere's judgment and changes had too often pushed them into further peril at every turn. She was going to listen to him from now on.

No one but him, and especially not Brot'an, was making the choices anymore.

Chap wheeled with a grating snarl and bit Magiere's ankle.

It wasn't enough to break the boot's leather, but it had to hurt. Magiere toppled on the bed and rolled away in startled anger. She never had a chance to say a word.

Chap went straight at Osha, snapping and snarling. A wolf doing so would have been frightening enough, and majay-hì were all bigger than wolves. Unfortunately, Leanâlhâm was too close and scrambled away to the bedside in terror. Chap did not stop snarling until wide-eyed Osha was pinned in the corner beyond the room's door. Only then did Chap slowly turn around upon the others.

There was Brot'an in the middle of the room, half-crouched.

Chap took a moment's pleasure at the shadow-gripper's tension. He glanced toward Leesil, calling up Leesil's memories of Leanâlhâm in the cutway last night—fully cloaked and hooded. He added a cascade of every single memory in Leesil that showed Chap himself ranging city streets at night.

Leesil flinched sharply, rubbing the side of his head. "Ah, seven hells. Knock that off! I get the point!"

"What point?" Magiere demanded, rising on the bed's far side next to him.

Chap grew still and quiet, and looked at Leanâlhâm, who was cowering at the near side of the bed. He shook himself all over and padded to the pile of gear in the corner. He jerked a rope loose from one of the packs, shaking it apart and wriggling his head through a loop of it. Taking up the stray end in his teeth, he padded back to the girl.

Leanâlhâm looked around at everyone with great worry. As Chap neared, head up, she had to look up to stare at him. But all he did was drop the end of the rope in her lap.

Brot'an said, "This is not going to work." Clearly, he understood and did not care for the idea.

Chap did not care whether Brot'an liked it or not as he waited for Leanâlhâm's understanding and her consent.

"You stay out of it," Leesil warned Brot'an.

But the elder elf would not yield. "Chap will be almost as obvious as you or Magiere out there. And he has already been seen at the guild."

"So we'll disguise him somehow. But it's not your decision," Leesil snapped. "It's his . . . and hers."

Chap stood absolutely still within reach of Leanâlhâm. He waited until some of the fright and confusion in her green eyes gave way to wonder and curiosity.

"It's your choice, Leanâlhâm," Leesil said. "You don't have to do this, but if so, he'll go with you."

Chap caught memories rising in Leanâlhâm of the majay-hì who protected her own homeland.

"He understands what you—we—say?" she whispered, still watching him. "Do all majay-hì?"

"No, just him," Leesil let out in a grumble. "And trust me . . . it's not always a good thing."

Chap waited until the last of Leanâlhâm's fear faded. In some ways, with her mixed heritage and bloodlines, she was so much like himself, like Leesil and Magiere—trapped between two worlds.

For every memory of the majay-hì that came to her, Chap held it there, crisp and clear, until the next rose. From the way they ran in her forests, sometimes in and out of the an'Cróan's enclaves, to those who occasionally gave birth to their young among the girl's people.

It was the way that Chap himself had been born, also trapped between worlds—a majay-hì and yet not.

Leanâlhâm leaned forward a little, perhaps wondering if he really did understand her.

"Yes," she whispered.

He poked his nose into hers, lapped his tongue over her face, and she started slightly in shock.

"Stupid," Osha spit out. "This stupid, stupid!"

"It's insane," Magiere added, and turned on Leesil. "How can you go along with this?"

"Both of you, put a cork in it," Leesil said. "It's settled."

Brot'an frowned, but his expression was more thoughtful than doubtful. "If the majay-hì is to play a . . . pet, as I assume, the guards may not give him notice, but the Anmaglâhk watching the castle will. They know him. So . . . how do we make a majay-hì look like a pet dog?"

Leanâlhâm slowly raised one hand and reached out. Chap tucked his head under the girl's fingers until they slid between his ears.

"Well, I've got one small notion," Leesil said.

Chap's ears went straight up. When he glanced away from Leanâlhâm, Leesil was smiling at him.

"After all," Leesil added, "Wynn's always said you're a filthy pig."

Chap did not like the sound of that . . . whatever it meant.

Chane sat on his bed, fighting the urge to claw off his own skin. He had taken a draft of the violet concoction—both a blessing and a curse—and dormancy did not come for him.

He watched the window, now covered with an old blanket. Even so, a glow filtered around the worn wool fabric from the sun outside, creating a bar of sharp light on the floor. He kept waiting for that bar on the scuffed planks to creep toward him.

Chane twitched hard, fighting for self-control, and clenched his hands on the bed's edge until he felt the straw mattress begin to tear under his hardening fingernails. Shade raised her head from where she lay on the floor, looked at him, and then dropped her muzzle back on her forepaws again. They both sat silently, waiting.

Neither was prepared for the too-soft knock at the door.

As Shade jumped to her feet, Chane flinched again and rose. He glanced uncertainly at her, and the knock came again. One of them had to do something.

Chane grabbed his dwarven sword, still in its sheath, from the bedside, and approached the door.

"Yes?" he rasped without opening it.

No one answered at first, but then a soft, wavering voice replied, "Umm . . . I . . . umm, have a message."

Chane flipped up the simple latch hook and jerked the door open. Vague recognition dawned when he saw a young man standing outside and staring up in fear. The unexpected visitor was slender and nervous, with his shoulders hunched inside his gray sage's robe. There were streaks of white in his unruly brown hair. When he glanced at the sword in Chane's hand, his eyes froze without a blink.

Chane leaned the sword against the wall next to the door. He had seen this one speaking with Wynn a few times at the guild. Usually he could not help bristling at Wynn's befriending any other man, but this young sage inspired no such jealousy.

With a trembling hand, the young man held out a folded piece of paper.

There was nothing written on the outside, but at the sight of it, Chane forgot everything else. He grabbed the note and shook it open. It was written in Belaskian, his own language.

This messenger is a trusted friend to be protected by all means. Official representatives of the law have assumed control of my confinement, but I remain where I am.

Without formal charges made before the people's High Advocate, my imprisonment may end soon enough. Give events another day and see what happens. If I haven't regained access to what I need, it will be pointless to stay. Do nothing—either of you—until you hear from me again.

If you haven't heard from me in two days, do what you must.

The tone and words were clinical and cryptic, but Chane knew their intention. No names or places were mentioned, so Wynn was still concerned about anything written down falling into the wrong hands. This time, she was likely taking precautions in case the messenger was intercepted and questioned. The young man would know little to nothing about what Wynn was really after, and almost no one would even be able to read the letter.

Chane read the note again slowly, trying to determine its full meaning.

Her reference to "official representatives" could only mean the city guard, likely Captain Rodian. That she remained where she was must mean the captain had not removed her; she was still in her room at the guild. The final cryptic line seemed clear.

Magiere, Leesil, and Chap would not know how or where to reach her—and, in truth, Chane preferred it that way. But Wynn was well aware that if all else failed, Chane was the only one who knew the lay of the keep and the exact location of her room. He would be the one to retrieve her.

He raised his eyes the young man. "What is your name?"

"Nik . . . Nikolas . . . Columsarn."

"How did you know where to come, who to give this to?"

Nikolas raised his head slightly. "Wynn is my friend and I bring her meals. She slipped me this note and made a passing comment about Nattie's inn." He paused. "I've seen you with her, so I knew who to look for . . . to describe to the innkeeper."

Chane frowned. This was not the safest method for communication, but he could think of nothing better.

"Can you carry an answer to her without detection?"

Nikolas nodded.

Even amid Chane's suffering, he felt an unexpected—unwanted—twinge of gratitude. The young man must be braver than he looked.

Chane tore Wynn's note into tiny pieces and shoved the remains into his own pack for later disposal. He pulled out a small writing charcoal and a journal with notes he had taken on the Begaine syllabary. Since almost no one here wrote or spoke Belaskian, he thought that Nikolas might be asked no questions if he was caught carrying a note simply written in Begaine, the compressed syllabic symbols of the sages. Even so, Chane's grasp of the syllabary was a work in progress with a long way to go.

It took him a while to stroke the symbols for words in his own language, acknowledging Wynn's instructions—and without using her name. Once he finished and folded the note, he rose from the floor and then hesitated in studying Nikolas Columsarn.

"What excuse did you give when you left the grounds?" he asked.

"An errand to the Upright Quill."

Chane winced. He had had a few dealings with "Master" Pawl a'Seatt of that private scriptorium. It was doubtful anyone besides him—and Wynn and Shade—knew the man was an undead. Even Wynn was doubtful after having seen a'Seatt visit the guild in daylight.

What if someone later asked at the scriptorium about Nikolas's "errand," only to find the young man had not been seen there? When Chane said as much, Nikolas shook his head.

"There actually is something I can pick up," he said, "so I won't look suspicious when I return."

Chane did not like the idea of any sage getting near Pawl a'Seatt, especially while carrying a note to Wynn. But he could not accompany Nikolas unless he covered himself fully, including with that mask and the glasses. That would only attract attention, even if he could last long enough to finish the escort.

Pawl a'Seatt hated other undead. The only way Chane had gotten clear of the strangely potent man had been by Wynn promising to remove Chane from this city. But Chane would never let a sage go into danger, especially not one that Wynn had asked him to protect.

He glanced at Shade and then back at Nikolas.

"Wait a moment," he said, closing the door.

Chane crouched before Shade, held up his left hand, and touched the brass ring that he wore to warn her. Then he slipped off the ring. The whole room appeared to shimmer like heat on a summer plain, and then his senses sharpened without the ring's influence on him.

"Shade," he said, cocking his head toward the door. "Go and protect that sage, but try not to be seen by . . ."

He was at a loss, uncertain if Shade would know Pawl a'Seatt by name. Instead, he closed his eyes and focused on the night when they had assaulted Sau'ilahk, the wraith, outside the Upright Quill. Chane had had to flee into the shop when Wynn had ignited the sun-crystal staff. Therein they had all been taken by surprise, finding Pawl a'Seatt in hiding, watching everything that had transpired in the street.

A'Seatt had seen Shade with Wynn, and Chane did not want him associating Nikolas with Wynn—not while Nikolas was acting as go-between. The young man hardly seemed capable of defending himself.

As Chane opened his eyes, Shade growled softly.

"You understand?" he asked.

She huffed once.

"When you get Nikolas back to the guild, return here. Lose anyone who might follow you. I will be waiting to open the back door."

She huffed again, and Chane surprised himself by saying, "Good girl."

He slipped the ring back on, then put on his gloves and cloak, pulling the cloak's hood forward to shadow his face. As he opened the door, Shade rushed past him toward the stairs, startling Nikolas.

Taking in the sight of Chane's cloak, Nikolas's expression shifted to alarm.

"You can't come with me," he warned. "I heard what happened last night, and if Captain Rodian sees you, he'll—"

"I am not coming with you," Chane interrupted, handing Nikolas the note and motioning the sage down the stairs.

Confused, Nikolas led the way. When they reached the bottom, Chane held the young man back, pointing to where Shade waited down the short passage to the back door.

"*She* is going with you," Chane said, "and do not argue with me. She will protect you and see you safely back to the guild."

Nikolas blinked. "Oh."

"Go out the front door," Chane instructed. "Head halfway down the street and wait for her to join you."

Nikolas blinked again but obeyed, turning to leave.

Chane immediately headed the other way. Reaching the back door, he checked his hood and averted his face.

"I will be waiting."

Bracing himself, he shoved open the door. Even under his cloak, he felt his skin tingle and sting. Shade bolted out, and he jerked the door shut, after which he slid slowly down the wall to sit on the passage floor. A thin crack of light seeped in from beneath the back door.

Chane inched a little farther up the passage. There was nothing more he could do for Wynn besides sit here and wait.

CHAPTER 10

Pawl a'Seatt didn't often go to his shop during the day. Uncomfortable as sunlight was, this was not the reason. In truth, his ability to walk in daylight remained a mystery to him.

He understood why the undead chose populated places in which to settle and hunt; he had done so, as well. Unlike them, a thriving city fed him to a degree, merely by his presence among so many. Though hunting was no longer a necessity for him, unlike other undeads, the longer he remained in close proximity to the living, the weaker and more listless they became.

In his earliest days—or, rather, nights—it had not been so. He'd once had to feed and exist only in the darkness.

He never discovered what had changed for him. It had happened gradually, over hundreds of years, though he did not always consider it a blessing. He now had to take great care in monitoring how much time he lingered in close company with others—especially the few people with which he interacted regularly. There were times when necessity, need, desire, or something else dictated otherwise.

Today, he had already made his habitual dawn visit to open the shop. When he entered a second time for this morning, this time through the back door, his late reappearance caused an immediate stir in the workroom. Perhaps his employees interpreted this as a harbinger of reprimand for not completing Premin Renäld's contracted project the day before.

Gangly and bony, Tavishaw took several furtive glances over the slanted top of his scribing desk, the rhythm of his scripting breaking each time like a stutter in the scratching upon the paper.

Even old Teagan glowered openly at being disturbed while inspecting Tavishaw's work. The scribe master was accustomed to running things his way during the days. Scrawny, shriveled, and half-bald, he peered at Pawl through round, thick-lensed glasses. His amplified pupils above his extended nose gave him the look of a gaunt hound spotting another canine sniffing about his yard.

And Liam began working so hastily that Pawl feared for the quality of the script.

Only Imaret appeared untroubled. Her pace never altered. She rarely even glanced at the content reference sheet beside her, as if the page was already imprinted in her young mind. Hers was a rare gift or talent possessed by only one other person Pawl had ever met. She quietly and efficiently scribed the index for the transcribed copy of the journeyor's journal submitted by Premin Renäld.

"How is it proceeding?" Pawl asked the girl, though this wasn't really why he'd returned.

"Almost done," Imaret answered without looking up. She was likely still cross that he'd been unable to tell her anything about Nikolas or what was happening inside the guild.

The tinkle of the front door's bell carried into the back room. Pawl grew mildly relieved at the prospect of anything that might distract him from his state of unrest. Master Teagan automatically headed for the front room, but paused at finding Pawl close on his heels.

"I'll see to it," Pawl said, ignoring Teagan's scowl.

Teagan followed him, anyway. But before they reached the door out into the shop's front, it swung inward, and there stood Nikolas Columsarn in his usual anxious state.

"Nikolas!"

Pawl stiffened at Imaret's outcry. He'd barely glanced back when she dropped her quill, and he frowned at the possible ruin of the index page. Imaret nearly knocked fragile old Teagan into the wall as she wormed through the short passage, past Pawl.

"Are you all right? Is the guild still locked up?" she asked, her voice too loud. "Why were the city guards called? Are they still there? How did you get out?"

Nikolas flinched repeatedly, as if every question were her little fist poking him in the arm. Pawl heard only silence behind him, and when he looked, Tavishaw and Liam were both staring.

"The guild is closed?" Tavishaw asked in surprise.

Pawl immediately placed a hand on Imaret's back and herded her and Nikolas into the shop's outer room. He would never get Imaret back to work while Nikolas was here.

"How did you know about the guild?" Nikolas asked.

"I was there last night," Imaret said. "I was worried for you."

"Why?"

"Why?" she echoed indignantly. "Because you were locked inside!"

Since the deaths of Elias and Jeremy in a nearby alley, Imaret grew frantic whenever she didn't know the whereabouts of the remaining few she cared about. On a more practical consideration, Pawl was concerned by how this affected her work. The only way to stabilize that was to allow this meeting to play out—and perhaps gain some insight for himself.

Nikolas frowned. "Imaret, I'm fine in there. No one even notices me."

At this evasion, Pawl seized control.

"What has happened?" he asked pointedly. "Why were the Shyldfälches summoned?"

Nikolas looked up at him. A sudden desperation turned the young sage pale just before he looked away.

"I don't know," he said quietly.

"You don't know?" Imaret asked.

Pawl raised one finger at her, and she fell silent. His centuries of experience with people told him that the young man was dying to speak, to pour out his personal troubles. When Imaret was about to go at Nikolas again, Pawl rested his hand on her fragile shoulder. She looked up at him, possibly annoyed, but remained quiet.

"Journeyor Hygeorht has been confined," Nikolas finally offered.

"Why?" Pawl asked.

"I don't know."

Pawl's frustration began to match Imaret's, but this time the truth of Nikolas's answer was plain on his troubled face. The young sage was at a loss.

"Why did you come here?" Pawl asked.

Nikolas still wouldn't look at him. "I thought to check and see if Premin Renäld's project was finished, maybe bring it back, and . . . I just needed to get out for a while."

Pawl could see this was not true. Why would Nikolas lie?

"The transcription is not quite finished," he said. "I'll have it delivered late this afternoon."

His words appeared to make Nikolas only more miserable. He was tempted to use intimidation to force Nikolas to talk, but he resisted. Whatever had happened with Wynn Hygeorht, Nikolas—if he knew anything more—would eventually tell Imaret something. And Pawl would hear of it.

"All right," Nikolas replied, turning away, but he stopped briefly to look at Imaret. "I have to get back, but I'll try to see you—both of you—as soon as I can." He attempted a weak smile. "If nothing else, Captain Rodian won't last much longer. He's been at it with one or another premin since last night and looks like he's eaten nothing but raw lemons for days."

Nikolas slipped out the front door.

"Bye, Nikolas," Imaret called after him.

"Back to work," Pawl ordered.

She shuffled through the opened counter section and into the back room.

Pawl walked to a front window and watched Nikolas head south along the street. Once the sage was out of the line of sight, Pawl stepped out the shop's front door. He spotted Nikolas's gray robe a block down and followed until the young sage turned the corner. When Pawl reached that intersection and peered around the candle shop there, he stopped.

A dark shadow emerged from the mouth of an alley running behind the shops. Pawl watched a long-legged black wolf, taller than any he'd seen, fall in beside Nikolas.

It was the same animal that had been with Wynn on the night she'd faced that black-robed undead outside his shop. Another undead had been there with her, one that Pawl should've dispatched for invading *his* city. But doing so with Journeyor Hygeorht present would have raised questions from her about him.

Pausing there in the street, Pawl let his thoughts turn.

Wynn Hygeorht had been confined. The guild had been locked down by the city guard, likely at the request of the Premin Council. All work on the translation project had ceased. Nikolas was full of something he was dying to speak of and yet would not. Now Wynn's black wolf escorted the nervous young sage out and about the city.

Wynn was the source, though not the cause, for both Pawl's reignited anger and his determination for its remedy, to seek answers regarding the white woman, his murderer and maker. Wynn had been the one to return with those ancient texts from afar. Whatever was happening—whatever had halted the translation project—it was somehow all wrapped around her. And she was beyond reach inside the guild's keep.

Pawl walked back toward his shop in silent, cold tension.

Chap and Leanâlhâm lingered by a street corner one block up the mainway from the guild's bailey gate, and he was itching all over.

Leesil was going to pay for this, one way or another.

Chap dropped on his haunches and pulled up one rear leg to scratch himself again.

"Bârtva'na!" Leanâlhâm whispered in panic, slipping into her own tongue. "Do not!"

A little cloud of black dust rose as Chap scratched. He tried to rub his itching face with a forepaw. All that did was raise a puff of soot around his face, and he sneezed.

"Please, Ch—majay-hì," Leanâlhâm insisted. "You will rub it off and be noticed."

Like her people, Leanâlhâm had an aversion to anyone imposing a name upon one of the sacred guardians of her homeland. She reached for his face, perhaps to stop his paw, but then paused. Whether she thought it irreverent to touch him or that he was just filthy, he did not know.

Chap was covered in soot. Or at least his back, tail, head, and most of his face were.

Disguise or not, it was wholly uncomfortable, and it was all Leesil's doing. Chap grumbled under his breath, unable to stop fidgeting and scratching. He was going to get Leesil back for this.

Before he and Leanâlhâm had left the inn, a plan had been made. Once again, Chap let the others proceed without interrupting. It gave them a sense of control, though he had his preparation in mind for how to contact Wynn. That deception was especially necessary for Magiere and Osha, who were the most worried about Leanâlhâm.

Their basic plan was sensible. He and Leanâlhâm would approach the gatehouse portcullis. If no one recognized Chap or reacted to him, Leanâlhâm would present herself as a visitor seeking Wynn.

Unlike Osha, Leanâlhâm had been taught Belaskian, the Farlands dominant language, by her deceased uncle and grandfather. Brot'an had tutored her in some basic Numanese, although how the old butcher had learned the tongue so quickly still bothered Chap. Leanâlhâm's heavy Elvish accent would simply support her guise as an acquaintance from afar, here to visit Wynn.

If she was refused entry, then it could be assumed that Wynn was indeed a prisoner—but her location would be in question. If Leanâlhâm was let in by guards but then refused by the sages, at least they would know Wynn was still on guild grounds. And in that event, hopefully, Chap could at least gain the inner courtyard in order to try what he wanted to accomplish.

That mattered the most. Somehow, they had to at least reach the courtyard.

Leanâlhâm had been ordered—both by Brot'an and Magiere—that at the first sign of trouble, she was to get out any way possible; Chap would take care of himself. The girl had promised this. Magiere had also instructed her to pay attention to any unsought memories that suddenly surfaced in her mind. This confused Leanâlhâm quite a bit, and even more when she was told why, for it was the only way Chap could warn or instruct her.

The problem, of course, was that Chap had not spent enough time watching for Leanâlhâm's memories. He could only call back a person's own memories that he had already seen in that same person's mind. Leanâlhâm was instructed that if she suddenly remembered—for no reason—their flight in secret from the attack of the anmaglâhk, she was to turn and flee. She had so badly wanted to be useful that she would have promised anything.

However, the prospect of this task and the reality were two very different things. Now Leanâlhâm glanced down nervously at Chap.

She was fully cloaked with her hood pulled up, and he could not help feeling humiliated by the piece of cord around his neck as a makeshift leash. Yes, it had been his idea, and with the other end clenched in the girl's hand, he had led her and not the other way around. Still, his discomfort got the best of him, and he disliked even the illusion of being anyone's pet.

Chap was well aware Sgäile and Gleann had protected Leanâlhâm from the world with a vengeance. Then Brot'an and Osha had taken up that role. This entire endeavor was outside the girl's experience. He wished he could reassure her, even if it was another lie.

She seemed to read his expression and said, "I am not afraid."

He could see that was not true.

"It is all right," she insisted. "I am ready."

Stepping out, Chap pulled on the leash cord until she stepped in beside him. When they finally passed through the bailey gate and approached the closed portcullis, he craned his head, peering through its broad beams. He saw only one guard standing inside, but he could not see much of the court-yard down the gatehouse tunnel.

Leanâlhâm came within arm's reach of the portcullis, and then Chap spotted another guard stepping into view at the tunnel's far end. Both guards wore red tabards over chain vests, and the nearer one had a helmet with a nose guard. The one pacing beyond the tunnel's far end had sandy-colored hair and a close-trimmed beard across only his jaw above a clean-shaven throat. His boots clopped softly on the courtyard's stone as he passed beyond sight.

"May . . . enter?" Leanâlhâm asked in broken Numanese.

"What's your business?" the closer guard questioned, glancing once at Chap.

"I am here . . . visit friend . . . Wynn Hygeorht."

The following silence left Chap tense. He was uncertain why until he realized the boots on the inner courtyard's stones had stopped echoing down the tunnel.

"No visitors today, miss," the guard said politely. "I'm sorry."

"Please . . . I come long way."

The sound of footsteps resumed. Chap spotted the guard with the close-trimmed beard turn into the tunnel's far end and head for the portcullis.

Rodian couldn't yet see who was outside the portcullis, but he was almost sure he'd heard the name of Wynn Hygeorht. As he approached the gate-house tunnel's outer mouth, he was surprised to see a slender girl—perhaps a young woman—in a full cloak with her hood pulled forward. Beside her was a very tall, mottled black and gray dog . . . or was it a wolf?

The girl was definitely no sage by her attire, but Rodian's guardsman partially blocked his view of the dog.

"What's this?" he asked.

"Just a girl . . . an elven girl," Guardsman Wickham answered with a nod. "Here to visit, she says."

As Wickham turned, he exposed the dog to Rodian's full view. The animal was indeed wolflike but taller, nearly as tall as the dogs used to hunt them.

"Who are you here to see?" he asked, stepping up to look through the portcullis beams.

The girl, or rather young woman, by her height, backstepped and dropped her head. Her face wasn't clear to his view, with the hood hanging to hide her eyes, but the dog was plain to see. Its strange blue eyes, tall ears, and tapered muzzle reminded Rodian of . . . Shade. Wynn's animal could be of the same breed, although he'd never before seen another like her.

The young woman hadn't answered his question.

Rodian worried he might frighten her off, and he wanted to know more about this odd pair. If she ran, he wouldn't have time to catch her with the portcullis down.

"Wynn Hygeorht," the young woman finally confirmed.

Rodian's first instinct was to arrest her on the spot and question her, though he'd still have to get her to stay put until the portcullis opened. Perhaps he might learn even more by letting this visitor actually see Wynn . . . with him present, of course.

"Open up!" he called above.

The young woman inched backward again, though the dog didn't, and the cord leashing the dog pulled taut and stopped her. The portcullis ground upward, and before it had even cleared Rodian's head, he ducked under.

"I'll take you to her," he said. Now he could see inside her hood.

She was pretty, even beautiful, with the large, slanted eyes of a Lhoin'na, though her skin appeared slightly darker than most of those people. She was indeed young, though that didn't always mean much with an elf. Pretty women did not affect Rodian, but what struck him the most was the way her green eyes shifted nervously about, always watching everything, always watching . . .

Rodian tensed. All Lhoin'na had amber-colored eyes, not green. Wynn Hygeorht had a penchant for the strangest of companions.

He took care with his manner, yet she still appeared afraid, and this raised his suspicions more. What was she hiding? He gestured down the tunnel with one hand.

"This way."

Turning his back on her, he walked up the tunnel but listened for the sound of her steps. What he heard first was the click of claws on stone. So the dog had immediately followed, and only then came the young woman's footfalls. When Rodian emerged into the courtyard, he barely had a chance to glance back and make certain she was there.

"Captain, what are you doing?"

Rodian looked ahead to find Domin High-Tower stomping toward him out of the keep's main doors. He let out a deep, slow breath and went to cut off the domin before the dwarf frightened Wynn's strange visitor even more.

Chap had gotten what he needed in entering the courtyard, but when he spotted the stout dwarven sage, he knew he might have only moments. He hoped what he was about to try would work, though he tried it only once before.

On the way to the Pock Peaks in search of the first orb, Wynn had been cut off from everyone and lost in a blizzard. He had searched hard for her, but without a line of sight, he had no way to speak into her thoughts. He had tried, anyway, and it had worked for one instance.

Leanâlhâm froze beside Chap as he looked to the right, to where Wynn had been hauled off the night before. There was no sign of her in any of the windows of the two-level building flush against the keep's southeast wall. Chap tried calling to her, anyway.

Wynn, I am here.

The captain sidestepped into the dwarven sage's path. "Can I help you, Domin?"

"I was passing the entry hall and heard the portcullis gears," the dwarf answered, not at all politely.

Chap scanned the courtyard's left side. The building there had no windows, just three doors along its length spanning the whole courtyard's side. A pair of double bay doors in the left half had been set high at its second level.

He tried again. *Wynn . . . are you here? Where are you?*

Unless he actually saw her, this whole attempt could be pointless. Even if she heard him, as she had in the blizzard, she would not be able to answer if she were locked away. She could hear his voice in her thoughts, but he could only hear her true voice. However, if he could at least see her, he would know where she was, and he could tell her they would come for her.

His anxiety grew. What if she was no longer here? Had they been lured inside . . . into a trap?

"Why have you raised the gate?" the dwarf demanded. "I see no sages coming or going. Supplies do not arrive at this time!"

Chap looked beyond the dwarf and the captain to the main keep ahead. A few narrow window slits marked its two upper floors. No one looked out of their panes, no one from whom he might glimpse any memories in the hope of stumbling on Wynn's exact location. He felt Leanâlhâm's small hand drop on his neck, and her fingers clenched his sooty fur. Perhaps in fear she'd finally overcome her reluctance to touch him. He glanced up, wondering what had caused this.

Leanâlhâm was looking up to the building on the courtyard's right side. In the last window on the second level, Wynn stood wide-eyed, looking down at them with her hands flattened against the panes.

Chap almost sagged in relief, and then Wynn's brow furrowed. A clear memory rose in his awareness as he watched her.

To his surprise, he became lost in it. He saw through her eyes as if he were she in a long-past moment. She—he—was locked up in Lord Darmouth's keep in a small room.

The memory flickered, though the setting remained the same. She—he—was now closer to the room's door. Light from one narrow window had changed, suggesting it was a different time of day. The door opened, and one of Darmouth's armed men stood in the passage outside.

"I do not tell you how to run your affairs," the captain retorted to the dwarf. "I fulfill my responsibilities as I see fit."

In the window above, Wynn's eyes closed, scrunching tight. The previous image went black in Chap's mind, and something more rose out of that darkness. He began to see a face—no, several faces—of armed men. They were dressed like the guards here in the keep.

One last flash of memory in Wynn came to Chap—that of Darmouth's guard coming to the other room's door.

And Chap had his answer.

Wynn's situation was more than some dispute with her superiors. She was indeed a prisoner, and these guards—this captain in the red tabard—now controlled her confinement.

Chap's relief at finding her faded. The situation was more complicated than he had hoped.

We are coming . . . soon. Do nothing to make them move you elsewhere.

With her hands pressed against the glass, Wynn nodded, looking so hopeful that he hated to leave her.

Only moments had passed since the dwarven sage had first called out. Chap was fully aware the exchange with the captain could end quickly. Then the creaking sound of the portcullis beginning its descent echoed out of the gatehouse tunnel.

With a last look at Wynn, Chap backed toward the tunnel's mouth, and Leanâlhâm followed without a sound.

Rodian cursed inwardly, wondering how he could explain a visitor being allowed inside. If he even mentioned the young woman was here to see Wynn, it would incite High-Tower all the more, perhaps enough to send him charging to Sykion.

How many more times could he play his authority as trump against whatever challenge these sages cast in his way? Reiterating that he was in charge and would handle things his way would soon wear thin, and the royal family would step in again.

High-Tower shifted to the left more quickly than his bulk suggested possible. His head tilted, and his slash of a mouth opened. The domin was surprisingly silent as he looked around Rodian.

Rodian couldn't help but look back . . . to find the girl and the wolf-dog gone as the outer portcullis thudded closed.

"Who was that?" High-Tower demanded.

Rodian didn't answer and bolted into the gatehouse tunnel. There was no sign of the pair beyond the portcullis, and he grabbed the shoulder of Wickham's tabard.

"Where is she?" he barked.

Guardsman Wickham blinked in alarm. "She left. I thought you sent her off."

Rodian clutched the portcullis's broad, upright beams, peering out to the bailey gate. As far as he could see over its top and up Old Procession Road, there was no sign of the elven woman with the strange eyes.

"Captain!" High-Tower shouted, and the crack of his voice echoed down the tunnel. "What is going on here?"

Rodian only cursed under his breath again.

A block down the main road from the bailey gate, Chap ducked around a corner with Leanâlhâm and peered back toward the sages' small castle.

"Something is wrong in there," Leanâlhâm whispered in Elvish as she leaned out above him. "We should return to tell the others."

But Chap lingered. With guards inside the keep and the place locked down, he wanted more time to look for any other security measures. In only a moment, he spotted one.

Another guard came into view, walking the top of the bailey wall's south half. The man paused on reaching the right-side small barbican, one of two framing the bailey gate. He leaned away, likely conversing with his comrade inside the portcullis, and then turned back the way he had come.

Chap hung his head. Of course there would be more guards than just the captain, one man inside the portcullis, and at least one in the gatehouse tower. Likely more than one walked the bailey wall, but he suddenly wondered about Wynn's trick of memory.

Where—how and why—had she learned to willfully recall and hold a memory as she had for him to see? In all their lost days together, Wynn had never done this. She did not need to, considering he could always speak into her thoughts and she had a voice. The meaning in those memories she had shown him could not have been clearer. And for her to so vividly reexperience a past moment with such clarity, and then overlay others like it . . .

"Majay-hì!" Leanâlhâm whispered. "We must go."

Pulled from his thoughts, Chap huffed once and turned up the road. If only there had been more time with Wynn. Perhaps she could have shown him even more with this new memory skill of hers. As he walked ahead of Leanâlhâm, he glanced back toward the keep.

A movement like a black shadow skulked along the bailey wall's base.

Chap wheeled and tensed as another form came into view behind that black shadow walking on all fours. Someone in a gray robe trotted toward the bailey gate, passing that shadow, that . . . tall, black, wolfish form. He lunged a step back toward the castle.

The rope in Leanâlhâm's grip snapped tight around Chap's neck. He heard her stumble, but he fixated on that dark form. The black wolf hung back, out of sight of the portcullis, as the sage in gray opened the bailey gate.

Shade lingered close to the bailey wall as the sage paused, looking back at her. She opened her jaws and snapped them shut. Perhaps she had barked at the sage, but no sound carried to Chap. The sage hesitated an instant longer and then hurried through, closing the gate.

Chap watched as his daughter crept toward the gate, but she did not reach it. Her ears pricked, as if she listened. From a distance, Chap heard the grinding and loud clanks of the portcullis being raised.

What was Shade doing out here escorting a sage to the guild? Why was she not with Wynn, where she should be?

"What is wrong?" Leanâlhâm whispered. "What are you looking . . . ?" and then she gasped. "Majay-hì! Another majay-hì . . . here?"

Shade's head twisted as she looked up the mainway.

Chap panicked, forgetting all that he had come here to do as his daughter stared up the mainway at him. The only thing left in his thoughts was the drive to make her understand how he could have done this to a daughter he had never seen before a night ago. A father she had never met had banished her from the world she knew to cross an ocean and a continent to serve a purpose that he could not.

He had suffered for two nights before going to beg Lily to do this for him . . . to do this to one of their unborn children. Even thinking back, he knew he would have made the same request. But here and now, all he wanted was to beg his daughter's forgiveness, to help her to understand why he had done this to her.

Chap clamped his teeth on the leash cord and pulled sharply.

Leanâlhâm stumbled. "What are we doing?"

He kept jerking on the cord until the last of it ripped from her hand.

"No, no!" she called frantically. "We must go back to the others."

There was so little time in this moment. Chap only hoped Leanâlhâm would remember what Magiere had told her. He called up the girl's brief memory from last night of Magiere and Leesil. He recalled these two images over and over. Then he butted Leanâlhâm's leg.

Her eyes widened as she almost fell. Instead of shock at the memories suddenly assaulting her, she shouted at him.

"No! You must come, too."

Chap huffed twice, and when she opened her mouth to argue, he lost his self-control. He snarled and snapped at her, again raising that memory of the inn's room. Her young face twisted with so much fright that he stopped. He wanted to rush after Shade, but he crept slowly forward and licked Leanâl-hâm's hand.

Confusion flooded her expression. She was still too unfamiliar with his ways. He shoved her with his head more gently this time. She knew what he wanted; he simply had to make her do it.

When he started to back up, to his relief, she didn't follow. She turned halfway, still watching him retreat. He did not turn around until she finally headed up the street. Only then did he wheel about to race up the road.

Chap stumbled to a halt. Shade was nowhere in sight.

Perhaps like the night they had met in the catacomb archives, she wanted nothing to do with him. Why else would she leave after seeing him again? He broke into a lope, heading up the mainway, but he did not make it far.

A woman screamed out.

He stalled amid an intersection a full block from the bailey gate as a woman in a shimmering cloak and white fur gloves grabbed her toddling little daughter out of his way. Other people drew away from him in alarm. He retreated, trying not to startle anyone else, but there were people in every branch of the streets around him.

"Wolf!" someone cried out, and two men with long staves in hand turned and looked Chap's way.

So much for soot and ashes and Leesil's idiotic disguise!

It did not matter that he still had a rope dangling from his neck. Or maybe that just made it worse, as if he had broken from captivity.

All Chap could think of was his daughter, and why she was not with Wynn.

Charging straight at the staff-wielding men in his way, he had to clip one of their legs to get through. At the crack of a staff on cobble behind him, he swerved and bolted on at full speed. When he reached where the mainway met the loop around the sages' castle, he slowed long enough to sniff the cobblestones nearest to the bailey wall. If sight would not help him, perhaps scent would.

Then he heard the running feet coming after him.

*   *   *

Én'nish had taken the day's watch over the guild castle. Perched on a rooftop along Wall Shop Row near the castle's front, she hadn't known quite what to think when a filthy majay-hì, its fur smudged and smeared black, walked up to the portcullis beside a slender, cloaked figure. The cloaked woman was too small to be the monster Magiere, but all the filth upon the majay-hì did not hide who he was. Én'nish knew on sight the one that the humans called Chap.

When the pair had come out again only moments later, Én'nish had been prepared to follow them. Something unexpected stalled her.

A black majay-hì appeared, apparently escorting a young male sage in gray. This majay-hì did not follow the sage into the keep, and Én'nish knew this one, as well. It had been seen by one of her comrades in the company of Wynn Hygeorht upon the sage's return to the city.

Én'nish could not fathom what any majay-hì would be doing this far from her homeland, let alone in the company of humans. She almost followed it, but only the one called Chap might lead her to the hiding place of the monster. About to pick up that abomination's trail, she was startled again.

Chap returned, only a city block ahead of two shouting men carrying staves. The majay-hì paused at the bailey wall where the black one had been moments before. Then Chap took off at a run, following the black one's trail.

To follow, Én'nish took a running leap and landed lightly on the next rooftop.

Still at the window, Wynn's stomach churned with mixed relief and worry.

Chap had come and now he knew where she was. He'd told her they'd be coming for her. It made her feel more secure than she could've imagined, but she'd already sent a message to Chane giving him two days. After that, she knew he'd be coming for her, and Chane was not always patient. He might not listen—might even try sooner.

Leesil was a master of infiltration; it was part of what he'd done in his youth. Now that Chap could tell Leesil where Wynn was, Leesil as well might not wait too long.

And if Leesil and Chane crossed paths . . .

Wynn's stomach knotted. All of her relief drained away. She had to get another message to Chane, and quickly. The midday bell had passed, so likely Nikolas would come with her next meal. She spun around, grabbing a sheet of paper from her little desk table.

"What are you doing?"

Startled, Wynn turned at the harsh challenge she heard in the passage outside her room. She'd almost not recognized that voice at first, for she'd never heard Nikolas sound hostile before.

"None of your concern."

Wynn froze at Dorian's cold reply.

"That is *my* duty," Nikolas almost shouted.

Wynn ran for the door and jerked it open. The first person she saw was the guard as he instinctively reached for the hilt of his sword. It wasn't Lúcan, and she didn't recognize him, but at the sight of her, he relaxed and turned his wary eyes back on the two sages.

Dorian stood in the passage, holding a tray with a bowl of soup and pot of tea. Nikolas stood a few paces beyond, nearer the stairs, his mouth tight and his hands clenched on a similar tray. Dorian eyed the Shyldfälche guard.

"Premin Sykion has instructed that I bring the journeyor's meals from now on," Dorian commanded. "No one but me."

The guard did not appear impressed. "I take my orders from Captain Rodian or Corporal Lúcan, and I've heard of no such change."

"Then you'd best check with your superiors," Dorian answered. "The instruction has already been given."

Without another word, Dorian pushed past the guard and came straight at Wynn. He didn't even pause, forcing her to back up into the room. When he entered, he went to the desk without even looking at her and set down the tray. The last thing Wynn saw was Nikolas's desperate face as he stood outside in the passage, and then Dorian quickly left, closing the door.

Wynn sank onto her bed's edge, with no way to get a message to Chane.

Chane sat leaning against the passage wall at the back of Nattie's inn, hoping he had done right in sending Shade off with the young sage. Too much time had passed. Or perhaps it just felt so as he quivered and itched, wanting to scratch off his skin and imagining the burning sun just outside the inn's back door. He hated this and longed for the oblivion of dormancy.

A wild, eager scratching outside the door was followed by a loud huff.

Chane quickly rolled to one knee, pulled his hood low, and shoved open the back door. Shade rushed inside and passed him, and he pulled the door shut. But as he turned about, he saw only her tail as she bolted up the stairs, huffing and panting in agitation.

Something had gone wrong.

Chane did not hesitate and followed Shade quickly, taking two steps at a time to where she sat panting and whining at their room's door. He opened it, only to have her rush into the room. Quickly stepping inside, he latched the door and crouched before her.

"What is wrong?" he rasped. "What happened?"

Shade rumbled and then whined again, and Chane's alarm grew. Without warning her, he slipped off the brass ring. She did not even snarl, but instead fixed her crystal blue eyes on his.

A memory rose in Chane's awareness.

He saw the moment when he had looked down from Wynn's window into the courtyard that first night back at the guild. He had seen Magiere, Leesil, and Chap step out of the keep's main doors with Wynn and Shade. Then he saw a flash of them being "escorted" out. The jumbled flashes made him dizzy until the memory seemed to narrow in scope and focus only on parts of the images . . . on Chap. This repeated and repeated until Chane jumped to his feet again.

"Chap?" he asked. "You saw Chap?"

Shade let out a sharp huff. She raced to the small, dingy window and rose, setting her forepaws on the sill. Chane joined her, though he flattened against the wall to one side when she pushed her nose around the canvas curtain's edge to peer down outside. He had no idea what she was trying to tell him.

Shade pulled her head back and looked up at Chane, and the same dizzying flash of memories came to him again. He glanced at the curtained window in alarm.

"Chap . . . is here?" he rasped.

She huffed once.

Chane quickly slid the brass ring on as Shade dropped and backed away from the window.

Chap scrambled after Shade's trail through streets, cutways, and alleys, stopping only when he could to test for her scent. He caught sight of her twice, but each time she somehow outdistanced him. Every time he took to an open street to catch up, he heard someone shouting near or far behind him. When he trailed her all the way into a seedy district, some of what he saw seemed familiar.

He was somewhere else in the very district in which Magiere and Leesil still hid. Then Shade's trail took another change.

Chap entered a long strip of worn buildings where the next cross street was too far off for Shade to have reached it so quickly. He backtracked, sniffing along the buildings' side walls until he picked up her trail in an alley. He followed it, until it ended at the back door of a bleached gray, wooden inn with two stories and a high-peaked roof.

He dug his claws into the rear door's gap.

No matter how hard he levered and pulled, it would not open. Shade could not have gotten in this way, and he doubled-checked that her trail did not continue farther along the alley. The stench of the alley's center gutter made it hard to be certain, but he could find no scent of her beyond that one building. His daughter had to have gotten through that door.

Shame at what Chap had done to his daughter began to wane. Anger began mixing with his bafflement. If Wynn was locked in a room at the guild, with city guards at the portcullis, what in the world was Shade doing out here alone?

He looked up and down the alley, prepared to slip around the block for a peek at the building's front. A stinging chill ran over him, making his fur stand on end. Instinctual fury followed, running through his flesh. His hackles rose and he snarled before he even realized why.

Choking in rage, Chap was almost overcome by the sudden, overwhelming presence of an undead.

It was somewhere nearby, and he turned a full circle to peer up and down the alley. Nothing moved in his sight, not even rats scurrying among the refuse and ash cans. He looked again to the locked rear door and up across the windows above it.

Chap swallowed down the need to cut loose a howl. *It* was inside the place where Shade had gone! Had she been hunting?

He charged and rammed the rear door. It bucked and crackled but did not give way. With his head ringing, he backed up for another run at it.

Then the sickening presence that heated him within suddenly vanished . . . as if it had never been there at all.

Chap froze where he stood, trembling with lingering fury, almost unable to think.

The door swung out so hard it knocked over an old crate for collecting kitchen scraps. A corpulent, middle-aged woman in an age-faded apron waddled out, wielding an upturned broom like a club.

"What in the Trinity of Sentience is goin' on out . . ."

She faltered, her angry scowl vanishing as she spotted Chap.

"Wolf!" she screamed.

Chap came to his senses as a large, old man burst out behind the woman.

"It's a wolf, wolf, wolf!" the woman screamed, ducking behind the old man. The sound of running feet and further shouts carried out the open door from behind the couple.

A snarl turned to a whine in Chap's throat as he wheeled and raced off down the alley.

All because of Leesil and his stupid, worthless disguise.

CHAPTER 11

Leesil had never been good at sitting and waiting. This situation was no exception. By the way Magiere paced the small room, she was little better. The *clap*-pause-*clap* of her boots was getting on his nerves.

She still limped, but he knew that would pass soon because of what she'd done to herself. That thought took away half his relief that she would be all right. To make things even more uncomfortable, Osha was up on the roof, Leanâlhâm was still off with Chap, and only Brot'an remained. He lay on the floor in a pretense of rest, but his eyes were open, staring into the rooftop's rafters.

All was quiet but for the monotonous sound of Magiere's boots.

Small talk seemed pointless, and Leesil didn't want to speak of anything important. Not while Brot'an was present. A sudden silence jarred Leesil from sulking, and he realized Magiere had stopped pacing as she turned to Brot'an.

"How could you drag a defenseless girl into this skirmish with your own kind?" she demanded.

Brot'an had shown little reaction to anything since last night, but he sat up as if this time the question unnerved him. Much as Leesil wanted an answer to this, among other things, he'd grown as tired of the question as the lack of an answer.

"Her presence with us was her choice, not mine," Brot'an said, sounding almost irritated.

This was more of an answer than they'd gotten before, Leesil noted. Not that it mattered, since it only raised more questions.

"Her choice?" Magiere stepped closer. "Why would she—"

A soft, rapid pound upon the door was followed by Leanâlhâm's nearly breathless, hushed voice. "It is me."

Leesil rolled up to his feet and unbolted the door. Leanâlhâm practically fell inside—alone.

"Where's Chap?" he asked.

A rush of confused Elvish and Belaskian spilled from the girl. He didn't follow anything but "guards on the gate . . . the walls . . . We had to leave quickly. . . ."

Leanâlhâm paused to inhale deeply amid panting.

"Slow down," Magiere said, limping over to the girl.

Brot'an was on his feet, listening to the exchange.

"Where's Chap?" Leesil demanded, louder this time.

Leanâlhâm looked at him. "A black majay-hì . . . came to the gate with a sage. When it left, the majay-hì . . . I mean Chap . . . wanted to follow the other. He made me . . . come back alone." She looked frantic for an instant, and then added, "I tried to argue, but he was very . . ."

She faltered, as if she couldn't find the right word.

"Oh, dead deities!" Leesil hissed under his breath.

The black majay-hì could only be Shade. Leesil watched Magiere sag, shaking her head. What was Shade doing outside the guild? What was Chap thinking, going after her and leaving Leanâlhâm alone? An angry tension filled Magiere's expression.

Leesil grabbed the door's bolt and looked at Leanâlhâm. "Which way did he head from the guild?"

The room's window bucked open. Osha swung inside in a panic, dropping too loudly on the floor. He looked straight at Brot'an and rattled off something in Elvish. Then Leesil heard distant shouts through the open window.

Brot'an sighed audibly. "We have a problem."

One voice carried from afar, and Leesil ran to the window, leaning out. Only a few words were clear above the clamor.

"Wolf! Get back inside!"

"Oh, seven hells!" Leesil groaned through clenched teeth. "What has the mutt done this time?"

Én'nish had been taken aback when panicked humans chased after Chap. Part of her wanted to end their pursuit of a sacred majay-hì. But he was not one of the guardians she knew.

He was an aberration that Most Aged Father had warned against.

She could do little but leap from one rooftop to the next in pursuit as Chap dashed through one street or alley after another, dragging a cord with one end looped about his neck. No matter his twists and turns, the crowd kept on growing and caught up again and again.

Én'nish wondered if this might be to her advantage.

All of the majay-hì's efforts were focused on escape. He would never see an attack from above. If she gained just an instant, should he evade his pursuers again and then pause, she could drop and knock him out, safely capturing him for Fréthfàre.

There was the problem of trying to drag off a large animal by herself. But in this she could finally express her gratitude to Fréthfàre—to the Covârleasa— for giving her a second chance. The capture of the deviant would go far in proving her worth in the purpose given by Most Aged Father.

Én'nish crouched low, watching as the majay-hì swerved into a cutway, and then she took a running leap across to the next rooftop. When Chap halted, looking both ways along the street before lunging out, she hurried along the roof toward the forward eaves at its far end.

Then she froze, losing track of Chap at a sudden movement below.

An overly tall, cloaked form was rushing down the cutway toward its street-side end, with a smaller form following behind. Én'nish kept still and quiet. There was only one of such size who could appear so suddenly, run so silently.

Brot'ân'duivé neared the cutway's end and peered into the street as the smaller follower caught up.

Sudden shouts drew Én'nish's focus away. The crowd rounded the last street corner, and Chap bolted ahead of them. When she looked down again, Brot'ân'duivé was gone. Only the smaller figure remained, lurking in the cutway's end near the street.

Chap couldn't believe how quickly the crowd had caught up this time. His pursuers were once again only a block behind him. He peered about, trying to identify anything as he ran, but it was all a blur. Nothing looked familiar.

"Cut it off!" someone shouted, and ahead of him, people turned to look.

A large man in a hide jerkin pulled a sword. More shouts, seeming to grow in volume, followed behind Chap. He slid to a stop, the pads of his paws burning as they scraped across cobblestones, and he looked wildly about. A young boy tried to run out of a shabby little building, all too excited at the sight of the "wolf." A bystander snatched the boy back.

For one foolish instant, Chap looked behind.

The original pair of men with their staves came trotting, huffing, and puffing after him. Behind them waddled a huge woman with a bosom like a shelf that bounced up and down as she waved a wooden rolling pin in the air. A grimy old man wielding a dung fork like a pole arm passed the woman, his gray, stubbled face set in grim determination as he gained ground on the men with staves.

Chap almost whimpered. How had his decision to track Shade come to all this? A soft triple whistle barely reached his ears, and he grew more frantic. Was someone now calling out dogs?

A scream of horror carried from somewhere behind the mob. "Another! Another one! Here!"

Chap took only one glance in utter confusion, for how could there be another like him? Had Shade now followed him? It did not matter that most of the pursuers stalled or turned to look the other way. Chap's head whipped back around, and ahead the man with the sword was coming straight at him.

That triple, shrill whistle came again, but from above, as if it were some bird. It was too precise, and what would a bird of prey be doing flying over a city?

Chap looked up.

A figure rose on the next rooftop down and to the left. Tall and lean of form, its cloak was tied up around its waist. It waved both arms and pointed to the building's far end.

Chap suddenly realized the building was the inn where he and his companions were staying. He had not recognized it amid the chaos in the street, for he had never seen it from the front.

A large, open-slatted crate came flying out of the cutway at the inn's near-front corner.

Feathers trailed behind it in the air amid the ruckus of squeaking pigeons. One man ducked aside with a shout of warning. The one with the sword had time only to turn his head.

Chap charged just as the crate crashed into the swordsman's face.

Feathers, squeaks, and wood rained around Chap. A pigeon bounced off the cobbles and hit him in the jaw, its thrashing wings blinding him for an instant. Amid curses and shouts, kicks and wild swings, Chap swerved and scampered through.

And there was Leesil, glowering at him from out of the cutway on the inn's far end.

Chap swerved into the cutway, claws scrabbling on the cobble, as Leesil turned ahead of him and ran toward the inn's rear. Leanâlhâm came running down the back alley's other way, catching them both at the rear door. It must have been the girl who had screamed out about "another one" to distract his pursuers.

And there was Brot'an, holding the door open.

Leesil nearly shoved Leanâlhâm through, and Chap rushed in after them. He did not quite reach a full stop, his paws sliding on the floor's planks, and he slammed sideways against the narrow passage's wall as Brot'an pulled the door shut.

Chap stood there wobbling on tired legs, too exhausted to feel even relief as yet.

Leesil crouched down and whispered harshly into his face, "What was all that about?"

Chap's panting broke as he glared back. After what he had just been through, did Leesil really have the audacity to be indignant?

"Quiet—all of you!" Brot'an whispered.

Leesil rose with Leanâlhâm, who peered wide-eyed around him toward the door. Chap turned to find Brot'an poised there, listening. Shouting grew louder outside, as if the crowd had followed into the alley.

"Where'd it go?" someone called.

"I don't see it. Maybe—"

"Who chucked that pigeon crate?"

"Never mind! Some of you get back to the street. Block the alley ends and check the cutways. That beast can't have gotten out of here."

The voices continued longer amid grumbles and arguments. In the momentary respite, Chap's numb relief at being rescued faded. All he had gained was of little use. Wynn was a prisoner. There was an undead in this city. And Shade had been very close to it.

As the shouting outside began to fade, Leesil headed for the stairs, urging Leanâlhâm along and up to their room.

"What did you do to cause all that?" he whispered.

Chap snarled at him this time. Leesil was no one to talk when it came to causing complications. And what good had his filthy excuse for a disguise accomplished?

A pigeon feather suddenly fell off Chap's head and down the bridge of his muzzle. He wanted to bite Leesil—bite him hard!

Én'nish landed silently on the inn's roof, and heard voices coming from an open window. She moved as close to the roof's edge as possible and flattened her body to listen. She spoke fluent Belaskian. Her first master had been an excellent teacher.

"All right, you. What went wrong?"

Én'nish stiffened, but not at the anger in those words. She knew that voice.

Hatred for Léshil took all of Én'nish's reason. Grief for her lost Groyt'ashia filled her with cold shudders. She breathed slowly through the pain and the maddened sickness it brought.

If only Léshil were alone . . . if only she could kill him, here and now.

She willed herself to focus only on her purpose. While she may have missed a chance to take the majay-hì to Fréthfàre, she had gained something far more important. She had found where their quarry was hiding.

A moment of silence followed Leesil's question.

"Did you learn anything about Wynn?"

That voice returned the rest of Én'nish's clarity. It was the monster, the one called Magiere. Three low barks answered her.

"You don't know?" Magiere returned sharply. "Leanâlhâm told me you saw her up in a window."

"She did?" Leesil asked.

Én'nish lost the next few sentences, for their voices grew too faint, but her body twitched slightly at that name: Leanâlhâm. Gleann's mixed-blood descendant was here. But how? Was she the one who had accompanied the other majay-hì into the guild's castle?

"Is Wynn a prisoner?" Leesil asked.

Én'nish focused on that question. She knew of the female sage only too well, had once even been forced to help guard the deceitful human through her people's forest. She had hated the little human even more upon learning that the sage knew their language. No human should be able to speak the language of her people.

Another silence followed, and then Chap uttered one low bark. So far, Brot'ân'duivé had not said a word, and neither had Leanâlhâm, if she was in there.

"All right, that's it," Leesil said. "No more skulking about. We're getting Wynn out of there."

"Finally," Magiere put in.

"Agreed," came a deeper voice.

Én'nish flinched at the sound of Brot'ân'duivé. Her hatred of him, traitor that he was, almost matched her bloodlust toward Léshil, but she also feared him.

"We need more information," Brot'ân'duivé went on. "Anything about the interior of the grounds and layout of the keep, and a sense of guard positions and movements."

A new voice broke in, male, lowly murmuring something in Elvish. Én'nish was tempted to hang over the eaves to hear more. She strained to listen, but the words were too soft.

Brot'ân'duivé had someone else with him.

Én'nish could not place the voice, but there had been an archer aiding the traitorous greimasg'äh in the skirmish last night. Who among the Anmaglâhk would serve Brot'ân'duivé? Another dissident, likely. Before she even completed that thought, someone closed the window, and all the voices became too muffled to hear.

Én'nish lay there a little longer, pondering. Magiere and Leesil had returned to get the sage after wherever they had been gone for so long. Wynn Hygeorht was now a prisoner among her own kind, and this small group's next purpose was to free her. As long as they followed this course, they—including Magiere—could be taken in the open at night, either before or after retrieving the sage.

It would not be a happenstance encounter this time. Én'nish and her comrades would be able to watch and wait, prepared. And Magiere would not be the only one out in the open. Léshil would never let his love go anywhere without him. If not for Most Aged Father's wishes for that monster . . .

Én'nish sank into grief again, where lost love bred only hate and bloodshed. It would be a far greater vengeance if Léshil had to watch his love die before she killed him. She ached to give him even one instant of the torment that he had given her for a lifetime . . . before he died.

The inn's back door opened again.

Én'nish slid back up the roof's slope until only her eyes breached the edge and looked down.

Brot'ân'duivé and Léshil exited into the alley, and she silently crawled along the roof to watch them head out along the cutway into the street. Brot'ân'duivé stopped cold, looking around, and Én'nish quickly pulled back and lost sight of them.

Had he heard or somehow sensed her? She did not look over the edge again, and instead crawled across the roof. She rose to a crouch and listened, but amid the sounds of the street, she could not tell which way they had gone. Rising, she ran. Her steps made no more sound than autumn leaves falling upon the shingles. As she leaped to the next rooftop, she never faltered in her flight to return to her own and report all that she had learned.

Though her hatred of Leesil and Brot'ân'duivé still poisoned her heart and mind, Én'nish was loyal to the Anmaglâhk first—and always.

Dänvârfij and Fréthfâre sat at the small table, discussing the watch schedule now that Magiere, Léshil, and the majay-hì had been spotted. But their numbers had dwindled, and their people needed sleep at some point.

Rhysís and Eywodan lay on the floor, resting for a quarter day, but both had been up all last night and through the morning. Tavithê and Owain were doing separate sweeps of the city, hoping to spot something. Én'nish was watching the guild's castle.

All of this had left the port unobserved, which made Dänvârfij uncomfortable.

"We could omit shifts at the port," Fréthfâre suggested. "We no longer need to spot arrivals now that our quarry is here."

"But if they decide to flee, a ship would be an option," Dänvârfij countered. "Sea travel is the most difficult to follow, and the easiest way to move a group. The greimasg'äh knows this. We must know if and when they make a move toward port to cut them off."

"If they are spotted there," Fréthfâre replied, "what good would it do? We would not be able to gather quickly enough to cut them off, especially if they do so in daylight. And Brot'ân'duivé will try to take the monster away in daylight, to throw us off."

"That would be risky."

"Which is why he would do it," Fréthfâre shot back. "It is the least likely option for the best way out. Unless we can find them in the city, we will never know when or how they move."

Dänvârfij fell silent at this. She still did not agree, though the reasoning made sense on the surface. And they were already stretched too thin.

"I will take watch on the guild tonight," she said. "Once Rhysís has rested, he can watch the port, at least at night. He needs less sleep than the rest of us."

Fréthfâre shifted in her chair. "It may be time that I take a hand in matters."

Dänvârfij looked away, fearing her companion might volunteer for watch duty. Then Én'nish crawled in the window, saving Dänvârfij from another uncomfortable argument.

"Covârleasa!" Én'nish breathed, looking to Fréthfâre as she rose from her crouch. "I have found them!"

A moment of chaos followed as Rhysís and Eywodan sat up and Dänvârfij leaped to her feet. Everyone began asking too many questions at once.

"Silence!" Fréthfâre ordered. "Let her speak."

Dänvârfij waited as Én'nish recounted a tale about the majay-hì, a wild chase through the streets, and a rescue by Brot'ân'duivé. In spite of Én'nish abandoning her post, the more she talked, the more Dänvârfij believed she had done right.

Magiere had been found.

But at mention of another name, Fréthfâre sat upright and whispered, "Leanâlhâm . . . here?"

Dänvârfij did not recognize this name at first. Then she remembered hearing of a mixed-blood girl as kin to Sgäilsheilleache. What would such a girl be doing here?

"Their words all surrounded the sage," Én'nish rushed on. "That is why the deviant majay-hì returned to the guild. The sage is a prisoner, and they plan to free her."

"We should assault their inn tonight," Rhysís said, "and take them all."

Silence fell for the span of a few breaths. Rhysís had not spoken much since the previous night when Owain had returned without Wy'lanvi's body. Apparently, Owain had gone back to the spot in the alley where Wy'lanvi had been assigned and found nothing. They all believed Brot'ân'duivé had taken the body.

Dänvârfij hoped only that the aging greimasg'äh still held enough respect for his people's burial customs. And if not, she could only pray that Wy'lanvi found his own way to their ancestors.

"Why do they want the sage?" she asked of Én'nish.

"I do not know," Én'nish answered. "But they are determined. Brot'ân'duivé is helping them."

Another pause followed, and though Dänvârfij's purpose, given by Most Aged Father, was to capture Magiere or Léshil, she began to wonder. The artifact had been removed from the ice-bound castle by those two, but Most Aged Father had also warned that the pair often relied on the sage for information. If those two now needed the sage so badly that Brot'ân'duivé assisted them, then the sage must know something essential.

"Our first task is to gather information about the artifact," Dänvârfij said slowly. "The sage may know more than Magiere or Léshil. That may help us understand how to handle it, once it is acquired. We will double our watch on the guild. When they come to retrieve the sage, we separate them, kill Brot'ân'duivé, and capture the others."

"No," Fréthfâre said, shaking her head. "Rhysís is right. They are unaware that we know their location and would not expect an attack tonight. When the sun sets, we move . . . and then kill the traitor and take Magiere and anyone else possible. The sage is not worth risking the loss of such a chance."

The others present, including Rhysís, looked uncertain, but not because of the difference between the two plans. Not one of them would ever choose to go against a greimasg'äh, but for Fréthfâre to countermand Dänvârfij in front of everyone was another matter.

Anmaglâhk functioned under a chain of command that began not with the highest or the eldest but with the first one given a purpose by Most Aged Father. That had been Dänvârfij. Even now, most of the others still looked on Fréthfâre as their wounded Covârleasa, though Most Aged Father had appointed someone new in her place back home. This shared command through Fréthfâre's sway over the others had more than once proven a difficulty.

Dänvârfij had no wish to further anyone's embarrassment by partaking in an open argument. She simply resorted to a higher authority than her own.

"If Magiere and Brot'ân'duivé want the sage so much," she said, "Most Aged Father would want us to capture the sage, as well. She is currently locked inside a human castle—a stable, stationary target. I believe this is how Most Aged Father would counsel us."

Dänvârfij looked to Fréthfâre and found the ailing woman studying her in return. For how could Most Aged Father's one-time prime counselor counter what he would obviously have advised?

"I could contact Most Aged Father and ask him . . . if you prefer," Dänvârfij suggested.

Fréthfâre's expression tightened slightly, but not from pain. She knew

was under orders to guard the grounds, he had brought more men than were visible.

There was a time when Chane would have simply scaled the walls and killed anything in his way. It would have been so much easier.

He had noticed one strange event while he and Shade lurked near the western corner of Old Bailey Road. He had been studying the keep's heights for signs of more guards when Shade huffed and directed his attention down the street.

At well past night's first bell, a wagon rolled onto Old Bailey Road at its southern corner and headed straight for the keep's bailey gate. The portcullis rose even before it arrived, and a city guard and a sage in midnight blue came out to open the bailey gate and let the wagon in. The vehicle was heavily laden, its cargo hidden beneath a lashed canvas tarp.

In the time Chane had spent among the sages, he had never seen a supply wagon arrive at night. Of course he could not have seen any arriving in daylight, but he had never even heard of nighttime deliveries before. He wished he could have learned more of this—although it was a minor puzzle among greater concerns, and he remained inside his room as much as possible. He was too afraid that he might miss . . .

A very heavy knock at the door halted Chane's pacing. He tensed with hope as Shade jumped off the bed. Chane was not certain who stood on the other side of that door, and he picked up his sword, pulling the dwarven steel blade from its sheath.

"Where do all-eaters guard the bones of the lost and forgotten?" he asked softly through the door.

"In Bäalâle Seatt," a low voice answered from outside.

Only one person besides him and Wynn knew the answer, as well as that ancient Dwarvish reference to mythical dragons: the *gi'uyllæ*, the all-eaters.

Chane jerked open the door and looked down.

A wide, solid dwarf stood there, filling the doorway. He was beardless, something uncommon among their males, with red hair that flowed to the shoulders of an iron-colored wool cloak tied about his thick neck. He no longer wore a stonewalker's black-scaled armor, but along with a double-wide sword sheathed on his hip, he carried a stout iron staff as tall as Chane.

Chane noted the burnt-orange wool tabard through the split of the visitor's cloak. The dwarf had once again "disguised" himself as a holy shirvêsh of Bedzâ'kenge—Feather-Tongue, the Eternal, the saint, of dwarven history, tradition, and wisdom.

"Ore-Locks," Chane whispered, not even bothering to hide his relief.

Ore-Locks held up Chane's message and cocked his head. "You sent for me?"

Safely locked inside their room at the inn, Leesil unrolled the newer Belaskian talking hide as he knelt down on the floor. Magiere crouched down on one side of him and Chap sat on the other. He had just returned from another outing with Brot'an.

Magiere was already fed up with how little they'd related of what they'd found during each scouting trip. Leesil now felt ready to share with the others. In the time that had passed since Chap's incident with the mob, a good deal had happened. For one, Leesil was still unsettled by what Chap had told them.

Shade was no longer with Wynn. Chap had tracked his daughter into a nearby neighborhood, where he'd sensed an undead near a broken-down inn. They would soon have to look into that. If they didn't, Leesil might have to fight Magiere to keep her from taking off to do so on her own.

Just knowing that Wynn was completely alone served to drive all of them, especially Magiere, to focus on freeing the sage. Once Wynn was safe, Leesil would deal with Magiere hunting an undead in a city crawling with anmaglâhk hunting her. He glanced quickly at his wife and finished rolling out the talking hide.

Brot'an stood near the window, which he'd opened a crack so he could hear anything outside. But he watched everyone in the room, mostly Magiere.

Osha and Leanâlhâm sat cross-legged against the wall across from Leesil, and Leanâlhâm peered down at the hide with deep curiosity.

There was no one on the roof, as Leesil expected everyone to be present. They all had a part to play concerning the other item on the floor: a broad piece of scrap cloth depicting a crude, charcoal-drawn layout of guild grounds.

"You think we ready . . . go tomorrow night?" Osha asked hopefully.

"Yes," Leesil answered, for he and Brot'an had been busy.

It still unsettled him more than he cared to admit how easy it had been to both scout and plan with Brot'an. Leesil hadn't consulted Magiere, and with good reason. She wouldn't like what they'd devised for her part in all of this.

Magiere's strengths lay in unyielding, blind determination. She would throw herself headlong at anything that got between her and those she loved. She was not subtle, and not half as devious as she liked to think—not like him. Where she was heated by fury, he could be coldly vicious when necessary.

"Good," Osha said. "Where start?"

Magiere glanced sidelong at Leesil and raised one eyebrow. He took in the sight of her beautiful, pale face, her mass of near-black hair with shots of bloodred glowing by the room's candle lantern. He felt the same sense of wonder he always had when he really *looked* at her. But he was in for a battle now—with her.

"Brot'an and I will start here," he said.

He reached out to the cloth map, pointing to a section of the bailey wall at the keep's back.

"You . . . and Brot'an?" Magiere asked too quietly, like the deceptive calm at the eye of a hurricane.

Chap snarled and huffed twice—loudly.

"There's no other way," Leesil rushed on. "He and I are the only ones skilled at infiltration. The anmaglâhk will be watching the guild, probably from more than one angle. Brot'an and I can't deal with that and the guards at the same time . . . or at least not when it comes time to remove Wynn."

He looked intently at Magiere. "You, Chap, Osha . . . and Leanâlhâm . . . have to run a distraction."

"Leanâlhâm?" Magiere repeated, her expression turning darker. "She's not going anywhere near this!"

Leesil hesitated. Deceit was his most ingrained skill, and lying came as easy as breathing to him, but not with her . . . he didn't lie easily to Magiere. But it was the only way to get her to do as he wanted.

"She can't stay here alone, unprotected," he said. "And we're going to need someone of suitable size and build for this ruse . . . someone smaller than the rest of us."

It was only half the truth, and that was nearly always the best lie. With Leanâlhâm in plain sight, she might be safer than left alone in this room. In turn, Magiere wouldn't let the girl go without her, and that would keep Magiere out of the way. Leesil also wanted no killing in this exploit.

It stuck in his gut that Magiere was his first concern in that rather than Brot'an. If things got too intense around her, there was a risk that . . .

Magiere already looked suspicious, and Leesil knew this wasn't over when she pivoted on one knee.

"What's the rest of it?" she demanded. "You're not going to—"

"I will help," Leanâlhâm cut in.

Everyone looked at her, and Leesil stifled a sigh of relief. Leanâlhâm took a hard swallow under all the scrutiny, but finally looked at Leesil and hesitantly leaned forward.

"I want to help Wynn," she said, sounding almost eager.

Magiere's mouth hung halfway open. Then she snapped her jaw shut, as if uncertain whom to shout at next. Osha, however, was frowning at Leesil.

"I not go with you?" he asked, displeasure plain in his broken words.

"No," Leesil answered, "because Magiere and Chap . . . and especially Leanâlhâm . . . are going to need you."

He had to turn this entire gathering back to the plan, and he quickly pointed to the bailey gate on the map.

"Brot'an and I have been watching the rotation of the guards. There are also loaded wagons coming regularly at the same time each night. They are always allowed through the portcullis."

Leesil glanced at Magiere. There was no less anger in her face, but she was looking at the map now.

"Always?" she asked.

Leesil glanced the other way at Chap, who was rumbling low in discontent, but he rushed on while he still had them distracted.

"All that matters is getting Wynn out," he said, "and making sure she can't be caught in the process. So there'll be no fits about who's to do what."

He waited for another argument, but it didn't come. Brot'an had been silently watching all this. The two of them had already agreed that Leesil should take the lead in this mixed group; he was the one the others might equally trust.

"It will work," he added, soft but firm. "But it will take all of us. We must all know our parts."

Chap began pawing the Belaskian letters on the talking hide.

"What does he say?" Magiere asked.

Leesil sighed. "He says he's not throwing a fit."

Chap wrinkled his jowls but dropped his haunches back to the floor.

"Are you ready to listen?" Leesil asked him, but then looked at Magiere. No one said a word.

"All right, then, this is how it's going to work. . . ."

When Chane finished explaining, Ore-Locks shook his head in astonishment.

"The sages would imprison one of their own?" he said. "If even half of what you say is true, then yes, we need to get her out."

"You doubt me?" Chane asked, not truly offended.

He had spent a fair bit of time relating the whole story of the past few days and nights. It was unsurprising that Ore-Locks had doubts without knowledge of how much Wynn had been through with the guild before now.

"No," Ore-Locks hurried to say. "I did not mean . . . just a figure of speech."

Not too long ago, Ore-Locks would not have cared a whit about offending Chane. Perhaps to both their surprise, they had become allies, if not friends. After they had located the orb at Bäalâle Seatt, Ore-Locks had taken it into safekeeping in the underworld of the Stonewalkers. The dragons, the all-eaters, had demanded that Ore-Locks become keeper of their orb.

"Once we get Wynn out," Ore-Locks went on, "where will you take her? She will not be safe here in this city. Perhaps not even inside Malourné's borders."

Chane had not thought that far ahead, and he glanced at Shade. She merely whined once. Neither of them had thought much further than freeing Wynn. Where would they go? Not only would the Premin Council be hunting for Wynn, they would likely use the city guard, as well.

"Dhredze Seatt might be safe for a while," Ore-Locks suggested. "But not at the temple of Feather-Tongue. Head Shirvêsh Mallet has ties to the guild. Perhaps in the underside of one of the settlements."

Chane was tempted. Of all places he had been in recent years, he had felt most at ease in the underground half of the dwarves' world—despite the fact that his height made him stand out too much. Ore-Locks's suggestion was welcome, but Chane viewed it as a fallback position. If he and Wynn were to find the remaining orbs, she needed access to resources that could help her translate the scroll. He did not know what she had in mind for their next step, but he doubted that she would agree to hide in a remote dwarven settlement. She was nothing if not focused . . . or outright stubborn.

She was determined to locate every orb before agents of the Ancient Enemy found them first. Chane had sworn to himself that her mission was his mission. But he also struggled with how to retrieve something desperately precious to him—for her.

Premin Hawes still possessed *The Seven Leaves of Life* and the *muhkgean* mushrooms and *anasgiah* flowers he had acquired. He was not leaving without them. And he still did not know what Wynn would want to do about Magiere, Leesil, and Chap.

That worried him the most. What did that trio's return mean for his future with Wynn?

Suddenly, the thought of vanishing into a dwarves' mountain with Wynn became more appealing. He would never admit it, but he was glad Ore-Locks had come to help. Chane had no one else to call on, and he could not do this alone.

"Dhredze Seatt it is," he finally answered, "but first we have to get Wynn."

"When?" Ore-Locks asked.

Shade's ears perked up at that.

"Tomorrow night," Chane answered. "We will be ready by then."

He rose and went to his pack, pulling out a torn sheet of paper and a charcoal writing stick. He knelt before Ore-Locks and waved Shade over, and began sketching an outline of the guild's grounds.

"We begin here," Chane said, pointing to the keep's front and glancing at Ore-Locks. "Considering some of your skills, the first step will be the easiest."

Ore-Locks and Shade leaned in to listen.

CHAPTER 13

Late the following night, Magiere hid inside an alley's mouth several blocks southwest of the Old Bailey Road loop. Chap stood at her side, peering around the building's corner into the open street, with Osha and Leanâlhâm just behind them. Magiere let out a slow breath that turned to vapor in the chill night.

She still thought much of Leesil's plan bordered on madness, but she hadn't come up with anything better. If all went well, they might have a chance at rescuing Wynn. *If* all went as planned. But this entire strategy still felt wrong to her. She should've been the one with Leesil, not Brot'an.

She could've covered Leesil's back while he scaled the bailey wall and then hauled her up by a rope. If the worst came, they'd always fought back-to-back to get out of anything . . . almost anything. Instead, she was standing in the dark with two young elves and a grumpy know-it-all masquerading as a dog.

Since when had she become the distraction, the decoy?

"Hear it?" Osha whispered.

Magiere heard nothing and glanced back at him. Osha was dressed in a heavy cloak with its hood pulled forward, shadowing his face. With his longbow strung, he reached over his shoulder and drew an arrow from his quiver. The arrow's feathers were so black that even Magiere had trouble making them out in the dark.

Leanâlhâm was dressed in a boy's breeches, a jerkin, and a shabby cloak. Leesil had scavenged up this clothing, and Magiere had refrained from asking him where and how. The girl had been eager enough back at the inn. Now she stood there shivering, gripping her cloak closed about herself from the chill, fright, or both.

"It come," Osha whispered.

At Chap's huffed agreement, Magiere finally heard the distant grind and creak of wagon wheels on cobble. She glanced back again at Leanâlhâm and then down at Chap.

"Both of you stay here, even if things go wrong," she ordered, and then raised her eyes to Osha. "Ready?"

Osha nodded once, and Magiere took off past him down the alley at a run. When she reached the alley's far end, she headed down the next street. She ran hard to get behind the wagon's path before Osha would have to step out in front of it.

Magiere halted at the corner where the side street met the mainway. But the sound of hooves came from her right and not left, up the way toward the alley's mouth. She had beaten the wagon and arrived at the next intersection too quickly. She leaned back against a shop's corner, head hanging, just listening.

As the wagon passed by, she ducked around the corner, flipped her hood back, and watched it roll up the street. She crept along the shop fronts, as any moment now . . .

A shadowy form rushed out of the next alley's mouth a dozen yards before the wagon.

Osha rooted himself midstreet and raised his bow, aiming at the driver.

"Stop now," he ordered.

In a creak of wheels and rattle of tack, the driver jerked the wagon team to a halt. Magiere came in behind it as quietly as she could.

"What's this about?" the driver shouted.

"I need wagon," Osha said.

Magiere crept toward the driver's side of the wagon.

Osha had his aim set on the driver's head, but even if he had to fire, it would not be lethal. The driver wouldn't know this, nor likely spot the oddity of the arrow that Osha had notched to his bowstring. When the plan had been settled back at the inn, Leesil had insisted there be no unnecessary bloodshed.

But he'd looked right at Magiere when he'd said it.

It stung her, heated her with anger, but she'd said nothing. He had his reasons, especially for what had happened up in the Wastes . . . what she'd done to save him when they'd fled that icy, white plain.

Brot'an had replaced the head of one of Osha's arrows with a lump of lead.

"Get out of my way!" the driver growled. "Or I'll run you down."

"No, you won't," Magiere whispered.

She never saw the driver's face clearly. The instant his head whipped toward her voice, she braced her foot against a front wheel spoke and lunged upward, slamming her fist into the side of his head.

His head whipped the other way as he toppled, the force sliding his body across the bench. As he tumbled off the wagon's far side, beyond Magiere's sight, Osha arrived. He stood over the driver, looking down at the man, as she came around to join him.

Magiere snatched the back of the driver's heavy canvas coat with one hand. Osha just stared at her. She ignored him and dragged the limp man to the side of the street and dropped him under a shop awning. Osha was still watching her as Leanâlhâm and Chap came out of the alley.

Chap began rumbling at her.

"Get ready," Magiere told Leanâlhâm. She still didn't want Leanâlhâm in the middle of all this, but events were now in motion.

Magiere headed to the wagon's rear and pulled back the tarp covering the load. She expected to find crates of goods, food, perhaps blankets, or even bundles of paper and racks of ink for the sages. She found something else.

The wagon was piled with folds of heavy canvas tarps or tents, coils of rope, lanterns, and a few hand axes. The nearest cask smelled of salt pork or jerky. At that, she jerked a canvas sack open, expecting to find dried peas or beans, or even just potatoes. It was filled with iron spikes, each having a side hook for lashings.

She stared in puzzlement at the piled canvas again, hesitating as Leanâl-hâm crept in beside her. Why would the guild go to such trouble to bring this stuff in under the cover of night? Why would they need these things at all? It made no sense.

"Quick," Leanâlhâm whispered. "We must go."

Magiere pulled the cask out, tossed it aside, and began shoving other items out of the way to make a space.

"Get in," she said.

Leanâlhâm climbed into the little hole Magiere made for her. Every instinct in Magiere rushed up, telling her to pull the girl out of there.

"It is all right," Leanâlhâm said, reading her face.

"You don't do anything other than what Leesil told you," Magiere answered harshly. "Once you're back out, you dive for cover at the first sign of trouble. You let Osha handle anything until Chap and I catch up. Do you hear me?"

"Yes," Leanâlhâm answered, nodding as she leaned back among the cargo.

Magiere pulled the tarp back into place and then paused as she grabbed its corner lashing. In only a blink, she jerked the cord with all her strength, and it snapped off short on the wagon wall's edge. Whoever unloaded the wagon would only find it broken. Should Leanâlhâm be forced to hide again on the way out, at least the tarp couldn't be tied down to hamper her.

Magiere rounded to the front as Osha climbed onto the wagon's bench and took the reins. He looked down intently at her and then glanced over his shoulder to where Leanâlhâm hid.

"I . . . I protect," he said.

"You'd better," Magiere answered, handing up his bow and quiver.

Osha stored his weapon under the bench at his feet, and Magiere stepped back, with Chap at her side.

"We'll be watching for you," she said.

Osha nodded, pulling his hood farther forward, and the wagon rolled off, heading for the loop of street around the guild's castle, still blocks away.

Chap whined once in agitation. Magiere dropped a hand on his head, stroking his ears once.

"That was the easy part," she said. "We'll have plenty to do soon."

Or so she hoped. Magiere tried not to think what might happen to any of them, including Leesil, if all of this didn't go as he'd planned.

Chane, Shade, and Ore-Locks hid around the corner where Wall Shop Row met Old Procession Road. They were only a block from the guild's bailey gate. Strangely, Chane was not even nervous.

They had gone over and over their plan. He was confident he would have Wynn out of the guild this very night. With that in mind, he unwrapped a bit of burlap that held something Ore-Locks had purchased for him that day.

Chane took out a small sandglass with a line drawn partway down around its upper half. He shook it briefly, until all the sand fell into the bottom, and then he set it down before Shade.

"As I said," he told her. "When I turn this over, wait until the sand fills the bottom to the mark."

She wrinkled a jowl in annoyance and huffed once.

Perhaps Chane had repeated this too often, and he looked to Ore-Locks. "Ready?"

Ore-Locks nodded, the tail of his bound red hair bobbing once.

Chane flipped the sandglass over. He turned quickly, running south along Wall Shop Row with Ore-Locks behind him. They left Shade alone with the sand already falling.

One block down, Chane swerved into a cutway between the buildings. He had already scouted this path two nights before. It was one of the only cutways where the backside of Wall Shop Row opened through the remaining sections of the "outer" bailey wall of the old guild castle.

There, at the cutway's back mouth, Chane and Ore-Locks stopped and crouched low. They peered out and across the Old Bailey Road loop at the inner bailey wall, scanning its top in both directions for any signs of city guards walking their circuits.

Chane believed he had timed this correctly, but was not taking any chances.

"Clear," he finally whispered, and scurried across and along the wall toward the bailey gate. When they reached the indented corner where the wall met the gate's nearside barbican, they stopped and listened.

Chane heard the guard inside the portcullis shifting on his feet from a long night of standing.

"Remember to look for the glove," Chane whispered.

"Of course," Ore-Locks answered, sounding almost as annoyed as Shade.

Once Chane and Ore-Locks were inside the courtyard, there would be no further chance for second checks. The plan then was for Chane to enter the keep's main building and make certain they had a clear path to the new library building at the back. With Captain Rodian in charge of guild security, there was no telling what safeguards he might have placed inside the main keep. Chane needed to check before Wynn was brought through there.

At the same time, Ore-Locks would go to Wynn's room and bring her quietly out and through the main keep to meet Chane in the library. After that, escape was a simple matter of going out a third-floor window. Chane would help Wynn scale down the back of the bailey wall.

But they had also planned for failure. If, for any reason, Chane could not get to the library and could not risk crossing the courtyard again, he would simply toss a glove outside the keep's main doors. If Ore-Locks spotted the glove in bringing out Wynn, he would have to try to take Wynn out by a secondary route.

Chane hoped that would not happen as he looked up the bailey wall and grimaced. Their only method for getting into the keep was another part he did not like.

"I will make it quick," Ore-Locks whispered. "But getting through the keep's own thick wall will be even less pleasant."

Chane nodded, and he took Ore-Locks's thick hand. There was an advantage to having a stonewalker on his side.

"Close your eyes if you have to," Ore-Locks said.

Chane wrinkled his nose an instant before Ore-Locks heaved him forward.

Dänvârfij crouched with Én'nish on the rear of a rooftop where Wall Shop Row met Old Procession Road leading up to the bailey gate. She stared down in puzzlement.

"Who are they?" Én'nish whispered.

Dänvârfij shook her head.

They had been standing watch on the front of the small castle when a tall, pale human, a red-haired dwarf, and the black majay-hì had appeared up the mainway and crouched around a corner in hiding. The two men had run south out of sight along the row of shops. It was not long before they reappeared southward, scurried across the street that looped around the guild, and crouched in hiding next to the southern barbican of the bailey gate.

This night, after more debating with Fréthfàre, Dänvârfij had surrounded the guild with her people. Rhysís was covering the northwest, Owain the back, and Eywodan on the southeast. Tavithê had gone to watch the port, in case Én'nish was wrong and their quarry tried to flee the city without the sage.

"What could they be doing?" Én'nish wondered aloud.

Dänvârfij had no idea. The human and dwarf certainly could not scale the wall there without being spotted. If they did, they would simply find themselves trapped in the inner bailey when a guard came along the wall's top, into view. She had half expected to see Léshil, Magiere, and even Brot'ân'duivé come this night, but not two strangers. How many in this city took covert interest in the guild . . . or the little sage?

Én'nish gasped. "Look!"

Dänvârfij already saw and straightened to her feet as the human below gripped the hand of the dwarf. And the dwarf thrust his other hand *through* the bailey wall's stone.

It was hard to be certain of what she saw next. It happened quickly in the wall's night shadows, out of reach of the great braziers on the gatehouse's front. But the color of the wall's stone appeared to flow up the dwarf's arm and over his body.

He stepped through the wall, pulling the pale human after him. Both disappeared into stone and were gone.

A moment of silence passed before Én'nish asked, "Do we move?"

Dänvârfij hesitated. What they had witnessed was disturbing, impossible. She had heard talk of mages among the humans, but had never imagined anything like this. The nature of the dwarves was still unfamiliar to her, as those people did not exist in her part of the world. But the two men were not their quarry, and they could not risk missing Magiere and Leesil.

"No," Dänvârfij answered. "We do not know what they are after. Should they be here for the sage or not, we can take them either way when they come out. We hold our positions . . . for now."

She was less certain than she sounded.

Panic rushed through Chane as Ore-Locks pulled him into the bailey wall. He did not struggle and focused only on gripping Ore-Locks's hand as darkness and cold enveloped him. The sensation of suffocation—though he did not require air—and the pressure all over him were no easier than the first time . . . when Ore-Locks had dragged him through a cave-in on their way to Bäalâle Seatt.

This time, the discomfort did not last as long. Almost before Chane knew it, he stood within the inner bailey among a narrow band of trees, looking at the keep's own taller wall. Still disoriented, he stumbled and then righted himself.

232 · BARB & J. C. HENDEE

Passing through stone was never easy, even for an undead. Ore-Locks was not as skilled as some of his brethren, the keepers of the honored dead in the depths below Dhredze Seatt. He could not take anything living with him through stone, which was a pity, because that would have made getting Wynn out far easier.

"Are you well?" Ore-Locks asked.

"I am fine. Go on."

He was not fine, but Shade would be on the move soon. The sands in the glass were still falling, and they had to be ready. Ore-Locks took off down the bailey, and Chane followed to where the keep's wall met the southern corner tower.

"This one is thicker," Ore-Locks warned again.

"Just go."

Ore-Locks took hold of Chane's arm and stepped into the wall.

The world went black and cold again, and Chane choked down rising panic.

Stone pressed in over every part of him, as if to crush him. Time froze in the longest of moments. Then, suddenly, the pressure vanished and air surrounded him again.

Chane heard the soft crackle of braziers somewhere nearby on the gatehouse tower, and the chill night felt almost warm compared to the cold of stone. He opened his eyes and looked up as Ore-Locks let go of his arm.

Below the night sky's stars, Chane looked over the end of the two-story stone barracks. Wynn's room was at the top near corner, but there was no window on the end of the building.

He dropped low and scurried to the building's corner, crouching with Ore-Locks near the old cistern. They were inside the courtyard, hidden in the shadows. Now the waiting continued as Chane peeked around the corner and across the keep's broad inner courtyard.

No guards were in sight, but that did not mean they were not there. From his present position across to the courtyard's northern corner, he could see only half the space. He could see the main keep's double doors, but not the opening to the gatehouse tunnel or the courtyard's western corner beyond that.

Chane possessed a decent internal sense of time, but the moments passed too slowly as he imagined sand trickling away before Shade's eyes.

"Any moment now," Ore-Locks whispered.

Leesil flattened against the side of a warehouse on Norgate Road near where it met the back of Old Bailey Road, which encircled the guild's castle. Brot'an leaned out slightly from behind him, and they both gazed on the back of the keep's bailey wall.

"Any time now," Leesil whispered.

Their next move had to be timed just right.

A guard in a red tabard finally appeared, walking the bailey wall around the eastern tower. The man kept on along the back wall, heading for the rear central barbican.

Leesil and Brot'an had chosen to approach from the rear because it was the only place where any part of the keep met the bailey wall. A large building had been built inside the bailey for some reason. They had no idea what was inside it, but its upper-floor windows were just within reach of the wall's top . . . with a short climb. The bailey wall itself, a good twenty feet high, at a guess, was another matter.

Leesil crouched, getting ready to run, and both he and Brot'an waited for the right moment.

Tonight, neither of them wore cloaks, and Leesil had even forgone his hauberk. They both wore long scarves that wrapped up and hid light-colored hair and the lower half of their faces. Only their eyes were left exposed.

Leesil's winged punching blades were strapped tight on his thighs, but he was uncomfortable with the two new weapons sheathed inside his shirtsleeves—an anmaglâhk's hook-bladed bone knife and stiletto. Brot'an had offered them to him, and Leesil knew they would be necessary, so he'd taken them. He was uncomfortably aware of only one possible source for the spares Brot'an had been carrying: the body of a dead anmaglâhk.

After all the questionable things Leesil had done in his life, it shouldn't bother him to use a dead man's weapons, but it did. He'd once possessed his own anmaglâhk stilettos and bone knife, at the time unaware what they'd meant or where his mother had gotten them. He'd traded one intact stiletto and a broken one to a blacksmith for his first set of winged blades.

He'd left his bone knife buried to the hilt in the throat of Lord Darmouth.

Losing those assassin's weapons had been no loss; there were always more weapons to be had. Losing his had been a relief. Now he wore them again . . . like an anmaglâhk.

The guard reached the large barbican jutting out from the center of the bailey's rear wall. He paused there, surveying the keep and the inner bailey, and then turned to look out at the quiet night city around the guild.

Leesil flattened against the wall in the dark.

The guard finally turned away, heading back the way he'd come in his half circuit around the wall's northern half. It would be some 130 paces before the guard walking the wall's southern half came into sight.

When the first guard was fifteen paces along his way, with his back turned, Leesil slipped from the shadows, heading for the wall with Brot'an close behind him.

Pawl a'Seatt had been too restless this night to even remain at the shop for closing time. Whatever was happening at the guild, what he did not know, ate at him too much. He'd left Teagan to close up and then hurried off before the scribe master could even express surprise.

Pawl had taken to the city's heights, heading toward the castle and keep of the sages.

Little might be learned in watching the grounds, other than to know how much the captain of the Shyldfälches had done to seal the place. But even that was something compared to the nothingness of waiting and wondering when the translation project might restart.

The Premin Council had locked up Wynn Hygeorht, and from that moment, all work on the project had ceased. Pawl was certain there must be a connection between her imprisonment and the stalled transcriptions.

Dressed in his voluminous black cloak and broad-brimmed black hat, Pawl now crouched upon a rooftop across from the guild's northern corner, where a short access road off Old Bailey Road connected to the Outwall Loop. He knew his behavior was probably foolish and certainly pointless, but he watched the northern circuit guard turn around at the rear central barbican for the sixth time since he'd arrived.

The city guard headed back along the wall. It would be a while before the one walking the wall's southern half appeared in sight at the keep's back.

Pawl hung his head, wondering again what he'd thought he could accomplish here.

Movement caught his left eye as something dark shot across Old Bailey Road.

His sight sharpened until the night grew bright in his eyes. Two figures, the second taller than the first, rushed for the bailey wall. They ducked in next to the jutting barbican's southern side where it joined the wall.

Another movement pulled Pawl's attention.

A tall figure stood up on a roof a few buildings south of him. It wore a dark, hooded cloak that bulked up at its back. The cloak did not swing freely, as he could see the figure's legs, and the figure crept to the building's edge, crouching as it looked down into the street. It appeared to be watching the pair that now hid on the barbican's far side.

Pawl silently ran and leaped to the next rooftop. Upon landing, he dropped low. He rose slowly, peering along the rooftops, but that other unknown figure still watched the street below.

He had seen similar tall figures moving about the city roofs once before. He had not sensed them as undead, so they had not particularly interested him until now. What was this cloaked figure doing, watching the guild? And who were the two below that this one took such trouble not to be noticed by them?

Pawl remained there in the dark only a few buildings away, watching and waiting.

*　　*　　*

Chane could still see the sands falling in his mind's eye, and yet Shade had not acted. Her first loud bark took him by surprise and made him flinch. She was finally outside the bailey gate, raising a ruckus to draw the guard's attention. Chane nodded one last time to Ore-Locks and stood up to make a silent dash for the keep's main doors.

He had barely cleared the corner when the barracks door opened outward.

Chane ducked back around the corner at the sound of hard boots stomping the courtyard stones. Peeking out with one eye, he tensed at whom he saw.

Captain Rodian strode out of Wynn's barracks.

Chane frowned, clenching his jaw. Had Rodian placed himself on night watch? Did he not have enough men to see to the keep? The captain was not some random guard, and would know Chane on sight.

At this unforeseen complication, Chane held up a hand for Ore-Locks to remain still. He then peeked around the barracks' corner again.

The captain stopped midway to the keep's main doors. He turned in the courtyard at the sound of Shade's barks echoing up the gatehouse tunnel. Striding toward the tunnel, he slipped from Chane's sight as he approached the tunnel's mouth, but his footfalls stopped too soon.

Shade's cacophony of snarling and howling continued, echoing loudly in the night air.

"Maolís!" the captain suddenly barked. "What's going on out there?"

"Not sure, sir," came an answer. "Should I go and see?"

The captain's footfalls began again, eventually echoing as if he had headed into the tunnel.

The courtyard was empty, but the captain would still be in direct line of sight to the keep's main doors. If he raised the portcullis to see to matters himself, would he recognize Shade? There was no telling what might happen then, or how long Shade could continue her distraction.

Chane did not hesitate. "Now," he rasped.

Ore-Locks pivoted and stepped straight into the barracks' end wall.

Chane hurried out, creeping along the barracks' front. As he passed its door, for an instant he was tempted to enter there, go straight to Wynn, and alter the whole plan.

Someone still had to secure the path, so he continued along the barracks to its far end and the eastern corner of the courtyard. There he paused in the shadows, looking between the keep's main doors and the gatehouse tunnel, in direct line of sight to them.

There was no turning back.

Chane inched toward the keep's doors with his eyes on the tunnel, determined to make certain Wynn and Ore-Locks had a safe path to the library.

CHAPTER 14

Rodian strode down the gatehouse tunnel.

He'd been spending as much time as possible at the guild. The key to learning what was really happening could only be found here—mostly through Wynn Hygeorht. When he reached Guardsman Maolís at the tunnel's outer end, he peered through the portcullis's thick beams.

"What's going on out there?" he demanded.

The path to the closed bailey gate was all clear, but he heard a dog in the street beyond it, making a commotion.

"Sounds like a dog having some kind of fit, sir," Maolís answered.

"Yes," Rodian replied dryly, "I can hear that."

Maolís was a solid guardsman with thick arms, carrot red hair, and a smattering of freckles across his small nose and broad cheeks. He also had an unusually firm grasp of the obvious.

Suddenly, Rodian thought of one very tall dog—or wolf.

Shade always tended to remain near Wynn, but she'd run off a few nights before. Then another "dog," very much like her, had shown up later in the company of a shy elven girl with strange eyes.

"Open the portcullis!" he called up.

Loud creaking and clanks echoed in the tunnel, nearly drowning out the dog's noise. When the outer portcullis was only halfway up, Rodian ducked under, heading quickly to the bailey gate. He pulled it open and looked down.

It *was* Shade, but she instantly fell silent, ears stiffening upright as she stared at him. She looked almost startled, at a loss over the gate actually opening, if such emotion was possible on a dog's face.

Rodian took a step and reached out carefully.

Before he could grab her scruff, she wheeled and bolted up the road toward the city. He started to run after her.

"Shade, stop!" he called.

Her tall form was nearly as black as night's shadows, and she stretched out her long legs into a full run. Before Rodian even reached the head of Old Procession Road into the city, Shade swerved right up Wall Shop Row a whole block away and was gone.

"Shade!" he called again, slowing to a halt in frustration.

What had the dog been doing out here? If she'd been howling to get inside—back to Wynn—then why run off the instant the gate opened? Why had she left Wynn in the first place?

Rodian fumed over losing the dog so quickly. He wavered, knowing full well that only one person knew the answer, and the Premin Council had barred him from questioning Wynn.

As if they could.

Something was going on here tonight, and he needed to find out what. Until he received a direct order from the royal family regarding Wynn, he was not going to tolerate guild interference in his duties. And besides, it was late. Sykion wouldn't even hear about his "visit" to Wynn until the morning, if at all.

"Lower the portcullis once I'm through," he called, as he pulled the bailey gate closed behind him.

He didn't even pause when he entered the gatehouse tunnel, but as he reached the courtyard, the bell for the first quarter of night rang out. And Lúcan called down from above.

"Sir, wagon coming."

Rodian stopped and sighed, and the nagging knot of tension in his neck tightened.

"Very well," he called back.

These wagons of late arrived the same time every night, yet there was no explanation for them. Even the sages wouldn't need this much of . . . whatever . . . all at once. Again, they were up to something. He could just feel it somehow. Questioning Wynn would have to wait.

Turning, he peered down the gatehouse tunnel. What had Shade been doing out there? He looked about the empty courtyard. Over the years, he'd trusted his sense of the order of things, and all this was definitely lacking a perceivable order. He headed back to the portcullis as he heard its gears and chains begin to grind again.

"Go unbolt the gate," he ordered. "I'll see to the wagon myself."

"Yes, sir," Maolís answered.

"When you're done, cut through the bailey and take the stairs up the wall at the eastern corner. You're to walk the back side, and tell Jonah and Angus to stick to their sides of the keep and the front. The more eyes everywhere, the better."

"Yes, sir." Maolís ducked out under the half-closed portcullis.

"Bring it back up!" Rodian called, and he waited inside the tunnel's mouth, watching for the wagon's approach.

Dänvârfij still perched on the same rooftop with Én'nish. So far, they had seen no sign of their quarry or the two strangers—human or dwarf—who had disappeared through the keep's outer wall. Although those two concerned Dänvârfij, she was focused on watching for Magiere or Léshil or even Chap. She knew better than to think she could watch for Brot'ân'duivé.

Every shadow in the world was a greimasg'äh's ally, defense, and weapon.

The only thing that might betray Brot'ân'duivé was if his new attachment to Léshil and the monster drew him into the open. Even so, could she actually kill a shadow-gripper by chance, let alone by the choice to do so? Sgäilsheilleache had killed her beloved jeóin and mentor, Hkuan'duv, but the act had cost him his life.

Én'nish fidgeted restlessly beside Dänvârfij, not at all as an anmaglâhk should, but Dänvârfij needed someone with her. If any messages had to be passed to the others on watch, this was the only way without someone abandoning his or her post. She was considering sending Én'nish to check in with the others when a loud barking and howling erupted outside the bailey gate.

"The black majay-hì!" Én'nish breathed.

Dänvârfij's hand tightened on her bow. She had let herself slip into distracted thoughts and not even noticed the dark form approaching. She watched in puzzlement as a guard with a close-trimmed beard hurried out to let the majay-hì inside, but it ran away from him. It was the same majay-hì that Dänvârfij had seen earlier in the company of the pale man and the dwarf.

Had they left the animal behind for this reason? Almost as soon as the majay-hì vanished down a city side street, the sound of rolling wagon wheels carried from down the loop around the castle. Dänvârfij leaned a little over the roof's edge.

Another mysterious wagon, like those from the nights before, pulled up to the bailey gate opened by another guard.

Dänvârfij settled back, watching. What was happening inside the guild this night?

As the wagon rolled through the bailey gate, Rodian nodded to the driver and turned to head up the gatehouse tunnel. Overseeing the wagon's unloading was an unwanted intrusion, but it had to be dealt with before he could rouse Wynn for a talk. Once he'd cleared the tunnel, he turned and waved the driver toward the courtyard's northeast side. Then he blinked and wrinkled his brow.

As the wagon emerged into the courtyard, two cloaked people sat on its bench. He was certain there had been only one when it arrived. The second figure was smaller and slighter than the driver.

Rodian shook his head. The second had likely been in the wagon's back, perhaps steadying the cargo. From the way the tarp bulged too much on one side, the wagon looked improperly loaded. As it pulled past him to stop before the northeast building, he could see where the tarp's back corner lashing had broken off under the strain.

He cared only that the process moved swiftly. The sooner it was finished, the sooner he could find out why Shade was running loose in the city.

As the wagon stopped under the second-floor bay doors, he headed for the storage building's central door to inform Hawes of its arrival. He didn't even reach the door.

Four sages in midnight blue came out and hurried toward the wagon. The bay doors above opened as a fifth swung out a winch arm and lowered a hook and line.

He couldn't fault their efficiency, though it was unnerving how they always seemed to know exactly when a wagon arrived. And not once was there any sign of a sage on watch for a wagon.

Rodian stepped back, observing as the cargo was unloaded. These dark-robed sages couldn't work fast enough for his limited patience tonight.

Timing was critical, as Leesil stood flattened in the corner where the bailey wall met the central, rear barbican. He listened to the receding footfalls of the northern guard walking away along the wall's top. When he no longer heard those steps, Brot'an turned before Leesil could.

"I will go first," Brot'an whispered, pulling out his hooked bone knife and holding out his other hand for Leesil's identical blade.

Leesil wavered and shook his head. "No, I'll go first. Chap gave me a better lay of the grounds."

This was a lie. Leesil—and Chap—had barely seen the keep's inside. Neither of them knew what waited within the large, three-story construction at the back. He badly needed to get Wynn out, but the last thing he wanted was Brot'an ahead of him, in case they ran into trouble.

Brot'an raised one eyebrow but didn't argue. He held out his bone knife and Leesil took it. Brot'an turned to face the corner between the wall and barbican and braced his arms.

"Up my back," he whispered.

Leesil placed both blades between his teeth, their handles out to either side of his mouth, and climbed up Brot'an's back. When he stood on Brot'an's shoulders, nearly seven feet up the wall, he took the blades in hand. Reaching as high as he could, he quietly wedged one blade tip into a seam between the stones. He tested the first blade's set with half his weight. When it held, he pulled himself up another arm's reach and set the second blade.

He repeated this over and over, trying to quell triggered memories of youth. There had been more than a handful of nights when he'd entered some lodge, keep, or stronghold in a similar fashion, seeking out whomever he'd been sent to kill.

Leesil shut off his thoughts, focusing on the slowly nearing top of the wall and barbican. When he reached up the last time, he set the first blade atop a crenellation between two of the barbican's merlons. He gripped the edge with his hand and pulled himself up, grabbing the discarded blade as he rolled into the barbican. Then he rose just enough to peer along the wall's top.

The northern guard was gone from sight, which was both good and bad. It had taken Leesil longer than he'd hoped to scale the wall. He leaned out between the merlons and dropped both bone knives. Brot'an silently caught them and began to climb.

Leesil crouched, peering southward. The southern guard hadn't come into sight yet. To add to his annoyance, in barely half the time it had taken him to make the climb, Brot'an cleared the wall and handed back one bone knife. Leesil quickly sheathed it and refrained from looking anywhere but the wall and the keep. He never glanced about at the quiet night city.

Both he and Brot'an knew they were likely being watched. Neither would do anything to let any anmaglâhk nearby know they were aware of them.

Hopefully, Magiere and the others would be able to draw them off soon, and right now, Leesil was more concerned about the city guards. The one thing they couldn't have was someone sounding an alarm.

He looked north along the wall one more time.

"Let's get to the . . ." he began, but never finished as he turned back.

Beyond Brot'an, something moved at the inner edge of the wall's top near its southern corner. Another guard, a third one, came up the steps out of the inner bailey.

Leesil held his breath and ducked as he jerked Brot'an's sleeve. Soon enough that new guard would come walking along the rear wall. Everything had now gone wrong.

Brot'an peered between the barbican's merlons, trying to find a line of sight. He dropped his right hand down at his side, and a stiletto slipped from his right sleeve as if of its own accord. The hilt settled into the shadow-gripper's palm as the new guard reached the wall's top.

Leesil was lost in panic—but not over the guard's approach. Before he regained his wits, Brot'an rose in a flash and appeared to lash his arm forward before he dropped again.

The stiletto was gone from his hand.

Leesil made a grab for Brot'an's arm, but the shadow-gripper snatched his wrist.

"Look quickly," Brot'an whispered, "or you will miss it."

Leesil barely rose for a peek. Killing had never been part of this. He should've never trusted Brot'an.

A dull thud sounded in the night.

The guard at the wall's corner stiffened upright as his head flinched to one side. For a blink, it looked like he stood there in stillness. As Leesil heard the soft clatter of metal on stone, the man crumpled on the wall's walkway.

Brot'an released Leesil's wrist and rushed down the bailey wall.

Leesil had no choice but to follow—though first he pulled the lashing on his right winged blade. If the guard was still alive, Brot'an was not going to finish the man off. But the old butcher never even paused by the fallen guard.

As Brot'an crouched and reached out to retrieve his fallen stiletto, Leesil slowed to a stop over the prone body.

He studied the still-breathing but unconscious guard with carrot red hair and a smattering of freckles. Then he noticed a darkening spot on the man's temple—from blunt force and not the point of a blade.

Brot'an retreated on all fours before rising with his stiletto in hand.

Leesil shook his head slowly, eyeing Brot'an. It was impossible that anyone could make a blade, let alone its hilt, strike from that far away in the dark.

"Get to the window," Brot'an whispered, "while I hide him."

Without another word, he hefted the guard's limp body and crept down the stairs into the bailey.

Still unnerved, Leesil hurried back to where the rear building met the bailey wall, determined to remain focused on the task at hand. The only thing that mattered was reaching Wynn. But he'd barely climbed up to the first window's sill when a whisper from behind made him stiffen.

"We are off in our timing," Brot'an said. "Get it open. The southern guard is already on his way."

Leesil bit back a retort. The window was of simple design: two opening sides, each with two columns of small panes, and an inner central latch. The latch came first, and if he couldn't get to it, he would have to score the frame and pop out a glass pane. The latter would take longer.

Pulling his new stiletto, he slipped the point between the window's two hinged halves. He pushed the silver-white blade inward below where the latch waited. The frame's wood creaked.

Leesil breathed in through his mouth and out through his nose, letting only one thought pass through his mind.

Focus on the task at hand.

Wynn knew something was happening. For several days, she'd seen no one but Dorian or small glimpses of a varied series of Rodian's guards outside her door. Most nights it had been Lúcan on guard, which gave her some strange comfort. Sometimes she saw sages or guards walking the courtyard, but they didn't really count. It was as if she had been all but forgotten, except for someone bringing her meals and guarding her door.

Wynn was well aware there were those outside the guild's walls who would try to come for her soon. And now, that made everything else even worse. They couldn't be stopped, and if things were different, she wouldn't have wished it so. But she'd been cut off from sending word to Chane and could only hope he still waited at least one more night, because . . .

Certainly, Magiere and Leesil wouldn't be that patient, especially after Chap had located her position. Surprised at how much she hated being out of control of her circumstances, Wynn wished there was some way to warn off Chane or the others.

There had been a time, in her early days with Leesil, Magiere, and Chap, when she'd not hesitated at being pulled headlong into adventure. And she'd sometimes regretted what came of it. She'd been so incapable and naive. Now, when she needed to act by her own choice, she couldn't. For two nights that nervous frustration had been building, until . . .

Wynn heard the distant sound of a dog, and she scrambled over the bed to reach the window.

The barracks windows, older than others in the keep, didn't open, so she pressed her ear against a pane. There was definitely barking and howling somewhere outside, though she couldn't fix the direction. It didn't matter, for there was no mistaking Shade's voice. That meant Chane was likely on the move.

Wynn closed her eyes, wishing fervently that Leesil had come for her first. It wasn't that she didn't miss Chane. He was the one she'd thought most of these past days and nights. But Leesil would know exactly what to do to get her out quietly, while Chane . . .

Well, driven or pushed, Chane was as much of a blunt instrument as Magiere. Wynn feared he might do something rash and get himself caught. But what was Shade trying to do out there?

Wynn longed to see her, to find out what was happening by sharing memories. Then a heavy footfall *inside* her room made her breath catch. She hadn't heard the door open, and she whirled around.

A bulky form kept pushing *through* the wall to the left of her door.

Any thought of needing a weapon, or the absence of her treasured staff, left Wynn's thoughts. The color and texture of stone flowed off the bulky form, until it stood fully within her room. It was the last person she would've ever expected to come for her.

Ore-Locks held up one thick finger across his lips in warning.

Wynn finally breathed again.

Dressed again like a shirvêsh from the temple of Feather-Tongue, he leaned his iron staff against the wall by the door. Without a word, he pulled the door open, and Wynn's panic nearly went through the roof. She rushed in behind him, expecting the guard outside to immediately step into the doorway.

Ore-Locks leaned out, looking left and then right, and the guard never appeared.

Wynn leaned around him. To her further shock, the guard sat slumped beside the door, apparently unconscious. Before she could ask, Ore-Locks grabbed hold of the guard's red tabard with one hand and half dragged, half carried the man inside, dropping him on the floor of her room.

"He never saw me," Ore-Locks said quietly. "Remember, I cannot be seen. No one must know I was here or why. It would damage the bond between the guild and the Stonewalkers."

For all Wynn's skill with languages, his claim might as well have been gibberish amid her shock. She couldn't get over the fact that he was truly standing there before her.

"How did you . . . ? Where did you . . . ?" she began babbling.

"We need to hurry," he urged. "Chane has gone for the rear library to make certain the way is clear. He will get you out a window and down the wall."

Suddenly, everything made sense. Chane had sent for Ore-Locks, and Ore-Locks had snuck Chane onto the grounds . . . right through its walls.

She couldn't help being moved, as Ore-Locks was taking a great risk. He was likely in trouble already with Cinder-Shard, head of Dhredze Seatt's Stonewalkers, for having left without a word to follow her in search of Bäalâle Seatt. The Stonewalkers were the ones who now secured the ancient texts Wynn had brought back, moving them to and from hiding as directed by Premin Sykion. If Ore-Locks was caught helping her escape, she couldn't imagine the repercussions. And, worse, guilt choked Wynn for an instant.

She kept a secret from Ore-Locks concerning his ancient heritage.

The ancestor he'd gone searching for in Bäalâle was Thallûhearag, the Lord of Slaughter, the little-remembered but worst of traitors in dwarven history. But Thallûhearag wasn't the villain that few still remembered from a dark legend.

His true name had been Deep-Root, and he had been a stonewalker like his descendant, Ore-Locks.

Deep-Root had sacrificed himself, when his people had gone mad, to stop the Ancient Enemy's forces from gaining a shorter path to what were now the Numan Lands. For the thousands that had died there, he had protected a hundredfold more in the north. All of this Ore-Locks now knew, but he didn't know what Wynn had kept from him.

Deep-Root had had a twin brother.

Wynn looked at Ore-Locks's disguise, that burnt-orange tabard of a shirvêsh of Bedzâ'kenge, and she cringed. Bedzâ'kenge—Feather-Tongue—had been Deep-Root's twin brother. Ore-Locks was the descendant of both.

Feather-Tongue was now among the revered dwarven Eternals, the dwarves' equivalents of patron saints. But Deep-Root was barely remembered, and only as the worst among the Eternals' opposites, the Fallen Ones.

The reasons for keeping all this from Ore-Locks were so complicated that Wynn pushed them from her mind. There wasn't even time to thank him for the risk he took for her.

"Get your staff and anything else you need," Ore-Locks urged. "You may not be coming back for a long while."

She winced, and at the sight of her, Ore-Locks looked about at the near-empty room.

"They took it," she said bleakly. "They took almost everything."

There was no time for more regrets. She wouldn't let the efforts of Chane, Shade, and Ore-Locks go to waste. After ripping a blanket off the bed, she hurried to her chest.

She bundled up what remained of her belongings: her old elven clothing, shorter travel robe, and a few other items. Then she went to the desk and grabbed the few remaining pieces of blank paper, some writing charcoal, her elven quill with the white metal tip, and a bottle of ink. When she turned about, Ore-Locks held her cloak, and he pulled it over her shoulders.

"This is all I have left," she said.

He nodded and hefted his iron staff. Pausing briefly at the door, and making certain the way was clear, he motioned Wynn to follow. They crept down the passage to the stairs, hurrying in silence to the door out to the courtyard. Ore-Locks held up a hand for Wynn to wait and then cracked the door open, peeking out.

"Is it clear?" she whispered.

He didn't answer, but rather leaned his head out, looking to the right toward the keep's main doors. It took too long, and Wynn leaned in on him.

"What are you looking for?" she asked.

"A glove," he answered.

"What does that mean?"

He straightened in some unexplained relief. "It is not there. We can go on."

Wynn was still baffled, and then she heard voices outside.

Ore-Locks peered out the open door's narrow space and froze. Wynn thought he was looking toward the courtyard's northern corner. Before she could lean in again, he backpedaled, nearly knocking her flat as he carefully shut the door.

"What?" she whispered in alarm.

"A wagon," Ore-Locks answered. "Sages are unloading it, and Captain Rodian of the Shyldfälches is out there with them."

Wynn wasn't certain how Ore-Locks knew of Rodian. The Stonewalkers were connected to the guild, the sages were connected to the royals, and the royals were connected to the Shyldfälches. Anything more just spun in her head amid the tension.

"Is he looking the other way?" she asked.

Perhaps they could slip out and hurry into the keep. They were hardly safe just standing here behind a door in an open passage.

"Let me look," she whispered, and stepped around Ore-Locks to crack open the door.

What she saw filled her with dismay.

Four metaologers unloaded cargo while a fifth was in the storage building's upper bay, working lines to haul up the loads. A driver and a smaller companion waited on the wagon's bench, and Captain Rodian stood beyond the courtyard's center watching all this with his arms tightly crossed.

Wynn quietly shut the door and slumped against it; she and Ore-Locks were not going anywhere.

CHAPTER 15

Chane had reached the keep's main doors without trouble. Once inside the entryway, he checked all ways before turning right and heading down the long passage along the front of the building.

When he reached the first side passage, he peeked around the corner. This way led between small divided chambers for classrooms, seminars, and the hospice, ending at the library's southeast door. With no one in sight, he took the turn and moved deeper into the main building's rear. When he reached the heavy oak door, he nearly sighed in relief.

This had all been much easier than anticipated.

When he pressed lightly on the door's handle, it did not move. He applied more pressure, but with no better result. The door was locked.

Confused, Chane pressed harder, using his weight to try to force it, but it held fast. He looked over the whole door in disbelief. In all his time among the sages, he had never heard of the new library being locked. Perhaps this was an error? Worse, since the door opened outward, there was no way he could force it. He could try to shatter its heavy planks, but doing so would take time and make too much noise.

What else could he try?

There were two other doors into the library: one at its center and one on its northwest end. One or both might be open. Still, he hesitated, wondering how close Ore-Locks and Wynn were to leaving the barracks. By the main building's layout, he would have to go all the way to the front in order to make his way to the central passage leading to the library's main doors. He would be right in sight of anyone coming in the keep's main doors.

But if he hurried and got into the library, and checked for a clear path to the window, he could unlock or force this door from the inside. Wynn and Ore-Locks could still enter as planned.

That seemed the only way.

Hurrying with care, Chane made his way back but paused short of the entryway with its overhanging cold lamp mounted above the main doors. Peering in all directions, he neither heard nor saw anyone. And then he turned right, slipping down the central passage.

There ahead of him was another high-mounted cold lamp, its crystal glimmering dimly above the library's central double doors.

When the window's latch slipped up on the tip of Leesil's blade, he pushed it open and crawled through into a narrow path. He landed on the floor beside a wall of bookcases facing the window.

Brot'an immediately climbed up and followed him in.

"A library," Brot'an whispered, looking over the shelves and then up.

Leesil gazed along the wall of books and bound sheaves and saw that the casements didn't reach the ceiling. He froze when he looked to their tops. He saw what had pulled Brot'an's attention.

Light from somewhere beyond the shelves shone upon the ceiling beams. Though it was very late, someone else was in here.

Leesil had hoped to find himself in an upper storage area or even an empty room. He hadn't thought of a library on the third floor of a building. He'd never imagined they would enter a place frequented by someone too obsessed with scholarly notions to just go to bed . . . like a normal person.

Then again, he should've anticipated this. The whole small castle was filled with sages. How many times on the road had he and Magiere gone to sleep while Wynn sat up by a campfire, scribbling in one of her journals? Here he was, creeping in on some unsuspecting sage like a thief in the night, and, worse, with an oversized assassin behind him.

Leesil took a long breath and motioned to Brot'an as he crept along the shelves toward the left end wall.

Chap and Leanâlhâm had explained exactly where they'd seen Wynn, and once Leesil reached the center courtyard, he'd know where to go. But first he had to search for a way through to that courtyard, and he only knew the general direction in which it lay.

Exactly what was he supposed to do, amid trying to find the stairs out of here, if he ran into some old bookworm hunched over an even older tome?

Leesil reached the end of the casements, where a path led along the library's southward wall. He peeked around the end, and halfway along the sidewall he spotted a set of downward stairs beyond more rows of shelves. A pot-metal lamp was mounted right above the stairwell.

A sage's cold-lamp crystal glowed softly within the lamp's glass.

Leesil couldn't help but curse under his breath as his anxiety broke. Some addle-brained sage had simply left a light on. With a sigh, he waved Brot'an onward and led the way, checking each row of shelves or open spaces as he headed for the stairs.

Rodian waited impatiently as the last of the wagon's cargo was unloaded. He wondered again why these supplies arrived in the night. Food stores might be delivered so late if the sages were preparing some special meal for the next day. The notion struck him as eccentric, but it *was* a possible explanation, if not for the contents of this wagon.

Lashed-up piles of canvas, clinking casks of metal, and coils of rope would make no decent meal. None of this had anything to do with stocking a populated keep no longer used for military purposes. Except for a few closed crates, most of it looked like gear for a large expedition afield—without any perceivable armaments.

How was all this being paid for, and to what purpose?

Rodian knew nothing of the sages' finances, but they had to be operating on limited accounts. Yes, they had their services among the people, running public schools in some districts and working with local trade and craft guilds. Most of that was likely financed by stipends from the kingdom's treasury. What little profit they were allowed to take in wouldn't be enough to cover all that he'd seen in a few nights. And how long had these wagons been coming in before that?

Either the Premin Council had built up funding beyond expectation, or someone outside these walls had a vested interest in whatever the sages were up to. Once again, Rodian saw the hand of Malourné's royal family at work when no one was watching. But to what purpose?

Once unloading was finished, the four metaologers disappeared inside as the fifth pulled the upper bay doors closed. The driver, who, like his companion, had not stepped off, turned the wagon, clucked to his horses, and headed back toward the gatehouse tunnel.

The driver was certainly tall, even sitting down. Rodian hadn't noticed how tall until now. Something about the short one on the bench—something familiar—bothered him, but he couldn't quite place it. He took a step as the wagon entered the tunnel.

Intuition told him to get a better look at these two silent wagon handlers. Then he glanced toward the dormitory barracks. It was even later now, and he still wanted a word with Wynn while all the other sages remained out of the way. That task was more pressing.

Turning, Rodian headed straight for the barracks door.

Peeking through the cracked barracks door, Wynn sucked a breath that actually squeaked in her throat, and she pulled the door shut.

"What?" Ore-Locks whispered in alarm. "What did you—"

Wynn clamped her hand over his mouth.

"Rodian!" she whispered. "He's coming straight toward us!"

Ore-Locks's eyes widened until the whites showed all around his black-pellet irises. He grabbed Wynn's hand, turned about, and then faltered. He appeared caught in indecision, looking at the stairs leading back up and the dark passage beside them.

"Not the stairs," Wynn whispered. "We'll get trapped up there."

The passage led through the keep wall to the initiates' barracks built long ago in the bailey. Ore-Locks immediately took off that way. They'd nearly reached the dim light of a cold lamp at the far end when Wynn's panic cleared in a realization.

If Rodian went to her room and found her gone, with the guard unconscious, things would quickly get much worse. He'd sound the alarm, and Chane would be in even more danger. But if she got to her room and blocked the captain from entering so late at night, she could play dumb about the missing guard. While Rodian left to find that irresponsible guard, she could try to get out again.

Wynn pulled back hard, but Ore-Locks dragged her along like a stubborn puppy.

"Ore-Locks, stop!"

He wouldn't, so she had to smack him across the back. He turned on her with a glower.

She whispered harshly, "I need to get back to—"

The latch on the courtyard door clicked, echoing down the passage. They both froze in the dark as the door began to crack open.

Wynn shoved Ore-Locks, though it didn't budge him a bit. Backing up, she flattened against the passage's wall and frantically waved him off, pointing at the other wall. He appeared to understand, though he hesitated, looking at her and then the door.

Hinges creaked as the door began to swing inward.

Ore-Locks grimaced as he turned and fled through—into—the passage wall's stone.

Wynn had no idea how to explain being found outside her room, but the repercussions would be worse if Ore-Locks was found with her. She crouched, out of the line of sight, and lay down to roll in against the passage wall's base.

It was a desperate, silly notion for hiding.

Rodian had begun pushing open the barracks door when a loud bang startled him. He turned, his hand reflexively dropping to his sword hilt. What he saw left him in more than mild surprise.

Premin Hawes burst from the center door of the northwest building, where only moments before the other sages had entered after unloading the wagon. She bolted for the keep's main doors, not even glancing Rodian's way.

For a moment, he was so stunned that he didn't move. The premin of metaology crossed the courtyard in full flight, the skirt of her midnight blue robe flapping around her narrow, booted feet. He couldn't remember ever seeing Hawes in such a state, and perhaps no one ever had.

He was just about to follow her when the dark-haired metaologer who'd hauled Wynn off a few nights ago came flying out the same door. The door banged recklessly against the wall and, at the noise, Hawes skidded to a stop, turned, and held out her hand.

"No, Dorian!" she commanded. "Go back and watch every area that we have covered."

Dorian gave a quick nod and went running back to wherever he'd come from. Hawes took two backward steps and then turned to race to the keep's main doors and disappeared inside.

Rodian was at a complete loss as to what all of this meant. What could Dorian possibly be watching from inside the northwest building? And what had Hawes meant by "covered"? He wanted to question Wynn, but something more immediate was happening.

Rodian took off at a jog after Hawes.

*　　*　　*

Dänvârfij crouched low on the rooftop as the wagon rolled out through the bailey gate. Én'nish was crouched beside her, and they both drew in a sharp breath at the same time.

Beside the tall driver on the bench sat a smaller, slender form in a full cloak, pants, and jerkin. Perhaps it was the driver's son or apprentice. But there had been only the driver onboard when the wagon had first entered the bailey gate and tunnel.

Dänvârfij tensed in indecision. First the pale human and dwarf had melted through the outer wall. Then the black majay-hì had raised a wild commotion at the gate, drawing out the guards before it had run off. Now a small, cloaked figure came out who had not gone in.

"Is it the sage in disguise?" Én'nish whispered.

Dänvârfij closed her eyes. Everything that had happened in this city since Magiere's return seemed to surround Wynn Hygeorht. There was no certainty here, but there was no letting the possibility slip through her hands. If it was the sage on the wagon, somehow she had slipped out of the castle with no help from Magiere or Léshil.

"Who is driving?" Én'nish asked.

Dänvârfij squinted but could not make out the driver's face, though he was quite tall. Too tall to be Léshil, yet not broad-shouldered enough for Brot'ân'duivé. She looked straight into Én'nish's too-eager eyes.

"Get Rhysís and go after them. Secure the sage at any cost."

Chane hurried toward the library's center doors caught in a pool of light from a cold lamp mounted to one side. Each of the frame stones at the arch's top held an engraved Begaine symbol for the guild's creed. He knew what they meant without struggling to read them.

Truth through Knowledge . . . Knowledge through Understanding . . . Understanding through Truth . . . Wisdom's Eternal Cycle.

It was a bitter notion after all that the Premin Council had put Wynn through.

He grabbed the right door's handle, twisted it, and found it locked. Gripping the handle harder, he threw his weight against it, knowing the effort wouldn't matter. For the first time since beginning this undertaking, real anxiety flooded through him.

It was not enough that they had locked Wynn away. Was the council now locking up any and all knowledge? How could he get Wynn out if he could not quickly and safely breach the library to clear her a path? He wondered if he should rush to the main doors and toss a glove out into the courtyard. Ore-Locks might yet get Wynn out another way.

Chane steeled himself. There was still one more library door to try, and he had to reach it quickly. But as he turned, one of the keep's main double doors swung open.

He backed up, not even looking to see who it was, and snatched the glass off the wall-mounted cold lamp. Pulling the lamp's crystal, he clenched it tightly in his fist to squelch its light and then flattened against the sidewall as he peered up the central passage.

Premin Hawes stepped into the entryway and quickly shut the main doors. She stood there for a moment in the entryway's dim pool of light. She was facing down the central passage.

Chane feared she had already seen him, but he kept still in waiting. Even if she had not, if she came straight on, she would soon enough.

One of the main doors opened again, and Hawes spun toward them, facing away from Chane.

Captain Rodian stepped inside, frowning at the premin.

Rodian was surprised to find Hawes still in the entryway. How strange, considering her panicked rush of a moment before.

"Is something amiss, Premin?" he asked, abandoning any pretense. "I saw you running and was concerned."

If she was equally surprised to see him, her expression didn't betray it.

Hawes was as composed as Rodian had ever seen her, once again the coldly observant premin of metaology.

"I was told someone was wandering about," she returned evenly. "Considering the curfew you set and your order to keep the library locked at night, I did not want some initiate's forgetfulness to cause trouble."

He stared at her, letting silence linger for three breaths. "How did you receive this word?"

"We have our ways of communication here," she answered. "Nothing that would hamper your security. I apologize for not having notified your men before acting on my own."

Rodian didn't move. "Such hurry . . . out of concern for an initiate?"

"All of our charges should be long abed. As you are here, perhaps you would assist me in checking the main building."

What Rodian wanted was to put her in a room until she gave him a real answer. He didn't believe her in the slightest, and had long since grown suspicious of anything said by any member of the Premin Council. She knew someone was in here, but Rodian seriously doubted it was a mischievous initiate up past bedtime.

Locking Hawes up might be a pleasure unto itself, but it would only gain Rodian more trouble from the royals, unless he could prove exceptional reasons.

"Should I call more men?" he asked.

"I think you and I can handle this." The premin turned halfway, glancing northward along the main passage. "Perhaps you could check up there while I head the other way. With the towers and library locked up, whoever is wandering about couldn't have gone far. We will meet back here shortly."

He was about to suggest they switch sides in the search, for Hawes had too quickly stated her preference. But he couldn't think of an adequate justification for the change and so he had to play along. Nodding, he turned northward at a slow pace along the keep front's main passage.

Rodian listened for the sound of Hawes's footsteps heading the other way.

Chane did not move a muscle as he watched the pair in the entryway. He gained no relief when Rodian disappeared from sight, heading north, for Hawes lingered. The premin stood there a moment and then suddenly, sharply, she turned and vanished in the other direction. Chane remained still, though it appeared neither the premin nor the captain had spotted him.

That was something at least, but too little. All of his plans were now ruined.

With those two wandering about the keep, it would not matter if he managed to force his way into the library. He had to stop Wynn and Ore-Locks before they entered this building and ran straight into the premin or the captain. But could he reach the main doors himself without being spotted?

He crept along the central passage's left wall toward the entryway. At a half dozen paces away, he slowed, watching the mouth of the main passage's northward half. Of the two now in the keep, if the captain spotted him first, Chane would have no chance to talk his way out. Then again, though Hawes knew him a little, she might be far more dangerous if she did not believe his excuses.

There was only one course left to Chane.

He pressed forward along the left wall, nearing where the central passage met the main one at the entryway. The main doors were so close, but he feared stepping into view. He lingered, listening, and then glanced the way Rodian had gone. Finally, he began slipping forward to peer around the corner after Hawes.

A hand shot out from Chane's left, in front of his chin. He was so startled he did not see where it came from, until its narrow fingers clenched the front of his cloak and shirt.

The forearm below that slender hand protruded from out of the passage wall's stone.

In shocked instinct, Chane pulled back, but he could not break free. Even before he could grab his sword hilt, the hand dragged him face-first into—through—the passage's left wall. Only one thought remained as he was swallowed into cold, dark stone.

That narrow hand could not have belonged to Ore-Locks.

Wynn tried to come up with some plausible excuse for being out of her room once Rodian spotted her. Maybe it would be better for Chane—and Shade—if she faced down the captain and took all consequences on herself. After all, what could Rodian do without formal charges? What more could the Premin Council do?

They still wanted her under their watchful eye, so they wouldn't make any legal claim against her. That would put her permanently in Rodian's hands and off guild grounds. Of course, there was still an unconscious guardsman in her room. That was something the captain would pin on her, though she doubted he'd believe she'd done it herself. But he'd still arrest her, thinking she might eventually give up who had.

Wynn closed her eyes and bit down on the tip of her tongue. No matter which way she worked it, there was no good outcome. And the moments just kept creeping along.

She opened her eyes, peering toward the door to the courtyard . . . and it was closed again.

Wynn just kept staring at it, waiting. She finally got up, hesitantly creeping back up the passage. When she reached the door, she pressed her ear to it and listened, but she heard nothing at all . . . except a shift on stone behind her.

A hand dropped heavily on her shoulder.

She inhaled in fright and whirled about with a clenched fist. A thick hand clamped over her mouth as another one caught her punch.

"Shush. It is me, you fool," Ore-Locks whispered into her face.

Wynn pulled his hand from her face, her heart still racing.

"Was that really necessary?" she hissed at him.

He rolled his eyes in a glower and pushed her out of the way. Reaching for the door, he cracked it open and peeked out.

"Is he gone?" she whispered, thinking that hardly likely. Once Rodian took after something, he was impossible to shake off.

Ore-Locks shot her an annoyed glance and cocked his head, motioning for her to follow. She was still shaking as she followed him out into the courtyard, but she was both astonished and relieved to find it empty.

It was not the time to question good luck, and she stayed right on Ore-Locks's heels as they inched along the barracks to the courtyard's corner. Chane must be wondering where they were by now, but Wynn was wondering something else.

Where has Rodian gone now?

Rodian walked his half of the front passage, past the common hall's main arch, and rounded the right-hand turn toward the library's north entrance. He passed the common hall's small side arch on his right and the kitchen's entrance across on the left. He peered into both, and both were empty, though he hadn't expected to find anyone there. When he reached the left-hand passage leading to the northern tower, he paused to check the library door at the turn.

It was locked, as it should be. He shook his head, wondering what Hawes was up to with this nonsense errand. Something was clearly happening here. And still, while he was here . . .

He glanced down the way toward the door to the northern tower. The cold lamp above him at the library's north entrance didn't cast enough light that far, so he walked past the kitchen's rear entrance and stopped to check the door across the way into the bailey's rear.

It was locked, as were the tower door and the door next to that for the archives below.

Rodian had had enough of this and exhaled in exasperation as he headed back. It was time to get some answers out of Hawes.

CHAPTER 16

Waiting alone in the alley with Chap, Magiere found that she had too much time to think. Much too much. Of all that she might've wished for tonight, the last was abundant time to think—especially while suffering in ignorance over what was happening with her companions.

She assumed that Osha and Leanâlhâm were on the way back. It depended on how long it had taken to unload that wagon. Leesil and Brot'an must have breached the keep by now. But every time Magiere blinked, she saw flashes of what she'd done in the northern white wastes to find and secure the second orb, to get Leesil and Chap out of that frigid land alive.

To return here and learn there were yet more orbs, that more of the Ancient Enemy's minions were on the move, searching as well, was too much. And the one person besides Chap who might have real answers was locked up beyond reach.

Magiere had such a burning urge to go after Wynn herself, and she glanced down. Chap was watching the street, his ears pricked up. She wondered if he'd caught any of these brief memories of hers. She didn't ask him or warn him to stay out of her head.

In truth, she wasn't worried about Chap. He'd had his own agenda from the beginning of all this and would see it through to the end. Neither was she worried about herself—at least not about her purpose for the future.

Leesil was another matter. There was nothing Magiere wouldn't do to keep him safe, even when he tried to stop her from doing so. All his life, he'd been either a slave assassin to a warlord or a slave to the open road or a slave to fates they couldn't shake, especially hers. All he really wanted now was to go home to their tavern, the Sea Lion, in the little coastal town of Miiska.

That had once been Magiere's strongest desire, next to him.

Over and over, the warm image of hearth and home had wavered like a mirage, just out of reach. Over and over, it had vanished more quickly as each seemingly insurmountable task had fallen on them. In the beginning, it had been *him* who'd kept her going, held *her* up in the face of it all.

How much had changed . . . and now there were two more orbs to find.

Chap suddenly rumbled, just once. Magiere found him watching her with his crystalline blue eyes.

She'd never told him, but she'd come to see him as the strong one among the three of them. Chap would face anything as long as the purpose was clear, and if it wasn't, he would hold everything in place until it was. He'd been the one to take the two orbs into hiding, so that no one but him knew where they were. How he'd accomplished that in the end he'd never said, but she remembered the way he returned to meet up with her and Leesil.

Chap had padded back into their sight as if he carried some internal burden that gave him unbearable shame. He would take whatever fate threw at him and snarl in its face, but upon his return, he'd been silent. He'd ignored any attempt Leesil made to get him to use the talking hide.

Magiere ran her hand down Chap's neck.

He hated being relegated to the "distraction" as much as she did. Like her, he hadn't been able to fault Leesil's plan or come up with anything better.

"Shouldn't be much longer," she said.

Chap's shoulders stiffened under her hand. An instant later, she heard the creak and clatter of wagon wheels on cobble.

Drawing her falchion, she rested it against her thigh as Chap shot across the alley's mouth to lurk at its other side. They were ready, for even when Osha and Leanâlhâm arrived, the "distraction" was far from over.

Én'nish flitted among the street's darkest shadows beside Rhysís as they followed the strange pair driving the wagon away from the castle. She let them get far enough away that not even a quiet disturbance would be heard or seen by the red tabard guards on the castle's bailey walls.

Rhysís pulled the pieces of his short bow out of the back of his tunic and assembled the two arms into their white metal handle. He and Én'nish paused once around a street corner. She waited while he strung the bow and pulled aside the shoulder of his tied-up cloak to reveal his quiver of short arrows. She had always found his skill set to be strange.

He was equally skilled—above sufficient—in everything an anmaglâhk valued: hand-to-hand, weapons, languages, subterfuge, interrogation, and tracking. But he had no skill of excellence. For some reason, this bothered her.

Most anmaglâhk were sufficient in most skills but excelled at one or two. She excelled in hand-to-hand, with blades or not, and her small size had more than once drawn an opponent into overconfidence. Rhysís also spoke less than any anmaglâhk she'd ever known—though he seemed to know Dänvârfij well. As a result, Én'nish didn't care much for him, though he was a sound partner on a hunt like this. At the moment, that was all that mattered.

She glanced back along the way they had come. The small castle was no longer in sight. As she looked down the street to the wagon now a block ahead, she raised one hand and brushed her thumb across her first two fingers.

At the signal, Rhysís notched an arrow, and Én'nish drew her stilettos.

The wagon suddenly turned a corner and passed out of sight.

Én'nish let out a grating breath. But as soon as they regained a line of sight, Rhysís would put down the driver. They could easily take the disguised sage to Fréthfâre, and then Rhysís could go to notify Dänvârfij.

This was not a difficult purpose to fulfill.

Én'nish broke into an open run along the empty street, with Rhysís close behind her. When she neared that corner, she swerved in under the last shop's awning. Then as she crept toward the corner, she made another silent gesture.

Rhysís ran wide in the street, raising his bow to aim down the alley, and Én'nish readied to duck around the corner.

An arrow's quick hiss broke the silence.

In the side of Én'nish's view, Rhysís suddenly twisted away, and he had not fired his bow. A vicious snarl erupted in the alley as she saw an arrow sticking through the fabric of Rhysís's hood. Its black feathers protruded next to his cloth-wrapped jaw.

Rhysís himself was unhurt.

Something glinted on Én'nish's other side, rushing at her head. She ducked and spun out before the alley's mouth.

The nearer pillar of the shop shattered, making the whole awning above begin to buckle. As she looked atop the wagon's bed in the side alley, the driver stood there with a long, curved, elven bow raised and readied.

There was no sign of the disguised sage.

Én'nish barely made out a face in the shadowed hood pulled forward over the driver's head. His amber eyes and dark skin with too-long features and . . .

It was Osha, the failure, and onetime student of Sgäilsheilleache. He must have been the one on the rooftops nights ago, the archer to whom Brot'ân'duivé had called out. Osha swung his aim toward her, another arrow already notched and pulled.

"No!" someone growled in the alley's dark. "Take the other. . . . This one is mine."

Out of the dark alley came the *monster*, stepping around the shattered remains of the shop column.

Magiere's sickening white skin caught the dim light of a street lantern up the way. She raised her heavy, one-edged sword, gripped it with both hands, and charged. The silver majay-hì bolted straight at Rhysís from the alley's other side.

It had all been a decoy, a trap. That was all that Én'nish had time to realize as she heard Osha's bowstring release and saw Magiere's sword coming fast at a downward angle.

Én'nish ducked and spun, hearing the sword pass too close to her head.

Magiere's falchion tip clipped the street's cobble, and she reversed her hands instantly to bring the blade back in a waist-high slash. This anmaglâhk seemed too small to be one of the an'Cróan, but that only confirmed what she guessed.

It had to be Én'nish beneath that hood and face wrap. The same who'd wanted Leesil dead when they'd entered the Elven Territories of the Farlands. The one who'd wrapped a garrote around his throat only a few nights ago.

Magiere was sick of these murderers coming at her—at Leesil—and she didn't resist when hunger boiled from her stomach into her throat.

The night lit up, searing her eyes as her sight fully widened. All she saw was the one who'd tried to kill her husband. Even a notion of capturing one of these assassins, forcing one to tell everything of Most Aged Father's plans, vanished from her thoughts as she swung.

Leesil had told her to just run decoy and get away. But he wasn't here.

Én'nish dropped and rolled under Magiere's arcing falchion. The vicious little killer rose to her feet without a stall and ran for the tilted awning above the broken column.

Magiere lost all self-control. She let the falchion spin out of her hands, clattering across the cobble, and she lunged after her prey.

Én'nish leaped upward. Her forward foot landed halfway up the awning's remaining support post. She twisted her torso back toward the street.

Even functioning on instinct, Magiere knew what to do. She rushed in before Én'nish planted her other foot and seized the woman's trailing calf before she could push off into the air. She pulled Én'nish off balance and heaved the small woman overhead toward the open street.

Én'nish shrieked and tumbled through the air as Magiere charged after her.

The small, forest gray form fell and tumbled across the cobble to slam against a wall at the street's far side. Magiere didn't slow to snatch up her falchion as her target clawed up to her feet.

Magiere didn't even *think* of a weapon. All she *felt* was a need to end anything that tried to harm her mate. All that remained was hunger and the drive to tear her prey apart with her hands . . . with her teeth.

Chap rushed the male anmaglâhk as he tried again to fire an arrow. An instant before he leaped, the bowstring released. He heard the arrow hiss away behind him as his forepaws caught his target square in the chest.

There was no time to look back and see if Osha had been hit.

Chap did not even have an instant for surprise that the anmaglâhk had not tried to evade him. They both slammed down on the cobble in a tangle.

He snapped and snarled, trying first for the man's face. The anmaglâhk took a swipe with his bow. Its thick center struck Chap's muzzle, and the pain briefly stunned him. Then he felt the elf's free hand push at his face. He snapped blindly at it, hoping to maim that bowstring hand. Instead, his teeth closed on a forearm, and he thrashed his head, tearing at it. Beneath the anmaglâhk's sudden outcry, Chap heard Osha's shout.

"Chap, move!"

But he did not—not until the anmaglâhk brought a knee up into his side.

Chap gasped and tumbled away as forest gray fabric shredded in his teeth. Somewhere nearby came a shriek that smothered the clatter of metal across cobblestones. When he rolled to his feet, trying to catch his breath, the anmaglâhk was already standing again.

The man's sleeve behind his draw hand was shredded and blood-soaked. Still, he held the bow steady, aimed in Osha's direction. He began to sidestep, his eyes shifting right just once, likely looking for his companion.

Chap took a quick step at that opening and then faltered.

Magiere's falchion lay in the middle of the street, and he raised his eyes and spotted her. He panicked at the sight of her twisted features. A raised memory of hearth and home would not reach through to her now, and Leesil was not here. There was only one other thing that might make Magiere respond.

Chap had to end this fouled exploit.

Still dazed, Én'nish tried to twist away as a blurry hand came for her throat. She barely whipped her head aside, for her opponent was now too fast and so impossibly strong.

The hand latched onto her shoulder and crushed its grip closed. Én'nish cried out in pain that made her sight darken, and she lashed out with a foot.

It connected with the inside of a knee. Her assailant instantly began to topple, but the grip held. It did not break until Én'nish's back hit the street. Those fingers bruised her shoulder muscles before she rolled away.

She rose, shaking her head to clear her senses amid pain. Then fear overrode anguish, anger, and hate. She looked into the face of a monster not three paces before her.

The white face beneath stray tendrils of black hair was covered in a sheen like a quick sweat. Tears rolled from narrowed eyes that were completely black, with no whites. Features twisted in rage and madness. An open mouth exposed the teeth, the fangs, of some animal.

This was the true face of the monster called Magiere.

Rhysís came into Én'nish's peripheral view, backing up the street's far side. "Break off!" he shouted in their own tongue. "Now!"

All the anger came back to Én'nish, but horror overwhelmed it again when the monster took a lunging step.

Magiere stalled at an eerie wail that pierced Én'nish's ears.

It was like the mewl of a large cat, but so loud in warning, as if rising from the throat of a dog. As that sound seemed to vibrate through Én'nish's bones, she shivered, and Magiere turned in its direction.

Én'nish spotted Chap lowering his head, and her spite resurfaced again. She held out a stiletto, pointing it at Magiere as she shouted in Elvish, and Rhysís instantly leveled his aim on the majay-hì.

*   *   *

"Think of your misbegotten mate and the love he took from me! I will suffer that for a lifetime . . . but I will see you suffer the same an instant before you die."

Chap caught every word of the smaller anmaglâhk's shout in Elvish, even as his wail to Magiere had left his throat raw. There was no mistaking Én'nish's voice.

Magiere twisted back at the woman's vicious voice, but she could not have understood those words. The anmaglâhk archer swung his aim toward Chap.

Before Chap could move, Osha lunged out in front of him.

"You shoot, you die!" Osha shouted, and then his voice dropped to a menacing whisper. "Even if I die . . . you die!"

Chap did not know why Én'nish had spoken in her own language. Perhaps the young woman had intended only Osha to understand and be rattled. It had not worked. Osha stood poised and steady, just the same, with an arrow fully drawn back, its black feathers almost to his dark tan cheek.

"We leave—now!" the other anmaglâhk barked in Elvish, but Én'nish hesitated and then took a step back.

Magiere started to lunge, and Chap went at her with a vicious snarl and snap. This had to end now. Neither side would win, even if half of them ended up dead.

Magiere wheeled on him, and as he looked into her fully black eyes, Én'nish's words still stuck in his head.

Think of your misbegotten mate and the love he took from me! I will suffer that for a lifetime . . . but I will see you suffer the same an instant before you die.

He kept rumbling as he closed on Magiere.

Én'nish's threat was real, though it mattered little. There was never a doubt that these assassins wanted Leesil dead almost as much as Magiere. One of them had a personal vendetta, and that was both doubly dangerous and potentially useful for the future.

Magiere stared at him, half panting from exertion or fury, but she did not move.

"Chap?" she whispered.

He almost collapsed in relief when she recognized him, but he quickly reached for her memories. Of all those he had glimpsed before in her, he had to find and raise those of Leesil amid her awareness filled with older, hate-laced recollections of Én'nish and other anmaglâhk. He flooded her with memories that might soothe her. But he was also aware of Osha, just to his left, stepping into sight.

Én'nish and her accomplice were gone.

"All right?" Osha whispered.

Focused only on Magiere, Chap was uncertain to whom the young elf spoke. When Osha tried to step around toward Magiere, Chap sidestepped and cut him off.

Magiere stumbled back against the street's far wall. Perhaps she was now aware enough to stay back.

Chap kept his focus on her memories. Her head sagged until her face was curtained by black hair, but her fingers twitched, clutching at the wall stones like claws.

Magiere sank into those memories of hearth and home. There was the moment of her wedding, of holding Leesil's arm as they walked down the aisle, with Osha and Wynn walking together behind them. The whole place was filled with their neighbors and friends in Miiska.

She didn't fight these memories and let Chap wash away everything else in her thoughts. But Wynn still waited, here and now, and Leesil was out there trying to get to her.

"Enough," she whispered, though it slurred between her teeth. "That's enough, Chap."

When she raised her head, the whole world was dark and dim again before her eyes. There was only Chap watching her, and Osha behind him, with his bow at his side and an arrow still notched to its string.

Magiere remembered so little of what had happened only moments before.

"We go now?" Osha asked insistently, though a slight frown wrinkled his high brow. "Go where Brot'ân'duivé say. . . . Follow plan."

Chap huffed once.

Magiere stared at Chap as Osha's words sank in. They were simply supposed to act as a decoy, draw off any lurking anmaglâhk watching the guild castle, and seed a little chaos among them.

They'd done their part. She took a deep breath and heaved herself off the wall.

With a last worried glance at her, Osha turned away. Chap lingered until Magiere actually followed and then fell in beside her. As they neared the alley's mouth, Magiere looked at the wagon, trying to peer beneath, but no one was there.

"Leanâlhâm?" she called.

Something moved at a near corner of the alley's mouth. Leanâlhâm stood looking out, wide-eyed, from the shadows.

Magiere faltered in the middle of the alley's mouth. The girl was supposed to have stayed hidden until they came for her. Had she been there all along and seen everything?

Osha passed Leanâlhâm and stopped short of the narrow space between the wagon and the alley wall. Leanâlhâm still looked at Magiere without blinking, stuck where she was at the alley's corner.

"Are you . . . all right?" the girl whispered.

"It's time to go," Magiere said, and reached out.

Leanâlhâm flinched and pulled back, and then so did Magiere.

Osha carefully put his hand on the girl's shoulder, turning her to follow him, but Leanâlhâm glanced back over her shoulder. It was too hard for Magiere to see her face in the dark of the alley.

No doubt the girl kept looking back at her as Osha led her away. Magiere stood there, unable to follow.

Once, as an invader in Leanâlhâm's homeland, Magiere had been asked, or rather intimidated into, something by Sgäile. Looking back now, it seemed like some forewarning of what had come later: Sgäile's own death. She'd agreed to watch over Leanâlhâm if she could. And she would protect that girl of mixed blood, now caught between worlds like the rest of them.

But how could Magiere protect Leanâlhâm from herself?

Chap huffed and nudged her leg, and Magiere finally followed him down the alley, where they left the wagon behind. It was no longer needed.

As Leesil crept through the strange library with Brot'an, he never wanted to see another library ever again. Most especially not one made by the sages.

Every time they cleared another row of shelves, casements, or little cleared spaces with tables and stools, he spotted a light ahead on the ceiling rafters. And every time he had to slow and peek about, only to find no one was there.

The absurdity of his task struck him anew. Yes, this had all been his idea, but that wasn't the point. Of all the things he'd expected to do in Calm Seatt, breaking Wynn out of her own guild wasn't one of them.

And who in seven hells left this many lights on all night?

He and Brot'an had even stopped to puzzle over one. Leesil was familiar with Wynn's crystal, but hers was powered by body heat, friction. What kept these others glowing in their wall mounts? He glanced about nervously. Did someone come at regular intervals to warm the crystals? If so, he needed to move faster.

"There," Brot'an whispered, pointing.

Leesil spotted the next staircase leading down. He quickly headed for it, and they descended—finally—to the last floor of this bookworm's labyrinth.

They neither saw nor heard anyone. Their only company was an overwhelming number of books, parchments, sheaves, tables, and chairs—and wall-mounted cold lamps spaced far enough apart to leave spaces of shadow among the casements.

Leesil glanced back at Brot'an, and the old butcher almost appeared to scowl. When they reached the inner wall of the first floor, Leesil hurried southeast, looking for a door. They found one—right below yet another cold lamp.

"Easy enough," Leesil whispered.

Brot'an didn't respond, and Leesil carefully gripped the door handle. He twisted slowly, and it didn't budge. He pressed harder, and then again with more of his weight . . . to no effect.

There was a reason why they'd found no sages about. The place was locked.

Dropping to his knees, he took a closer look. The door was heavy, but the light from the lamp above exposed a simple lock plate. The only problem would be light spilling out the door once it was opened and thereby drawing attention.

He glanced up, about to tell Brot'an to remove the crystal once the door had been unlocked, and then noticed a glint above the lamp. Something was higher up, near the ceiling, and it didn't look exactly like another crystal.

It was set in a pewter oval like a bulky pendant, though he couldn't make out how it clung to the wall. It wasn't cut in facets; this "crystal" was almost round or domed, with perhaps half of it sunk into the pewter. He couldn't be certain, but it appeared the pewter frame was etched with a pattern or maybe tiny markings.

Leesil turned back to the task at hand.

"Take the lamp's crystal out," he told Brot'an. "Once I have the door unlocked, tuck it away so it doesn't betray us. We might need it later."

He had no reluctance at stealing from the guild, not after they'd locked up Wynn.

Brot'an shook his head. "Let me unlock the door."

"I've got it."

Reaching behind, Leesil pulled out his shirt's tail and removed a long, slender box from inside the back of his shirt. He set it on the stone floor before opening it.

There was empty space within that had once held his own lost bone knife and two white metal stilettos. He folded back a panel on the lid's inside and revealed an array of slim tools of dark metal. Most were about the size of a noblewoman's hatpin. Choosing two, he studied the lock as Brot'an crouched, glowing crystal already in hand.

"Where did you get that box?" Brot'an asked.

Leesil had no intention of sharing his youth with Brot'an or explaining that the box had been a gift from his mother the day he turned seventeen. That was a birthday he would much rather forget. Without answering, Leesil went to work on the lock.

Chane fought to stifle panic when he realized he could not move.

The hand that had clutched his shirt and cloak and pulled him into the wall let go as soon as he felt air again on his face. But more than half of his body remained trapped in stone.

He could not turn his head; the back of his skull was held fast. With only his eyes, he looked wildly about, but the room was too dark even for him to see much.

It appeared to be a gathering place, a small room of arranged benches facing toward the small chamber's left side. In the right far corner was a closed door, and from what he remembered, it must lead out into the main passage along the keep's front. But that was all he could see without being able to turn his head.

Except for a figure standing ahead of him in the dark little seminar room, and it certainly was not Ore-Locks.

Its robe was so dark it appeared almost black, though Chane knew it was midnight blue. The garment covered a slight form that reached up with one narrow hand to pull back a matching cowl. The other hand came out of a pocket, bearing the harsh light of a cold-lamp crystal.

Premin Frideswida Hawes appeared before Chane.

Every time he grew warier of her skills, she became even more dangerous than he had imagined. She watched him silently from well beyond arm's length, her bristling gray hair and hazel eyes glittering in the crystal's light. It did not take Chane long to realize what had happened.

She had not gone south down the main passage. Instead, she had slipped into this room and waited for him to draw near in heading toward the entrance. Somehow she had sensed him enough to seize and pull him through—no, into—the wall. The only things he could move now were his face, his eyes, and most of his left hand.

Chane could not remember ever being this helpless.

Panic and then rage began to awaken the sleeping beast within him—and it rose in a frenzy, wanting to break free. As his senses sharpened further, he knew his eyes would lose all color; his teeth would begin to shift, exposing fangs; and in the beast's panic, he could not stop himself from trying to pull free.

All of his hunger feeding him strength did no good.

Still, Hawes studied him like some creature easily captured for her chill curiosity. Though her jaw was clenched tight, her expression remained otherwise unreadable.

Chane fought to stop the change but could not, and surely she saw all of it. He was helpless against himself and helpless against her. And he hated both conditions, but he remained silent.

Shouting would only make things worse, endangering Wynn and Ore-Locks, should they hear him and come running. Even if he were about to be finished off, here and now, he would do nothing to betray Wynn.

Hawes raised one hand, and her fingers twitched once, as if making a quick gesture.

"What are you?" she demanded.

Perhaps it was the sound of her voice in this silent room that caught Chane off guard. Was this a chance to distract her, to keep her here for a while? In that at least, he might keep one obstacle out of Wynn's way. He bit down, trying to force the beast within back into its cell.

With a sense of hysteria, he wondered if telling her the truth would stun—rivet—her all the more.

To his shame, he was afraid. If he gave an answer she did not care for, she might easily shove him back inside the wall, not knowing how to finish him. She could leave him there, forever unseen, forever undead in a tomb no one would find, let alone try to open.

"I told you once," he rasped, trying to keep calm. "I am the one who keeps Wynn safe."

"That is what you choose to be . . . not what you are."

"Does it matter?"

Hawes went silent for a while. "Did Wynn truly find Bäalâle Seatt?"

The sudden shock of her question numbed the last of Chane's cunning. How had the premin even known what he and Wynn were up to the last time they had left this place? He had never been a skilled judge of people—only because he didn't care about anyone besides himself and Wynn, for the most part. Something in Hawes's tone and her stillness—and now that question—left him wondering.

Had he had misinterpreted what was happening here? Did Hawes genuinely want answers and see this as the only way to get them?

"Yes," Chane answered.

He saw her reaction, though it was only the barest, briefest widening of her hazel eyes. Hawes wanted the truth for the sake of it, so unlike her counterparts on the Premin Council. If he was going save Wynn—if not himself—his only chance was to answer her.

"What were you seeking there?" Hawes asked.

"A device . . . an orb of stone . . . used by the Ancient Enemy. Wynn believes there are more, and she is determined to find them before minions of the Enemy do so first." At this, Chane couldn't stop, but bitterness leaked into his maimed voice. "She has done so on her own, as no one *here* sees fit to help her!"

Hawes blinked, but her eyes remained fixed on him. The motion was too much like that of an owl at rest, eyeing a mouse. But it had been a reaction, perhaps a startling one for this premin.

"Not entirely true," she replied. "What purpose do these . . . orbs . . . serve?"

Hawes, like all on the council, must have read Wynn's journal accounts of what had happened in the six-towered castle in the Pock Peaks. She knew at least of the first orb's discovery. Did she also know of the one Chane had found in Bäalâle Seatt, the one Wynn had handed over to Ore-Locks?

"I do not know," he answered. "The few who might are desperate to claim them, so I assume they have great power."

"The few?" she repeated sharply.

Almost instantly, without the sound of a step, she closed on him . . . close enough that he could have grabbed her if only he could have gotten free of the wall.

"The one called Most Aged Father among the elves of the Farlands," Chane answered. "Minions of the Enemy . . . perhaps some of the elves of this continent . . . and Domin il'Sänke."

Hawes's eyes narrowed as she hissed, "Ghassan il'Sänke?"

The reaction confirmed one thing: Chane had warned Wynn more than once against trusting that Suman sage. That Hawes was shaken, even openly angered, by the foreign domin's awareness of the orbs did not mean she was any more trustworthy.

What did Hawes want with the orbs?

Chane tried to turn away from the subject.

"Wynn has been forced to fight this out on her own!" he accused, suddenly unable to contain his anger. "Except for Shade and myself! Your council has been the most consistent obstacle in the way of the only one who has tried to do anything worthwhile in this."

Hawes blinked slowly again, watching him. She did not offer any defense of her council.

Chane suspected the premin had already known half the answers to her questions. Was she simply testing him?

"Why did you break in here?" she asked. "To steal her away?"

Chane hesitated, uncertain. Would the truth cause Hawes to rouse the guards to check on Wynn? Hawes looked almost tense as she waited for his answer.

"Yes."

Premin Hawes once again became the cold, calculating observer as she stared at him.

Fear washed through Chane that he had said too much.

CHAPTER 17

Wynn crept along the barracks behind Ore-Locks until they reached the courtyard's eastern corner. Ore-Locks pushed her back as he inched out along the main building's wall. He peered toward the gatehouse tunnel and finally straightened to wave her forward. There was no one else in sight, and Wynn scurried after him to the keep's main double doors.

They slipped inside, finding themselves in the empty entryway where the passage leading to the library's center doors met the main corridor along the inside of the building's front. Wynn cringed a little at the cold lamp above the door, which exposed them too much.

"We are to meet Chane inside the library's southeast door," Ore-Locks whispered.

"This way," Wynn answered, turning right and stepping past him.

Almost immediately, his large hand clenched the back of her cloak. He pulled her one-handed back behind himself, as if she weighed no more than a puppy.

"Stop doing that!" she growled.

"Shush!" he whispered, and then headed onward.

Trying to be quiet, they quickly made their way to where the next left turn led to the library's southeast door. Once around the corner, they nearly ran for that door. Wynn exhaled in relief once they stood before it. This was going much more smoothly than she'd anticipated, and she gripped the door's handle and twisted it.

It turned only a fraction of what it should and clacked softly to a stop.

"No!" she rasped through her teeth.

"Shush!" Ore-Locks warned again.

Wynn grabbed the handle with both hands and tried to twist it again, and still the door wouldn't open. Her frustration turned to anger.

That damn Rodian—this had to be his doing. It wasn't enough to lock her up. He had to lock up the whole keep.

She braced her feet, prepared to heave on the handle with all of her little body. Ore-Locks's hand quickly closed over both of hers, and she glared at him. He only glared back. He was much better at it.

Too much noise, he mouthed.

Wynn stared at the door. Perhaps Ore-Locks could slip through the stone wall to get inside. Then again, he couldn't take her with him, as he wasn't as skilled in that as his brethren. Even Chane had difficulty in walking through stone with Ore-Locks, and Chane was dead.

"Chane could not have opened it, either—or it would be open," Ore-Locks whispered. "We should head back and find another route, as planned."

But he appeared hesitant as he glanced back up the passage.

If Wynn understood right, Chane would've left a glove outside the main doors if he couldn't secure this path. There had been no glove. So where was Chane? She waved to Ore-Locks as she stepped back up the passage. Ore-Locks quickly followed, not letting her get ahead of him.

"There are two other entrances," she whispered. "One to the north and one straight in from the entrance. Perhaps he got in through one of those and hasn't had time to let us know somehow."

Ore-Locks shook his head, his red ponytail switching across his broad shoulders.

"Maybe," he answered. "We will check the center doors first, as they are nearest. Just remember that I cannot be seen by anyone but you."

A part of her wanted to tell him to flee on his own, straight through the walls, now that he'd gotten her out of her room. After all she had put Ore-Locks through in their hunt for Bäalâle, she wasn't about to have him suffer in being arrested with her. But for as far as this plan had gone, she doubted he would willingly leave her.

That he'd come to help her at all, at Chane's request, left Wynn even more guilt ridden over the secret she'd kept from a tortured man who was a keeper of the honored dead of Dhredze Seatt. And stranger still . . .

It appeared Chane had a friend in Ore-Locks. For as little as was known or believed in Wynn's land concerning the undead, Ore-Locks, as a stonewalker, with their way of life, should hold any being like Chane as an enemy.

As they reached the passage's end, Ore-Locks held out his free arm, blocking Wynn's way. He set his iron staff's butt silently on the floor stones and peered a long while around the corner toward the far entryway. Finally, he hefted his staff and nodded to her.

Wynn took a step, and Ore-Locks immediately halted. Before she could ask, he grabbed her arm, hauling her back around the corner as he retreated. She frowned at his sudden panic, for she hadn't seen anyone out in the main passage.

"There's no one there," she whispered.

"Footsteps," he countered.

Wynn heard nothing, but she watched Ore-Locks's eyes wander. He lowered his head, and at first it looked like his eyes half closed, or he was looking at his feet. Wynn did the same, studying his great boots planted firmly on stone, and then she remembered . . .

Stone and earth were everything to the dwarven people. They lived upon and within it, even listened to it, and more so for a stonewalker. Ore-Locks could hear—feel—sound through stone in touching it. He had never been wrong in this in the brief time Wynn had known him.

"The weight of man," Ore-Locks whispered, his eyes still half-closed.

"Wearing boots . . . somewhere north of us . . . inside this building . . . and closing."

Wynn tensed and looked toward the corner and some four feet of the main passage still in view. A man wearing boots hard enough for that faint vibration to carry? Was one of the guards inside, walking sentry? Or was it Rodian, and that's why he'd disappeared from the courtyard?

"He is coming toward the front passage!" Ore-Locks whispered.

Wynn jerked once on his sleeve and ducked out into the main passage before he could catch her. She turned southward, hurrying farther down, away from the entrance and all other ways into the library.

Hawes whirled around, away from Chane, and went still. He followed her intense gaze to the chamber's closed door. With his senses still widened, he made out two sets of hurried footfalls—one light, one heavy—rushing away down the front passage beyond that door.

Hawes stood there too long. Obviously she had heard those faint footsteps, though he was not certain how. His fear of her began to fade as another concern took its place.

"Wynn needs help," he said, breaking the long silence, "more than I can give. The weight of it all is too heavy for her."

Hawes stood there a little longer before her head alone turned, like some gray predatory owl noticing him again. Without a word, she closed the distance between them and grabbed his hand that protruded from the wall.

Chane panicked, fearing that with a mere touch she would entomb him in stone. She was slight, and yet it had been easy for her to jerk him halfway through the wall.

Hawes whispered something so brief and quiet that Chane did not catch it. She pulled lightly upon his hand.

Suddenly, he felt as if he were encased in mud or at least something softer and more pliable than stone. He lunged forward before that sensation vanished, and as soon as he was free of the wall, he sidestepped away from Hawes.

Once again he had lowered himself to ask for her help. As yet she had not said no. Much as he did not wish to damage a potential alliance, he was not letting her touch him again.

She turned her back on him, as if this meant nothing to her, and walked away.

"Remain here until I return," she said.

She cracked the chamber's door enough to peek out, and then widened the opening, leaning out to look the other way along the passage.

"Premin," a low male voice called from outside.

Hawes's head instantly rotated to the right. She pulled the door wider, causing it to creak loudly, and then stepped out and shut it.

Chane was alone, still too lost in confusion to even rush to the door.

Wynn scurried southward along the main passage with Ore-Locks right behind her. Her eyes were on the passage's far right end and the door into the initiates' lecture hall. It was one place no one might look, and at least it had another door in its rear, leading elsewhere. Then she heard those more distant footsteps echoing down the corridor from behind her.

Any moment, some guard or even Rodian himself would step into the main passage's northward end. And she panicked even more.

A loud creak filled the passage, much closer behind than those footsteps.

Wynn's breath caught as she looked frantically about. She heard Ore-Locks stop, and she turned to look behind. With no choice, she grabbed the nearest door handle on the passage's left side.

"In here!" she whispered.

Ducking through the door, she found that Ore-Locks had already appeared inside—straight through the wall—and she realized they were in one of the smaller classrooms. She closed the door as Ore-Locks inhaled, held it, and shook his head.

Wynn slumped against the side wall beside the door, panting from fright. For the moment, they were hidden, but again they'd been cut off from escape. And where in the world was Chane?

Rodian's footfalls echoed down the northern passage. As he reached the turn into the front main corridor along the building, he saw someone lean out of a door just beyond the entryway. The figure was too dark to make out beyond the entryway's dim light, but he knew who it must be.

"Premin," he called.

Hawes turned her head, her cowl now down, and looked straight at him. She stepped out and closed the door, walking up the passage to pause and wait in the entryway.

"Is everything well?" she asked as he reached her.

He looked past her to the door she had closed. "Is something amiss in there?"

"I mislaid one of my notebooks earlier today. I thought to check for it while looking around."

His gaze dropped to her empty hands.

"It must be somewhere else," she added. "I will have to retrace my steps in the morning."

"Did you find your wayward initiate?"

Hawes shook her head slightly, only once, and turned for the main doors, reaching for a handle. "I may have been . . . misinformed."

Rodian wasn't fooled by this maneuver amid their conversation; she was trying to draw him out of here and back into the courtyard. He had a choice to make quickly: either see what she'd been up to or follow her and dig further into what she was hiding. With regret, he chose the latter.

Hawes was already outside, holding open the door. To both their surprise, as Rodian stepped out, Dorian came running toward them across the courtyard.

"Premin!" he began in a rush. "You must . . ."

At the sight of Rodian, Dorian's voice failed.

Of course it did, and Rodian simply stared, daring the young metaologer to finish. These sages would hardly allow their smallest inner workings or secrets to reach his ears or eyes. His anger began rising.

Dorian backed up in silence, still looking at Hawes. Rodian turned on the premin as well, ignoring the reticent young metaologer.

"I assume something else is now amiss," he said, not bothering to make a question of it.

"All appears to be as it should," she answered. "At least for immediate concerns. My apologies for taking your time. I will leave you to attend to your own concerns, as I . . ."

She paused, glanced once at Dorian, and then looked casually about the courtyard.

"I should see Domin High-Tower," she finished, "concerning distribution of stores that arrived this evening."

"At this time of night?" Rodian asked.

"He is often up late in his study."

The premin's casual manner was as much out of place as her earlier mad dash across the courtyard to reach the main building. Rodian looked directly at Dorian as he spoke to Hawes.

"Exactly what did you mean earlier when you told this one to stop and—"

"Captain!"

Lúcan's shout jarred Rodian's concentration. His corporal came jogging across the courtyard from the door to one of the gatehouse's inner towers. Lúcan halted with a curt nod to Rodian.

"Sir, one of the men on the wall is missing,"

"Missing?"

"Jonah reported when he came to the front on his last half circuit. He hadn't seen Maolís anywhere along the rear wall."

Rodian's stomach felt as if he'd swallowed a rock, and he turned on Hawes. "Corporal, escort the premin to her study and see that she remains safe there."

"Captain," Hawes said, "I am perfectly safe on my—"

"I insist," Rodian interrupted. "Your council called me to protect this place against intruders. One of mine is missing, leaving a breach in security."

She breathed in quickly, as if about to argue further.

"For your own protection, Premin," Rodian continued, "as now required of me. Corporal?"

Lúcan turned to Hawes and gestured toward the courtyard's northwest side. Hawes hesitated a bit longer, as if uncertain what to say. But what could she say?

She finally gave Rodian a slight nod and turned to walk off ahead of Lúcan. Dorian backstepped after the pair, still watching Rodian.

"Return to your duty, Dorian," Hawes ordered.

As soon as all three entered the northwest storage building, Rodian turned at a jog for the gatehouse tunnel. Upon reaching the portcullis, he looked out and up through its beams.

"Jonah, are you there?" he called out.

"Yes, sir," his guardsman answered from above in the tower's gear room.

"Rouse Angus and get down here—now!"

Rodian turned back up the tunnel. If there was an intruder, he would no longer be spotted from the walls. He was already inside.

"Hurry," Brot'an whispered.

Leesil bit his lower lip against a retort. He was doing his best, and with this lock, Brot'an wasn't going to do any better. Through the picks, Leesil felt something inside the lock that wasn't normal. He should've expected that it wouldn't be easy getting through a keep of sages so paranoid about secrets that they'd locked up Wynn. But that didn't account for the poor latch on the library's upper window.

He set upon the lock again, trying by feel to open it.

"Hold the light closer," he said.

Brot'an did so, though the crystal was now dimmer than before.

"Rub it," Leesil said. "That should fix its light."

With a frown, Brot'an did so, and the crystal brightened a bit.

Through his picks, Leesil felt something give. "Got it," he breathed.

Brot'an raised the eyebrow with the scars running through it, stepped back, and pocketed the crystal. Everything went dim but for light on the ceiling from some other faraway lamp in the library.

Leesil tucked away his tools and rose. He gripped the handle and looked to Brot'an, who nodded. He opened the door, prepared to step out into some passage through the keep. Well, there was a passage, but it was too dark to see anything beyond half a dozen yards.

This building built in the keep's old inner bailey was flush against the keep wall. When he and Brot'an had surveyed it from outside the grounds, they knew somehow it had to have an entrance into the keep's main building. They'd anticipated a locked or barred door in what they'd discovered was a library, but . . .

"Give me the crystal," Leesil said in a low voice, and held out his hand.

Even before Brot'an dropped it into his palm, the crystal's light exposed the problem.

Leesil cursed softly under his breath.

Of course there would be a passage connecting this building through the keep's old, massive wall. He had simply hoped that the sages, likely living on stipends from their local monarchy, wouldn't waste money on a second door.

But there it was, another few yards down the dark, narrow passage.

Leesil strode to the second door, gripped its handle halfheartedly, and gently twisted. Of course it was locked. With a sigh, he handed the crystal back to Brot'an and crouched to pull out his tools once more.

Chane tried to listen at the door of the small room, hoping to hear whatever might be said outside. He was almost certain that the other voice out in the passage belonged to Captain Rodian. Then came the muted sound of the main doors opening, and perhaps a third voice outside before the door swung shut. It had all been too quick, too quiet, and nothing more reached him.

He stood there in indecision.

Hawes had told him to wait, but she had not returned. What had she been talking about with the captain? Who was that third voice out in the courtyard—where Ore-Locks and Wynn would have to come through? Had Hawes herself somehow run afoul of Rodian's guards?

Chane had heard two sets of footsteps earlier, but they could have belonged to anyone. He had lost track of time amid all these mistakes and mishaps. Those steps could have even been Rodian and one of his guards searching the keep.

With the captain moving freely about, in and out of the courtyard, it seemed unlikely that Wynn and Ore-Locks had reached the main building. Perhaps they were still stuck in her room. If so, Wynn would be watching out her window, waiting for the courtyard to clear.

Chane needed a way to check and see, without having to step into the courtyard—or drop a glove outside the main doors. He could wait no longer for Hawes and cracked open the door, wincing as it creaked.

Inching it open, slowly broadening his view, he found the whole main passage empty for as far as he could see. He crept out, heading northward toward the kitchens.

There was one route to where Chane might view Wynn's window across the courtyard: in the top of the storage building, well above Hawes's study in the underground floors.

"Can you feel any vibrations?" Wynn whispered, huddling with Ore-Locks behind the door of the dark room.

"Nothing," he answered.

A tentative hope rose in Wynn. She pulled her cold-lamp crystal from her pocket and rubbed it. Soft light illuminated Ore-Locks's clean-shaven, broad face. His brow was furrowed in frustration.

"I'll have a look," she said.

"Do not—let me," he said, and turned to the wall beside the door.

"What are you doing?"

"Having a look."

Ore-Locks pressed his face against—into—the stone wall. The stone's dark, mottled gray texture began to flow over him, as if he were becoming the stone itself.

Wynn grabbed the back of his cloak and heaved before his ears sank out of sight. Ore-Locks straightened up as his head came out of the wall.

"What is it now!" he whispered sharply.

"What if someone sees you like that?"

He leaned into her face. "Do you think you and your little crystal would attract less attention?"

"I was going to cover it," she argued.

"You will still have to lean out in plain sight to look far enough up the passage."

"At least I wouldn't look like a gargoyle's head sprouting from the wall!"

"You are a lot of—"

"*Don't* . . . you say it," and Wynn leaned in to him this time. "I'm sick of people telling me I'm so much *trouble*."

Ore-Locks's mouth tightly closed in a flat line. One of his eyebrows rose higher than the other.

"Oh, fine!" she said, and he turned away, putting his head into the wall.

Even after the times Wynn had seen this before, it was still disturbing to see stone practically flow through and over him, as if it were turning him into a statue. It stopped halfway down his great bulk once he'd finished leaning out through the thick wall. Only from his waist down did he still stick out in the room, but he was taking too long.

Ore-Locks suddenly lurched back into Wynn. She grabbed his cloak again to keep herself from being knocked over. His jaw was clenched, and in the silence of the little room, Wynn heard the creak of another door out in the passage.

"This is ridiculous," she whispered.

For the first time since Ore-Locks's appearance, he looked truly infuriated. "Everything around you turns ridiculous!"

Wynn bit back a retort. After all, he wasn't wrong.

Leesil managed the second lock quickly, now that he knew what to feel for. A click answered his manipulations. He tested the handle carefully, nudged the door just a little to see that it would open, looked up at Brot'an, and nodded. Then he hurried to gather his tools. As he stood up, Brot'an pocketed the crystal.

Leesil inched the door open, but upon looking out, he found himself staring up a long, empty passage. By its make and stonework, it should be part of the keep's main building. He'd hoped to keep any encounters to a minimum, but even at this time of night he hadn't expected to run into *no one*.

Had the city-guard captain called a curfew? Well, if so, then so much the better.

He shrugged at Brot'an, and they both stepped through the door.

Leesil led the way, and when they neared an intersection at the passage's end, he flattened against the right wall as he slid forward. He watched to the left of the main passage, until he reached the corner, and then carefully turned to face into the wall. Tilting his head, he used only his left eye to peer to the right up the long, broad passage.

By the length of the last passage they'd entered, he guessed that this main corridor ran parallel to this building's inner wall. The courtyard had to be beyond it, just outside.

A light halfway down spilled illumination into the long, broad passage, but he couldn't see a lantern or lamp. There was some type of recess there on the left. Beyond it, the passage continued northward, too dark to clearly see its end. For as few lights as were here, perhaps that recess held a door out into the courtyard.

Leesil backed around the corner and whispered, "There's a possible way out just up ahead."

Brot'an nodded, urging him on, and Leesil rounded the corner.

Rodian reached the courtyard again as Angus and Jonah came out of the gatehouse's inner northward tower. He waved them toward the keep's main doors and then followed, sweeping the entire courtyard with his eyes.

Jonah reached the doors first, and both men paused and waited.

"I want a full search of the interior," Rodian ordered. "Every room, as fast as we can move without missing anything."

"Yes, sir."

Jonah pulled the doors open and Angus stepped inside. Rodian was about to follow his men when a muffled shout stalled him.

"Sir!"

Turning, he spotted Lúcan half stumbling out a door in the northwest building . . . and he was alone.

"Go!" Rodian ordered Angus and Jonah, and then trotted to meet his corporal.

Chane had just darted past the entryway to get away from its light, and he began to make his way up the main passage's northward half with care. He was still uncertain if Rodian and Hawes were the only ones who had come into the main building.

If he could reach the kitchen and cut through its rear access, he would end up on the lower floor of the old granary and stables now used for storage and workshops. Once he'd reached its top floor, he might get a look across the courtyard to Wynn's window. But he'd gone only few paces past the entryway when he heard a sound so quiet—almost nonexistent—that a living being might have missed it.

Flattening against the passage's outer wall, he looked behind himself, southward along the main passage. Light spilling from the entryway made it hard to be certain, but beyond that glimmer he thought he saw the darkness move.

For one instant Chane thought of turning and running, and then it struck him that he would have more clearly heard a guard on patrol. In the dark beyond the entryway, Chane thought he saw a figure approaching, perhaps slightly crouched in stealth.

Something—someone—had covertly entered the keep.

Chane drew his sword but kept it out of sight at his side so it would not reflect any light. Whether an invader was after Wynn or something or someone else, he was not letting it remain here. Then he saw something more—another, much taller shape in the dark—coming up the passage as the first one drew near the entryway's light.

The first one was half bent over, creeping. Of medium height, the figure's face and hair were hidden by a long wrap of dark cloth. Chane glimpsed the same on the taller one; it was now clear that both were male.

Neither were guards or sages.

The first one froze, almost straightening, and stared up the passage, as if he saw Chane hiding beyond the entryway. Chane saw slanted, amber eyes; he was facing a pair of elves. What were any of the Lhoin'na doing here, sneaking in like thieves in the night?

Chane was not about to ask even as he stepped out from the wall, raising his sword.

All of the waiting and hiding and waiting was wearing on Wynn and turning her stomach into a knot. Wherever Chane was, he too had to be panicking by now. His simple plan had gone completely awry.

"We have to go!" she whispered. "If you don't try the door again, I will."

Ore-Locks grimaced, looking uncertainly at the door.

"If we're caught in here together, it will look even worse for you," she added.

With his mouth tight, Ore-Locks reached for the door, but his hand stopped halfway.

"Oh, what now?" Wynn whispered in frustration.

He pointed down at the floor, and for at least the fourth time tonight, Wynn wanted to groan. He must have felt something in the floor stones, yet another *someone* walking past outside in the passage.

Ore-Locks stood still, watching the door, even as he asked, "By the ancestors, how many of your people go wandering about in the dark? It is like one of my people's tram stations out there, at the end of the workday!"

Wynn had no answer. Once again, he wasn't wrong.

Leesil stopped before the entryway, seeing the cold lamp mounted above the broad and stout double doors in the recess halfway up the broad corridor. He was uncomfortably aware of being too exposed.

Something beyond the entryway in the passage's other half caught his eye, something too light-colored to hide for long in the dark.

He fixed on a form flattened against the passage's outer wall, and then he straightened just a little. He swung his left hand down, reaching for a winged blade strapped to his thigh. The form beyond the doors' recess stepped away from the wall . . . with a longsword in its hand.

Leesil heard the soft sound behind him of something sliding out of cloth. He knew Brot'an had drawn his blades. All Leesil's plans drained away, like alley sludge into a city sewer under a downpour.

Killing had never been part of his plan. Whoever this other man was, he was neither a guard nor a sage and had no like compunction against bloodshed. And any noise would quickly draw attention from elsewhere.

The shadowed figure took a step, and the barest bit of light from the recess touched him.

Leesil saw pale features inside the cloak's hood . . . and then he couldn't breathe.

The pale man with jaggedly cut red-brown hair hanging around his face just glared, slowly lifting the tip of a sword made of strangely mottled steel.

It was Chane.

Shock and hatred made Leesil break into a mild sweat. An undead, one of the worst he'd ever met, was inside the keep among all these defenseless sages, including . . .

Leesil's throat went dry. Chane should be an entire continent and ocean away. And he was here, and Wynn was here.

What had that naive little sage done this time?

Leesil jerked out a winged blade, snapping its sheath lashing in half.

Chane froze as the taller elf drew two long stilettos out of his sleeves. Both blades appeared too light-toned for normal steel. He tilted his sword up, raising its tip in preparation, and the shorter elf ripped something out of a sheath on his thigh. Chane instantly fixed on that weapon.

He knew it, and he looked in the first elf's eyes, glaring back at him.

Chane froze in indecision. It was Leesil.

Leesil inched to the far edge of the entryway and shifted sideways, clearing the way for his taller companion.

Chane's hunger rose as the beast inside him thrashed in panic for self-preservation. Despair came, as well. It was all truly over now.

Magiere, Leesil, and Chap must have devised their own scheme to reach Wynn. In such a sick turn of fate, they had launched their attempt on the same night as Chane. Now he had run right into one of them in his own attempt to rescue Wynn. Even if he had been willing to explain, Leesil would never hesitate long enough to hear him.

Chane's promise to Wynn became worthless under the hate in Leesil's amber eyes. He braced himself, ready for Leesil to close in, and kept one eye on the taller elf with the stilettos.

Then he heard one of the main doors open.

Flattening against the passage's wall, he watched Leesil and his tall companion do the same on the entryway's far side, and then Chane leaned his head out, trying to see.

Two guards with red tabards over chain armor stepped through one of the main doors.

Chane's thoughts went blank for an instant. How much worse could this situation become? And then . . .

Anyone who cared for Wynn had to remain free in here, especially any who were capable of finding, protecting, and rescuing her. It simply could not be him.

Chane knew Leesil would think exactly that. Between the choice of getting to her or getting rid of him, Leesil would choose Wynn. And Chane knew what had to be done.

He stepped away from the wall into full view, sword in hand. To his frustration, neither guard looked his way. Before Leesil could shout a warning at them, Chane snapped his sword tip against the passage wall.

At that sharp ring of steel, both guards looked his way, and their eyes widened.

"Stop!" one of them shouted.

Chane took off up the passage, heading north, as two sets of running, booted feet sent echoes chasing after him.

This time, Wynn clearly heard an unfamiliar voice shouting "Stop!" out in the passage. Only an instant of confusion came and went before she thought of Chane.

He must have tried another route into the library and been spotted. He'd have to fight, perhaps kill a guard, to avoid being captured. If they captured him, locked him up in a cell—even one without a window—by dawn they would see him go dormant. Anyone checking on him would find a dead man . . . until he rose again at dusk.

In being seen here, Chane's skulking would cause a guild-wide alarm, and it would all get even worse.

Wynn grabbed the door's handle, and Ore-Locks reached out to stop her.

"We have to go now!" she whispered, and jerked the door open.

Leesil's mind went blank as two guards raced away up the passage's other half after Chane. A barrage of horrors from the past flooded his emptied head, rushing in on him all at once.

Chane had been with Welstiel when they'd all converged upon the icebound castle of Li'kän, that ancient undead. That had been where they'd found the first orb, and Wynn had found all of those old, rotting books she'd so desperately wanted to bring home, though there were vastly more than they could carry. But to get that far, they'd fought against healer monks turned to feral undead by Welstiel . . . and Chane.

Osha had been badly injured, as had Chap, who had also nearly been pulled over the side of an abyss. Chane had been there, in the middle of it all.

The night before, Chap had sensed an undead in this city, in Calm Seatt. It had happened somewhere near where Shade disappeared. And Shade was supposed to be with Wynn.

Every time Chane crossed their path, it always had something to do with Wynn.

Leesil snatched up the amulet hanging about his neck. Magiere had given it to him long ago, once she no longer needed it to track undeads. It always glowed whenever one was near.

It wasn't glowing even a little as he dangled it before his face. It would've by the time he'd even entered this building, but it hadn't even grown warm against his chest to warn him. Yet Chane had been standing there, barely a dozen paces away.

"We move on," Brot'an said quietly.

Leesil startled to awareness, looked at the main doors, and everything seemed wrong now. An extra guard had appeared on the wall. Two more had come into the building from the courtyard. There was no way to see what was going on out there. Something had changed since he and Brot'an had scouted this place.

"No," he answered. "There will be more guards outside, so we need to find a way from one building to the next. We head back to this passage's far end and look for another door that might lead into the structures along the keep's southeast side . . . where Chap spotted Wynn."

He didn't like taking blind paths in desperation, but he saw no other choice. As he turned, he found Brot'an looking up the passage where the guards had now vanished. The distinct pucker of a scowl showed between the butcher's feathery eyebrows, but he finally nodded in agreement.

Leesil stepped beyond Brot'an, leading the way, and then stopped.

Just beyond the first intersection they'd come out of into the main passage, a door swung open.

CHAPTER 18

Chane gauged his speed to stay just in sight of the guards. He needed to give Leesil time to slip through and hopefully find Wynn, while keeping these guards out of the way. It was galling to find himself actually helping that half-blood, but there was no other option where Wynn was concerned.

"Stop!" a guard shouted somewhere behind him. "By order of the Shyld-fälches!"

Did they really think *that* was going to work?

Beyond the common hall's front archway, he rounded the passage's corner and took off at full speed. He raced by the common hall's narrower side arch and the kitchen entrance across from it.

Much as he was tempted, he could not duck into the kitchens just yet. The guards were too close, and he had to lure them farther away from the main entrance. Some parts of the main building were familiar to him; other parts were less so. Stuck with what little he knew, he was already growing frantic.

Chane skidded to a stop where the passage turned left before the library's northern entrance. Down that turn lay the north tower, where High-Tower had his study. Short of that was the door leading to the inner bailey's backside. That was likely locked up due to Rodian's security measures. No doubt the same had been done for the tower's door or even the archive's stairwell to its left.

He noticed the kitchen's side door across from the rear exit into the bailey. Then he heard the guards round the previous corner.

Chane bolted off, running for the kitchen's side door, a place he knew little about. But if he kept the guards busy long enough, perhaps he might still find a way through the kitchen into the storage building.

He still needed a look across the courtyard to see if Wynn was trapped in her room.

Wynn pocketed her crystal before rushing out into the dark passage. Ore-Locks pushed past her, and this time she didn't argue. There was little to see in the dark except the dim glow of the entrance's cold lamp, hidden from view.

"The shout came from up there," Ore-Locks whispered.

Wynn barely made out his chin jutting northward along the main passage.

"We have to find Chane quickly," she whispered back, "before he—"

Ore-Locks leveled his iron staff, and Wynn backed up. She had to duck left as he suddenly twisted the staff into a swing before grabbing it with his other hand. She heard a sharp clang of steel against the staff's iron.

Wynn caught a glimpse of a dark figure stumbling into the passage wall beyond Ore-Locks. Almost instantly, a taller figure rushed forward out of the darkness at the dwarf. She didn't have time to moan as she dug for her crystal. If these were guards, hopefully Ore-Locks could knock them unconscious without serious harm.

As the iron staff recoiled from the first strike, Ore-Locks arced it straight down in the tall one's path. That one hopped into a midair crouch that made Wynn's eyes widen. The staff struck where its feet had been.

Small bits of stone went flying from the impact, but Wynn's gaze was still fixed on the tall form appearing to hover for an instant in the air. He was just too tall to have moved so quickly, and between wraps of black cloth covering his lower face and hair were large amber eyes. One of those eyes glowed out through a set of four parallel scars.

Wynn recognized his half-hidden face.

The front end of Ore-Locks's iron staff recoiled off the floor. He turned its momentum sideways across the passage, and Wynn had to duck the staff's back end once more.

The staff struck the left wall. Like a controlled ricochet in Ore-Locks's great hands, its tip bounced off, arcing back across the passage, and then down at the first figure trying to push off the right wall.

"Valhachkasej'â!" that one snarled, raising his arms to block at the last instant.

Wynn saw two white metal winged blades on his arms.

"Ah no!" she breathed.

The staff struck the blades and slammed Leesil into the passage wall.

"No . . . no! No!" Wynn cried.

She tried to grab Ore-Locks, but he swung the staff back at Brot'an. Wynn ducked the staff's butt again, and when it passed, she threw herself atop Ore-Locks's broad back, trying to grip with her legs as she fumbled to cover his eyes with her hands.

"Stop!" Wynn shouted. "Everyone . . . stop it now!"

Rodian was still calculating which guards to move where when Lúcan had reappeared out of the northeast storage building. Since that ugly night, when the young corporal had been left so marred, he rarely expressed any open emotion. Now his hair was disheveled and his tabard was slightly askew, as if he'd been running. He looked distraught.

Rodian trotted across the courtyard, meeting Lúcan halfway.

"What's happened?" he asked, slowing to a stop.

"The premin is gone!"

"What? How?"

"I showed her into the study and shut the door. Then one of those other handleless iron doors down there opened. Two dark-robed sages took one look at me, glanced at the premin's door, and then ducked back inside before I could question them. Something wasn't right, and I opened the study door to check on the premin. She wasn't there anymore."

Lúcan shook his head, dropping his gaze.

"I don't know how, sir," he continued. "Believe me, she couldn't have snuck by me, and there's no other way out of there."

Rodian wasn't going to blame his corporal, and he guessed that someone like Hawes was in little danger on her own. But he wanted to throw up his hands in frustration.

May the Blessed Trinity of Sentience take pity on him—*just once*—trapped again among sages!

"Watch the portcullis," he ordered Lúcan. "I'll handle this."

Finding Hawes was unlikely, though he wondered where she'd gone and how. The premin had been doing something inside the main building, besides a faked search for a nonexistent initiate.

Rodian strode off for the keep's main doors.

Wynn saw Brot'an freeze to stare back at her.

"Get off me," Ore-Locks growled.

She looked at Leesil and then Brot'an again as the tall elder elf pulled down his face wrap. It was the only time Wynn could remember seeing the master anmaglâhk astonished, at least as much as she was.

"What are you doing here?" she breathed in shock. "Leesil, what's going on?

Ore-Locks pulled her hands off his eyes. "You know these two?"

Leesil righted himself, wobbling. He shook out one arm and rolled a shoulder. When he jerked his face wrap down, Wynn melted in relief at the sight of his familiar features.

"Will you get off . . . *now*?" Ore-Locks repeated.

Wynn slid off Ore-Locks's back and ducked around him, and then her relief wavered. "Leesil?"

He didn't make an inappropriate joke or come to give her a quick hug. He didn't even look at Ore-Locks after being slammed against the wall twice.

Leesil stood there, eyeing her coldly.

Wynn's stomach knotted up again. Something was terribly wrong.

He stepped toward her, making Ore-Locks tense up, and then passed right by her. He headed down the passage, away from the main doors.

"Come on," he said without looking back.

"But Leesil—" Wynn began.

"Now!" he snapped, never breaking stride.

"Who are these two?" Ore-Locks demanded.

"Friends come to free her," Brot'an answered. "As have you, it appears. Introductions can wait."

Brot'an tucked his stilettos back up his sleeves and waved Wynn after Leesil, who'd paused halfway down the passage but hadn't looked back.

Wynn's thoughts cleared enough to race in another direction. Chane had to be in trouble, and she turned to Ore-Locks.

"I'm safe with these two, so you need to—"

"What? No! I will not just leave you with—"

"Yes, you will," she cut in. "You have to go find *him* . . . help *him*!"

Ore-Locks's glare drifted from her to Brot'an and back again. Then they all heard a door handle ratchet up near the entryway up the passage.

Brot'an snatched Wynn by the arm and dragged her after Leesil. When Ore-Locks tried to intervene, Wynn waved him off.

"I'm safe," she whispered. "Now find him and get him out of here!"

She tried to look back and see if Ore-Locks did as she asked, but she kept stumbling as Brot'an dragged her in his longer strides. They rounded the corner toward the library's southernmost entrance, and Ore-Locks was gone from sight.

Wynn pulled away from Brot'an and ran after Leesil. When she caught up, he kept on. He didn't even acknowledge her presence until they reached the first door to the library—which was open. With barely a glance, Leesil grabbed Wynn's wrist and pulled her after him down that narrower passage to the second door.

Wynn had no idea how he knew where to go, and his grip was too tight. What could she possibly have done to make him so angry?

This no longer felt like a rescue.

Rodian stepped through the keep's main doors into the entryway and heard a distant, faint shout. He thought it was Jonah's voice, and then pounding footfalls carried faintly from somewhere up the main passage's northern half. As he was about to head off that way, something caught his eye.

He pivoted in the other direction and peered down the passage's southern half. Had he seen a glimmer of light down there? Had something moved in the dark between him and that brief glow?

He squinted but saw nothing, yet he was certain he hadn't imagined it. Then came the heavy scrape of a boot.

Pulling his sword, he turned south down the main passage. His steps quickened the farther he went, and still he saw nothing in the dark. When he reached the first left-hand turn into the passage to the library's southeast end, again there was that soft, brief glow.

The library's southeast door was open, and the glow had come from beyond it and the passage to the second door. How could both doors be unlocked?

Rodian broke into a run for the library door.

Chane ducked through the kitchen's side door and around the long butcher-block table. He heard the guards coming nearer and quickly looked about.

Wynn had once mentioned leaving kitchen duty by way of a back door to the storage building. Footsteps suddenly pounded right by the kitchen's side door. Chane ducked low, for the guards had caught up quicker than he had hoped.

"Do you see him?" one guard called.

"No. He's fast. . . . Check the doors at the end while I check this one."

Chane heard one set of footsteps hurry off along the passage toward the north tower. Likely the other had turned to check the rear door into the bailey. Once they found all doors locked, they would have only one route that he could have taken—into this kitchen. He was growing very tired of this and glanced quickly along the kitchen's back.

There was a door, but it faced rearward instead of to the left, in the direction of the storage building. If he took that door and stepped into some scullery, he would be trapped.

The frustration was too much. He wavered at the decision between ducking out the kitchen's main entrance to outdistance the guards in reaching the keep's main doors and finding somewhere else to hide. That would put him in a bad place, as well. The guards might even hear him and turn back toward the main entryway, and into Wynn's way if she and Ore-Locks came in.

There was one option that might keep the guards searching here a little longer. He half crawled between the kitchen's preparation tables.

"Everything's locked up," one guard called.

"Same here," the other replied. "And so . . ."

Chane rose and bolted through the kitchen's main doors. He slipped across the passage through the common hall's side arch and flattened against the inner wall to listen.

Wynn couldn't help feeling sick as Leesil dragged her up the stairs to the library's top floor. He hadn't spoken or even looked at her. What could have happened to make him treat her like this?

Leesil never let things fester. If he didn't like something, he spoke up—or he got devious in manipulating things to his own liking. Here and now wasn't the time, but Wynn knew the moment would come once they got out of here. Still, she didn't care for the waiting.

When they stepped onto the top floor, Leesil picked up the pace, and Wynn was a little surprised to find herself hauled along the library's south wall. It was the same route to the same window by which she'd once brought Chane into the guild . . . the same route Chane was supposed to check for her and Ore-Locks.

With little choice, she hurried after Leesil with Brot'an behind her.

"Psst."

At that cut-off hiss behind Wynn, Leesil stopped and turned to look, as did she.

Brot'an had halted and turned in the path between the wall and rows of casements. With his back to Wynn, she saw stilettos already in his hands as he set himself. She shifted, trying to peer around Brot'an toward the stairs they'd come up.

"Out of sight!" Leesil hissed and grabbed the back of her cloak and tunic.

He tried to thrust Wynn between the book casements, but she caught a glimpse of red rising up the stairwell beneath the cold lamp above the steps. She grabbed the casement's end to hold herself in place.

Captain Rodian stepped out onto the floor, sword in hand and his gaze fixed on Brot'an.

"No!" Wynn shouted.

The captain's eyes widened at the sight of her, though Brot'an didn't even flinch. Leesil again tried to shove her between the casements. She stomped on his foot, and as he stumbled with a curse, she grabbed the back of Brot'an's belt.

"Don't!" she begged.

Brot'an didn't turn, and Wynn looked at Rodian and shook her head. The captain's gaze shifted once to her, his sword still poised, and he fixed on Brot'an once more.

"This isn't what it looks like," Wynn said quickly. "I have got to get out of here. . . . That's all they're trying to do . . . to get me out."

Rodian didn't speak.

He studied her for a long moment and then shifted a little leftward. Perhaps he was trying to get a better look at Leesil, and Wynn tightened her grip upon Brot'an's belt. This was so bad that she couldn't even imagine the repercussions, no matter who won out in this moment.

Rodian slowly straightened and lowered his sword. She watched the captain's brow furrow and his mouth close tightly. He exhaled through his nose. Finally, he just shook his head—and he turned away.

The last Wynn saw of him, he descended the stairs, casually slipping his sword back into its sheath. He was gone almost as quickly as he'd appeared.

Wynn stared after the captain as Brot'an straightened before her. She was jarred into a flinch at Leesil's caustic whisper behind her.

"How many people in here tonight are trying to get you out of your own mess?"

"This is not the time or place," Brot'an whispered.

But Wynn spun around to eye Leesil, not really catching all that was hidden in his comment.

"Me?" she shot back. "You think all of this is just about me?"

Her voice shook with anger, but it felt better than misery. None of them had the slightest idea what all of this was really about—none but her. They would understand soon enough, and then maybe they'd see the scope of things, and how much worse it might all become.

"It's always about you," Leesil said flatly. "Every time we turn around, you're doing something . . . with someone . . . to get—"

"Oh, shut up, Leesil," she cut in, "and get me out of here!"

Relieved by her own anger, for it did wonders to shut out the fear, she didn't even wait for Leesil's shocked reply. Wynn pushed past him, heading for the library's rear window.

"What are you doing in here?"

If Chane had had a heartbeat, it would have skipped at that whisper. His whole body clenched as he whipped his head back to look across the common hall.

There, beyond the tables and benches, stood Ore-Locks, frowning at him. The dwarf's face was reddened, as if he had recently made some strenuous exertion.

Chane put a finger across his lips in warning. As Ore-Locks hurried between the tables, a dozen questions flooded Chane's thoughts. One stood out above the others as he motioned Ore-Locks toward the other side of the archway.

Chane mouthed, *Where is Wynn?*

Ore-Locks returned only, *Safe.*

That was not enough. But then Chane heard footsteps across the passage in the kitchen.

Ore-Locks's red eyebrows rose, and he peeked around the archway's edge.

Guards, Chane mouthed, and held up two fingers.

Ore-Locks scowled at him.

"He must have doubled back!" someone shouted. "Come on."

Ore-Locks leaned back out of sight.

Chane had had enough, and there was only one option left. When he heard a guard step into the passage outside, he snapped his fingers, trying to pull the man's attention. But in a stroke of bad luck, as the guard stepped through the arch, he glanced the other way and raised his sword at the sight of Ore-Locks.

"A'ye!" the dwarf shouted. "Behind you."

The guard's head began to turn.

Ore-Locks brought his staff down on the man's helmet with a dull *clank.*

The man's eyes rolled upward, and as he crumpled, the second guard ran through the arch, swerving to grab the staff's end with one hand. Sword up, he rounded on Ore-Locks.

Chane snagged the shoulder of the man's tabard and jerked him about. His fist cracked against the guard's jaw, dropping the man in his tracks.

Ore-Locks stood beyond the heap of two guards, glowering at Chane.

Without waiting, Chane grabbed the top guard and dragged him farther along the common hall's inner wall before dropping him.

"Where is Wynn?" he asked urgently.

Ore-Locks dumped the other guard a short way up the other side.

"Heading out through the library, no thanks to you," he retorted, and then paused with a seemingly confused shake of his head. "Some others came after her . . . two Lhoin'na wrapped up like thieves."

Chane knew exactly whom Ore-Locks meant and slumped in relief—at least briefly. This was not all of what he had wanted. Wynn was safe, but she would soon be back with her old companions, including Magiere.

"Did she call one of them Leesil?" he asked, needing to be certain.

"Yes," Ore-Locks answered with a surprised blink. "You know him?"

Chane nodded bitterly. "Yes . . . I know him."

"Enough dawdling. This is over, and we should leave now . . . before you attract any more attention."

Moving fast for his bulk, Ore-Locks ducked out the archway and stalked off into the kitchen. Chane followed, at a loss for what the dwarf was up to. But it became all too clear once he caught up to Ore-Locks, standing before the kitchen's rear wall.

"Brace yourself," Ore-Locks said, and without a moment's grace, he grabbed Chane's wrist.

Chane never got out a word as he was jerked into the wall. Darkness, cold, and smothering silence swallowed him whole. He had not counted on leaving this way. Then again, nothing this night had occurred as he had planned. Wynn was free, but in the darkness of stone, Chane felt only bitterness, not relief.

After all that had happened, the guild would be locked up tighter than ever before. Worse still, should Wynn somehow be granted access to the resources required to decipher what remained in the scroll, should she ever be allowed within these walls . . . he would not.

The guards, and Premin Hawes, had seen him breaking in at night. The Premin Council would soon learn of this.

It had been only a few nights since he had come to terms with what was required of him. If he wished to remain at Wynn's side, her goal, her mission, had to be his, as well. If he wished to have any existence that involved the guild, he had to abide by it and watch over all within it, regardless that some did not belong here.

Perhaps he was one of those who did not.

In Chane's effort to help Wynn, all seemed lost to him, including her. He could not even imagine how she would contact him now—considering whom she would be with.

He felt the comparative warmth of chill night air on his face, and the darkness outside appeared bright for an instant as he was hauled out of the stone by Ore-Locks. He nearly stumbled at suddenly standing in the shadows of the inner bailey between the northern keep tower and the northwest outer building. He had enjoyed peace and quiet, more than once, in the guest quarters there. That was lost, as well. He looked at the thick bailey wall before him, behind the leafless trees.

"Once more," Ore-Locks whispered.

Chane nodded, steeling himself, but he could never be ready for his last glimpse of the guild.

Pawl a'Seatt had not moved from the rooftop near Norgate Road. Neither had the tall stranger that he watched one rooftop away. That cowled figure with the tied-up cloak still crouched at the rooftop's edge, watching the guild grounds, and Pawl wanted to know why.

Then the cowled man tensed almost imperceptibly.

Pawl looked to the keep as someone climbed out a rear library window and dropped to the top of the bailey wall. This figure was slender, his face and hair covered by wraps. It was one of the pair who had scaled the wall and entered earlier through that same window.

The slender man stood up, looking both ways along the wall, and then turned to help someone else. A smaller figure came out the window. The second one dangled over the sill and dropped with steadying help from the first one, who then watched as a third figure—the tallest one of the original pair—came out last, his face and hair still covered. That one dropped straight from the window's edge, landing in a crouch.

Pawl focused most sharply upon the newer figure, the smallest one. Two had entered, and three had come out. He saw no sign of this being a capture or kidnapping. The reasonable alternative was a rescue, and there was only one person Pawl had heard of who would count as any kind of a "prisoner" within the sages' keep.

Even in the dark cloak and high, soft boots, it could only be Wynn Hygeorht.

The translation project had been stopped shortly before Pawl heard of Wynn's incarceration. It was unlikely that her freedom would start it again, and more likely that it would prolong its pause. He wondered whether to halt her flight himself.

The shorter of the two men handed something to the other one. After a brief exchange, the tall one tossed a rope's end over the bailey wall's side. The shorter one climbed down and stood waiting, and then Wynn took quite a bit longer to follow.

To Pawl's mild surprise, the tall figure dropped the rope over the side and scaled quickly down the wall using two blades. In an astonishingly brief time, all three crept southward along the base of the wall. And then Pawl looked back to the cowled stranger on the roof.

That one had risen, gripping a strange short bow by its silvery white metal grip, and reached behind his back, beneath his tied-up cloak. When his hand came out, his fingers pinched the end of a short arrow. He notched the arrow and aimed down at the trio below in the shadow of the bailey wall.

Chane nearly gagged in relief as Ore-Locks pulled him through the bailey wall onto the northwest side of Old Bailey Road near Switchin Way. They were finally out, and Chane focused on the moment, unable to face this night's outcome.

"We need to find Shade," he rasped.

They had left her at the keep's front, but Chane could not be spotted near the gates. How unexpected that it bothered him to think of Shade waiting out there alone.

Ore-Locks cocked his head toward the west tower down the way. "We can try to get to the front if we . . ."

He fell silent, and Chane followed Ore-Locks's fixed stare.

Something . . . someone dark stepped from the shadows of the wall and into the street. Chane did not need to wait as she pulled back her cowl. Even if she had not been wearing the midnight blue robe, he would have recognized the way she moved. But he had no idea what the sudden appearance of Premin Hawes meant here and now.

She stepped steadily up the street toward him, and then he noticed she held something slung over her shoulder. His puzzlement grew, as did Ore-Locks's wariness, as she stopped an arm's length away.

Premin Hawes rolled the strap off her shoulder and held a pack out toward Chane.

"You did not wait as instructed," she said calmly. "Under the circumstances, I thought you would prefer to hold on to these yourself."

Still confused, Chane took the pack from her and looked inside. Within it he found the cloth-wrapped bundles of the dwarven mushrooms and the flowers he had scavenged from the plain outside the lands of the Lhoin'na. There was also the precious text *The Seven Leaves of Life*.

Profound relief came first, followed by suspicion.

Why was Hawes doing this? Did she wish to help in Wynn's cause, or was this just a ploy to gain his trust for some other purpose?

"She is out of the keep," Hawes said.

Chane tensed.

"Tell her that if she has need to send for me," Hawes added. "But she must not return here . . . not yet. Do you understand?"

Ore-Locks was watching them both in silent puzzlement. He had no idea what was happening, let alone why the premin of metaology came out unaccompanied in the night to speak to a Noble Dead who had invaded her guild.

"I understand," Chane said, and he did, in part.

"Good," she said, turning away. "Keep her safe."

He hesitated, despair beginning to close in on him again. "I do not know if I will see . . . she is with other companions now."

"She will come to you," Hawes called without looking back.

"How do you know?" he asked.

"I know."

Premin Hawes neared the bailey wall and stepped *through*, not *into*, stone.

Chane watched the wall appear to buckle or perhaps ripple around her like a disturbed vertical pool of water. She vanished completely through the wall, and the ripples in the stone quickly settled. For a moment, Chane was tempted to touch that spot and feel its solidity for certain.

At a guess, Hawes could not travel distances through earth and stone like a stonewalker. Unlike them, she probably found no barrier, even wood, an impediment at all.

Chane thought of Wynn and of Hawes's final prediction. Perhaps they did have one ally inside the guild—a subtly powerful and potentially dangerous one, who also sat on the Premin Council. But how was he to tell Wynn any of this?

"How . . . how did she?" Ore-Locks mumbled, and then his mouth just hung open.

In spite of everything, Chane could not stop a slight smile. He clutched the pack with his precious components, and then a bark broke the silence. A dark form loped toward him along Old Bailey Road.

"Shade," he said quietly, waiting for her.

Her shape often made him forget the intelligence of the majay-hì, equal to or perhaps even greater than that of people, though differing greatly. Or so Wynn had said more than once. Shade must have been roaming the road, watching for them, or perhaps sniffed them out.

Ore-Locks glanced up at the bailey wall's top, but as of yet, Chane had heard no guard's footsteps coming their way.

"We should get out of sight," Ore-Locks said.

Chane agreed, and with little else to do, they all headed for the Grayland's Empire and Nattie's inn.

Pawl rose, poised as the cowled stranger turned slowly, tracking the trio below in the street with his bow drawn. But Pawl could not be certain at which of the three this lurker aimed.

Everything that had happened around the guild somehow pointed to Wynn Hygeorht.

Everything Pawl needed from the transcription project concerning the white woman of centuries ago might also be linked to the young sage.

And the figure on the rooftop had not drawn his bow until after Wynn had appeared.

Pawl took off at a run across the roof. Swiping off his broad-brimmed hat and ripping off his cloak, he pulled his blade from behind his back.

Too dark for steel, the hardened iron blade was barely the length of a shortsword, with a handle of only rough hide straps wrapped around its bare tang. In the night, no one would see the strange, rough, but evenly patterned serrations of its edges. That blade was the only relic of his living days, of his own people long gone from the world . . . and nearly gone from the fragments of his own memories.

Pawl took his last step at the edge of the roof as he threw his blade at the cloaked figure across the street. Then he leaped into the air to a height no one would have believed if they had seen it. The blade was too heavy and unbalanced to strike true, but all he needed was to stop that archer.

An instant before the blade struck, the man whirled out of its path. The blade hit the roof beyond the archer and tumbled away as Pawl arced across the street in midair. The stranger instantly spotted him.

An arrow struck low in Pawl's shoulder and punched through skin and muscle.

He landed and charged on without slowing. Another arrow hit him dead center in the chest.

He heard and felt his breastbone crack as the second arrow's head pierced his heart, but he never even slowed. A third arrow punctured him just to the left of the second. He closed on his quarry and saw the man's—the elf's— amber eyes suddenly widen above the dark gray-green wrap across the lower half of his face.

The stranger dropped his bow and reached quickly up his sleeves.

Pawl closed the last step at a full run and slammed his hand into the would-be assassin's throat.

Bone cracked audibly as the elf's head whipped forward and then back. His feet left the shakes as force drove him backward under all of Pawl's strength and speed. The body hit the roof, flopping and sliding across the shakes until it rammed into and caught on a chimney, toppling one tile off its top.

The stranger lay there unmoving as Pawl went to look down over the roof's edge.

Old Bailey Road was empty. Wynn and her two companions were gone, never aware how close she, or one of them, had come to death. Yet Pawl was no closer to what he needed, though he had halted an event that could have further hindered his answers.

He began pulling arrows out of his flesh and bone. The one through his chest took both hands.

Black fluids spilling from his wounds would never show against the black cloth of his attire. He would have to burn his tunic, though, to be certain the evidence was never found. Dropping the last arrow, he walked to the corpse caught on the chimney and ripped away the face wrap.

He had never heard of assassins among the Lhoin'na. Nor had ever seen one with such near-white blond hair or such a dark complexion. He had counted at least four others like this in his nightly roaming. How many of these were in his city?

And why were they after Wynn Hygeorht?

Leaving the body where it lay, Pawl retrieved his ancient, serrated iron blade. There was nothing more he could learn here. At a run, he leaped over the street again to the nearest rooftop, heading for home.

Dänvârfij grew nervous in the dark above Wall Shop Row. She had been waiting for a report since Én'nish had gone to fetch Rhysís and go after the wagon. Too much time had passed, and one or both should have come to her by now.

Worse, without Én'nish, there was no one to send off to check in with Owain and Eywodan. If anything happened outside her view, she would not know it. She hesitated at leaving her post and missing Én'nish's return, but it was not wise or safe to allow so much time to pass without an exchange of information.

Dänvârfij stood up, heading for the roof's edge. A light *thud* sounded behind her, and she turned.

Én'nish rose from her jump as Rhysís landed lightly beside her.

Had any prisoners already been delivered to Fréthfâre? Then she saw that Rhysís's right forearm was bleeding, and his cloak was torn.

"What happened?" she asked.

"A trap . . . a decoy," Én'nish answered, "to pull some of us away. They know we are watching the castle."

"Of course they know. Brot'ân'duivé is with them!" Dänvârfij quickly tempered her anger. "What do you mean by 'decoy'?"

Rhysís would not look her in the eyes as he answered. "The half-undead woman, the majay-hì, and . . . another of us pulled the wagon around a corner and were prepared for us."

Dänvârfij stared, uncertain she followed all of his meaning. "Another . . . of us?"

"Osha is now with Brot'ân'duivé," Én'nish hissed. "Another turned traitor."

Dänvârfij chilled at this disturbing news, though, in retrospect, it was not a complete surprise. Osha had been there, like Dänvârfij, when Sgäilsheilleache and Hkuan'duv killed each other. She had never understood how someone as untalented as Osha had ever gained Sgäilsheilleache as his jeóin. And after that encounter, when she had fled, Most Aged Father had instructed her to wait on the ship that retrieved her. Soon enough, Osha had come, though her presence aboard the vessel surprised him.

And later it had been Brot'ân'duivé who had extracted Osha from questioning by Most Aged Father.

Osha, inept as he was, appeared to always be in the company of the most skilled. And now . . .

Determination that fed on hatred and desire for vengeance could be more powerful than skills. Dänvârfij knew this, had seen what it had done to Én'nish. She had seen it in the eyes of Rhysís after the night Wy'lanvi died. How could this be happening to her caste?

Until Sgäilsheilleache and Hkuan'duv, no anmaglâhk had ever turned on another. Rhysís blamed Brot'ân'duivé for the death of a friend, and Osha most likely blamed . . . *her* for the death of Sgäilsheilleache. For with Hkuan'duv gone, there was no one else left for Osha's vengeance.

In all of Dänvârfij's life, the only thing she had never questioned was the loyalty of her caste to each other and their people. This had dried like a fallen leaf in a growing drought and began to blow away like dust, not only with the death of Hkuan'duv, but upon the treachery of Brot'ân'duivé.

"Was Osha the driver?" she asked, forcing herself to remain focused.

"Yes," Én'nish answered.

"Who was the smaller one?"

"I do not know. That one was missing when we caught up and were ambushed. We thought it more important to break off and report."

Dänvârfij nodded. "Nothing more has happened here. Én'nish, go and check with—"

Another light *thud* upon the roof interrupted her. Eywodan jogged across the shakes, the tan skin around his eyes looking almost gray when he drew near.

"Owain is dead," he said before even coming to a stop. "I found his body."

Én'nish sucked in a loud breath, but again Dänvârfij felt as if she barely understood the words. She could not speak.

"How?" Rhysís asked quietly.

"It had been too long since exchanging reports," Eywodan answered. "I grew concerned and went to his position. I found him . . . still on the rooftop."

"You left his body?"

"Yes!" Eywodan snapped, his scant exposed skin turning grayer. "I feared others of us might be ambushed, and I ran to help the living! We can retrieve the body later."

Chagrined, Rhysís glanced away. "So the traitor kills yet another of his own."

Dänvârfij still could not speak. It was hard to believe they had lost Owain to more of Brot'ân'duivé's treachery, but Eywodan surprised her by shaking his head.

"I do not think so," he said. "Owain's entire throat had been crushed by what appeared to be a single blow. That is not the way we kill . . . not even a traitor."

This had gone far enough. Finding her voice, Dänvârfij turned to Rhysís.

"It was wrong to hold out for the sage," she said, "especially once we knew where our quarry hid. We go to their inn tonight, make sure they have all returned, and then take them. But foremost, we kill Brot'ân'duivé."

Rhysís's eyes glittered softly, his bow still assembled and in hand. Perhaps he envisioned the shot that would take down a greimasg'äh.

Dänvârfij knew it would not be that easy. All of them knew that to kill Brot'ân'duivé would cost one or more of their lives.

"Only then do we attempt capture of the others," she continued. "Kill the majay-hì if you must, and Osha, but Magiere and Léshil must be taken alive."

Dänvârfij would have preferred to pull Tavithê as well from the port watch, but it was more important to reach the inn and take their quarry by surprise.

"We go," she said, running for the next rooftop.

Rodian stood inside the keep's entryway, facing an openly outraged Premin Sykion with Domin High-Tower beside her. Both had been awakened due to the gravity of the situation, and although Rodian knew his report would cause shock, he was glad of it.

For once Sykion had lost her veneer of motherly wisdom and superiority. She looked so livid that she might snatch his own sword from his sheath to run him through.

But Rodian preferred open hostility. It made people careless.

"How could someone of your position and authority allow this to happen?" she demanded.

Beneath her rage, he heard a quaver of fear in her voice.

"How could you let one girl slip through your fingers?" Sykion went on.

He let her rant a little longer, before he replied in a purely professional tone.

"The effort to free Journeyor Hygeorht came from multiple directions. They had obviously anticipated that any one infiltrator might fail . . . and would then attempt a distraction. Four of my men were injured trying to stop them, and it appears that Journeyor Hygeorht has quite a few contacts outside these walls who do not share your view of her."

Angus and Jonah had been found in the common hall, and although both appeared to be recovering, he was worried that Jonah's jaw might be cracked. A young guard named Benedict had been discovered unconscious in Wynn's room. Maolís had been found in the inner bailey below the eastern tower, having taken a nasty blow to the side of the head. But upon waking, he had no idea what had hit him.

Rodian hadn't bothered questioning any of his men for long. It would've led to nothing, and another notion had been brewing in his thoughts since the moment he'd turned his back on Wynn and her masked rescuers.

At the sight of Sykion's pinched and reddened face, he couldn't hold it back any longer.

"I apologize for the temporary loss of Journeyor Hygeorht," he said. "I assure you that my second-in-command, Lieutenant Branwell, will begin arrangements for her arrest warrant, and we will comb the city."

Pausing, he pulled a small notebook from his belt and a slender, paper-wrapped writing charcoal from his pocket.

"You need only give me the formal charge, Premin," he added, "and I will have her back in jurisdiction soon enough."

Sykion blinked, and Rodian stood calmly with his charcoal poised over a blank page.

"Charge?" High-Tower finally managed to ask.

"A proper search will be costly," Rodian returned. "I can hardly justify that without a formal charge of criminal activity. And it is necessary for the warrant. You do want Journeyor Hygeorht recovered—I mean, *arrested*—do you not? That is all that the Shyldfälches have the authority to do."

Rodian waited, watching Sykion's flattened expression.

Before taking this position, he had sworn an oath upon the Éa-bêch, the first book of law for Malourné. Twice in his service he had broken or bent the law himself—once for the greater good, and once when Duchess Reine offered him Snowbird as a gift. He was not allowed to accept such gifts, but he'd wanted to keep the horse.

The present situation was entirely different.

As of yet, Wynn Hygeorht had committed no verified crime, let alone been found guilty in the people's court. The Premin Council and the royals had forced her incarceration, circumventing Rodian's own sacred oath of service. Ambitious as he was, he would not be cornered into breaking the law a third time.

If Sykion could name a crime that had been committed, Rodian would be forced to hunt down Wynn himself. But he had a feeling that was not going to happen.

Sykion actually sputtered in finding her voice. "You . . . yourself . . . just told us four of your men had been injured."

Rodian raised an eyebrow. "You wish me to charge her with assault? Do you believe Journeyor Hygeorht attacked them personally?"

Sykion glanced away. "We simply wish you to bring her home."

"The journeyor is a free citizen," Rodian returned. "She decides where she calls *home*. I have no authority to force her to return here if she wishes to be elsewhere. And so, without a formal charge . . ."

He let those words hang.

Sykion's gaze darkened again. "You are well aware this matter is sensitive to the guild. Tomorrow, I will speak with the council and decide our best course of action. I will also speak with the royal family about what happened here tonight . . . about your inability to secure one small, four-towered keep inhabited by no one but scholars."

"You do that," Rodian said, and he stepped out of the main doors, into the courtyard.

He wasn't quite as sure of himself as he sounded.

Dänvârfij was unconcerned when she and her companions reached the rooftops around their quarry's inn. She sent Eywodan to check and found that no one was inside the room that Én'nish indicated. In truth, Dänvârfij was relieved.

This meant that when their quarry began to return, she could make a proper head count and watch for Brot'ân'duivé. But the night grew too long, and with it grew her anxiety.

"They should have returned by now," Én'nish whispered.

Dänvârfij agreed. "Go check the room itself. See what you find inside."

Én'nish was off immediately, reaching the window, prying the latch, and slipping inside. The rest of them waited, poised to act, as Dänvârfij watched the top window without blinking. Én'nish was not inside for long.

She swung out, scrambling to the inn's top, and came at an open run to leap across to the adjoining roof. Dänvârfij's stomach turned hollow.

"Empty!" Én'nish related. "Everything is gone. Not even a blanket re-mains."

Dänvârfij dropped to her haunches, chin on her knees as she stared at the window. Brot'ân'duivé had again slipped out of reach, somewhere beyond the next shadow . . . and the next.

Magiere busily helped Osha and Leanâlhâm set up their new quarters on the east side of what Brot'an had called the Graylands Empire. Chap merely climbed on a bed and lay watching the room's door. Magiere still wasn't certain if Brot'an and Leesil had been merely cautious or outright paranoid in changing locations. But looking about, she found little cause to com-plain.

This room was larger and possibly had been two rooms joined into one at some time. A hearth with an iron hook rod for cooking food and two good-sized beds helped fill the space. There was a stout table, along with several chairs.

So, they had all they needed for the time being. Still, Magiere kept trying to find something to do, anything to keep from glancing at the door again as some sound drifted up from the inn's common room.

And Leesil still didn't come.

He and Brot'an should've gotten Wynn and arrived by now. So many things could've gone wrong, even beyond what she imagined. Chap seemed no less worried. More than once, he got up and went to the window, rising on his hind legs and placing his forepaws on the sill to look out. He always gave up and returned to the bed—except for the last time, when his ears straightened up, and he went to sniff at the door.

"Soon!" Osha said too sharply.

Magiere was not the only one that Chap was making more anxious.

"Come," Osha said, looking to Magiere and then Leanâlhâm. "We make tea."

He picked up a chipped water pitcher and headed for the charred teapot near the hearth.

Chap's ears suddenly rose and stiffened again, and he was up on all fours atop the bed. Magiere almost snapped at him, and then the door did open.

Leesil stepped in, leaving the door wide.

Magiere took a rushed step toward him but halted as Wynn stepped in with Brot'an right behind her. Magiere almost collapsed in relief. Of course Leesil had succeeded. If he knew anything, it was how to sneak about without getting caught . . . most of the time.

"Magiere!" Wynn cried, running at her. "Chap!"

Magiere didn't even finish returning Wynn's slamming hug before the little sage rushed away and nearly threw herself on top of Chap. But as Wynn rolled off Chap and sat up on the bed's edge, her small mouth gaped.

"Leanâlhâm?" she whispered. "Osha?"

Osha met Wynn's gaze, and whispered back, "You are . . . well."

The relief in his voice was unmistakable, like someone discovering a wound had healed instantly. The whole room filled with tension all over again, not that Osha noticed as he stared into Wynn's wide brown eyes.

Magiere wanted to groan. Those two had unsettled issues between them, which she'd hoped would remain so, and then she noticed Leanâlhâm.

At Wynn's arrival, Leanâlhâm's eyes had brightened for the first time since her arrival with Brot'an. She'd taken only one step to go greet Wynn when everyone heard Osha's whisper.

Leanâlhâm instantly halted and looked across at Osha, who still watched Wynn. The girl's features went slack. She dropped her gaze, averted her eyes, and backed away.

Magiere had no time to wonder at this, though the girl's reaction worried her. What mattered was that Leesil was all right, and that he'd managed to get Wynn back. But when Leesil turned to shut the door, for some reason he didn't turn around again. Magiere went over, stepping in at his side and reaching for him. Before she touched his arm, he pulled down his face wrap.

His features were strained and tight, as if he held in something awful. His expression changed even more. He didn't look at Magiere, but she'd seen that kind of anger in him before. The kind that went so far that it turned him focused and chilled to the point of frightening.

Magiere gripped his arm, drawing closer to him. "What is it?"

Finally, he held her eyes with his own. When he answered, the words were loud enough for all to hear.

"I saw Chane in there . . . inside Wynn's guild."

CHAPTER 19

Chap tensed on the bed as Leesil spoke those words.

Wynn turned toward where Leesil stood by the door, his back still turned, and it was only Magiere's steady glare that waited for the sage. Chap knew Magiere was an instant away from open rage.

A small part of him almost wished to let the foolish little sage face such a consequence. Even in their scant time together a few nights ago, he had seen the change in Wynn since their journey here from the Farlands. She was serious, more in control, perhaps even a little hardened. Most of her wide-eyed wonder and naive curiosity had grown faint. Her wispy, light brown hair was a mess, and her pretty, olive-toned features were unreadable.

And Chap still grew angry with her.

What does Leesil mean?

Wynn twitched at his voice in her head and turned her face toward him, but she was silent, perhaps trying to decide how to answer. Before, whenever Wynn was cornered into an admission about Chane, her expression would be awash with guilt and shame—and sometimes defiance. A rush of words would always follow as she tried to defend herself.

Not this time. She said nothing.

"What do you . . ." Magiere began, and then looked at Leesil. "Was he with her?"

"He was looking for her," Leesil answered, now turning about to eye Wynn. "I'd bet my life on it. Wasn't he?"

"Yes," Wynn answered.

"You knew!" Magiere accused, both her hands clenched into fists. "You knew he was coming for you."

Osha stared at Wynn, and Chap saw a frown begin to crease the young elf's brow. Unlike Magiere and Leesil, his expression turned sad. Leanâlhâm's eyes kept flicking back and forth between everyone in startled confusion.

Chap did not want an open fight to play out in front of either of the young ones, but this matter was getting worse by the moment, and Wynn's reasoning was in serious question.

"Who is this Chane?" Brot'an cut in, clearly unsettled by the turn this night had taken.

Leesil jerked the scarf from his neck, unraveling its folds around his head.

"A killer," he snarled. "A so-called Noble Dead . . . a vampire."

"Not anymore," Wynn said.

"Could he be the one that Chap sensed while he searched for the other majay-hì?" Brot'an asked.

At that, Chap lost track of all else.

Where is my daughter? Why is she not with you?

Wynn turned her head slightly. "She's with him."

Chap lost hold of his own anger.

You put my daughter in the company of that . . . thing?

"Who is with who?" Magiere demanded.

"Shade . . . is with Chane," Wynn answered quietly. "He's been helping her to protect me since last autumn."

Osha now looked almost as unhappy as Leesil.

"Chane . . . he is . . . ?" Osha began, but faltered, perhaps not knowing the right words in Belaskian. With an exasperated exhale, he continued in Old Elvish. "Was he the tall one in the castle? The one attacking us with those mad monks?"

Neither Leesil nor Magiere would understand him, but Chap did, as well as Wynn. She didn't look at Osha or answer him. She didn't need to.

Magiere took a step toward Wynn. "There's an undead loose in the city, and you didn't *tell* us."

"I didn't have time," Wynn answered, standing to face her. "And I told him to stay away from you."

"You told him . . . ?" Magiere choked on her words.

Chap saw her irises enlarge, turning black, and he glanced at Leesil with a huff of warning.

Leesil put a hand on Magiere's shoulder and whispered, "Easy."

The room fell silent.

Chap did not know what to think. It seemed Chane had been with Wynn—and Shade—for nearly half a year, so he must have gone to . . .

He was with you in that lost dwarven stronghold.

"Yes," Wynn answered aloud.

Chap saw hints of the old Wynn in her face—lonely, lost, and uncertain.

"I had to find the next orb," she continued, still facing Magiere. "I couldn't travel alone, and Shade wasn't enough protection. Chane is . . . He is more than . . . He is nothing like what you remember."

This was the wrong thing to say to Magiere. Even Chap suddenly lost his anger as Magiere wrenched free of Leesil's grasp.

"Nothing like?" she said right into Wynn's face. "No more killing to feed . . . or just for the pleasure of it?" Her voice lowered to a threatening growl. "And what do you think it took for him to reach you again? How many died along the way for him to cross an ocean and a whole continent alone? How many men, women . . . even children—"

"No." Wynn shook her head.

"You couldn't count them for that distance! You couldn't even imagine it."

Wynn shrank back, looking into Magiere's suddenly glistening face. Chap stood poised to lunge into Magiere, who was visibly shuddering before Wynn.

"This time I'll see his ashes," Magiere whispered, "after I take his head a second time."

"Enough!" Leesil shouted, and he grabbed Magiere, wrenching her away.

Magiere spun away, unable to look at Wynn anymore. She bit down, clamping her jaws hard against the hunger that her rage called up. Of all the things Wynn had done, of the foolish choices she'd ever made, harboring that monster was too much. Magiere stood facing the wall, trying to hold on to reason.

"Get it under control," Leesil whispered in her ear. *"Now!"*

She was trying, but all she could think of was that undead—that thing called Chane—who had come at her and those she loved more than once. Now he was here . . . again because of Wynn. She couldn't stop shaking, even as she tried to focus on breathing and nothing more. And as she half turned from the wall, she saw large, slanted green eyes in a young, frightened, tanned face.

Leanâlhâm stood only a few steps to Magiere's left, and the girl was watching only her. The girl didn't belong in the middle of all this. After what she'd likely seen in Brot'an's company, what she'd seen earlier this night . . .

Magiere shriveled inside at the way Leanâlhâm looked at her. She turned away and buried her face in the crook of Leesil's neck. She had to stop this, to find any way to let go of all the anger Wynn caused. She felt Leesil's hands grip her upper arms, holding her there. His grip suddenly tightened, and she heard him whisper.

"Leanâlhâm . . . no, don't!"

Magiere stiffened and flinched at another touch upon her back.

"Is the wound . . . not truly healed?" Leanâlhâm asked softly.

There was no way the girl could think that what she'd seen was caused by a wound. Not even a scar remained on Magiere's thigh for how it had been willfully closed. And that small hand on Magiere's back pressed flat and firm.

"Are you . . . *ill* . . . again?" Leanâlhâm asked.

The lie in the girl's question, so blindly forgiving, was too much to bear. Magiere still couldn't look at Leanâlhâm, though her hunger vanished.

"She's all right. . . . She'll be fine," Leesil lied, as well.

"No matter what you think," Wynn suddenly said, "I *had* to reach the orb. You, of all of us, should understand that, Magiere."

Leanâlhâm's hand remained as Magiere turned her head to look at Wynn.

Chap could not guess what Wynn had been through and that still needed to be uncovered. But it changed little where an undead was concerned.

"That's all that matters now—gaining the rest of them," Wynn continued, "before the Enemy's minions do so. And if not for Shade—and Chane—I would've been dead . . . more than twice."

"How could you accept protection from *him*?" Magiere returned.

"Because you weren't there!" Wynn answered, her voice quavering slightly, and she looked at Leesil and then Chap. "None of you. You left me, and I had to reach the next orb once I discovered there was more than one."

In spite of Wynn's accusation, Chap's anger did not fade.

Chane had murdered countless people to sustain himself . . . or, as Magiere said, for the pleasure of the kill. He had helped Welstiel slaughter a remote outpost of healer monks, turning some of them into feral vampires. He had helped burn to death a ship of the elves, and perhaps was the one responsible for throwing a female an'Cróan hostage over the side as a diversion. He had tracked Magiere to the Pock Peaks and fought at Welstiel's side, even if he had betrayed Welstiel in the end.

Now Wynn had induced Chap's daughter to accept the company of that sadistic undead.

Chap would not allow this.

There was no excuse, no reason, that Wynn could give that would keep Chap from finishing Chane the instant the chance came. But his anger over these transgressions was cut cold by one question.

"What next . . . *orb*?" Brot'an asked quietly.

Chap's fear of discussing anything in front of these elves doubled. Brot'an knew only what Wynn had foolishly written in a journal that she'd sent off with Osha on the young elf's return to his homeland. Oh yes, Chap knew of that journal, though by what he had gleaned from Wynn's memories, it had not been specific regarding what they had found. There was only a reference to an "artifact."

Chap huffed twice at Magiere with a clack of his jaws and then turned on Wynn with a snarl.

We will speak of this later. Brot'an knows too much as is . . . because of you!

Wynn flinched but ignored him, and stepped closer to Magiere.

"There are more important things at stake than your hatred for the undead," Wynn insisted. "Chane retrieved a scroll from that castle, the very one Li'kän was trying to get me to read. Without Chane, we'd all be stumbling blindly about, more clueless than the Enemy's minions!"

Chap growled and snapped his jaws more loudly this time.

"Don't make excuses," Magiere shot back. "He *is* one of the Enemy's minions. You, of all people, know that!"

Chap glanced sidelong at Brot'an, who remained fixed on the two women. What would it take to keep these two quiet? And if Wynn kept this up, Magiere's calm might break again.

"The scroll has the only hints to finding all five orbs!" Wynn argued.

That pushed Chap over the edge, and he lunged off the bed, snarling at both of them. There seemed nothing to be done short of biting one of them, though all he did was snap and snarl.

Wynn, enough!

But Wynn's words finally caught Magiere, as well. "He took a scroll from the castle? Did you know when we left that place? What else have you been holding back?"

"I didn't know until he found me here in Calm Seatt," Wynn countered. "When you arrived, I didn't have time to tell you before we got separated."

"Tell us where he is," Leesil ordered, "before he kills again."

Wynn stared at him as if he were a stranger.

Chap did not know what to do to keep this from escalating further. He agreed with Leesil, but the secrets Wynn was spilling had gone too far—much too far.

"Where is this scroll?" Brot'an asked, his voice still quiet.

Wynn glanced his way, as if really seeing him for the first time. "What are you doing here? What are any of you doing this far from your homeland?"

"Protecting Magiere," Brot'an answered. "Protecting the . . . orb she has from Most Aged Father."

Wynn studied him. "Truly . . . you're here to help us?"

"Yes."

Chap turned his rumbling toward Brot'an, but when he looked back, the expression of finality on Wynn's face terrified him.

"Good," she said. "Chane has the scroll."

Wynn, shut your mouth!

"No," she said flatly, looking down at him. "We're in no position to ignore any help we can get—from *anyone*—and that includes someone as experienced and skillful as Brot'an."

She glanced over at Leesil, who was no more pleased than Chap.

"But not from *anyone* who isn't honestly trying to help," she added.

Leesil's eyes brightened with some of Magiere's fury, but before he could respond, Wynn pulled up her hood and drew her cloak around herself.

"I'm going to Shade . . . and Chane," she added. "If we're to locate the remaining orbs, we need that scroll, and we need both of them."

"No, you're not," Leesil said, and he stepped in her way before Magiere could make a move.

"Yes, she is," Brot'an said.

Chap stood stiff. He was not fooled by the butcher's willingness to help, and he did not need to wait to catch any of Brot'an's well-hidden memories. This was a ruse, another twist and manipulation, like the one Brot'an had used in a final moment to get Leesil to kill Lord Darmouth.

As soon as the shadow-gripper learned what he needed, he would go after the other orbs himself—alone. The worst part was that Chap still needed to learn the same for himself, and Wynn had hidden that knowledge with Chane.

And worse, the last thing he needed was Brot'an and Leesil assaulting each other, forcing all present to take sides.

"I will keep her safe," Brot'an added. "Léshil, you must accept that she is right . . . in this, at least. If there are more of these artifacts, and Most Aged Father and his agents do not know of them yet, it must remain so. That is the purpose here that comes before all personal issues."

Chap had his own concerns, and he closed on Wynn.

I am going with you, as well.

She looked down at him in surprise, and then sudden relief, but that expression quickly vanished, replaced by suspicion.

"Only if you mean to help," she said.

It was not a request . . . and you are not going alone with Brot'an.

She crouched down, leaning in close to whisper in his ear.

"We need Chane on this. If you hurt him, Shade won't be the only one unable to forgive you."

He could not believe what he heard. But neither could he let her leave without him. This was not the Wynn he knew.

She rose and turned to Leesil and Magiere. "I'm sorry you're angry, but there is no time for more explanations . . . ones you wouldn't accept, anyway."

Leesil shook his head and looked away.

"Just go," Magiere breathed.

Something had broken between those three, and Chap doubted it would ever be mended. And though he hated to admit it, Wynn was correct about one thing.

What mattered most was gaining the orbs. That took precedence over outrage . . . and betrayal.

Osha and Leanâlhâm still watched in quiet confusion, though for Osha there was also pain in his long features. Chap thought Wynn might go to him, for the way she looked at him, almost longingly, with equal sadness over not having seen him in so long.

But then Wynn turned quickly and left. Chap waited just long enough to trail Brot'an out the door.

After walking away from Sykion and High-Tower, Rodian felt an unwanted wave of exhaustion. He tried to remember the last time he'd slept.

As he made his way toward the gatehouse tunnel, he saw Corporal Lúcan at the far end, standing before the portcullis beams. In the last day and night, the corporal hadn't looked much better than Rodian himself felt, and four of their comrades were now recovering in the guild's hospice. He paused near the small tower that contained the gatehouse's mechanics.

"Lúcan," he called out. "I'll have the portcullis up in a moment. Ride back to the barracks and tell Branwell to gather four men and come relieve us. Then you get some sleep."

"Yes, sir."

After Rodian reached the gear room, he gave his orders. By the time he returned to the courtyard, Lúcan was gone. Events of the evening rolled through his mind, and he wondered what would come next with the dawn. Would Sykion come at him with some unexplained charge against Wynn? Would he finally get any hint as to what was actually going on here?

His thoughts wandered too much as time passed quickly. He heard horses' hooves and headed down the gatehouse tunnel to the open portcullis. There had been little point to closing it until reinforcements arrived.

Branwell came riding through the bailey gate, followed by four men. The lieutenant dismounted and strode up to face Rodian. He held out a folded piece of paper with a royal seal.

"I was told to give you this immediately, sir."

Something in Branwell's voice sounded a little too satisfied. With reluctance, Rodian took the message and broke the wax seal.

It was a summons to the royal castle.

* * *

"Owain is dead, and you took no prisoners?" Fréthfàre asked from her chair.

Dänvârfij had no illusions about this moment, now that she had returned and begun her report. They had gone back for Owain's body. It now lay in the room's corner, wrapped in a scavenged blanket and spare cord and awaiting rites. Dänvârfij did not know how that would be accomplished here in this stinking human city. Fréthfàre would use tonight's failure to her own advantage, feeding her own hunger for vengeance as well as seizing more control over their purpose.

The room felt small and hot, though the fire had gone out. Rhysís, Én'nish, and Eywodan stood in uncomfortable silence.

"Where is Tavithê?" Fréthfàre continued, resting her head against the chair's tall back and looking down her nose.

"Still on watch at the port," Dänvârfij confirmed.

"So . . . we are six now and have not a thing to show for it."

Dänvârfij nodded, though only five were of active use. In the rest, Fréthfàre was not wrong. This mission had been a slowly escalating set of failures since the beginning, as Brot'ân'duivé shadowed them across the world, picking them off one by one. While Fréthfàre had made most decisions along the way, this night's failure—and loss—rested on Dänvârfij alone.

Even with their numbers so diminished, the success of their purpose was all that mattered. She braced herself, not wishing to allow Fréthfàre any more of this self-righteous indulgence.

"We need to disperse and relocate our quarry," Dänvârfij said, ignoring Fréthfàre's last accusation. "And we cannot discount the guild. We cannot confirm whether they freed the sage."

Her focused tone had the desired effect, drawing attention from Rhysís and Eywodan and even Én'nish. All appeared to welcome the prospect of new orders. None of them wished to stand here with Owain's body lying only a few steps away and yet so far from their people's ancestors. They would have no more idea how to address that than she did. But at least Owain would not be found by humans, and his weapons and belongings were safe among his own caste.

"Rhysís and I will watch the guild," Dänvârfij continued. "For now, Tavithê remains on the port watch. Én'nish and Eywodan will begin covering areas with public lodging. Sweep the streets, as well, but keep hidden as much as possible. We will locate our quarry by process of elimination."

"Should we not report?" Fréthfâre asked. "Most Aged Father will want to know our status. I'm sure I could manage to make my way out of the city to the nearest free trees."

Dänvârfij glanced down at the crippled ex-Covârleasa. This was another problem they rarely spoke about.

The Shapers among their people had not produced any new word-wood for the Anmaglâhk, specifically made from Most Aged Father's own tree home, so that his caste could communicate with him. Not one new word-wood had been finished since the death of the healer named Gleannéohkân'thva, leaving only one member of Sgäilsheilleache's family: Leanâlhâm.

Word-wood was in short supply, so their group possessed only two. Dänvârfij had one, and Fréthfâre the other.

"It would be best if you remained here," Dänvârfij said. "I will report to Most Aged Father at the first opportunity."

Fréthfâre studied her for a moment. "Be sure you do."

Chane paced his room at Nattie's inn, uncertain what to do with himself. Shade lay near the door, and Ore-Locks stood restlessly nearby, likely wondering if he was still needed or if he should return to Dhredze Seatt.

Chane did not know the answer.

Ore-Locks shifted his weight for the fourth time, his expression thoughtful. "Where do you think those Lhoin'na might have taken her?"

"They are not Lhoin'na," Chane answered. "They are an'Cróan, a separate elven people from—"

Shade leaped to her feet, whining and wriggling as she rushed the door. Almost instantly, Chane heard a soft knock outside.

"Chane, it's me."

Even via a whisper through the door, he knew Wynn's voice. Nearly sick with relief that she'd managed to come somehow, Chane rushed the door as Shade scooted out of the way. When he jerked the door open, he did not have long to look upon Wynn. His gaze rose above her head, and he tensed.

Behind her stood someone incredibly tall and too broad-shouldered for his frame. Chane recognized that one's clothing, for it was the same elf who had been with Leesil inside the guild's keep. Now there was no face wrap inside the cloak's deep hood. Lighter-colored scars in dark skin skipped over the elder an'Cróan's left eye.

A canine head thrust forward around Wynn's hip to snarl at Chane.

"Enough of that," Wynn said, not even looking down at Chap.

Before Chane could move or speak, Shade tried pushing past him to get to Wynn. She stopped short at the sight of the tall, silver-gray dog in the hallway. Chane knew exactly how Shade felt.

How could Wynn expose them like this? And how could she bring Chap anywhere near him?

Shade began to rumble.

"No family squabbles, either!" Wynn ordered.

Shade went quiet, but Chane focused again on the tall stranger . . . who was watching him in turn. The man's face was still and emotionless, with eyes that never blinked.

"This is Brot'an," Wynn said. "I promise it's all right."

Chane backed slowly out of the way.

Wynn hurried inside, pulling Shade with her. She dropped to the floor at the room's center and gathered the dog in her arms.

"I missed you so much," she said, and then looked up at Chane. "And you."

At the moment, it humiliated Chane how much she affected him with two simple words. He stepped aside against the room's wall, allowing the tall elf and Chap inside his room.

Ore-Locks stood watching all of this, though he had retrieved his iron staff and rested it on the floor in his hand.

"Brot'an . . . Ore-Locks," Wynn said in gesturing to each.

"Yes, we almost met a short while ago," Ore-Locks replied, and the tall elf nodded politely.

"Wynn, what are they doing here?" Chane asked.

Chap had not settled and still rumbled slightly with each breath. The fur on the back of his neck bristled, but he kept looking between Chane *and* Shade. Shade shifted around Wynn's other side, placing Wynn between herself and Chap.

That action left Chane wondering why. Was not Chap her sire?

"We need them," Wynn answered.

Chane found her watching him purposefully.

"And they need us," she continued, stroking Shade's back one last time. "Lines are being drawn and may result in some unexpected alliances. You have the scroll?"

The question stunned him. "Wynn?"

"They know about the scroll," she told him, "and I meant what I said. If we're to locate the final orbs, we have to accept any allies with skills who can help. Both Chap and Brot'an have . . . skills that are more than useful."

Chane had already made up his mind to put his faith in her, but he had never imagined this. With Chap here, why had not Leesil and Magiere come at him, or had Wynn managed to keep his location secret from them until now? He glanced once at Chap, who bared his teeth slightly.

If Wynn wanted him to work with Chap and this elf, what could he say?

"We may have one more," Chane said.

"One more what?"

"Ally . . . at the guild . . . perhaps."

Wynn blinked, and Chane watched a flicker of hope instantly fade to worry upon her face.

"You mean Nikolas?"

"No. Premin Hawes."

Wynn looked at him as if he were out of his mind, for Hawes was part of the council that had caused all of this trouble for her.

Ore-Locks added, "She told us if you needed help, we could send her word. When she spoke, I believed her."

"As did I," Chane added.

Wynn sat upright, as if panicked. But then, trembling, she sank back to kneel beside Shade. Chane could see her hesitation, followed by hope.

"All right. If we have Hawes, that changes some things," Wynn said.

"Who is this Hawes?" Brot'an asked.

"A premin of metaology, highly placed in my guild," Wynn answered, looking at him, "with access to . . . resources I can no longer get near. She can help us—me—with translating the rest of the scroll."

Chane did not care for her familiarity with this an'Cróan. She obviously knew him from before this night.

Wynn suddenly winced and held up one hand. "Chap, stop! Too fast. I don't know. . . . We'll need to get her a message."

Chap was fully focused on Wynn, and Shade snarled at him.

Chane stepped rapidly to Wynn, and Chap's focus shifted instantly to him.

"What is happening?" Chane asked.

"Chap wants to know how we'll contact Hawes," Wynn answered, rubbing her temple. "He has . . . many questions. Too many at once."

Wynn had told Chane about this odd method of communication, how Chap's mental voice was far more sophisticated and direct than Shade's. Chane did not like hearing only one side of the conversation where Chap was concerned.

"He's not wrong," Wynn continued. "If we are to find the last two orbs, we must get the rest of the poem translated."

"Last two?" Ore-Locks asked sharply. "You mean last three."

Wynn winced again. "Chap, stop it!"

She put her palm on the floor to support herself. Shade ducked around Wynn, growling in Chap's face, and of all unexpected things, Chap flinched.

Chane felt almost completely in the dark as to what was going on here—and he did not like that, either.

Wynn pushed Shade back and spoke directly to Chap. "They need to know!" She then looked up at Chane. "Magiere, Leesil, and Chap recovered a third orb in the northern wastes. Chap has hidden it . . . along with the orb of Water."

That made no sense at all, for Chane had seen the first orb in the ice-bound castle. How could a majay-hì hide two, each so large that even he or Ore-Locks would have difficulty carrying one? The dog could not have dragged two off on his own.

"That leaves two for us to find," Wynn said. "We have to locate them as quickly as possible."

No one spoke for a moment.

Chane was uncertain how to feel at this abrupt knowledge, but in truth, the news was not unwelcome. If a third orb had been recovered, then Magiere, Leesil, and Chap *had* proven themselves useful. He had imagined himself, Wynn, and Shade having to find the last three—with all three endeavors placing Wynn in growing danger. He could not care less what became of Magiere, Leesil, or Chap, but perhaps Wynn was correct. Their assistance might end this dangerous exploit more quickly, and keep Wynn a little farther out of harm's way.

"Then we need to contact this Hawes," Brot'an said. "I assume she wishes to keep her willingness to help a secret?"

"Yes," Chane answered. "We cannot risk exposing her, or she can do nothing."

"I may know a way," Wynn said, though her brow creased. "Nikolas has a friend at the Upright Quill, and I believe that shop is still delivering work to the guild. If this friend can get a message to Nikolas, he can get it to Hawes."

She stood up with an expression of firm purpose. "Chane, do you have some paper?"

"You are not considering going yourself?" he asked, incredulous.

"Why not?"

"Because half the city guard could be looking for you! Or me . . . or

Shade. She was the distraction, right in front of the guild, that let Ore-Locks and me get inside."

Chane could feel an argument coming and braced himself.

"No one saw me," Ore-Locks said quietly. "I will take the message."

"What?" Wynn turned to him.

"No one but the premin saw me," Ore-Locks continued. "My people are common enough here that few would give me notice. I am the only choice among us." He looked at Brot'an. "I believe you would stand out, and up, far too much. No offense intended."

"No offense at all," the elf answered. "It is sensible."

Chane studied Brot'an. Though he would never trust this stranger, the tall elf appeared to lean toward the side of reason. That counted for something.

"Then it is settled," Chane said.

Wynn sighed. "Very well."

Once again, Rodian waited in the luxurious sitting room at the royal castle, with its walnut-legged couches and dyed silks of shimmering seafoam green and cyan. Upon arrival earlier, two of the Weardas had escorted him here and then left. The double doors were closed, and he was alone.

Although worried—perhaps more than worried—he refused to leap to conclusions. Sykion couldn't have sent word this quickly, so the summons couldn't possibly involve this night's events. Yet here he was.

The double doors opened.

Captain Tristan stood in the opening. "His highness, Prince Leäfrich Âreskynna."

Rodian refrained from a whispered expletive. He would be forced to deal with the prince again, at least in part, depending on who else might appear. His discomfort grew as Prince Leäfrich strode in by himself, without his sister, Âthelthryth, a white-robed elf, or even Duchess Reine. Dressed in loose breeches and an untucked linen shirt, the prince halted before Rodian and then glanced back.

"Close the doors," he ordered.

Tristan backed out and obeyed, leaving Rodian alone with Leäfrich.

"We were informed of trouble at the guild," the prince said without pre-amble.

Rodian hesitated, not entirely certain what had been related. "If I may ask, by whom?"

"You may not. Explain yourself."

The discomfort growing in Rodian's chest turned to wariness. "There was an infiltration, possibly from several points of entrance. Four of my men were injured, but not critically. Journeyor Hygeorht escaped."

"You mean she was taken? You allowed one of our sages to be abducted."

Of all the ambushes Rodian had considered, this was not one of them.

"No, highness," he replied. "She had been locked up, illegally, by the Pre-min Council, and she took part in her own escape."

"She was stolen from her home, and you allowed it," the prince retorted. "You will begin a search immediately. You will put every able Shyldfälche into the streets, and you *will* recover her."

Therein was the slip—"recover," not "rescue."

"And if I locate the journeyor and she does not wish to go back?" Rodian asked.

"Your duty is to recover her." Leäfrich came closer. "I do not see how I can make myself clearer."

The skin over his narrow features was pale, and there were dark circles under his eyes.

"Your fitness of duty is now in question," the prince continued, "and you are being given one chance to answer for your negligence."

Rodian stiffened, but his reaction came from more than just the threat. No one of the royal family had ever spoken to him like this. Perhaps his secret ambitions had crept too high at times, but he was still the commander of Shyldfälches.

"Pardon, highness," he said slowly. "But I would like to know how Prin-cess Âthelthryth or your father prefer this matter to be handled. I am accustomed to taking orders from them, and as this issue involves the guild, either the king or the heir should be informed."

"What makes you assume they are not?" Leäfrich asked quietly. "My father is unwell, and my sister is at his side. They are kept fully informed, and at present I carry out their wishes. I have the power to rescind appointments at the highest levels until they say otherwise."

Leäfrich paused, no doubt to let his last statement sink in. "You allowed one of our sages to be stolen from her bed. If she is not safely recovered within four days, I will put Lieutenant Branwell in charge of the search."

Rodian was careful not to let his expression betray him, though his stomach rolled.

"Find her." Leäfrich said, and then strode for the doors. "Tristan!"

The doors opened, and the prince exited without slowing. The captain of the Weardas stood waiting, his hand still on one door's handle. But Rodian stared after the prince until Leäfrich was gone from sight.

Sworn oaths or not, one thing had been made crystal clear: Rodian had no choice but to hunt down Wynn Hygeorht. He hated this tangled web more than he'd hated anything in life. Nearly dropping from exhaustion, he realized how badly he needed sleep.

As he started for the doors, several memories nagged him. He knew he couldn't rest until he'd checked the one place where Wynn had commonly been found in the past whenever there was trouble.

CHAPTER 20

Pawl wasn't ready to go home, so he stopped by his shop. The Upright Quill was long closed up, all of his employees gone home, and he unlocked the front door and stepped inside.

In his mind's eye, he still saw the strangely dark-skinned elven archer, dead and broken against a rooftop chimney, as Wynn Hygeorht fled the guild with two highly skilled infiltrators.

But how was any of this connected to the translation project?

He paused in the dark at the front counter, distracted by a stack of recently scribed pages awaiting approval. Teagan should've seen to those before closing, but the old scribe master had been suffering from sniffles and chills the past few days. Perhaps that had worsened.

Pawl reached for the top sheet. His hand stopped, fingers poised above the stack. He raised his eyes first, then his head, peering about in the dark shop.

It was past the midnight bell, yet he felt something . . . alive. Stepping back, he turned sideways and glanced at the nearest of the two windows, one to each side of the front door.

Faint light from some outer street lantern seeped through cracks of the left-side inner shutters, but he sensed nothing nearby outside. Quietly, he flipped the counter's hinged section, stepped behind it, and then pushed through the swinging doors into the large back workroom.

Weak light glowed from the workroom's left side, and he walked past tables and stools to the back of the room. Glancing toward the one oil lantern still lit and nearly out of fuel, he found Imaret. She was fast asleep on a high stool, her head resting on her arms atop a small pile of papers on her slanted scribing desk.

Pawl stepped closer, hovering over the small girl left alone in his shop.

What was she doing here so late, and why hadn't Teagan seen her home? The situation was not only annoying and against his rules but unsafe should Imaret wake and head home alone. There were lurkers in the city like none he could remember. Some watched the guild, waiting to murder.

Yet Imaret, like Nikolas, was still foolish enough to . . .

Centuries had come and gone—so many that Pawl couldn't remember exactly when he'd last foolishly become concerned beyond necessity with any mortal. Even those few were now fragments, barely clearer than his oldest memories.

An old, one-legged sailor relegated to tending a secondhand shop . . .

Some pompous princeling too eager to flee his family's disinterest . . .

A dog so obsessed with protecting its owner's property and family that even after the home was abandoned, it still stood guard . . .

A woman of insane wisdom . . . a vicious elven priest among the trees . . . a slave from a distant land, a brigand, a village elder, a would-be tyrant . . .

And now a child scribe of singular talent, and a young sage touched too soon by death.

Pawl could not truly remember his mother or father. They were but faint, blurred images in his mind. He didn't remember if he'd had siblings, let alone been the elder brother of a younger sister. But had he been Imaret's brother, he would have already come hammering upon the shop door, looking for her.

Still, Pawl grew angry with himself.

This was his city, his territory, and all within it were fixtures of that setting, their necessity varying by degrees. All were impermanent—everything was impermanent but him. All else passed, leaving only loss. Even when memory of loss alone decayed over time, it left another sense of loss, knowing *something* had been forgotten.

He could not endure more such attachments.

"Imaret," he said, and then louder when she did not stir. "Imaret!"

She opened her eyes, blinked, and rolled her head to look up at him.

"Master?" she whispered.

"What are you doing here?"

She sat up too quickly, teetering for an instant atop the stool, and then looked about as if uncertain where she was.

"I . . . I wanted to finish this," she stuttered, and picked up the top sheet on her desk.

Pawl did not take it, though he saw what it was: a moon's-end report for the accountant who often patronized the shop. The fastidious outsider always requested Imaret to do the transcription. Though she had no extraordinary talent for numbers, it didn't matter; one sound read of the characters on a page and she could duplicate them from memory.

"Master Teagan was feeling worse," Imaret rambled on. "I told him I could finish, that it wouldn't take me long, and I'd get home quick enough before dark, but I . . . must've dozed off . . . didn't hear the bells."

"Your parents will be worried," Pawl returned, "if they haven't come looking for you already and you didn't hear them knocking. I will be the one to answer for this."

"No, you don't need to . . . I mean, yes, you should take me home, but you don't need to explain anything. They won't . . . be worried."

Her gaze shifted nervously away and she blinked again.

This was the second time the girl alluded to something wrong at home. Pawl had far too much on his mind, with no wish to be entangled in the personal affairs of his employees. But still . . .

"What's wrong?" he asked.

Imaret remained quiet for a moment. Pawl folded his arms as she purposefully avoided meeting his eyes.

"Early this winter," she began quietly, "we found out that Mama was going to have another baby. The three of us were so happy. . . . But she's not young, and something happened. She lost the baby this last new moon. She was sad for some days, and then more days, and then she didn't get out of bed anymore."

Imaret sniffed before going on.

"Papa tries to make it better. That's all he does now, but it doesn't help. No one cooks food anymore . . . no one knows when I'm there . . . or not there."

Pawl remained perfectly still and silent. Rationally, he should say nothing at all, for this was not his burden as long as Imaret remained functional in his shop. But still . . .

"I am older than you think," he began. "I have seen such things before. It may improve."

She tilted her head to one side, peering up at him. "You think?"

"Perhaps." He paused, trying to find a comparison. "Like a sharp paper cut when you are handling freshly trimmed sheets, the wound is quick and startling. The pain lingers long after. But with enough time, it is nothing but scar and memory, and even . . ."

He stalled a bit too long. "And even these can fade . . . with time."

Imaret appeared somewhat consoled, though his words were certainly no answer for a parent's neglect. They were all that Pawl could offer without becoming more involved. She climbed off the high stool, prepared to leave before he had even said so.

"What time is it?" Imaret asked.

"Past midnight. Set your quills and brushes to soak. Your parents may be more worried than you assume."

She scurried about cleaning up her desk, and Pawl waited in silence. She had just set to cleaning her quill heads when a knock carried from the shop's front room. Imaret turned, one quill still in hand.

"Who could that be?" she whispered.

Pawl glanced down to find her right behind him, peeking around his leg.

"Wait here," he instructed.

He grabbed the dimming lantern off its hook before heading out to the shop's front. That anyone came knocking so late was unusual, more so if expecting to find anyone on the premises. Such conditions rarely meant anything good waited outside, and he opened the front door, ready to demand an explanation.

Pawl stopped before a word escaped.

A cloaked dwarf carrying a stout iron staff stood outside, looking up at Pawl with a frown. He was clean-shaven—unusual for a male dwarf—and something about his features and red hair brought Domin High-Tower to Pawl's mind, though this one's hair was not shot with steel gray.

"We are closed," Pawl said coldly. "Come back during the business day."

"You are Master a'Seatt?" the dwarf asked, and when Pawl didn't answer, he went on in a low voice. "I have a private message for you concerning one of your scribes."

Again, Pawl hesitated, glancing along the street at all the shops, now dark and shuttered for the night. It was doubtful this had to do with Imaret's tardiness and parents, yet the coincidence bothered him. Still, it was only a dwarf, and he stepped back to let the visitor inside. Before he could even close the front door, he heard the swinging doors behind the counter.

Imaret emerged from the back room, disregarding his instructions, and peered over the top of the counter. Perhaps she thought it might be Nikolas, though it was far too late for even one of his visits. To heighten Pawl's wariness, the dwarf fixed on Imaret's dusky young face and dark, kinky hair curling in all directions.

"Are you Imaret?" the dwarf asked.

That captured Pawl's full attention, and he stepped between them. "Who are you?"

The dwarf raised one red eyebrow. "I am here on behalf of Journeyor Wynn Hygeorht. She believes your people might willingly get a message to a Nikolas Columsarn at the guild, who in turn could deliver it to Premin Hawes in private."

"Nikolas!" Imaret gasped.

Pawl raised one finger at her for silence, though he kept his eyes on the dwarf.

"What is in this message?" he asked.

"Simply a request to meet, though Journeyor Hygeorht does not wish this to be known by anyone else. There are difficulties with the guild that she would like . . . solved. Premin Hawes has offered assistance."

Pawl studied him. Difficulties with the guild, solutions and private meetings outside of that place . . . What did it all mean? The one thing he wanted more than anything else was for the translation project, and his attached transcription work, to proceed—for the pieces of those ancient texts to once more flow through his shop. Any difficulties between Wynn Hygeorht and the guild might be linked to the work's halt—or not. Any solution might solve both those impediments—or not. But Pawl was not involving one of his scribes in such subterfuge.

"All that's required is that this message reach Premin Hawes?" he asked.

The dwarf frowned. "Yes, but—"

Another knock sounded, this one much sharper and louder than the first.

Pawl started slightly, sensing another close-by life outside his door. What was going on that his shop should become the center of midnight activity? Suddenly the latch turned and the front door opened, for Pawl had not locked it upon letting in the dwarf.

Captain Rodian stood in the opening, and his gaze shifted away from Pawl at the sight of the dwarf.

"Forgive the late intrusion," the captain said, still not looking back at Pawl. "I did not expect to find you conducting business so late."

"Yet you enter just the same," Pawl returned.

"I stopped by, on the chance you were here, before checking at your residence."

The last implication set Pawl on edge. How did Rodian know where he lived unless the man had checked the commerce records for all shop owners?

Even during the unfortunate business last autumn, Rodian had never set up a meeting at Pawl's home.

The dwarf ignored the captain and looked at Pawl. "May I count on you for this . . . translation?"

He held out a folded paper. One edge was ragged, as if torn off.

Pawl hesitated. If events were to continue as he hoped, then he could not refuse. His shop had worked with Hawes on projects for her various journey-ors. If he visited the guild tomorrow and told the guard at the gate that he needed to see her, even if they kept him waiting at the portcullis, she would come. There was no need to involve Imaret or Nikolas.

Pawl took the folded sheet. "The work will not be completed until tomorrow. You may expect the results after dusk, at a guess, and no sooner."

"My thanks." And as suddenly as the dwarf had appeared, he slipped out and was gone.

"A bit late for a customer," Rodian commented, closing the front door.

"Or for a visit from the Shyldfälches," Pawl countered, and then gestured to Imaret. "One of my scribes worked too late. I need to get her home, so please . . . be brief."

"I am looking for Journeyor Wynn Hygeorht," the captain said.

Pawl slipped beyond suspicion but remained silent. This was one too many synchronicities in one night.

The captain went on. "She was taken from the guild tonight, and in the past, when . . . difficulties have occurred for her, she's been found here more than once. I simply wished to check again. Have you seen her?"

"Taken?" Pawl repeated, ignoring the rest, and then grew angry with himself for sounding so incredulous.

He knew better than to expose any reaction to one such as the captain. From what Pawl had witnessed, Wynn Hygeorht had not been "taken" by anyone. Whether the captain knew so or not was in doubt, but the implication of Rodian's choice of word warned of further complications.

"Have you seen her?" Rodian repeated.

"No."

"What about you, miss?" Rodian asked.

Pawl turned the full intensity of his gaze on Imaret. She in turn glanced more than once between him and the captain.

"No . . . no, I haven't seen Wynn in a long time," Imaret answered.

Rodian nodded and turned to Pawl. "I thought not, but had to check. Don't be alarmed if you see one of my men somewhere outside tomorrow. The royal family is anxious to have the journeyor found and returned safely. So we must cover anywhere she has connections."

Pawl remained outwardly passive at his shop being put under watch. "Of course. Thank you for informing me beforehand."

"And you will let me know if you see her . . . or her dog. You know the one."

"Certainly."

With the superficial exchange concluded, the exhausted-looking captain nodded and headed out the door. As soon as the door shut, Imaret rushed out from behind the counter, straight at Pawl.

"What's going on?"

"I don't know. Now get your cloak, before we are further delayed."

He waited as Imaret scurried off to the workroom, but his thoughts turned to her again. He knew the owner of a local eatery who owed him more than one favor. Tomorrow, he would make arrangements to have cooked meals delivered to Imaret's house each morning until further notice. He made a mental note, as well, to tell Teagan to find some local girl for a maid to visit the home at least once per quarter moon . . . until further notice.

Chap was familiar with the social discomfort observed in humans during awkward silences. However, as a member of the Fay, born into flesh within a majay-hì pup, he had rarely been affected by such.

Yet here in this dark little room, he was in the company of a bloodthirsty monster obsessed with Wynn, his own estranged daughter, and an elven butcher willing to murder his own kind as long as it served his agenda.

How could this not be awkward?

Almost as soon as Ore-Locks had left to the deliver the message, Brot'an dropped to the floor, sitting cross-legged to wait. Was not that what anmaglâhk did—wait as if without care until the moment to strike, always listening . . . watching everything?

The sight did not unsettle Chap. He had expected nothing else, especially from Brot'an. What did unsettle him was the sight of Chane sinking down to sit on the bed's edge, with Wynn joining him, sitting close enough that her shoulder touched his upper arm. Then Shade sidled in against Wynn's outside leg.

The three of them looked so . . . together.

"Chane, hand me the pitcher and basin," Wynn said. The sudden sound of her voice was startling in the silent room.

Chane reached for the chipped basin and a pitcher on the tiny table beside the bed. He handed these to Wynn, who immediately poured water and set the basin on the floor for Shade to lap.

Chap had sent Shade to watch over Wynn, but it appeared the caretaking went both ways.

"Are you thirsty?" Wynn asked.

Chap looked up from watching his daughter and found Wynn watching him.

No, I am . . . fine.

He would have rather shouted into her thoughts, demanding why she sat there next to that *thing* . . . that walking corpse. He wanted to force an explanation from Shade as to why she tolerated this, as well. His daughter was majay-hì; aside from their guardianship of elven lands, their kind protected the living from the undead.

Chap did neither of those things. He feared that if he did, he would receive no answers and only weaken the tentative thread holding all of them together. For Wynn was right about one thing. The lines being drawn here were going to create unexpected, unwanted alliances. No matter how abhorrent, these alliances could not be refused . . . for now.

They all sat in silence, except when Wynn briefly questioned Chane about how he and Ore-Locks had managed to escape the keep. Chane's even shorter answers in his voiceless rasp made Chap's skin crawl beneath his bristling fur. It felt as if more than one night had crawled by when they all heard heavy-booted steps outside the little room's door.

"It is me," a low, deep voice whispered outside.

Chane went to open the door, and Ore-Locks stepped inside.

"Did you find anyone at the shop?" Wynn asked.

"Yes, your Master a'Seatt . . . and the girl," Ore-Locks answered. "I passed on the note, and I think we should hear something by tomorrow night."

Wynn closed her eyes in relief.

"There is more," Ore-Locks went on, his thick red eyebrows scrunching. "That captain, the one with the trimmed beard, stopped by the shop before I left."

Wynn's eyes snapped opened again. "Rodian? What did he want?"

Ore-Locks shook his head. "I left before he did, but thought it worth mentioning."

Wynn looked troubled, but Chap was relieved. With the message delivered, their goal accomplished, this unsavory encounter was at an end.

We have plans to make and things to discuss back at our own quarters. We go . . . and Shade should come, too. She belongs with us.

Wynn looked at him. "You and Brot'an go back. Shade and I are staying here. These *are* our quarters."

Chap jumped to his feet in shock, as if he had not heard her correctly.

Brot'an stood up instantly, looking between them. It appeared he was becoming more adept at knowing when something had passed silently between Chap and another.

"What is happening?" the elf demanded.

"Chap thinks it is time to return to Leesil and Magiere," Wynn related. "He's right, but Shade and I are staying here. In my message to Hawes, I told her to come to me . . . here. You two go back and let the others know what is happening."

Chap could not hold back a snarl. *No! If you or Shade remain, then so do I.*

"You can't," she told him calmly. "Leesil will never believe anything if Brot'an's the only one to report back. You have to go with him."

Brot'an kept glancing between them, at a loss for having heard only half of what was said. Chap was in no mood to have Wynn explain, nor for any more of her nonsense.

And what will Leesil say when I return without you? What will Magiere say . . . or do?

"Tell them I have to meet with Premin Hawes. They will understand— they have to."

"No, they will not," Brot'an spoke up. "You will leave with us, little one."

This time it was Brot'an who received Wynn's glare of warning. "Don't think you can tell me what to do."

Chane stood up, towering over Wynn, and Shade rose from her haunches, as well. Ore-Locks stood watching in confusion, his iron staff in one hand; he took hold of it with his other on witnessing Chane's and Shade's reactions.

Wynn looked nothing like the young woman Chap had once known, the one who had depended on him for so much. She appeared far too much at home as she rose between Chane and Shade. In his own quest to stop the Enemy, to locate the orbs, had he lost her? Or had she lost him?

"Go tell Magiere and Leesil what's happened," Wynn said. "If they don't understand now, they soon will. When I've spoken with Premin Hawes, I'll let you know everything I've learned. Then . . . we plan our next move, and not before."

Chap considered knocking her on her backside and dragging her off. Twisted as it was, Brot'an would most certainly aid him. But in looking at Wynn, it seemed even that would come to nothing. He saw there was truly nothing he could say or do to make her leave this place.

It was a deeply unsettling realization.

*   *   *

Still shaking from anger and fear, Magiere stood before the closed door. She could barely believe what had taken place. Wynn might believe that lines were being drawn, but for Magiere, if that meant a murdering undead like Chane was an ally, the line separating the living from its worst threat had been erased.

Over and over, she remembered demanding to know how Wynn could accept Chane's protection. She couldn't stop thinking of Wynn's answer.

Because you weren't there. None of you.

Had Wynn had no choice but to accept Chane's help because everyone else had abandoned her?

Even amid guilt, Magiere couldn't accept that, and, still trying to silence Wynn's voice in her head, she turned her eyes to Leesil. She had no idea what to say to him. How could they just stand here and wait? Neither of them had ever been any good at that.

She believed in taking a fight head-on. He believed in coming at it from the side before anyone saw him. Neither approach seemed possible now.

"We should use this time," Leanâlhâm said. "Who knows when we will have a moment again to do anything for ourselves."

Unexpectedly, Magiere had Leanâlhâm to thank for easing the tension. She studied the girl's slender face, smooth brown hair, and those startlingly green eyes that should have been amber.

"What do you suggest?" Magiere asked doubtfully.

Leanâlhâm stepped to the hearth. "Leesil, will you start a fire so we can cook?"

Her Belaskian was simple, but she spoke it well—far better than Osha, considering he was an anmaglâhk.

"Magiere, you help Osha with his words," Leanâlhâm went on. "If we travel together, seek orbs together, he must learn to speak better."

"Now?" Osha asked, though he didn't turn from his vigil at the window.

"Yes, now," Leanâlhâm answered, and she began digging through a pack to retrieve a small pot, raw potatoes, and a few green stalks Magiere couldn't identify. "Do you have something more important to do?"

Magiere caught the quaver in the girl's voice. She remembered that moment between Osha and Wynn, on Wynn's first arrival, and how Leanâlhâm had reacted. That situation bore watching, and Magiere reached out to touch Leesil's shoulder.

"Get a fire started. We have to eat."

She then went to drop on the floor across from Osha at the window's other side, still hesitant at the notion of language lessons amid all of this. She couldn't help remembering how Wynn had once done this. Most of the Belaskian Osha knew, he'd learned from the sage.

"Leesil, do you have a knife?" Leanâlhâm asked.

"Nothing I'd let you use on potatoes," he answered, gathering sticks from a pile near the hearth. "I'll find you something."

Everything seemed so normal and, although the illusion didn't fool Magiere, she was grateful that the girl tried just the same. Doing something—anything—was better than staring at the room's closed door.

Osha put his back to the wall and slid down to the floor. He glanced over, watching Magiere with some unspoken concern. Leanâlhâm wasn't the only one exposed to Magiere's growing problem. Suddenly, even language lessons seemed better than facing that.

"How did Wynn do this?" Magiere asked bluntly.

Osha tilted his head back against the wall, his long, white-blond hair falling away from his face.

"She . . . talk," he said, a bit too wistfully. "Ask question. Make me answer. Scold if I talk Elvish."

What Magiere truly wanted to ask was what Osha and Leanâlhâm were doing here. But by the way these two obeyed Brot'an's every command, resentfully or not, it was too soon to press for answers.

Osha lowered his head, as if sad, and Magiere regretted turning his thoughts toward Wynn.

"I'll give it a try," she said. "You're certainly doing better than Leesil did with your language."

Osha lifted his head and blinked twice in puzzlement.

It had been a long time since Magiere had first entered the Elven Territories with Leesil, Chap, and Wynn. Along the way, Wynn had tried to tutor Leesil in Elvish, though it turned out to be the wrong dialect. Almost immediately, they'd been intercepted by anmaglâhk, including Sgäile and Osha. Since Osha was the most amiable among that escort, Leesil had thought to try out his new language skills.

Osha had paled in shock, flushed with fury, and drawn a stiletto. Wynn had to rush in, frantically trying to explain. Whatever Leesil had *tried* to say, it had come out wrong . . . and as a possible insult to Osha's mother.

Magiere cocked her head toward Leesil and then winked at Osha.

Osha rolled his eyes, snorted, and covered his mouth, trying to stifle a laugh.

"I not this bad," he whispered, but loud enough to be overheard.

Leesil paused at the hearth long enough to shoot him a scowl.

"I *am* not *that* bad," Magiere corrected. "Now tell me about the voyage across the eastern ocean."

Osha turned serious, his thin lips tightening into a line as his jaw muscles clenched. He looked away, remaining silent.

"Not about Brot'an's little secrets," Magiere added. "Just the ship, the crew, the food . . . the day to day."

Osha half smiled, nodding. *"Ath, bithâ!"*

"No Elvish," Magiere said. "I don't understand it, anyway."

In halting, broken phrases, Osha began telling her of his seafaring experiences among humans. Magiere listened, sometimes correcting a word or two. For the most part, all that mattered was that he could make his meaning clear.

Across the room, as the fire began to crackle, Leanâlhâm and Leesil spoke of mundane things, while he located a spare dagger and started on the potatoes.

"Those pieces are too big," Leanâlhâm admonished. "Slice thinner."

"That'll take all night," Leesil argued.

"If you do not, they will have to cook all night."

She set the little iron pot's handle onto the hearth's arm and swung the pot in over the barely flickering flames. Magiere listened to Osha, but found it was not long before Leanâlhâm gently dropped a number of eggs still in their shells into the water. The potatoes followed, along with the greens she'd cut up.

After a while, Osha grew frustrated with fighting for new words he didn't know. Soon after, he was saved from further struggle.

"All right, you two," Leesil said. "Come eat something."

They shared a late supper, maintaining the illusion that all was normal. But once the meal was done, they fell back into silent waiting—until the door opened.

Brot'an stepped in, followed by Chap.

Magiere climbed to her feet. Part of her was still enraged and heatedly hoping to talk some sense into Wynn about this insane notion of accepting help from *anyone* who offered.

Brot'an shut the door, and Magiere's thoughts went blank. It took two breaths before she could speak.

"Where's Wynn?"

Chap stalked right by her toward the hearth with a breathy exhale through his teeth.

Brot'an didn't answer at first, and then said, "Wynn has chosen to remain with her other companions."

Leesil had allowed Leanâlhâm's domestic activities to suppress his own sense of betrayal and panic. He'd been on the verge of feeling almost himself again. Then Brot'an had returned and answered Magiere's question.

Leesil was on his feet, but he didn't speak to Brot'an. He turned on Chap.

"You left her there . . . with *him*?"

Chap clacked his jaw and then huffed twice.

"It was not his choice," Brot'an added.

Magiere stepped between the two, caught at the room's center as she tried to pick one of them to go at. She finally fixed on Brot'an.

"Wynn would not leave," Brot'an said before Magiere got out a word. "Forcing her would have accomplished nothing."

Leesil was at a loss, puzzled by how visibly uncomfortable Brot'an looked.

"I tried to dissuade her, as did Chap," Brot'an continued, ignoring Magiere, and turning to Leesil. "You did not see her there. She is in no danger, and perhaps where she belongs for what she must do . . . for all of us."

Leesil took a step, but Magiere got in his way as she rushed to the bed. It had been stupid to let Brot'an go in the first place, as he cared nothing for Wynn other than what she might accomplish for him. In one motion, Magiere grabbed her cloak from the pile on the bed and pushed right past Brot'an for the door.

"Chap, you show me where she is—now!" Magiere half shouted. "She's coming back, one way or another."

Leesil nodded. "I'm coming, too."

"You cannot," Brot'an returned, his voice rising above its usually calm, firm state. "She has set careful plans in motion, ones worthy of her intelligence. A message has been sent to a Premin Hawes at the guild's castle, who will meet with Wynn to assist in translating the scroll that was mentioned. Wynn will then come to us. By tomorrow night, we may know the location of another orb."

No one had a response to that, and Leesil struggled over what to do.

"Wynn has become a warrior in her way," Brot'an said, "to hinder the Enemy, to stop another war. Would you dismiss her efforts?"

Leesil turned on him. "And what about you helping us, helping her . . . all out of the *goodness* of your heart? In seven hells! What are you really doing here?"

Brot'an narrowed his large amber eyes; one glared through the cage bars of old scars.

Leesil didn't expect an honest answer, and nodded to Magiere as he headed for the door.

"I do not trust Most Aged Father," Brot'an said, freezing Leesil in his steps. "No more than I would trust the Ancient Enemy to retreat into hiding. I would keep these orbs from them both. Wynn is driven by this purpose, and I would join her in it . . . even if I must go through you."

Brot'an shifted around Leesil in a lunge that forced Leesil to back up.

"What are *you* really doing here?" Brot'an echoed.

Leesil was momentarily rattled. Brot'an may have a bagful of other secrets, but in that smaller part where Most Aged Father was concerned, he was telling the truth. Leesil looked to Magiere.

She watched them both, and he clearly saw pain and fear in her dark eyes at Brot'an's words. Like Leesil, Magiere had frozen in doubt. Only Chap remained as he'd always been concerning the master assassin. He rumbled, jowls pulled back partway.

Leesil hadn't received even one recalled memory from Chap, and likely neither had Magiere. For all Chap's hatred of the old butcher, he hadn't tried to argue against Brot'an in any way.

Leesil realized how hard this night must have been for Chap. Chap cared deeply for Wynn, and he'd lost a daughter because of it.

They couldn't go to Chane's inn and drag Wynn away.

"What . . ." Leesil tried to say. "What now, then?"

"A plan," Brot'an answered, "to escape this city, once we have a destination."

Leesil closed his eyes. Another journey, another orb, another journey, and then what? How many times would it repeat, the next time getting harder than the last? Even succeeding wouldn't make anything better, likely only worse.

He felt Magiere's fingers sliding into his palm, and he gripped her hand.

"If you are going to plan," Leanâlhâm said almost too quietly to hear, "then Brot'ân'duivé and the majay-hì should eat while you talk."

Again, the girl's plain manner cut the tension by half.

Leesil pulled Magiere toward the hearth. Osha joined them next, and finally Brot'an. But Chap lay down in the middle of the room, facing away toward the door. Leanâlhâm brought him a plate, but he didn't even sniff at it. Slowly, while Brot'an ate, they all began to talk.

"The city guard won't be a problem," Leesil said. "Those anmaglâhk are something else."

Osha nodded. "They watch all . . ." He faltered, switching to Elvish as he spoke to Brot'an.

"Exits," Brot'an finished for him. "If they have enough, they will have someone watching any way out of the city."

Leesil reached over and grabbed his pack and pulled out the talking hide, though at present, Chap showed no interest in conversation.

"Where will the anmaglâhk focus now?" Leesil asked, and then shook his head. "No, never mind. It doesn't matter. Wherever we're headed will likely be a long way off. That means a ship or a long trek over land. There's only so much we can do until Wynn gets back."

Brot'an nodded once. "The numbers of the anmaglâhk on your trail have dwindled, though I do not know their actual count. Another issue is that they will have word-wood devices—one or more. If so, once we are free of the city, and should they learn of our direction, they could report it to Most Aged Father. Though my people are a long way from here, he could still deploy more of his loyalists to intercept us . . . again, depending upon our destination."

Leesil hesitated at that one unique word—"loyalists."

Brot'an, and even Leesil's mother, Nein'a, were part of a long-standing and silent, dissident faction among the an'Cróan, including some among the Anmaglâhk. Had the situation in the Elven Territories now escalated further? It seemed unlikely that Brot'an would make such a slip. Or had it been intentional? And what was Leesil's mother doing even now, somewhere across the world?

"Wynn said there are two orbs left," Magiere put in. "We don't know which one we'll go after first. We'll need to pick one before we even know where we're going."

"Unless we go after both," Leesil added.

Magiere and Brot'an focused intently on him.

He already knew how this suggestion would affect Brot'an. Even now, the shadow-gripper was calculating what to do should they split into two groups. Leesil didn't look at Magiere, as that would've invited another argument. He went on before she could start in on him.

"We have to get this over with," he said. "And whichever orb is closest, those who go after it will have to stall for those who will make the longer journey."

"How?" Osha asked. "Decoy?"

"No, at least not like the last," Brot'an answered. "We gave them something hidden in plain sight that they could not resist looking into, something obvious to uncover. That will not work a second time."

"Or . . . we could be even more obvious," Leesil countered. "Give them something so plain to see that in their panic, they won't think to second-guess it."

Magiere sighed in frustration, and Leesil knew she was sick of this roundabout approach. But Brot'an's eyes widened almost imperceptibly.

Only Leesil would've caught it while looking into those old eyes. As the master anmaglâhk nodded slightly in agreement, Leesil grew sick inside.

Once again, he found himself thinking too much like the old butcher—and he hated that. But if it got Magiere out of here alive, he could live with it.

CHAPTER 21

The following night, Wynn sat on the floor, tearing roasted mutton into small bits for Shade. Chane refused to let anyone leave the room, since only he had been seen around the inn. He brought back prepared food for the rest of them. Strangely, Ore-Locks ate little. Well, little for a dwarf.

Wynn had slept much of the day in the bed with Shade, as they were both exhausted. Ore-Locks had merely laid out a cloak in the corner of the room on which to rest. Fortunately, he didn't snore much. Once, when Wynn had stirred, perhaps in the midafternoon, she'd glanced over the bed's edge at Chane lying dormant directly in front of the room's door.

She couldn't help feeling there was something odd about him. He didn't appear quite so . . . dead, as he lay there. She'd then noticed his hand shift slightly where it rested on the hilt of his dwarven longsword still sheathed and laid out beside him. She'd never before seen Chane move in dormancy, not even slightly.

She was already awake again before sunset, as was Shade, who also glanced at Chane more than once. The moment it became almost fully dark at dusk, Chane sat up, rose, and went to wake Ore-Locks.

Shade wasn't even startled. However, Wynn was.

She'd looked at Shade resting with her head on her paws. Although Wynn had nothing to base her suspicions upon, she couldn't help wondering if Shade knew something about Chane that she didn't—a silly thought. Of course, she didn't ask either of them about this. What could she ask?

Then Chane had stepped out to see to the food, and the evening had moved on.

Shade wolfed down a whole pile of mutton bits in one bite.

"Don't eat so fast," Wynn scolded.

She didn't care for mutton, but there were roasted potatoes, goat cheese, and dark forest bread to choose from. Chane stood at the window, looking down into the street, as Ore-Locks sighed and fidgeted in the corner.

"Do you think she'll come?" Wynn asked.

"She will come," Chane answered. "If the message reaches her."

It was still difficult for Wynn to believe that Premin Hawes was willing to help. Though she kept such doubts to herself, a tiny part of her worried this might just be a way to track her down. But Chane seemed convinced, and he had a penchant—an actual gift—for knowing when someone lied, if he could focus on such detection.

Chane lifted the canvas curtain's edge with a fingertip, and a streetlamp outside lit his pale features. Wynn studied his clean, long profile.

She'd always liked it, from the first night they'd met back in Bela at the shabby guild annex she was trying to help establish. Standing there in the dim light, he looked like the young nobleman she'd first taken him for, before she knew . . . what he really was. But he wasn't the only one who now filled her thoughts.

Wynn was still stunned by the ache that stabbed her inside when she'd seen Osha. All else had flushed from her mind. She thought only of his companionship in the long journey into the Pock Peaks in search of the orb. More had happened after that.

Days after Magiere and Leesil's wedding, when they'd all reached Bela, the capital of Belaski, Osha had to leave early from the inn. One of the an'Cróan's living ships, a Päirvänean, lay in wait up the coast to take him home. She'd followed him to Bela's bustling docks, not yet ready to lose him—though another part of her reason was to give him a journal she'd written of certain events to pass on to Brot'an.

All along the journey out of the Pock Peaks, Magiere had warned Wynn about any intimacy with an an'Cróan. It was a warning that had once been given too late to Magiere concerning Leesil, who was a half-blood.

An'Cróan bonded for life, and some were unable to survive the loss of a mate.

Even when Osha said good-bye, turning up the busy waterfront through the crowd to head north out of the city, the way he'd looked at Wynn made her ache. He didn't want to leave her, and she hadn't been ready to let him go. Any warning was forgotten as she ran after him.

Wynn had shouted for him, though he hadn't heard her until she'd almost caught up. When he did stop and turn, she threw herself at him, grabbing for his shoulders to pull herself up.

"Do not forget me," she'd whispered as his arms closed around her.

Wynn lifted her head, clumsily thrusting her mouth against Osha's. Then she'd turned and run, fearing to even look back. Until last night, that day on the docks had been the last time she'd seen him.

Chane was not the only one who had followed her across the world, and Chane was not the only one who had stood as her guardian.

Chane turned from the window, gazing down at her.

"Thank you," he said.

"For what?"

"For coming back to us. For not staying with them."

Wynn felt like she might burn to cinders inside and come apart.

"Chane, what did you think I was going to—"

Shade growled, and Wynn jerked around. The dog kept growling at the wall just to the left of the bed.

A dark-sleeved arm emerged out of the wall's old planks.

"Wynn!" Chane rasped.

Ore-Locks rushed around the bed as a shoulder and the skirt of a robe followed the arm. Chane was right above Wynn, but he didn't step around her or try to pull her back.

Amid Wynn's fright, she noticed that neither of them appeared alarmed—only intense. Then the full outline of the dark robe was inside the dim room, and it wasn't black.

The light of her cold-lamp crystal on the bedside table clearly showed a deep, midnight blue. One narrow hand reached up to pull back the cowl.

Premin Hawes looked down at Wynn with two sparkling hazel eyes in a face almost elfin in its narrowness of chin. She stood there, looking about at the others. A canvas pack hung over one of her shoulders, a wrapped parcel under that same arm, and in her other hand . . .

At the sight of the sun-crystal staff, Wynn almost stopped breathing.

"Would it not have been easier to use the door?" Chane asked dryly.

"Footsteps upon the stairs or a knock might be heard," Hawes answered. "I have no wish to be noticed here."

She set the parcel and pack on the bed and held out the staff.

Wynn was still sitting on the floor, wondering what had just happened.

"I thought you might like these possessions returned," the premin said.

Wynn recovered enough to scramble up and grab the staff. She still couldn't catch her breath for a thank-you, though she'd have done anything to express her gratitude.

"The book you asked me to bring is in the pack," Hawes said, "though I read passable Sumanese."

Wynn wouldn't let go of the staff and fumbled to open her pack with one hand. And then she stopped, taking stock of the contents.

Aside from an old lexicon or dictionary of Sumanese, there was her journal—the one she'd encrypted with notes from all of the others she'd burned. However, in the message she'd sent to Hawes, she'd risked giving detailed instructions regarding both her location and needs for a reference on the oldest Sumanese dialects. Given Hawes's choice of guild order, it did not surprise Wynn that the premin knew some Sumanese. Languages were part of all sages' schooling, though primarily that of cathologers. But many of the recovered secrets of metaology had come out of the Suman Empire.

"Nikolas had no trouble getting the message to you?" Wynn asked.

Hawes raised one eyebrow. "Master a'Seatt delivered it."

"A'Seatt?" Chane hissed.

Wynn was taken aback, as well, and as if reading her reaction, Premin Hawes let out a slow breath.

"It might clarify much to tell each other everything," the premin said, "if we are to be of assistance to one another."

Wynn had already concluded that, but there was something else in the premin's response. Hawes hadn't just offered assistance; she expected something in return. What Wynn needed was beyond price, and she'd learned not to trust gifts. Perhaps it would be best to make the premin go first.

"Agreed," Wynn said, and rushed on. "Why are those wagons coming into the guild every night? What are they bringing?"

Hawes was quiet, though Wynn couldn't tell if this was caused by indecision, reluctance, or something else. The premin's expression, or lack of it, offered nothing.

"Supplies for an expedition," Hawes suddenly answered.

"Expedition? To where?"

"To the castle where you found the ancient texts. According to your report, you retrieved only a small fraction of what is there."

Before Wynn uttered a word, Chane beat her to it.

"They must not!" he rasped. "Did they not read of what is trapped beneath that castle? Premin, you have to—"

"Making a plan is still far from executing it," Hawes cut in.

"Then why do they already amass supplies?" Chane countered.

Hawes remained fixed on Wynn as she answered. "Assembling a group with even a slim chance to reach that place—should your accounting of the route be detailed enough—will take time. Even should they have a chance to succeed, the effort and what might be gained may prove pointless . . . or unnecessary, in comparison to immediate concerns."

Wynn didn't like the way Hawes studied her.

"I have answered your question," the premin said. "Do you have something to share with me?"

Wynn looked at Chane. He nodded and pulled the old scroll case from inside his shirt.

She reached into the pocket of her robe and pulled out a wrinkled sheet of paper as they both settled upon the floor. Chane pulled the lid off the case and unrolled the ancient leather scroll with its blacked-out surface.

An alliance with Hawes would be all or nothing, and they'd just chosen all. The premin crouched, frowning in puzzlement at both paper and scroll.

"This is what we've translated so far," Wynn explained, spinning the wrinkled paper around so that the premin could read it.

The Children in twenty and six steps seek to hide in five corners

The anchors amid Existence, which had once lived amid the Void.

One to wither the Tree from its roots to its leaves

Laid down where a cursed sun cracks the soil.

That which snuffs a Flame into cold and dark

Sits alone upon the water that never flows.

The middling one, taking the Wind like a last breath,

Sank to sulk in the shallows that still can drown.

And swallowing Wave in perpetual thirst, the fourth

Took seclusion in exalted and weeping stone.

But the last, that consumes its own, wandered astray

In the depths of the Mountain beneath the seat of a lord's song.

Wynn went on. "The Children were the first physical manifestation of the Noble Dead—vampires—somehow created by the Ancient Enemy . . . thirteen of them. The 'anchors' are the orbs, and you can see from the poem that there are five—one associated to each of the classical elements. At the war's end, the Children split into five groups and scattered to hide the orbs."

"You said you translated this?"

"Some of it, but Domin il'Sänke corrected much of it for me."

"Il'Sänke?" Hawes repeated with a subtle bite in her voice.

"The poem itself is in an ancient Sumanese dialect . . . Pärpa'äsea, I think he said."

The premin peered between the paper and scroll. "What poem? What does this blotted-out scroll have to do with any of this?"

Wynn realized how much more she'd have to reveal about herself if they were to continue.

"The poem itself is written in the fluids of one of the Children . . . beneath a black coating of ink."

Hawes raised only her eyes, and Wynn felt like she'd just alerted some sharp-eyed predator to her presence.

"How did you read what was written therein?" Hawes asked quietly.

Wynn glanced at Chane.

"The short version," he said.

Wynn ignored whatever criticism he implied.

"I made a mistake a few years ago," she began. She described how she'd ended up with mantic sight, able to see traces of the Elements—or at least Spirit—in all things.

"You dabbled with a thaumaturgical ritual?" Hawes asked. "What irresponsible fool taught you that? And yes, I know the particular one you used."

Wynn didn't want to go farther down that path. "The taint of it remained stuck in me, and now I can call up mantic sight at will."

"But not end it," Chane interjected.

"Trouble," Ore-Locks muttered. "Nothing but trouble."

Wynn ignored them both. "I am able to see—"

"The lack of Spirit within the characters beneath the coating," Hawes finished. "Because the words were written in the fluids of an undead . . . fluids taken from a body that no longer had the potency of true life . . . and something even beyond a lack of Spirit."

Wynn fell silent. Domin il'Sänke wasn't the only one who'd underestimated the premin. It hadn't struck Wynn before how much Frideswida Hawes truly knew, but it made sense. No one of lesser ability could've become a master, and then a domin, let alone a premin of metaology.

"Yes," Wynn confirmed. "But I can't maintain the sight for long, or it overwhelms and sickens me."

"You are fortunate it hasn't been the death of you . . . in mind, if not body," Hawes uttered. "Had I known, I would have removed—"

"No!" Wynn cut in. "It's all I have to get at what we need."

"And how did you learn to call it up at will?" Hawes demanded.

Wynn hesitated.

"Il'Sänke!" Hawes whispered. "That deceitful . . . What else did he teach you?"

Wynn had never seen the premin so unguarded in her emotions. "He tutored me on how to control the sight—that and how to ignite the staff."

Hawes appeared to calm, though her demand left Wynn puzzled and worried. She wondered what else the premin thought Ghassan il'Sänke had taught her. She had long suspected there was no affection between the premin and the Suman domin, and il'Sänke's underestimation of Hawes's thaumaturgical abilities seemed to be at the core of it.

Had she been wrong? Was there something greater than that between those two? However, none of it mattered now.

"We've recovered three of the orbs," Wynn explained. "There are—"

"Three?" Hawes repeated.

Wynn closed her mouth. Explaining all this was taking more time than she'd imagined.

"Yes. You know of the first found in the castle through my journals of the Farlands. There are still two left to locate. If I call up my sight and copy more of the poem, can you help decipher it?"

Hawes looked down at the translated poem and the first stanza.

"That was the 'anchor' of Water, in 'exalted and weeping stone,'" she whispered, as if speaking to herself. "And you found the next in Bäalâle Seatt, the one of Earth, which 'consumes its own.'"

Wynn grew frightened. No one but those who'd gone with her to Bäalâle should know that. She looked quickly at Ore-Locks and found the dwarf carefully watching the premin.

"Where was the third found?" Hawes asked.

"In the Wastes, up north . . . perhaps in the ice, though I haven't learned much more about it."

"In other words, someone else—not in this room—found it. Perhaps even one of your trio of evening visitors that were ejected."

This was getting to be too much, and still Wynn could do nothing but wait.

Hawes studied the poem again. "'That which snuffs Flame' is obviously for Fire, and 'water that never flows' is obviously the ice of the Wastes . . . hence your third orb. What remains are Air and Spirit."

Wynn only nodded. Though she'd already guessed which three orbs they'd acquired, having these conclusions confirmed—and knowing for certain which two were left—provided some needed certainty. But to have Hawes say so, reading it here and now, as if the conclusions were so obvious . . .

Wynn worried about how much the guild had gleaned from the ancient texts.

"And every metaphor describes the destruction of an Element," Hawes murmured.

Wynn had thought so, as well. Much as she agreed, something more now seemed missing by the way Hawes stared at the translated parts of the poem.

The first orb Magiere had carelessly opened, and Leesil and Chap had described all of the underground cavern's clinging moisture raining inward into the orb's light. The memories of Deep-Root in ancient Bäalâle Seatt that Wynn gained from the dragons had hinted that the orb of Earth was used to tunnel in under that seatt.

"I've suspected they were five tools for such use," Wynn said. "I'd imagined they could be used as weapons, each of the five."

"No, not weapons," Hawes whispered. "Not five . . . but one . . . altogether."

Wynn was immediately lost, even as the premin looked up at her.

"Reason it through," Hawes instructed. "What would happen to any target as the focus of all five orbs, as each one obliterated an elemental component?"

Wynn realized the answer but couldn't speak it.

"The target would cease to exist," Chane whispered for her.

"A'ye!" Ore-Locks added in shock.

"In theory," Hawes confirmed, lowering her gaze to the paper once more. "Think of what power was required to create them. It is . . . unimaginable."

Wynn heard Shade begin to rumble, but she didn't need that warning. She watched Hawes as the premin rambled on, seemingly lost in thought.

"Among the oldest fragments that the guild has recovered concerning the war, there is no record of these 'anchors,' let alone such a use for them. If this was their intended purpose, and they were not put to that unknown use, then the question remains: what was the intended target?"

Wynn's burdens, ones she would now heap upon all others in the search, grew tenfold.

"The target does not matter," Chane rasped.

Wynn took a quick glance and found him watching Hawes.

"All that matters is that they are never used," he added.

Hawes didn't respond, and Wynn felt more trapped than ever in having asked for the premin's assistance.

"Do you have any idea what the other two stanzas mean?" Wynn asked. "Any notion about locations or areas to look? Or if I call up mantic sight and try to copy more from the scroll, can you help decipher it?"

Hawes tightened her mouth. "I should do so myself. You have no training for this, regardless that you've toyed with some ability you should not have."

"No," Wynn said. "This isn't the only way the sight has served me."

"Wynn!" Chane whispered in warning.

"I don't care what the sight costs me," she continued. "I'm not giving it up! I need to see those words for myself."

Hawes pierced her with those hazel eyes. "You do not trust me?"

Wynn bit her tongue as she heard Ore-Locks inhale and hold it. There was no safe answer to that question. She wasn't certain she trusted Hawes at all—not now—and there was nothing to do about it.

"Will you help me?" Wynn asked, and a moment of silence followed.

"These anchors . . . these orbs you've found," Hawes finally said. "Are they well hidden, so that nothing of the Enemy might find them?"

"Yes," Wynn answered.

Chap had hidden Water and Fire himself, and Ore-Locks had hidden Earth with the Stonewalkers. The orbs were as far beyond the reach of the Enemy's minions—and the reach of anyone else—as they could be.

"Oh, troublesome girl!" Hawes breathed in resignation. "Yes, I will help you."

A day passed, night came again, and not one of Rodian's men had caught a glimpse of the tall and black wolfish dog, let alone one missing sage. Wynn and Shade were nowhere to be found. Now at his desk, having turned over guild security to Branwell, Rodian stared at a map of the city's districts.

He had only three more days.

In all honesty, he wasn't certain Prince Leäfrich could make good on his threat, but even an attempt would prove beyond embarrassing. Rodian didn't know what he would do if he actually found Wynn. But he had to find her at any cost now that the prince had blindsided him with this ridiculous abduction story.

The abrupt change was likely Sykion's doing, incited by his insistence that she either make a formal charge or drop all notions of incarcerating the young sage. No doubt Sykion would spread word that he'd allowed a young female sage to be "stolen from her bed."

The whole situation made Rodian's stomach ache.

But still, for more than one reason, he had to locate Wynn. If he had a chance to speak with her, no doubt she could at least refute the premin's story. There was no knowing what would happen after that, for it all depended on what, and how much, Wynn was willing to say.

An expected knock sounded on his office door, and he immediately called out, "Come."

The door cracked and Lúcan stuck his head in, steel gray hair dangling into his eyes.

"Anything?" Rodian asked.

"No, sir," Lúcan answered too quietly, perhaps wishing he had better news. "I've placed a man up the block from the Upright Quill, and two are sweeping all ways near the guild. A score are out searching the streets, but it's as if the sage is gone . . . perhaps already fled the city."

"No." Rodian shook his head. "She put up with a lot to remain on guild grounds for as long as she did. Whatever she needs is in there, and she's not the kind to walk away."

Lúcan swallowed hard. "So far, we've had no cause to enter any buildings."

"What are you suggesting?"

"Well . . . perhaps a general search order from the High Advocate. We could start knocking on doors and going through inns tomorrow."

Rodian stood up. Permission for invasive searches without evidential cause was rare. It had been granted only twice in his memory: once for a missing foreign dignitary, and the second time for the assassin who had later killed the same. But if his men could search every inn in Calm Seatt, they might find something to help. Or, at least, when rumors spread, it might flush Wynn out. She had to be holed up somewhere.

And since Rodian had been ordered by a prince of the realm to find a sage kidnapped from her bed, amid the outrage of the guild and the royalty, the High Advocate might be swayed.

"First thing in the morning," he said with a slight smile. "A very wise . . . cunning . . . suggestion, Corporal."

Lúcan matched that smile as he nodded and stepped out, closing the door.

Rodian sank into his chair. Chances were still slim, but perhaps he might still find the journeyor within three days.

Wynn sat cross-legged on the floor with the blackened scroll before her, as she prepared to call up her mantic sight. She never looked forward to this sickening process, and it was difficult to stop once it started.

Chane brought her quill with the white metal tip, an ink bottle, and a blank sheet, and set them on the floor beside the scroll. He also prepared to steady her hand, if need be.

"From the stanzas so far, the rest will likely be just as veiled," Hawes said, "and there may not be more concerning locations. In the main ascendancy dialects of Sumanese, look for *rúhk* for 'spirit' and *shàjár* or *sagár* for 'tree.' 'Life' would likely be *hkâ'ät*. 'Air' is *háwa* or *hká'a*, which are also used for 'wind,' though sometimes that is *hawä*. Since your time in this state is limited, scan quickly for any words you can sound out as similar to these."

Wynn nodded. Shade sat off on her left, and neither Shade nor Chane approved of what she was about to do. Both were silent nonetheless, knowing this was the only way to gain what they needed—they hoped.

Ore-Locks had never seen this, but he watched intently from out of the way.

"Are you prepared?" Hawes asked.

"I guess . . . I mean, yes," Wynn answered.

She lost sight of the premin as the woman stepped around behind her. Then Wynn heard a whisper close to her ear.

"Begin."

Extending her index finger, Wynn traced a sign for Spirit on the floor and encircled it, and she heard Hawes whispering something more, something unintelligible behind her.

At each gesture, Wynn focused hard to keep the lines alive in her mind's eye, as if they were actually drawn upon the floor. She scooted forward, settling inside the circle, and traced a wider circumference around herself and the first pattern. It was a simple construct, but through it, she shut out the world as she closed her eyes.

Wynn felt for that thin trace of elemental Spirit in all things, starting with herself.

As a living being, in which Spirit was always strongest, she imagined breathing it in from the air. She imagined it flowing upward from the wood of the floorboards . . . from the earth below the inn. In the darkness behind her eyelids, she held on to the first simple pattern traced upon the floor. When that held steady, she called upon the last image she needed.

Amid that pattern before her mind's eye, she saw Chap.

As she'd once seen him long ago in her mantic sight, his silver-gray fur shimmered like a million silk threads caught in the glare of a blue-white light. All of him was enveloped in white vapors that rose from his body like slow-moving flames.

Moments stretched, and mantic sight still didn't come. The ache in her knees threatened her focus.

Wynn clung to Chap—to the memory of him—burning bright behind the envisioned circle around the symbol of Spirit. Vertigo suddenly threatened to send her falling into the darkness behind her eyelids.

"Wynn?" Chane rasped.

She braced her hands on the floor. As she opened her eyes, nausea lurched from her stomach, up her throat, and seemingly into her head.

Translucent white, just shy of blue, dimly permeated the wood planks beneath her hands and knees. She raised her head slowly, carefully, and the first thing she saw was Shade. Wynn knew what to expect, but foreknowledge didn't help much.

For the first instant, Shade was as black as a void. But beneath her fur, a powerful glimmer of blue-white permeated her body—more so than anything else in the room. Traces of Spirit ran in every strand of Shade's charcoal fur. Her eyes were aglow, burning with her father's Fay ancestry.

Wynn had to look away.

"Chane!" she called through gritted teeth.

"I am here. Work quickly."

Only then did she feel a hand resting lightly between her shoulder blades, but it wasn't Chane's. Through it all, she kept hearing those soft, indistinct whispers behind her from Premin Hawes.

Wynn half closed her eyes as she turned her head, looking for Chane as the only normal image in the room. For while Chane wore the brass ring, even her mantic sight couldn't reveal him for what he was.

He appeared exactly the same, unchanged, as before Wynn had called her sight. He was her anchor.

Taking in a deep breath, she finally looked down at the scroll. Its surface was no longer completely black . . . to her.

The coating of old ink, spread nearly to the scroll's edges, had lightened with a thin inner trace of blue-white. Whatever covered the words had been made from a natural substance, and even after ages, it still retained a trace of elemental Spirit.

Within that space, pure black marks appeared, devoid of all Spirit.

"Wynn?" Hawes asked.

"I see the words now," she whispered.

Those swirling, elaborately stroked characters weren't written as in the other texts. Short lines began evenly along a wide right-side margin. Written from right to left, they ended erratically shy of the page's left side. The lines of text were broken into stanzas of differing length.

"But the dialect is so . . ." she whispered.

"Sound out what is possible by the characters you recognize," Hawes instructed. "Find anything similar to what you heard me speak."

Wynn's dinner threatened to come up as she tried to reach for her elven quill.

Chane grabbed her wrist and guided her hand as she dipped the quill and dropped its point to the blank sheet. Then something halfway down the scroll caught her eyes.

". . . and the breath of wind . . . sands . . . were born . . ." she said aloud, but she couldn't follow most of the writing.

Wynn stopped reading aloud and quickly began copying as much as she could by rote. She had scrawled only a few lines when a sharp wave of vertigo rose inside her.

"Wynn!" Chane rasped.

Almost instantly, she felt the premin's hand press between her shoulder blades, as if Hawes had felt that wave. Wynn's vertigo decreased as the premin's unintelligible whispering stopped.

"That is enough," Hawes ordered.

"No!" Wynn tried to say, still choking. "I need . . . more."

The quill was suddenly snatched from her grip. A narrow hand flattened over her eyes, blocking out everything, as she heard another whisper, shorter and sharper than the last. The nausea vanished as Hawes pulled her hand away from Wynn's eyes.

"Try sitting up," the premin said.

Wynn straightened on her knees, opened her eyes, and turned on Hawes in outrage.

"I barely wrote anything!"

Chane, still crouched close, grabbed her upper arm. "Wynn, that is enough for—"

"No!" she snapped, still glaring at the premin. "Why did you stop me?"

Hawes reached around her for the sheet upon which Wynn had written. "You collected something, but you were growing too unstable. You need instruction before another attempt."

Wynn only glared, wondering what the premin was up to. She finally calmed enough to ask, "Anything of use?"

Hawes reached out for the elven quill, not even appearing interested in its white metal tip, and began scanning what was on the page. She scrawled and stroked as Wynn waited, unable to see exactly what Hawes wrote.

"'The Wind was banished to the waters within the sands where we were born,'" the premin read aloud and then paused. "The 'we' may be a reference to the Children."

"How are we to know where any of the Children were born?" Chane asked.

"The war is believed to have begun in the south," Hawes answered. "Somewhere in the region of what is now the Suman Empire. And likely the 'empire' was only separate nations at that time. This line may hint at some place near where the Children were first born, or created as servants of the Enemy. But . . ."

Hawes fell silent, frowning slightly as she stared at the page—until Wynn grabbed it from the premin's hand to look at it. Hawes had scrawled the exact words she'd read in Numanese, using the Begaine syllabary.

"And 'Wind' more likely refers to the orb of Air," Wynn replied. "But the rest makes no sense. The only known desert of 'sand' is south of the Sky-Cutter Range. But there are no waters in that region. How could there be, since it's a desert?"

"You are still missing the full context," Hawes admonished.

Wynn thought about that for a moment. "You mean time?"

"Yes. What is in this scroll was written a thousand or more years ago . . . at an educated guess. What we call the Forgotten History may be even older than that. And how much can a world, or any one region, change in that much time?"

Wynn glanced back at il'Sänke's translation of the first stanza.

> *The middling one, taking the Wind like a last breath,*
> *Sank to sulk in the shallows that still can drown.*

It clearly referred to the orb of Air, but it offered no help in connecting it to the new phrase she had just copied. And neither phrase explained how to find water, let alone a body of such with shallows, in the middle of sand, or any other type of desert.

"How do we . . . ?" she began, not even sure what to ask.

Premin Hawes no longer looked at anyone or anything. She appeared to be focused across the room on the blank wall. More disturbing was another rare betrayal of emotion on her narrow face. Her eyes closed to slits exposing slivers of cold gray irises around black pupils. Her features twisted in a blink of revulsion as she spoke.

"I can think of only one person who might decipher such a location—if this new hint is that."

Before Wynn could press for more, the premin looked at her.

"We have much to discuss," Hawes said, "and much to do. You will need access to the guild and to me directly."

Wynn saw little hope in that.

"If she goes back," Ore-locks replied, "Premin Sykion and the council—your council—will lock her up again."

"Perhaps not," Hawes countered.

Chane crouched down beside them. "What do you mean?"

Hawes only looked at Wynn. "I have only one answer, and you may not like it."

The premin half turned where she knelt, retrieved the parcel she'd left on the bed, and handed it to Wynn. Still lost, Wynn took it and pulled the tie string to unwrap the outer canvas.

Inside was a midnight blue sage's robe.

Nearly half the night had passed, but neither Magiere nor the others with her had mentioned going to bed. They all waited to hear from Wynn. At the three bells of midnight, Brot'an finally got up to go find out what was keeping Wynn. Chap had immediately risen to follow him, as had Magiere and Osha, much to Leanâlhâm's alarm. Before Magiere got far, Leesil grabbed her arm.

"Let Brot'an go alone," he said.

As Magiere tried to pull free, Chap snarled at Leesil. Osha ignored him entirely, but Brot'an stood in his way. Leesil shook his head, hanging on to Magiere.

"Your going at Wynn again isn't going to hurry her along. Everyone, sit down. And Brot'an . . . make it quick!"

Brot'an nodded, slipping out the door before Chap or Osha could follow.

Magiere had turned on Leesil, but he wouldn't back down.

So now Magiere and the rest waited even longer for Brot'an's return. Leesil tried to distract everyone with a sketch of the city's districts that he and Brot'an had made during their scouting trips.

Osha merely sank down below the window as he asked, "Will work?"

"Depends on what Wynn has to say," Leesil answered, "and who's going where. But yes, the plan has a chance . . . and some flexibility."

Magiere's feelings toward Wynn were still too conflicted to agree with Leesil, even after he explained their options in the face of not knowing where to go once they left the city.

"If anmaglâhk split?" Osha asked. "If not to gather, then they—"

He was cut off by a light double knock on the door. Before anyone moved, it opened.

Brot'an stepped in with Wynn and Shade—and a cloaked dwarf carrying an iron staff.

Osha immediately rose and fixed on only Wynn.

Magiere had seen a few dwarves about the city, but none up close—as she had on their journey north into the Wastes. One in particular she had gotten to know a little. Much as this stranger caught her attention, her gaze quickly shifted to the open door as she reached for her falchion leaning against the bed.

Brot'an shut the door, but Magiere didn't relax. Chane hadn't come. It should've been a relief, but it wasn't.

Last night, Wynn had been disheveled, wearing a wrinkled gray robe. Tonight, she was dressed in her old elven pants and tunic from their time among the an'Cróan, with an open cloak thrown over the top. She carried the long staff with the odd leather sheath covering its top. Her hair was pulled back into a tail. Chap's daughter, the black majay-hì, pressed up against the sage, as if anxious at being among so many strangers.

Then Wynn looked at Osha, and her gaze lingered on him. As he seemed about to speak, she looked away, gesturing to the dwarf.

"This is Ore-Locks Iron-Braid," she said. "He can be trusted."

Leesil had mentioned the dwarf last night, but this one was nothing like the one Magiere had met in the earliest days of their journey to the northern wastes. Unlike that fierce and boisterous warrior, Wynn's companion was clean-shaven and wore a simple orange vestment under his cloak. He was quiet, intently watchful, and simply nodded to all in place of any greeting. Not at all dwarfish by what little Magiere knew of these strange people.

"You learn . . . news?" Osha asked Wynn.

"Yes," she nearly whispered without looking at him.

Magiere shook her head slightly over the trouble that remained for those two.

Wynn pulled off her cloak and leaned her odd staff in the corner behind the door. As she stepped closer, standing before Leesil's sketch on the floor, Shade followed her. She looked down at Magiere sitting on the floor with Leesil and Chap.

"Can we talk?" she asked bluntly. "Can we make plans?"

Magiere waited for Leesil to answer, but he didn't, and apparently neither had Chap, in his own way. Magiere found herself stuck in the role of peacemaker, something she was never good at and was not in the mood for right now.

Nodding once, she gestured to the open paper map. "Don't think we have a choice. You're the only one who knows where to head next."

And wasn't that an annoying twist of fate?

Wynn settled on the floor, resting a hand on Shade's back.

In a happier memory, in what seemed a lifetime ago, Magiere recalled waking in Leesil's arms for the first time after they'd finished driving Welstiel out of the capital of her homeland. They were preparing for another journey, and Wynn had burst through the door of the little inn's room, shouting, "I'm coming with you!"

She'd seemed almost a child back then, full of wonder, and nothing like the hardened young woman who now knelt on the floor. This woman solved mysteries and uncovered secrets that others wouldn't admit existed.

Wynn half turned, looking back. "Ore-Locks, grab a stool and join us. And Osha . . ."

She never finished, but Magiere saw her swallow hard, perhaps breathing too quickly.

"So . . ." Leesil began awkwardly. "This premin came to you? You have a direction for us?"

Wynn studied him. "Yes."

Wynn kept as calm as she could, but her heart pounded. It might've been the clear rift between herself and Magiere, Leesil, and Chap. Yes, that was most of it: knowing how much they opposed Chane having anything to do with what had to be accomplished. She'd expected them to be opposed but never thought it would fray and tear the ties they had to one another.

Yes, it was all that, but it was also Osha.

She felt him watching her, and she wanted to turn to him. This was not the moment or the place for that. She fought to shove aside memories of the time they'd spent together, up to that final instant on Bela's crowded docks.

How different he looked now, and it was more than that he no longer dressed like the Anmaglâhk. She desperately wanted to know what had happened to him. Then there was poor Leanâlhâm, of all people, here with the others. Worse, the young girl looked as much changed as Osha in the past two years, perhaps a little taller, and not at all happy to see Wynn. They had at least been friendly in the Farlands, for as little as they'd gotten to know one another. What had made Brot'an bring Leanâlhâm here?

Shade was no help in easing the tension. She pressed in against Wynn, as if everyone here were an enemy.

This was not going to be easy. But with the possible exception of Leanâl-hâm, everyone in this room had the skills needed to track and obtain the remaining two orbs. Wynn finally had some real help besides Chane and Shade. She wasn't about to lose that now.

She steeled herself and looked Chap in the eyes.

"We didn't decipher much," she said. "We know the three recovered orbs are for Water, Earth, and Fire. So we're searching for Air and Spirit."

You are certain?

Chap glanced again at Shade, who continued to ignore him.

"Yes," Wynn answered him, and then turned her attention to Magiere. "We were able to decipher that the orb of Air is somewhere in the south, possibly in the Suman Empire or the great desert just north of it."

"On this continent?" Magiere asked, and all traces of stiffness vanished from her expression. "We're that close?"

"Close?" Wynn repeated. "Have you seen a map of this continent? Do you know how long it will take to reach the Empire, how large it is, and the desert even more than that?"

"Hopefully you've got more to go on," Leesil said.

Wynn shook her head. "Not exactly, but Premin Hawes has a suggestion. It is risky, but I can't think of anything else, and we need to move quickly."

"What is this suggestion?" Brot'an asked.

"I have an . . . acquaintance in the guild's Suman branch, a domin of metaology named Ghassan il'Sänke. He helped in deciphering earlier parts of the scroll . . . and in combating the undead."

The last part gained Magiere's full attention, and Wynn gestured to her staff leaning in the corner.

"He created that for me," she said. "The crystal emits light akin to the sun. We know what that can do to Noble Dead, vampires, and others."

Leesil stared at the staff, both of his white-blond eyebrows arched. "Truly, it can— Wait. What *others*?"

Wynn didn't want to get sidetracked into explaining about Sau'ilahk, the wraith.

"I've seen other kinds of Noble Dead," she answered. "We'll deal with that later. Domin il'Sanke also believes the Ancient Enemy, so-called,

384 · BARB & J. C. HENDEE

may . . . will return. Premin Hawes believes that if anyone can decipher more of the cryptic clues we've extracted concerning the orb of Air, it might be him."

Wynn briefly explained about the limited details hidden in the poem versus all the centuries that had passed since it had been written. It was daunting that time itself may have rendered useless what little geographic hints were hidden in the scroll.

"So what's the risk?" Leesil asked. "It's not hard to see you're less than thrilled with bringing this Suman in on what we're after. Why? Whose side is he on?"

Wynn took a slow breath. How could she explain about il'Sänke?

"From what I've seen—learned—he's as determined as my guild branch's Premin Council to keep any portents secret from the masses. The difference is that he's not in denial, at least to me. He knows as much as I do, though perhaps about different details."

"So your Premin Hawes thinks this il'Sänke may know more?" Magiere asked. "Maybe something specific about where to look for another orb?"

"She does . . . and neither of us has a better idea. But we share with him only the clues related to the orb of Air . . . and nothing more."

"Then we go south," Magiere said. "But what about the last orb, the one of Spirit?"

Wynn looked at Magiere and then Leesil, feeling bleak. Leesil had fallen silent, and stared down at the map. She felt Chap watching her, but beyond his previous brief comment, he had said nothing at all. Wynn had to wonder about the changes in all three of them.

Magiere had always been the one who wanted to be done with all this and just go home. Yet now she was the only one openly pushing forward, while the other two remained silent.

"We've learned nothing yet of the last orb, which means . . ." Wynn faltered, her voice quavering as she continued. "We're going to have to separate into two groups."

She had no idea how they'd take this, and braced for the outrage.

Leesil's amber eyes only flickered, and he sat up, leaning toward her.

"We already knew that," he said quietly, "and planned for it. Two groups will be necessary for at least one to escape this city without the Anmaglâhk being able to follow quickly enough."

Both his manner and close proximity brought Wynn some relief.

"There are loose ends," Magiere grumbled, and she looked to Chap.

Chap sat rigid beside Magiere. Again Wynn didn't hear one word from him in her head. She wanted to know what he thought about all this, that he still believed they shared the same goals. Chap liked to be in control, and events were pressing forward right over the top of him.

"There are still preparations to make," Leesil said. "We'll need help with some of it, since we don't know anyone here besides you."

Confused, Wynn answered, "Yes, of course. But I need to speak with Chap . . . alone."

Leesil scowled in suspicion, but Wynn cut him off before he could speak.

"Talk with Ore-Locks about what you need," she said, and then got up. "If he can't come up with something, we'll figure it out."

"Wynn . . ." Magiere began. "What is this about?"

Wynn headed for the door, for there was one thing she'd learned that no one else should know just yet—no one except Chap. For it to be made clear, she would need to force Shade to face her father.

"Shade, come on," she called. "And Chap?"

Magiere visibly calmed, looking at Chap and then Shade, as if she'd suddenly understood something. Leesil sighed, rolling his eyes.

"Get going," he told Chap, "and get this settled before we have to set things in motion."

Wynn said nothing to correct Leesil and Magiere's misguided assumptions. She let them believe what they wanted to. What she needed in privacy with Chap had nothing to do with healing the rift between a father and a daughter.

Chap rose and headed toward Wynn, but as he passed too close, Shade sidled away from him. Wynn couldn't tell if Chap reacted or not; he simply stalked out the door to wait on the landing. Still, Shade wouldn't budge.

"Now!" Wynn commanded.

Shade rumbled and finally headed out.

Wynn could feel Osha watching her, but she didn't dare look back at him. She was about to follow Shade and Chap when she heard the first part of a conversation in the room behind her.

"What do you need?" Ore-Locks asked.

"Well, to begin," Leesil replied, "two wagons, some good-sized trunks, as we've a lot to haul with us that will have to be loaded early. And especially a ship to take our cargo and three passengers . . . departing at night."

After a long pause, Ore-Locks answered, "It is possible . . . what more?"

Wynn left them to their plans and closed the door, wishing Brot'an had said something—just so she'd know he was occupied. She found Chap waiting at her feet with his head down, and Shade sat two steps down the stairs with her back turned.

She cared for them both so much, but there was no time to deal with issues between them. What she wanted Chap to know she couldn't risk saying aloud, and that was why she needed Shade.

"Shade, show him," Wynn whispered. "Everything that happened . . . everything that was said with Premin Hawes."

Chap looked up at her. *What is this about?*

Wynn put a finger over her lips, for she wouldn't speak any of it out loud. Only Chap could know what she'd learned. Most especially, it had to be kept from Brot'an, but also from Osha and Leanâlhâm, who were too much under the greimasg'äh's influence.

"Shade," Wynn whispered.

Shade swiveled only her head and eyed Wynn, long and hard.

"Please," Wynn added.

Shade finally turned about, eyeing her father much like she would've an enemy or threat. She put her forepaws up one step and stretched her head out.

When Chap looked up at Wynn in uncertainty, she waved him toward Shade. He hesitantly slipped his head against his daughter's. Wynn wished that touch, the sharing in memory-speak, could've been just for them. They needed that, no matter how much Shade resisted, but that wasn't the reason.

The secret was still only a guess, but even that could be dangerous for what it might mean. Wynn knew the instant Chap learned it from Shade.

He lurched back, spinning on the landing, and his head nearly hit Wynn's leg. All Wynn did when he looked up was slowly nod. Even before she glanced toward the door and those muted voices beyond it, Chap did so, and his hackles rose.

She wanted more time to talk with him, but that couldn't be here and now. Even trying to use memory-speak with Shade and have her pass it along to Chap would take too long. The others were waiting, and the longer she remained outside, the less likely they would believe this private moment was about Chap and Shade.

The secret was not about the five orbs, but of five parts to one weapon, or so it had been guessed. The last who should ever know of this, even for all he had done for those Wynn cared about, was the master assassin.

Brot'an was here for a reason: to keep his own kind and Most Aged Father from getting to Magiere and what she'd recovered. What could—would—Brot'an do for such a weapon himself if he learned of it?

It was bad enough that Wynn had sent that journal with Osha to be given to Brot'an. It was the worst outcome of how naive she'd once been. When she looked down again, Chap stood glaring at the door. He began to shake with hissing breaths between bared and clenched teeth. He understood the implications of what Shade had relayed to him and exactly why Wynn had dragged them out into the hallway. Upon reaching for the door, she faltered at Shade's memory-words in her head.

—I . . . understand . . . too—

Shade ignored her father, watching only Wynn.

"I know you do," Wynn whispered.

At that, Chap looked between them, and his ears stiffened. *Know what? Was . . . is she. . . . talking to you?*

Wynn hung there, still gripping the door's handle. Shade was talking to her—in a way. It was only by having learned to isolate certain sounds—spoken words—from memories seen inside of Wynn, and also by Shade's learning what they meant. On the other hand, Wynn could only *hear* Chap, as a true Fay, in her head because of the taint left in her from a failed thaumaturgical ritual.

Wynn's eyes widened at a notion. Aside from being a Fay, Chap had been born into a majay-hì body the same as his mate Lily . . . and his daughter, Shade.

"Oh . . . have I got a useful trick for you," Wynn whispered, and then smiled.

Chap's ears fell, flattening in apprehension.

Wynn only giggled. "And it's going to drive Leesil to fits!"

Back inside the room, as Chap sat with Wynn before the sketched map on the floor, Leesil finally looked up from the map's other side at everyone.

"Is that clear enough?" he asked. "Any last doubts?"

Chap knew there were—he had plenty himself. Yet no one, not even Brot'an, had offered anything better. Leesil looked at Wynn kneeling beside Chap.

"Can you and Ore-Locks take care of what we need?" he asked.

She, in turn, looked up at the dwarf standing behind her, but when Chap glanced back it was at his daughter.

Shade lay removed from everyone, especially him, lying in the far corner next to the pile of gear Osha had stored there.

"It can be done," Ore-Locks said with a nod.

"Then it is time," Brot'an cut in. "I will escort you back to your inn."

As Wynn rose, Chap got up, as well, turning about for the door. Brot'an was already there.

"No," he said, shaking his head once. "I alone will take them."

Chap snarled, stalking straight at Brot'an, and Wynn's hand dropped on his shoulders. He looked up at her, his jowls still curled back.

You are not to be alone with him.

Wynn frowned at him.

"Dawn will come soon," Brot'an said, drawing Chap's attention. "And . . . respectfully, you are the hardest to move through the streets without being spotted."

Chap merely stared in Brot'an's eyes until Wynn closed her little fingers in his scruff.

"Don't you have something to *say* to them?" she asked, and glanced over her shoulder.

Chap knew Wynn was looking at Leesil and Magiere.

"What now?" Leesil grouched.

Chap was not looking forward to this. After the last additional thing that Wynn—and Shade—had shown him outside the room, he already felt shamed . . . and stupid. And Wynn had been right.

Once Chap showed—*told*—Leesil, he was going to throw a fit. Probably a big one.

The instant Brot'an opened the door, Shade hopped to her feet and scurried through. Wynn scratched her fingertips quickly on Chap's scalp and whispered, "Get it over with." She followed Ore-Locks out, and the last to leave was Brot'an.

"Chap?" Magiere called. "What's going on?"

He slumped, hanging his head, and finally turned about. First, without looking at Magiere or Leesil, he snatched up the talking hide in his teeth and dropped it on top of the sketched map. He might need it to help clarify what he was about to do.

Leesil looked at the hide with a frown, but Chap did not start pawing the letters. Instead, he began messing about, as Leesil would say, with all of the memories he had ever dipped from within his lifetime companion. It was not easy to find all that he sought, and Leesil flinched more than once.

"Will you get to the point already!" Leesil snapped, and then suddenly he went flat-faced and held his breath.

Magiere was watching Leesil. As he stiffened all over, she grabbed him and shook him. Still, he just stared back at Chap. Before Magiere could speak, Leesil's left eye twitched.

"What was that?" he whispered.

Chap did not know if Leesil asked if he had heard right or at all. It was one thing for Chap to call up a series of memory fragments inside Leesil or Magiere to make his intention clear as a communication. It was entirely another matter to call only the sound of voices from those long past moments— and, again, even harder to pick out and raise particular words or phrases arranged in the right order.

Chap was the one who had the headache this time. It went all the way into his eyes and ears. But it appeared he would not need the talking hide after all, and he repeated those fragmented spoken words gleaned from Leesil's memories.

—not—remember—only hear—my—words—from the—past—voices— . . . *—I—can . . . speak—and you—hear—me—now—*

How Shade had figured out how to do this left Chap in dismay. Then again, she had grown up with her own kind, unlike him. She knew only memory-speak, as Wynn called it, from the very beginning. She never had to deal with spoken language until finding Wynn, while he was still not as skilled at memory-speak as other majay-hì.

This new trick with memory-words would be useful, but it was not easy to do.

Leesil's expression began to darken.

"All of this time," he whispered, "before we even knew what you were . . . could do. . . . You've been messing around in my head."

Osha finally spoke up. "Why Léshil be angry to Chap?"

Even Leanâlhâm was staring in worry.

Leesil lunged from where he sat, shouting, "Come here, you mangy mutt!"

Chap tried to retreat, but his back paws did not catch. He ended up on his rump as Leesil dived for him with one outstretched hand. Magiere jumped on top of Leesil's back, pinning him to the floor, as Leanâlhâm scrambled on hands and knees to shield Chap.

"Do not touch him . . . speak to him that way!" the girl shouted at Leesil. "You will treat majay-hì with respect!"

"Respect?" Leesil echoed amid frantic breaths. "That deceitful, conniving—"

Leanâlhâm swatted him across the top of his head. "I not warn you again," she added emphatically.

"Leesil, what's this about?" Magiere demanded, still holding him down.

Leesil glared at Chap beyond a surprisingly angry Leanâlhâm, and he whispered, "It's him . . . talking at me . . . in my head."

"Well, what did he show you?" Magiere asked.

"Not memories . . . words!" Leesil barked, and tried again, unsuccessfully, to get out from under her. "He's putting *words* in my head."

Chap cowered behind Leanâlhâm, even as the girl looked back at him over her shoulder. Puzzled astonishment spread over her face. Osha, too, looked completely dumbstruck.

"Chap talk now?" he asked.

Magiere was watching Leesil, but she glanced sidelong at Chap in suspicion. So far, only Leesil truly understood what was going on, and Chap swallowed hard, waiting for Magiere to catch up.

"Why didn't you figure this out years ago . . . oh, great and wise Fay?" Leesil asked.

That brought back Chap's spite. He called up Leesil's own memory of a Chap covered in soot, scratching himself raw, and then added in broken memory words.

—*You—not—think of it—either*—

Leesil just glared at him.

"Wait," Magiere said too quietly. "He can talk . . . in our heads?"

"Yes," Leesil hissed.

And Magiere leaned forward atop Leesil, peering down at him. "So he can yammer at us, order us about, anytime he wants?"

Leesil let out a groan, or maybe it was a deep whine. He dropped his forehead against the floor. Magiere let out a sigh as she dropped on her butt beside him.

Chap rumbled and flicked his tongue up over his nose at both of them.

Just before dawn, Brot'ân'duivé took Wynn and her two companions, Shade and Ore-Locks, back to their inn. It was a long, slow process of moving the sage, the majay-hì, and the dwarf from one hiding point to the next as the city began to awaken for the day. But when he left them at their inn, he did not return to where Magiere and the others hid.

There was a task he needed to complete, and best done without the others knowing. He slipped through the shadowed alleys and cutways toward the guild's small castle.

Although Brot'ân'duivé would not say so, he thought Léshil's escape plan was as sound as any he could have formulated himself. The half-blood's mind worked well, likely from his mother's training, when he was not distracted. He possessed an innate ability to see what others might *do* and build upon those possible reactions. In spite of this, there was one long-term risk that Brot'ân'duivé wanted removed.

Any contact the anmaglâhk in this city had with Most Aged Father could easily lead to other teams being sent out into the world. In addition, the ones already here might split up if they had the means to remain in contact and coordinate with each other.

At least one of those options had to be removed—especially the second one. And there was a step to add to the plan that the others could not know about.

He wanted all of his enemies following Magiere and Léshil . . . and himself. Undead or not, Wynn's vampire would be a poor match for even a few trained members of Brot'ân'duivé's cast, though this was not his only reason.

Dawn and dusk were the most common times for agents abroad to check in with Most Aged Father or with others out scouting or on watch. With their numbers dwindling, Dänvârfij would be the one to do both.

A few streets from the guild, Brot'ân'duivé scaled the back of a small shop and slipped from roof to roof, out of sight of those below. He paralleled Old Procession Road from two blocks south, pausing often to watch the city's skyline. Something moved on a rooftop two blocks north, where Old Procession Road met Old Bailey Road, right across from the castle's bailey gate.

Brot'ân'duivé shook his head once. They must be spread thin, and have grown desperate, to put a scout in such an obvious position. It would be so easy to eliminate one more of them.

From his crouched position, at first he could not identify the one. He did not know all who traveled with Dänvârfij and Fréthfâre, even after following them for a year. The one suddenly scuttled to the roof's edge and hung its head over.

Brot'ân'duivé rose a little, wary of betraying his own presence against the city's skyline. Almost immediately, the one on the roof returned to the side facing the castle. Brot'ân'duivé did not need to know more. He took off north across the roofs, running in plain sight.

Someone else had passed by in the street below, checking in with the watcher on the roof. When he reached the last roof's side over Old Procession Road, he flattened as he peered over the edge.

A slender, tall form walked away in the early dawn. It wore a plain cloak, but that hid nothing from him. He saw its soft leather boots, dyed forest gray, and pant legs that matched. The way the figure moved, each step planted in a silent, flat step, was unmistakable.

Brot'ân'duivé watched Dänvârfij slip along the northwest run of Old Bailey Road, heading for some side street. She peered up toward the other one still on top of the roof.

Brot'ân'duivé could now see that the other figure was male. When that anmaglâhk shifted on the roof's edge, on hands and knees, the male kept his right knee off the roof's shakes.

Brot'ân'duivé realized it was Eywodan, likely the oldest member of the anmaglâhk here in this city. Years ago, Eywodan had assisted flood victims of Brot'ân'duivé's own clan. Eywodan's knee had been broken by rushing debris when he had waded into the swelling river. Brot'ân'duivé had carried him to a healer.

Brot'ân'duivé pushed away that memory and any sickness it brought. Eywodan was now the enemy, as well as Dänvârfij, Fréthfâre, and all of Most Aged Father's loyalists. Any who still followed that twisted, maddened patriarch could no longer be seen in any other way. But Brot'ân'duivé lingered, for an enemy was sometimes made so by the actions of another—by his action. One mistake made in fury and hatred had led to all of this, though it had been spurred by Most Aged Father's fanaticism.

Brot'ân'duivé had made that mistake. There was no changing it now, and he would not succumb to regret.

He watched until Eywodan looked the other way in scanning the guild's castle and the loop of street around it. With the street below clear and empty, Brot'ân'duivé dropped over the edge to land silently upon the cobblestones. He ran through the alleys and cutways, searching for a vantage point to catch sight of Dänvârfij. When he spotted her around a street corner in the early, dim dawn, he stalled.

She had doubled back beyond the castle and was heading south.

In scouting ventures with Léshil, Brot'ân'duivé had discovered there were not many inns or way houses in the southern district. That area did hold one of the city's landside exits. Could Dänvârfij simply be checking on another sentry? Had she placed someone to watch that exit?

It seemed unlikely, unwise, to spread their numbers so thin and still search for Magiere. Or had they given up the search and now merely waited and watched?

The sun had fully crested the rooftops in the east when Brot'ân'duivé finally watched Dänvârfij walk along a city thoroughfare and out the city's southern exit. He waited but a few moments and then followed, lingering inside the great gate's arch.

She only traveled a short way before stepping off the road into a grove of fir and pine trees.

This was what Brot'ân'duivé had hoped for. He waited until she was out of sight for three breaths, and then he walked out of the city before drawing his blades, keeping them under the folds of his dangling cloak.

Dänvârfij sank to her knees before a tall fir tree, its lowest branches high enough to hang above her bent head. She dreaded making this report, and yet she longed for guidance. Reaching inside the front of her forest gray tunic, she withdrew an elongated oval of smooth, tawny wood no bigger than her palm. She reached out and pressed the word-wood against the tree's trunk and whispered.

"Father?"

I am here, daughter.

Most Aged Father's voice filled her mind with welcome calm. She should have reported sooner and not let shame keep her from him.

"I have much to report," she said. "The white woman is here. We have seen her, and she has seen us, but we have not captured her yet."

What is the delay?

Dänvârfij closed her eyes. "Brot'ân'duivé now protects the woman and her companions. He has taken Wy'lanvi and Owain from us. Counting Fréth-fâre, we are now six. I have allowed the others only a quarter day or night of sleep between search or watch duty. But we are spread thin in a human city of such size."

She did not wish to sound as if she were making excuses for their lack of success. She simply wished him to know the true situation. No immediate response came, though she had not expected one. The loss of two more at the hands of the traitor would strike him hard. Even the thought of a greimasg'äh killing other anmaglâhk was so unthinkable.

So he is still there, in the city?

"And another," she answered, though this part was not something easy to tell him. "The faltering one, Osha, is with him. There is also the last survivor of Sgäilsheilleache's family . . . Leanâlhâm."

Osha . . . and Leanâlhâm . . . in a land of humans? What are they doing with the traitor?

His tone was so shocked that Dänvârfij wished she had not been the one to deliver such news. The rent in her caste was deepening. It had become more than just a few among the people sympathizing with dissidents both inside or outside of the caste. Osha was no longer anmaglâhk, and Leanâlhâm was just an orphan, and yet both had stepped into this civil war.

Dänvârfij ached, thinking of her people and wondering how much worse things had become since she had left home. She could not ask.

Do you have a plan?

The abrupt shift caught her off guard but was welcome.

"Of a kind. Our quarry has been trying to reach the sage, Wynn Hygeorht. That woman may hold something of importance. She has been imprisoned by her own kind, and it is my hope that Magiere and Brot'ân'duivé will try to free her before fleeing the city. When they come for the sage, above all else, Brot'ân'duivé will die, and we will capture the others."

You have sentries on all city exits?

"No, only on the port and the guild's castle. The others are sweeping the city, trying to gain a location."

Pull in everyone. Focus on the guild and all ways out of the city. You will not find Brot'ân'duivé until he chooses to show himself. Wait, and take your quarry in the open, once they are encumbered with too many to protect. This is the only way to keep the traitor from slipping away.

"Yes, Father."

His guidance made her settle at ease once more. Perhaps now was a chance to ask how he was, how efforts at home progressed . . . but a shadow shifted among the branches around her arm.

Dänvârfij's heart hammered as a shimmering white stiletto thrust through the branches for her heart. She twisted out of its path at the last instant. A booted foot shattered the branches and smashed the side of her head.

She rolled blindly away, trying to regain her feet. In her blurred sight, she saw a glint and kicked out as she rose on one knee. Her foot never connected, though that spark on white metal vanished.

Lunging backward and up to her feet, she reached for her own blades. She knew whom she faced even before her sight cleared, and she could not help being afraid. The very shadows of the fir's branches appeared to cling and glide over a tall, broad form like a second cloak as it—*he*—stepped out from between the trees.

Brot'ân'duivé, the traitor, stood fully in the dawn's light.

This was the first time in the long, dark journey from Dänvârfij's homeland that she had seen him face-to-face, seen those scars that skipped over his right eye. She was no match for him. Another greimasg'äh might not have taken him.

Brot'ân'duivé took another silent step, not even disturbing the leaves and needles on the earth.

She jerked out her stilettos and almost instantly realized her failure. As much as the traitor had been killing her brethren, killing her was not truly why he had come, for she held a stiletto in *both* hands.

Dänvârfij had dropped her word-wood at the tree. That was what he had come for.

Her life would be only a secondary gain next to that. She had lost even before she had a chance to strike at him. Her thoughts raced to scavenge anything from this moment.

Dänvârfij did not fear death; she feared failure of purpose, of her people . . . of her beloved patriarch, Most Aged Father. What was life to her other than service in silence and in shadow?

She quickly backed all the way to the open road and stood there in plain sight of any guards at the city gate. Even dull-witted humans would fix on a fight on the open road. Brot'ân'duivé would never call such attention to himself.

The greimasg'äh followed only to the last tree off the road and came no farther into the open.

Dänvârfij grew sick inside for her loss but sheathed her weapons, jerked off her face scarf, and pulled her hood back. With her face fully exposed, like any other visitor to the city, she turned and walked slowly toward the gates.

For a moment, she almost expected to hear a blade spinning through air.

It never came, and one military guard merely smiled at her as she passed through, into the city.

Now there was only Fréthfàre's word-wood, and it had to be guarded. Without it, they would be cut off from Most Aged Father and lost alone in this foreign land far from home.

Brot'ân'duivé watched through a tree's branches as Dänvârfij slipped back into the city. Killing her would have been an additional advantage. He did not admire her wisdom of retreat. He noted only that she was after all an anmaglâhk; she knew when, where, and how to cut her losses.

Turning back through the trees, he crouched beneath the branches of that one fir. There upon the needle-coated ground at its base lay the tawny oval of word-wood. He picked it up, prepared to destroy it, and then hesitated. There had been too many times in the past year when he had failed within himself, as he did so now when his spite and fury rose.

Brot'ân'duivé pressed the word-wood against the fir's trunk.

"Do you hear me, old worm in the wood of my people?" he whispered. "One day, I will come for you . . . again!"

No voice entered his thoughts, and after the longest moment, he was about to pull the word-wood from the bark and crack it.

Unlikely . . . but if ever, then I will be waiting again, dog . . . in the dark.

CHAPTER 22

Two mornings later, before the sun had risen, Wynn knelt by the back door of Nattie's inn and fastened a note to Shade's collar. Chane stood right behind both of them.

"Remember, give it only to Rodian," she said, and stroked Shade's neck as she drew up memories of the captain and the second castle of Calm Seatt. "Try to find him at the barracks first."

She wished Shade didn't have to be the one to put events in motion. Hopefully the dog could locate the captain somewhere other than the guild, as that place was likely watched by anmaglâhk.

Shade huffed and scratched the door.

With reluctance, Wynn cracked it open, and Shade slipped out and took off up the alley. When Wynn turned about, Chane looked troubled.

Dawn was close, and he needed to get back to their room.

Chane had a cloak—provided earlier by Brot'an—draped over his arm. It was not the drab cloak that the master anmaglâhk had been wearing as his traveler's disguise, but instead, it was the forest gray cloak of an anmaglâhk. Wynn didn't want to know where Brot'an had gotten it.

"Is everything else set?" Chane asked. "The trunks, the wagons . . . the inserts for the boots?"

"Yes, yes," she answered, nervous now that the first step had been taken.

"Ore-Locks arranged everything and kept me out of sight. I wish he was coming with us tonight, but he can't risk being seen in the middle of all this. There can be no oddities to put off the anmaglâhk."

"I will be there," he reminded her. And then he added grudgingly, "Lee-sil's plan should work, though he should not have involved you."

Wynn stifled a sigh. Chane had been fretting enough for both of them about her part in what was to come. But yes, the plan *should* work. Getting Rodian to agree to what she asked in Shade's message would help in that. All they could do now was wait.

"We should get you to the room," she said.

Chane didn't move.

"What's wrong?" she asked.

"There is something I haven't told you. Shade knows . . . but for some reason, she did not pass you any memories or try to tell you of it."

"Tell me what?"

Chane glanced away, and then blurted out, "I have managed to create a concoction, a potion, that allows me to remain awake during the day. I cannot go outside, but I will not fall dormant. I wish to be awake today, to help with preparations."

Wynn stared at him. "A potion? What . . . how long have you . . . ?"

He raised one hand to ward off questions. "For some time. I feared telling you because some of the components are questionable, and I based my experiments on a sample I obtained from Welstiel." He looked her straight in the eye before she could say anything about the last part. "You are the one who said we can no longer afford to refuse help on our side . . . from wherever it is offered. My being awake today will be helpful."

Wynn just stood there, taking this in. Chane could be awake during the day?

Once, she would've exploded at him for touching anything, using anything, that had ever belonged to Welstiel. She couldn't deny that the pack of toys Chane had taken from Magiere's undead half brother had been of some use. From the brass ring he now wore to the etched steel hoop that conjured

heat, there had been more than one moment when they wouldn't have succeeded in past endeavors. But the thought of Chane re-creating anything
uncovered by Welstiel and then consuming it . . .

To her surprise, though she was concerned, she wasn't angry. She'd never
admit it, but the thought of having his help all day brought relief. One part
was almost unbelievable, though.

"Shade has known about this?" Wynn asked.

"For a short while, just after she and I escaped from the guild."

"Why would Shade ever keep a secret for you?"

"I have wondered," he said. "It might be the ways of the majay-hì. Or . . .
she's more pragmatic than you know."

Wynn started slightly as the implications sank in. "So, yesterday, all day,
you were just lying there on the floor, pretending to . . . sleep . . . and she
knew it?"

Chane nodded once. Of all that Chane or Shade had ever done in Wynn's
company, this struck her as the most unsettling. They'd both been a pain in
her backside with their separate overprotectiveness. Now they were in actual
collusion about it.

"And there are side effects to this potion, aren't there?" she said. "That's
what all that hiding away on the sea voyage to the Lhoin'na was about. You
were . . . sick . . . every time you finally came out of your cabin."

He didn't—couldn't—deny it.

"It is nothing that will hinder me," he replied. "I am accustomed to it
now, so long as I do not prolong its use too far. I simply wanted you to know."

Shade was well on her way to Rodian, and right now, they had a great deal
to accomplish. Wynn walked past Chane and headed for the stairs.

"Let's get to work on those boots."

But soon enough, Wynn was going to make Chane show her everything—
including anything else he was hiding in Welstiel's pack of twisted little toys.
And Shade had better not be in on any more of it.

*　　*　　*

Rodian stepped from the barracks that housed his office and walked out into the courtyard of the second castle that housed Malourné's military. The sun was just cresting the keep's forward wall, and he knew it was too early to check in with the High Advocate.

It was the morning of the third day since he'd been summoned before Prince Leäfrich, and he hadn't slept all night.

So far, Rodian had been unable to convince the High Advocate to grant him a general warrant, but this didn't surprise him. The prospect of Shyldfälches pounding on doors was disruptive to the peace, yet Rodian hadn't given up. Last evening, he'd succeeded in convincing the advocate to send word to the royal family about his request. He had a feeling it would be granted.

Prince Leäfrich was likely under great pressure from the Premin Council to find Wynn.

Rodian slowed as he passed through the courtyard and watched the shadows of the keep's wall creep away as the sun rose higher. Even without the warrant, he'd not been idle.

His men swept the city on double duty, even gaining some of the military's regulars for assistance. All district constabularies had been alerted and given descriptions of Wynn Hygeorht and her wolfish black dog, with orders to detain either. So far, it seemed as if the little, precocious sage had just vanished.

Rodian rubbed his tired eyes, and then the sound of barking cut through his overburdened thoughts.

"Here! Stop that!" someone shouted. "Wait . . . isn't that . . . ? Get it!"

The barking only increased, mixed with snarls that echoed up the gatehouse tunnel.

It took only an instant before Rodian bolted into the tunnel.

The outer portcullis was already raised, and he doubled his pace. As he rushed out the tunnel's other end, he found three of the regulars trying to encircle a tall, charcoal black dog, which was snarling and snapping as it evaded them.

Shade was quick and agile, and gave them a lot of trouble.

One soldier spotted Rodian and held back for an instant. "Sorry, Captain. We can't get a grip on it . . . without getting bit."

Shade spun around, and at the sight of Rodian, she froze. Her racket dropped to a steady rumble.

He had no idea why his appearance would halt the dog in her place, and then he spotted one oddity. Wynn's dog had never worn a collar that he'd ever seen, yet a strip of gray wool was tied around Shade's neck. There was a piece of paper wrapped around that fabric.

"Back off, all of you!" Rodian ordered.

The three regulars exchanged confused glances but obeyed, standing poised around Shade but well out of reach. Slowly, cautiously, Rodian took two steps.

"Easy, girl," he said.

Shade continued to tremble and rumble, but she stood there watching him. Stranger still, she took a step toward him, though it made him hesitate in turn. Much as he wanted to know what was on that paper, he had no desire to get bitten. Shade was rather a large animal, and easily had the advantage of height over any common wolf.

The closer Rodian came, Shade matched him in slower steps, and grew quiet. Reaching down, he ripped the note off the collar and took a step back. He peeled open the torn paper, quickly reviewing its contents. He'd already guessed whom it was from. The note was short, but when he finished reading, he was left mentally numb.

Part of him wanted to curse; another part nearly melted in relief. He read the brief note again and weighed the scales of what Wynn was asking him to do—with no explanation and no promise on her part.

What choice did he have?

He could certainly pin down and lock up Shade, and make Wynn come to him to get the dog back. But that wouldn't get him the answers he wanted—needed—for what was going on inside the guild and between its Premin Council and the royals.

No . . . he had no choice. But he needed a quill and paper if he was to answer Wynn's note. He looked down at Shade, who tilted her head.

Backing toward the gatehouse tunnel, Rodian said. "Come?"

Shade trotted after him.

Chane knelt on the floor, working on the heel of a boot. He remained externally passive, but how he felt on the inside was another matter.

Telling Wynn the truth this morning about the concoction—or at least the one he had completed so far—took away one burden. He still hid the secret of the white flower petals and dwarven mushrooms—the *anasgiah* and *muhkgean*—and the hint of their use in *The Seven Leaves of Life*. He was also worried about the risks Wynn would undertake tonight.

He had no contention with the plan that Leesil had devised, only with the fact that Wynn was actively involved. If Leesil was so clever, why not come up with a plan that kept Wynn out of danger?

Chane was also unhappy about a visitor due to arrive any moment, and it was not long before that hesitant knock came at the door.

Wynn looked up from sewing padding into the shoulders of the forest gray cloak Brot'an had provided.

"It me," a soft voice said through the door.

Wynn swallowed and tried to clear her throat. "Ore-Locks, would . . . would you . . . ?" she stuttered.

The dwarf went to unlatch the door, and a tall, cloaked elf immediately stepped in. His amber eyes quickly found and locked on Wynn. This one was younger than Brot'an, with a long face, and loose, white-blond hair. Chane had seen him before and hated him at the time.

Once, in the Pock Peaks, this one had offered his full protection to Wynn—and she had accepted. Much later, when he had been injured, she had watched over him to the point of threatening Chane to keep away, though he had had no harmful intent in that moment.

"Osha," Wynn said tentatively, clearly aware of the strain in the room. "Come . . . in."

Chane still did not like him.

Osha did not even glance at Chane, either avoiding contact or because he was too fixated on Wynn. As he stepped closer to her, she put down the cloak and picked up Leesil's stained and tattered green scarf. Reaching up, she put her hand on Osha's arm.

"Let's see how this looks," she said. "Can you show me how he ties it up?"

Osha knelt beside her, taking the scarf.

Chane paused in his own work and had to fight to keep his hands from clenching.

"I think I hear Shade," he said, and hurried out the door.

He had heard no such noise but would have taken—made—any excuse to leave. He descended the steps two at a time to get away from that room.

Cracking open the inn's back door only a fraction, he hid behind it, against the daylight. A short while later, when Shade did arrive, she did not need to scratch. She poked her head inside, peeking around the door at him, and he widened the door for an instant, then shut it after she slipped in.

Shade trotted up the stairs and Chane followed, though not quickly enough; his reprieve from what waited in that room was far too short. Shade was already scratching at the room's door, and in her makeshift collar was a folded slip of paper, though not the one Wynn had sent.

Wynn jerked open the door from the inside before Chane gripped the handle. She snatched the paper as Shade stepped into the room. Chane was left standing on the landing as Wynn fumbled to open the sheet. One quick read, and she raised her eyes to him.

"He'll do it," she said, exhaling.

Chane ushered her back from the doorway and reluctantly followed her in and shut the door. No matter that the next step had been achieved, he watched Wynn already fretting again. Her gaze roamed as she looked at nothing, and he knew her thoughts were tangled up with what came next.

The cascade of events had begun and would not stop until all of this was over and done.

"We need to get word to the others," she said, and turned to Ore-Locks. "Leanâlhâm must leave as soon as the first wagon arrives. Can you go tell Magiere?"

At the mention of Magiere's name, Chane almost flinched.

Ore-Locks nodded, retrieving his staff from behind the door.

The plan may have been Leesil's, but whenever Magiere was around, she was always at the heart of more risks to Wynn's life. Chane could not help wondering how different things might have been if Magiere had never come back.

"Are you all right?" Wynn asked him.

"Yes . . . I am fine."

If nothing else, he would be with her this night. And if all went well, Magiere would soon be gone again.

Midafternoon, Leanâlhâm stood alone, outside the inn, dressed in Wynn's cloak with the hood pulled up. Behind her on the inn's porch were two large trunks and two crates of weathered wood planks. When she spotted a wagon rolling slowly up the street among the people coming and going—so many human faces—her stomach began to quiver.

The driver pulled his horses to a stop as another man beside him jumped down.

"You arrange for transport to the docks, miss?" the driver asked.

"Please," she answered carefully. "Thank you."

Brot'ân'duivé had coached her on what to say and how to say it. As with most foreign languages, more so this new one of Numanese, she understood more than she could actually speak.

At her silent direction, the second man loaded the crates and then the trunks, or, rather, he tried. When he attempted the first trunk, he grunted and could not quite lift it. The driver immediately hopped down to help.

"Begging your pardon, miss," the driver asked with a friendly smile. "What did you pack in there—rocks?"

Leanâlhâm tried to smile in turn, though nervousness made her small lips twitch. She looked away and down as she said, "Only some books . . . many books."

Brot'ân'duivé had thought this the best answer if needed.

"Books, eh?" the other man said, shaking his head.

The two men tried to lift the first trunk, but then thought otherwise. They dragged it to the wagon's back before heaving it up. The first trunk landed on the wagon's bed with a loud thump, and the wagon rocked. So it went with the second trunk.

"That's everything," the driver said, "Come on, miss. Up you go."

Leanâlhâm wavered. Once she boarded this wagon, there was no turning back. She had to manage this part of the plan alone. It would be the rest of the day and into the night before Osha—and Brot'ân'duivé—finished their tasks and rejoined her. She was frightened to be out in this strange, foreign place without Osha.

Brot'ân'duivé was dutiful to all his people, keeping them safe, including her. But Osha was truly good and kind, and as wounded by loss as was she. Perhaps even more.

"Miss?" the driver asked impatiently.

Leanâlhâm inhaled deeply. She took the driver's hand and let him pull her up onto the wagon's bench, as the other man climbed in back. There was nothing else she could do now that the cargo was loaded.

The wagon rolled down the street, farther and farther from the inn. In a surprisingly short time, the driver pulled up at the port. The waterfront and docks were filled with even more people than the street outside the inn, and none of them looked anything like her. The men unloaded the two trunks and two crates, carrying them off to the third pier, which she indicated as instructed by Leesil.

Leanâlhâm found herself waiting again, this time for a skiff to take her out to a ship.

The men headed off down the dock as the driver called out, "Safe voyage, miss."

For some reason, those words touched her, as if he truly wished that for her. She wanted to thank him but stumbled on the words, and then he was lost in the waterfront crowd. She checked the latches and straps on both trunks to make certain they were secure and then looked out over the great bay, past the docked ships and those beyond, toward the open sea. She looked anywhere to avoid seeing all the people around her and feeling so out of place. And yet . . .

Another voyage upon water awaited, with nothing to do but to ache for a home that no longer existed—at least not for her anymore. Had it not been for Osha on the journey here, she could not have borne sailing farther and farther from the only land she knew. At least she would still have him for company, and he would soon be far away from Wynn Hygeorht again.

That last thought filled Leanâlhâm with shame. Osha deserved something—someone—to cherish for all that he had lost and the burdens he now bore.

"Hold there!" a masculine voice commanded.

Leanâlhâm whirled in fright and saw an armed man in a red tabard. The way he looked at her as he strode up the dock clearly meant those words were for her, and she had no idea why.

She froze as he neared, and he dropped his head a little to peer directly into the hood of her cloak. Then he frowned and cocked his head in puzzlement, likely seeing her dark tan skin, her slightly narrow face, with those large, slightly slanted eyes that were green instead of amber. Then he looked over her cloak, the one Wynn had given her, and shook his head.

His manner changed instantly, and he stepped back, bowing slightly.

"Pardon, miss. Didn't mean to alarm you." Then he looked up and out beyond her. "Is that your skiff coming?"

Leanâlhâm followed the city guard's gaze out over the bay. She did not know if this skiff came for her, but she quickly nodded just the same. Whether it was this one or the next, she would soon be on a ship, waiting for nightfall.

CHAPTER 23

Not long past dusk, Én'nish still crouched upon a warehouse roof overlooking the southern end of the waterfront. Though she peered north along the high warehouse roofs, she could not make out Rhysís positioned at the northern end.

A few nights past, Dänvârfij had ordered a cease of all searches in the city. Tavithê was placed on watch at the city's southern gate, and Eywodan on the north exit, which spilled out onto the road leading up around the bay to the peninsula said to be the home of the dwarves. Dänvârfij herself took watch over the guild's castle.

They were all disciplined in long spells of wakefulness, but lack of sleep had begun to take its toll. Én'nish hoped someone from Magiere's group of misfits and traitors would show soon.

The city's guards had not been making her task any easier. They had been seen conducting their own sweeps through the city. Eywodan had surreptitiously learned they were looking for the sage, whom they claimed had been abducted from the guild. The city guards had been questioning people, using both the sage's description and several possibilities of attire.

Én'nish and her people now knew that Wynn Hygeorht was no longer inside the guild's castle.

She checked in with Rhysís at each bell that rang during the city's day, but neither of them had spotted anything noteworthy. Earlier, Rhysís had reported something that gave Én'nish a fragment of hope. A slender woman in a full cloak had arrived at the docks with luggage, and one of the city's guards had approached her almost immediately. The cloak the woman wore had somewhat matched a description that Eywodan had overhead the guards mention.

Rhysís had not been able to draw close enough to see the woman's face, but the guard had quickly departed. So it could not have been the sage, and the young woman was soon loaded onto a boat that rowed for a ship anchored in the bay. And Wynn Hygeorht would have never left the city alone.

Most Aged Father had been clear on this point. Magiere's people were fanatical about remaining together; they had proven so more than once. Still, Én'nish studied that one ship in the bay until dusk, never noticing anything of interest.

Her eyelids drooped and she shook herself, opening them. Sleep could come once their purpose was complete.

A patch of darkness in the street below moved of its own accord.

Én'nish twisted around, scrambling to the side of the warehouse's roof. A shadow that moved was now their greatest fear after Dänvârfij had told them what had happened when she had gone to speak with Most Aged Father.

Brot'ân'duivé, the traitor, was hunting them again.

She stuck only the top of her head over the rooftop's edge, just enough to look downward. Had it been only imagination and exhaustion addling her wits? The darkness moved again, and this time she saw it clearly.

It stepped through a pool of light cast by a street lantern, and Én'nish held her breath.

The near-black majay-hì silently padded toward the waterfront's far end and Rhysís's position. But along the way, it swerved into a side path and reappeared a block farther into the city on the double-wide street behind the waterfront.

Én'nish climbed the roof to its ridge and ran to leap to the next rooftop . . . and the next. When she was one rooftop away from Rhysís, she clicked her tongue five times. He rose like a dark silhouette sprouting from the shakes, and she pointed his attention toward the rear of that building. When he spotted the majay-hì, his return gestures indicated a question.

Follow?

She was torn, not wanting to split up if the dog led them to something important, but also reluctant to leave the port unwatched.

The majay-hì stepped into the light of another lantern. In that light, a shadow passed suddenly over the dog's head. Én'nish padded silently to the roof's rear edge for a better angle of view.

A cloaked figure walked right past the majay-hì, vanishing out the other side of the lantern's light. The majay-hì followed, but even the brief glimpse made Én'nish freeze. The figure had been taller than any human, with broad shoulders for such a stature. Its cloak and hood were a familiar forest gray.

Brot'ân'duivé had appeared and met up with the sage's black majay-hì, and he was clearly dressed for a hunt.

Én'nish rose on the roof, looking toward Rhysís in the same instant that he looked at her. For the first time, she was glad that she had teamed with him rather than with Tavithê or Eywodan. Dänvârfij was incapable of understanding anguish and the need for vengeance. Én'nish did not see either as a fault; they were imperatives for justice.

As Rhysís began assembling his short bow, Én'nish held up one hand to stop him. He paused, as if with great effort.

They could not yet kill Brot'ân'duivé. The traitor and the majay-hì were on the move—but to where? Any attack now would cut them off from the answer. If the greimasg'äh had slipped up in exposing himself, he might also expose the location of Magiere and the others.

Rhysís finished with his bow just the same and slung it over his shoulder. He stood waiting as Én'nish backed up to take a running leap across to him. Together they followed their quarry from across the waterfront's rooftops. This was what Én'nish had been waiting for, and they picked the trail of their target.

The majay-hì and Brot'ân'duivé were not difficult to follow, but that in itself left Én'nish wary. At the end of a row of slightly shabby shops across the street below, the pair stopped at the mouth of a broad cutway nearly as wide as the street itself. In that space stood a wagon with a team of two horses.

Én'nish slowed, ever more cautious as she crept to the roof's rear edge and leaned out to look.

The wagon rolled out into full view, turning the corner with its team pointed away up the street. As it stopped, a short figure stood up in its back. This small one wore a gray robe and full cowl: the sage. But even more than that, the driver riveted Én'nish's attention.

With his back turned to her where he sat on the bench, reins in hand, she still saw his hood was half pulled down. Over his head was an old, green scarf that held back long, white-blond hair. She had seen that scarf once before.

The sight of Léshil flushed Én'nish with sudden heat.

The sage stepped to the wagon bed's rear, patting her thigh, and the black majay-hì leaped up to join her. The greimasg'äh followed, and Én'nish heard the flick of reins. The wagon rolled away behind the waterfront, heading north through the city's bay side.

Én'nish grew more confused and anxious with each heartbeat.

The wagon could only be heading for the city's northern gate, but where were Magiere, Osha, the girl called Leanâlhâm, and the deviant majay-hì they called Chap? Most Aged Father wanted prisoners for questioning, but the primary need was to capture Magiere. Why would Brot'ân'duivé try to escape with only Léshil, the sage, and the younger majay-hì?

Én'nish locked eyes with Rhysís. They had to act now while Brot'ân'duivé remained in sight. All they need do was kill him from above, or at least incapacitate him. They would then gain Léshil and the sage as hostages.

She longed to kill Léshil, but she accepted that he would be a valuable bargaining tool. Most Aged Father's given purpose came first, but there would come a time for revenge. She nodded to Rhysís.

Rhysís stood up, notching an arrow and drawing it back. In a blink, they would never again have to watch their own shadows for a traitor. Rhysís grew still, turning so slowly as he tracked his target. The bowstring released.

Én'nish's gaze flicked to the street below.

The arrow struck Brot'ân'duivé dead center between his shoulder blades.

The greimasg'äh fell back, tumbling off the wagon's rear to flop facedown on the cobblestones. The sage cried out, and Léshil heaved on the reins. But his own words were lost in the sharp hiss of another arrow from Rhysís's bow.

The second arrow struck Brot'ân'duivé's back directly above the first and over his heart.

Én'nish instantly drew her bone knife and set its hooked point into the roof's edge. She swung over the edge, feeling for any purchase with her foot to quickly reach the street. She dropped, still too high up, hit the cobblestones, and rolled. When she was up again, she waited only long enough for Rhysís to follow.

She heard more shouting and saw the wagon turn a corner. Frantic, she drew a stiletto with her other hand and bolted up the street. In that instant, she lost focus on her purpose. Even Léshil slipped from her mind at the sight of the greimasg'äh lying still in the street.

Two arrows in his back were not enough for all those whom the traitor had killed. Neither she nor Rhysís or any of them would find relief until an anmaglâhk blade was thrust true through Brot'ân'duivé's heart. Then they would leave him to rot in the stench of this human city of dead stone, far from living trees and the burial ground of their people. And when Léshil followed that traitor into death, Én'nish's beloved Grôyt'ashia could finally find peace among the spirits of their ancestors.

Én'nish slowed to creep in upon Brot'ân'duivé's body, her eyes fixed on the arrows protruding from his back. Suddenly it was not enough to make certain he was finished. She wanted to look into his face a last time, to see those scars that marred his flesh as much as treachery marred his spirit.

"What are you doing?" Rhysís whispered. "The others will elude us!"

Still, she reached down.

With her stiletto poised, she gripped the shoulder of Brot'ân'duivé's cloak and tunic and jerked. Both arrows snapped as he flopped over, but another clatter drew her eye as the greimasg'äh's cloak fell open.

There was a sword on Brot'ân'duivé's hip, the sheath's end having been cut off short and sewn shut with leather laces. She looked to his face and faltered in panic before she could strike.

The face in the hood was not Brot'ân'duivé.

It was human and too pallid for such a quick death. Long features were half obscured by tendrils of red-brown hair. The eyes in that face suddenly opened and narrowed on her.

Én'nish flinched as a hissing rasp escaped his mouth and she stared into irises like colorless glass.

"Chane's hit!" Wynn screamed out as he'd fallen onto the street.

Almost immediately, the wagon tilted as it rounded the corner too fast.

Wynn tumbled against the side, and Shade lost her own footing. Wynn tried to sit up and look for Chane, but the back of her robe was grabbed from behind. Someone pulled her off her feet and barked "Down!" As her butt hit the wagon's bed, the wagon lurched to a halt. She barely caught a glimpse of a flapping cloak as the driver vaulted from the bench and ran along the wagon's bed.

Osha ripped the green scarf from his hair, and it fluttered down upon a wagon sidewall as he leaped out the wagon's back.

He landed in the outer street, his bow and a black-feathered arrow in hand, and he simply dropped his quiver at his feet. Shade launched off the wagon, as well, stopping at the cutway's corner as Osha notched his arrow. Wynn scrambled to follow them.

"Where he?" Osha shouted, drawing back the arrow.

Wynn was confused, wondering if they'd lost Chane, but then she knew Osha meant the captain, Rodian.

"We didn't get far enough," she answered as she reached the corner and joined Shade.

Back down the street, she spotted Chane trying to get a grip on the smaller anmaglâhk—who kicked out and rolled away across the cobblestones.

As that one gained its feet, Wynn thought it might be a woman, but a second one, clearly a male, turned his bow up the street at the sound of voices.

Wynn heard the sharp hiss of a bowstring's release, but the anmaglâhk hadn't fired yet. Then . . . a black-feathered arrow appeared to sprout below his left collarbone. He yelped, his aim wobbling, and his shot went high as he stumbled backward.

Shade was snarling but did not rush out—perhaps because Osha had already reached down for his quiver and another arrow.

The smaller anmaglâhk shrieked like an animal. She quickly backed toward her crumpling companion and threw a stiletto up the street before Osha had risen from his crouch. Instantly, there was another blade in her hand.

"Osha!" Wynn shouted. "Shade, go!"

Shade bolted out and down the street as Osha pushed off sideways from his crouch. The stiletto snagged in the side of his cloak before he hit the cobblestones. He never slowed and rolled to one knee, trying to draw the second arrow.

The wounded anmaglâhk dropped his bow, ripped out the arrow from his upper chest, and drew his blades as the small one flipped her second stiletto for another throw.

This was all happening too fast, and Wynn saw everything coming apart before her eyes.

"Down there!" came a distant shout from up the street. "You two—round through the next street and cut them off."

Wynn sucked in air as she looked the other way beyond Osha.

Shyldfälches in red tabards and chain armor came running through the night. Ahead of them was Rodian on his white horse.

Én'nish was lost and stunned, even in fury, at the sight of the pale man inside Brot'ân'duivé's cloak. Now he was on his feet, a shortsword in hand—and the remains of both arrows still stuck out of his back. She took a quick glance up the street toward the other disguised one . . . that had not been Léshil.

Osha stared back at her along the shaft of an arrow drawn in his bow. He did not fire, even as the little sage ran to his side and a shout carried from farther up the street.

"Down there! You two—round through the next street and cut them off."

Én'nish saw city guards running toward her, one on a white horse quickly outdistancing the others. In horror, she realized this was not just another decoy but a trap. She could not even risk taking her eyes off the pale man to look back at Rhysís, but they both needed to flee. Neither of them could be taken here.

"Beside the warehouse," she whispered as she spun.

She threw her second stiletto down at the charging black majay-hì, and the sage screamed. Én'nish heard a guttural rasp from the pale man now behind her, and his rapid footfalls warned of his charge as she grabbed for Rhysís. A sharp hiss in the air gave her only an instant's warning as the majay-hì lunged aside and her blade careened off the cobble.

Én'nish threw herself against Rhysís half an instant too late. The sharp sting of something burned across the right half of her back. She did not slow at the pain of an arrow tearing her tunic to skim her flesh.

"Run!" she ordered, dragging Rhysís toward a path between the buildings and the docks at its far end.

Rodian saw Wynn standing midstreet beside a man with a bow and long blond hair. Then he spotted the one she called Chane and the black dog. They were trying to surround two others wearing gray outfits and with the lower halves of their faces covered.

In spite of the bizarre sight, it was instantly clear who was the threat. Then the gray pair broke through the dog barring the way and ran between two warehouses.

Rodian swung out of the saddle as Snowbird slowed. "Lúcan! Angus! With me!"

He took off running after the fleeing pair as he pulled his sword.

"Rodian, no!" Wynn shouted. "Don't follow them."

He ignored her, rounding the corner in pursuit.

Wynn wanted to curse at the captain, but she turned quickly to look up at Osha. This was the moment to get him out of here, as planned, while the city guard was occupied.

"Go," she whispered. "Now, before the captain returns . . . with a lot of questions."

Osha looked down into Wynn's eyes, and for an instant, she regretted that she'd never taken a moment with him in these past few days and nights. There had been too much to do, and too many burdens on all of them. And then there was Chane, so close by.

Osha didn't say a word, didn't blink, as his gaze roamed her face like someone seeing something he'd lost and suddenly found.

"Hurry!" Wynn urged, glancing once toward where Rodian had gone. Already other guards were in the street around them, but they were too busy heading for various other ways to the docks.

When Wynn looked back, Osha was gone.

She hadn't heard or felt anything; he just wasn't there anymore. In that moment, she was the one who felt as if she'd found something she'd left behind only to have it vanish before her eyes. She hadn't even thanked him or said good-bye this time.

Shade appeared at her side and looked up the cutway toward the wagon. Wynn looked, as well, perhaps hoping, but there was no sign of Osha. She ran to the wagon, looking in its back for one thing. But the long and narrow canvas bundle that Osha had brought with him was gone, as well.

It was so strange the way he had insisted he bring it rather than stow it with the rest of the gear to be loaded on the ship. Stranger still, he treated it as some burden that revolted him.

Wynn was suddenly aware of someone behind her, and she cringed in shame.

"Are you all right?" she asked, unable to look back.

"Yes . . . only one partially penetrated," Chane answered. "The wood plank did well enough, but you will need to pull the other arrowhead out."

As she turned around, Chane dropped to one knee and looked away. She found two broken-off arrows in his back. One protruded more than the other, the back of its white metal head still showing through Brot'an's forest gray cloak.

Wynn quickly jerked that one out, for it had only stuck in the plank that she'd fastened onto Chane's back before they left the inn. They'd known whom the anmaglâhk would shoot first, and that had been why they'd dressed Chane in the anmaglâhk cloak and boots that Brot'an had acquired.

The other arrowhead was deeper in Chane's back. Wynn could feel that the plank had split on its impact.

"Brace yourself," she whispered, but she hesitated as she gripped the second snapped-off shaft.

It was coated in Chane's black fluids, which had already soaked into the cloak. Her grip slipped as she pulled, and she felt him flinch once. She finally had to wrap a corner of the cloak around the splintered shaft's end.

Chane winced as the arrow came out, and the black stain spread through the cloak and across his back. There was nothing more to do, as they'd have to wait to remove the broken plank.

"It will heal," he whispered as he rose.

Several guards stood nearby, and Wynn worried about how much they had just seen. It was night, and even real blood didn't look red in the dark. She held on to Chane's forearm as she looked toward where Rodian had gone. Now all they could do was wait for the captain's return.

That, too, was part of the plan.

Rodian nearly collided with two of his men as he ran out of the path's far end at the dockside. Lúcan caught up with him, but Angus lagged behind.

"Where are they?" he demanded.

The two guards before him looked about, shaking their heads.

"We never saw them," said the first. "And they didn't get by us."

Lúcan rushed out, peering both ways along the waterfront. He stepped to the left of where one pier jutted out into the bay and looked down toward the water below. Rodian watched his trusted corporal take a slow breath as he looked about again—and then he cursed several times.

It was as if the strangely garbed pair had vanished. What was it about them that had kicked all of his instincts into alarm? And Wynn Hygeorht still waited in the keeping of his men.

Rodian called Lúcan to follow and strode back between the warehouses. When he came out onto the backstreet, Wynn stood there beside Shade. She looked far too composed for his waning patience. Behind the pair stood that tall, pale bastard who'd struck Snowbird on his escape from the guild grounds.

Rodian glared at that one, at Wynn and the dog, and then looked around. There was one more who was missing—the one with blond hair and a bow. It didn't matter as much as it should have, for he had found Wynn Hygeorht.

"Who were those people?" he demanded. "And why did they come at you?"

Wynn shrugged. "I don't know, but I feared turning myself in until I had enough protection from you. And now I am safely in your custody."

Rodian clenched his jaw to keep from shouting. "You expect me to accept that?"

"I assume your orders are to return me to the guild."

He paused to take a few breaths. Angry and confused as he was, his ultimate problem had been solved. Wynn *was* in his custody, and with no bloodshed. Forcing calm, he clung to that and tried to ignore all the questions nagging him. But in spite of everything, he still wasn't prepared to force her back to the guild if she didn't want to go, and as of yet, no one had filed a formal charge against her.

It would have been much easier for him if he just did so. That was what the royal family wanted—demanded.

"I want some answers," he said.

"I'll try," she replied, "but I have a few requests."

Rodian raised one eyebrow at her continued audacity. "And what are those?"

"That my companion and dog be allowed to come with me . . . and that they can stay with me at the guild."

The Premin Council had not filed any charges against Wynn Hygeorht or her tall companion, let alone the dog. Wynn's request seemed a relatively benign—and unnecessary—condition. Rodian could certainly file assault charges on the one called Chane, but it was too damn much trouble.

And Wynn was just too calm about it all, as if she already knew.

"What else?" he asked.

"You will take me to the gates of the guild and stop there," she went on. "Then you will find Premin Hawes and bring her out—alone. I won't go inside without her first coming to get me."

That was a puzzle greater that any other she'd given him. Hawes had hardly proven herself obliging to Wynn.

"And last . . ." Wynn said, heading toward the wagon.

Rodian waved off his men about to close on her. She reached into the wagon's back and returned with a wrapped parcel in hand.

"I'll need a private moment someplace," she said, "to change clothes before we get there."

Rodian shook his head. He'd salvaged his public reputation and immediate position, but it remained to be seen how he stood privately with the royal family. And yet . . .

"When all is done," Wynn added, "and when there's time, I'll tell you what happened here, what happened to me at the guild . . . as much as is possible."

CHAPTER 24

Brot'ân'duivé stood in the shadows of a warehouse adjacent to the docks and watched one particular ship anchored in the bay. He noted the rise of the moon and listened for the city's night bells to gauge the proper timing.

He was not given to regret, but he had laid a final task on Osha, a risk as well as a burden. Osha was the only one who could accomplish it, and Brot'ân'duivé hoped the young one would manage this final piece of the plan well enough.

It was one piece that Brot'ân'duivé had added and not shared with the others.

Dänvârfij was unable to cast off doubt and fear of failure as she watched the guild's castle. She still could not believe she had allowed Brot'ân'duivé to take her word-wood. He had known exactly how to hobble her team. Now there would be no effective way to split her forces, should the need arise. No doubt, if he found out where they hid, he would come for the second one held by Fréthfâre to cut them off completely from Most Aged Father.

The guild grounds were quiet, with little activity aside from guards walking the bailey wall. Dänvârfij's eyelids drooped, and she forced them open, angry with herself.

A bird's chirp carried in the night air. She ignored it until the third quick repetition.

She turned on the rooftop at that calling for attention from an anmaglâhk. It had come from the building's side, from Old Procession Road leading to the bailey gate.

Had something happened? Which of her team had left a post to come to her?

She crept to the roof's side and peered over the edge.

A tall figure in a light brown cloak stood below with his hood thrown back. His hair was as white-blond as hers. Some long, narrow object wrapped in canvas was strapped across his back with a length of twine running over his left shoulder. Over that same shoulder hung a traditional an'Cróan curved bow rather than the assembled style of the Anmaglâhk.

The bow was fully strung and readied, though strangely its string was over his shoulder's back and the bow hung forward next to his left arm. A quiver protruded above his right shoulder, and the arrows within it had black feathers.

Dänvârfij watched Osha look about. Was he reckless enough to show himself in the open, alone? Or was this some trick or trap?

"Dänvârfij, are you here?" he called out in their own tongue.

He strolled to the wide street's far side and paused, his back to her as he looked toward the bailey gate. Dänvârfij slipped her hand into the back of her tunic, reaching for the parts of her bow.

Osha cocked his head, though he did not look up her way.

"We must talk," he called, as if he knew she was near.

She drew her bone knife instead of her bow's handle, and hooked it on the roof's edge. Whatever he had come here for, he had to be stopped from calling her name again. It was not a long drop from a shop's roof. She rose from her landing, bone knife in hand, and he turned to watch her.

He appeared calm and did not move at all in the street, but he looked as tired as she felt. She took a step.

"Far enough," he warned.

She halted and kept her voice lower than his. "What do you want?"

"Nothing but to be done with you . . . all of you."

His voice sounded so weary beneath his anger, but Dänvârfij felt no pity for him. "The damage is done; you are a traitor in trying to kill your own!"

"I have killed no one," he returned.

"You tried, and that is enough. For that, your life is forfeited."

The instant she took another step, he shrugged his shoulder. The bow dropped forward and he snatched it with one hand as the other quickly pulled an arrow from the quiver.

Dänvârfij faltered, for the distance might still allow him to fire. She needed room to evade, so she could then close before he drew a second arrow.

Osha simply held the arrow's notched end between two fingers, not yet setting it to the bowstring.

"I could have killed one of yours the night they came after the first wagon," he said. "And again this very night. Those two should soon be coming to you."

Deep within a corner of Dänvârfij's mind, she understood his loss and the need to lash out. He had lost his teacher, as she had lost hers, in the same instant when the two had killed each other . . . over the pale-skinned monster called Magiere. But she had not acted on those drives as Osha had. She had not abandoned her beliefs, her caste, her oath, and her people.

"I came to tell you that Brot'ân'duivé has left the city," Osha went on, bitterness and spite plain in his voice. "He slipped past yours and has taken Magiere, Léshil, and Chap on a ship bound for what is called the Isle of Wrêdelyd. You will not catch them, and there is nothing left here for you."

Her throat closed up. This could not be possible. It was a lie!

"I do not care if you believe me," Osha said. "I am sick of all of you. You are no better than him . . . if you think killing your own will save our people. They need saving only from you . . . and him. I am done with Brot'ân'duivé, as I am with you."

Dänvârfij was almost overcome by the urge to attack, but his words burned in her ears. Had he truly abandoned the traitor greimasg'äh? Had she truly let her quarry escape?

"If you do not believe me," Osha said, "then go and see for yourself."

He told her of the inn where they had all been hiding, yet he still did not move or turn away. Was this the truth—had she failed yet again in her purpose? Had Brot'ân'duivé slipped away once more, and this time taken what she and hers had sought?

She had to reach the docks. Then another chirp in the dark startled her.

Without thinking, Dänvârfij glanced up the street into the city, and then looked back in panic.

Osha was gone.

She almost ran out to look for him. There were few ways he could have taken in that brief mistake of hers, but too much had been already lost. She turned, running for the shop's wall to reach the roof once more.

As Dänvârfij finally gripped the roof's edge, pulling herself up, Én'nish was waiting for her rather than on watch at the waterfront.

Brot'ân'duivé remained unseen in the night shadows outside a waterfront warehouse as he waited for Osha. Once the skiff came in for its arranged final trip, he would have to step out to meet it at the dock. If the skiff arrived and found no one waiting, it would simply leave.

He did not fear being seen once he left the shadows, for he believed Léshil's plan to pull the anmaglâhk away had certainly worked. Even now, Osha should have found Dänvârfij or one of her comrades near the guild's castle and panicked them into gathering in an effort to verify his story. Osha was then to return to the waterfront to board the ship.

The best of the lie that Brot'ân'duivé had formulated for Dänvârfij had been that it was the truth. Dänvârfij and Fréthfâre would be in full panic once they found Magiere's last hiding place was empty. By the time they converged on the waterfront, any ship they managed to board and search would give them nothing.

Magiere would be long gone, and they would have to wait to follow her.

Brot'ân'duivé wanted them to wait—and to follow. For in all the plans concerning the orbs, there were three factors that concerned him the most.

First, he had had to choose whom to follow in going after only one orb at a time. Following Magiere was the only true choice, though Wynn Hygeorht seemed to know much more about the devices.

Second, keeping his enemies far from as many facts as possible meant keeping them away from the young sage. And again, that meant keeping their focus on Magiere in their ignorance. But this also served Brot'ân'duivé's final concern.

And last, Dänvârfij, Fréthfâre, and all with them would never give up. It would not matter how many ways he found to hamper them. If he was to keep them from completing their purpose, they would have to be brought within his reach. They must follow Magiere—and him—and he would not leave one of them alive in the end.

His people's freedom from Most Aged Father depended on this, just as their survival in what would come might depend on these unknown devices of the Ancient Enemy.

The waterfront was far beyond sight of the small castle of the human sages, yet Brot'ân'duivé looked up the street between the warehouses and into the city.

Three bells for midnight rang softly across Calm Seatt, and still there was no sign of Osha.

Whatever had happened to the young one, Brot'ân'duivé could only hope that Osha had fulfilled his final task. There was no time for worry, disappointment . . . or even grief, if the worst had happened. In that last concern, he had one dark hope.

It seemed impossible that Osha could have died. No, not for the sake of the unexplained fate that had separated the young one from the life he had wanted most of all. Osha had to be alive, which meant he had *chosen* not to return as instructed.

Brot'ân'duivé looked toward the bay and saw the skiff coming in. He slipped from the shadows and headed silently up the nearest dock, waiting until the skiff arrived and a heavily bearded sailor climbed up the ladder.

"Any baggage?" the man asked.

Brot'ân'duivé shook his head.

"Then we'd best go. Captain wasn't thrilled with this delay for a late-night pickup."

Brot'ân'duivé hesitated. "One moment," he said, and looked again toward the city.

"You waitin' for someone else?" the sailor asked.

Brot'ân'duivé lingered, ignoring the sailor, until he heard the man sigh. Then he turned and followed the sailor down the ladder into the skiff.

Leanâlhâm stood at the ship's rail, waiting for the skiff to return. In the last year of crossing the world, she had waited too many times. However, the worst of this instance was not being without the certain protection of a greimasg'äh but wondering when Osha would finally return.

It was so dark across the water to the lights of the human city, and waiting yet again grew to be too much. As late as it was, she needed something to fill the moments. It did not matter anymore if she took up her final task without Brot'ân'duivé.

Leanâlhâm turned away, ignoring the stares of two sailors on deck. She descended the ladder below the aftcastle to hurry for the cargo bay. She paused at its door long enough to turn up her oil lantern and then peeked inside, making certain no sailors were in there. The bay was only half full, and thankfully the two trunks were in easy reach and not buried beneath other cargo. She set down the lantern and crouched before the first one.

"I am here," she said, struggling with the strap buckles on the slightly smaller trunk. "One moment."

It took longer than that before the straps were free. She pulled a cord with a set of keys over her head to unlock the trunk's catch. It took both hands for her to heave the lid open.

Magiere sucked a deep breath and struggled out of the ball she was curled into inside the trunk.

"Are you all right?" Leanâlhâm asked.

Magiere struggled up to her feet, scowling as she worked one stiff knee and growled, "Leesil is never planning anything again!"

"Oh, quit whining," came a muffled voice from the other trunk. "It worked, didn't it?"

The other trunk suddenly vibrated amid an erratic thumping from within.

"Hey!" Léshil shouted louder. "For the last time, Chap . . . get your butt out of my face!"

Leanâlhâm's mouth gaped.

Magiere groaned under her breath. "Let's get them out of there . . . before Chap gets bitten."

Leanâlhâm crawled to the second chest, waiting as Magiere quickly undid the straps, and then she fumbled once while getting the key into the lock.

"Hurry up, already," Léshil cried out.

Magiere quickly heaved open the lid. Inside the trunk, Leanâlhâm found Chap almost upside down atop Léshil, who was crushed at the bottom.

"What took so long?" he demanded.

"Oh, quit *your* whining," Magiere answered.

"Yeah? Well, you had a private 'room,'" Leesil retorted. "Next time, you get to bunk with his sacred stinkyness."

"I said there won't be a next time," Magiere warned.

Leanâlhâm could only imagine how awful the afternoon and half a night had been for these three, locked up like this. Even with a water skin each and some air holes punched low in the trunks' sides, it must have been more than stifling.

Chap launched off the top of Léshil's stomach, and Leanâlhâm had to duck.

Léshil made a retching sound. "Ow! *Valhachkasej'â*, you mongrel!"

Leanâlhâm gasped at Léshil's curse. As Chap landed on the floorboards behind her, she gripped the trunk's edge, leaning straight into Léshil's face.

"You do not speak to him that way!" she admonished.

Léshil lurched away, his back flattened against the trunk's far side. "But he . . . I only . . ."

"He is a sacred guardian of my people!" Leanâlhâm shouted, too outraged for any of his excuses. "You will show respect."

Léshil just blinked twice and looked up at Magiere.

Magiere took in Leesil's dumbstruck face, and she held up both hands. "I'm not getting into the middle of this."

Leesil's eyes narrowed on Chap, though he clenched his mouth shut in an angry pout under Leanâlhâm's steady glare. It didn't help that Chap peeked around from behind the girl and flicked his tongue out and up over his nose.

This had to be more than just the girl reacting to Leesil's and Chap's foul moods. Leanâlhâm had been left on her own for too long, too worried about all that was happening beyond her reach.

Magiere reached down and grasped the girl's arm, pulling her. "Come on . . . we could all do with some fresh air."

Leanâlhâm grasped Magiere's arm in turn. "No! You cannot be seen. . . . What if all did not go right . . . the other anmaglâhk come for the ship . . . or someone here betrays you?"

"We'll be fine," Magiere assured, though more than ever she realized how difficult things were going to become with Leanâlhâm to watch over. "Brot'an set up the timing and they should both be aboard soon. We'll be out of port before anyone knows it."

Leanâlhâm calmed a little, though she still looked uncertain. She wouldn't let go of Magiere's arm.

"Yes," someone said. "The sails are being set."

Magiere spun, pushing the girl behind her as she reached for her falchion. Her hand never found the hilt, as her sword was still in the first trunk. There was Brot'an in the hold's doorway. As he stepped in, Leanâlhâm ducked around Magiere.

"Greimasg'äh!" she breathed in relief.

Leanâlhâm seldom appeared glad to see the elder of the anmaglâhk, but she now smiled at the sight of him. Brot'an only nodded and, pulling down the hood of his cloak, stepped right past her toward Magiere. So little could ever be read on Brot'an's scarred face that the slight wrinkle of his brow put Magiere on edge.

"What now?" Leesil asked.

Obviously he'd caught the flicker of expression, as well, though Chap was strangely silent. Brot'an looked between them, perhaps considering his words, and that started Magiere worrying even more.

"Where is Osha?"

At Leanâlhâm's question, Magiere spotted the girl outside the hold's doorway and peering down some outer passage. Brot'ân'duivé's mouth visibly tightened, and he didn't look back at the girl.

"What happened?" Magiere asked, growing alarmed.

"*Ahäichei* Osha?" Leanâlhâm nearly screamed at Brot'an.

When he still didn't answer, she turned and ran out of sight up the passage.

Magiere shoved past Brot'an, racing after Leanâlhâm, as she felt the ship lurch under rising sails.

Dänvârfij did not know what to expect as she ran out onto the waterfront with Én'nish.

"What do we do?" Én'nish breathed.

Dänvârfij stood there, staring at the few ships still in dock. If Osha had spoken the truth, then none of these vessels would gain her anything.

Én'nish had little more to offer on the way here. She could only relate that there had been another decoy, and that Rhysís had been wounded but was well enough to have returned to their quarters on his own. In that, Dänvârfij truly worried that Osha had spoken the truth.

Rhysís should not have been outdone by the likes of Osha, that pathetic excuse for one of her caste on whom Sgäilsheilleache had taken pity. But Osha had beaten Rhysís with a bow.

Dänvârfij tried to see out across the great bay, but in the dark and over the distance, she could not make out whether there was an outbound vessel. What could she do now?

Footsteps on wood rose behind her, and she spotted a large human male in a striped shirt and long coat of shaggy black fur striding down a pier toward the shore.

"Wait here," Dänvârfij told Én'nish.

She quickly pulled down her face wrap and hood. Stepping slow and steady, she gave the heavy man time to spot her before going to meet him.

"Pardon," she said. "You are a master here?"

He stopped, looking her up and down and then straight in the eyes, for she was as tall as he. She was obviously a foreigner, but most likely he would mistake her as one of the elves of this continent that she had heard mentioned twice in her time here.

"Ship?" she asked. "Bound for the isle?"

This was the only hint Osha had given her. Her Numanese was not perfect, but that last word would be enough for the man to understand her intention.

"You mean Wrêdelyd?" he asked. "You looking for passage?"

"Yes."

"Sorry, the only ship I've heard bound for there just set sail." He shrugged and pointed off toward the waterfront's north end. "Leave word with the harbormaster about where you're staying. When the next ship headed that way comes in, he'll let you know."

She could not even bring herself to shake her head as she tried to think of what to do next. Nothing came of it other than that she would have to explain all of this to Fréthfâre.

Dänvârfij turned away from the man without even a thank-you. She had let the monster—and any whereabouts of the artifact—slip from her grasp again.

Brot'ân'duivé now had both.

The following night, Chane paced alone in the guild's inner courtyard. Events of the recent days and nights were fresh in his mind. He was a little surprised, perhaps annoyed, to find himself missing Ore-Locks's company.

They'd arranged for the dwarf to head back to Dhredze Seatt as soon as Leesil's plan had been set in motion. Ore-Locks's tasks were done, and after all he had learned of the orb—the orbs—he had grown increasingly anxious to return home.

In that, Chane had agreed. No matter that the orb of Earth was hidden away with the Stonewalkers; he trusted only Ore-Locks where the orb was concerned.

Tonight, Wynn had gone to the main library to search for all possible routes, should they start a new journey soon. The library held more recent maps versus those in the archives, but Chane suspected that she wanted to be alone with her thoughts. A little time on his own was not unwelcome, either, now that a calm had settled over the guild, though he wished she had not grown so quiet.

Upon their return the previous night, as promised, Hawes had brought them in and dealt with the council. An instant storm rose over Wynn's change of order. It seemed that simply changing robes was not all there was to this, and a petition process was required first. The arduous review and examination would be much the same as for any apprentice first applying for jouneyor status.

Fortunately, Premin Hawes had handled that, as well, or at least Chane assumed so. No one on the council, nor Domin High-Tower himself, had come at Wynn with any further requirements. Likely Hawes had simply told them it would be easier for her to keep an eye on Wynn if they waived any re-petitioning. Still, many an eye among the guild's populace would turn Wynn's way at the sight of her new midnight blue robe. On the surface, she would be treated like any other sage of rank, or so Hawes had proclaimed.

In Chane's view, Wynn's change of garb carried an extra warning not to tamper with a journeyor under the cold, watchful eyes of the premin of metaology. That was enough for now, but he wondered what hid beneath that protection. He would not forget the premin's reactions to Wynn's greater knowledge of the orbs and what lay within the scroll that he carried.

He kept pacing a circle around and around the empty courtyard.

The sight of Wynn in that dark robe still made him uncomfortable, but she and he were allowed back into the guild, though there had been no warm welcome. As soon as Hawes and Wynn uncovered any hints to the possible location of the orb of Spirit, he and Wynn would be gone again, and perhaps that was best.

As he walked, the soft clap of his boots seemed to echo too much. He paused at the strange sound, and only then did he hear the second set of steps. Raising his head, he followed the sound to the mouth of the gatehouse tunnel.

A tall figure came toward the courtyard from within the tunnel's darkness.

Chane wondered who could possibly be visiting here at this time of night. The obvious answer was Captain Rodian, though after the council's long meeting with Hawes, they had dismissed his guards and reopened the portcullis. Still, the captain had not been fully satisfied with what Wynn had told him about elves, assassins, and the escape of her hunted friends.

Something was not right about that figure inside the tunnel.

Rather than the hint of a red tabard or the glint of mail sleeves, the visitor's clothing was too drab and dark to make out. Then it drew nearer to the tunnel's inner end and the great braziers burning on the gatehouse's inner wall.

It was cloaked and hooded, with a bow in hand and a quiver of darkly feathered arrows protruding above its shoulder. Some other narrow bundle stuck out beside the quiver. Even when the figure stepped fully from the tunnel, Chane was not certain who it was. Then he looked at the bow again.

Osha paused as he entered the courtyard and brushed back his hood.

Flames in the iron brazier above him made his white-blond hair shimmer with flickers of fiery orange. Amber eyes in his long, dark face matched that same burning intensity as he stood there.

Chane had not missed the way Osha had looked at Wynn, and more so, the way she had responded. His hands shook slightly, lowering to his sides, but since returning to the guild, he had left his swords in his room. It was improper to walk in this place bearing weapons.

Osha was supposed to have rejoined the others and fled the city.

As Chane locked eyes with Osha, he knew there was only one reason why the young elf had not done so. . . .

Wynn.

EPILOGUE

On the third day at sea, as Magiere stood alone at the ship's bow rail, the Isle of Wrêdelyd came into sight. There they would have to find a ship heading south for the Suman Empire and its westernmost nation, called il'Dha'ab Najuum, the seat of the emperor and home to the Suman branch for the Guild of Sagecraft.

Magiere wondered if she should tell the others to pack up, but at a guess, the ship wouldn't make port for a while. Leesil was suffering his usual seasickness, and she didn't want to drag him from his bunk too soon. Besides, ministering to his moans and groans gave Leanâlhâm something to do while Chap kept an eye on both of them.

On the first night aboard, when Leanâlhâm had learned that Osha hadn't returned with Brot'an, Magiere had been forced to stop the girl from rushing for the skiff. After that, Leanâlhâm had fallen into a state of dark, silent sorrow. Regardless of how Brot'an matter-of-factly assured them all that Osha was alive and well, it did little to soothe the girl.

If Osha was all right, they all knew where he had gone: to Wynn. That Leanâlhâm's sorrow remained, even in believing he was safe, meant just as much.

Magiere wasn't certain how to keep the girl safe, let alone how to deal with Leanâlhâm's broken heart. She only hoped it went no further than that, and not as far as whatever had happened long ago between Osha and Wynn. But all this wasn't what had set Magiere—and Leesil and Chap—on edge concerning Brot'an's claim that Osha was all right.

Something else was missing in Brot'an's assurance.

What had Osha been doing that only Brot'an seemed to know? Had it been Brot'an who'd given Osha instructions that the young elf had disobeyed in part or whole?

By midday, the isle drew closer beyond the peninsula of the dwarfs, and Magiere turned to head below. She stopped short, flinching on instinct, in finding Brot'an standing silently off behind her.

She hadn't heard him approach, let alone come up on deck. How long had he been standing there watching her?

His hood was down, and his long, streaked hair blew about his face in the wind, whipping over the four scars that jumped his eye. For all of Leesil and Chap's hatred and mistrust of him, Magiere had been willing to give the master anmaglâhk some benefit of doubt. Brot'an was nothing if not capable. He had fought for her life before his own people and had helped Leesil get them all out of Calm Seatt.

No, Magiere had no issue with Brot'an's abilities, as long as a common purpose was shared between them. But what truly motivated him? For whatever war he might be waging against his own caste, he was still Anmaglâhk and a so-called shadow-gripper. Nothing changed that.

The sailors were busy prepping for harbor, and Brot'an stepped to the side rail a few paces off. Magiere realized this was the first moment that he and she had been completely alone together.

"What are you doing here?" she asked bluntly. "It's more than keeping me out of Most Aged Father's reach. What else drove you so far from your people? And why would you ever allow Leanâlhâm, let alone Osha, to come with you?"

He gripped the rail, leaning against it as if weary, and looked down on the water rushing past the hull. Magiere couldn't help noting how large his hands were for an an'Cróan, with long, tan fingers and thick sinews and a few age spots.

"What happened to you up in the cold wastes of the north?" he asked in turn. "Something about you—between you and Léshil—has changed, as well as in the majay-hì, Chap." Finally, he looked over at her. "What did you have to do to gain that orb of . . . Fire, was it?"

Magiere held her tongue.

This was something she hadn't told anyone. Even she and Leesil had spoken almost nothing about it, and Chap only watched her with as much suspicion as she now watched Brot'an.

The old assassin believed in doing whatever was necessary. Of all people, he might understand—or not. Was it possible his secret was even uglier than hers?

Sooner or later, one of them would make the first slip.

Perhaps he knew, as she did, that this might cause a fall, a shattering of an alliance from which they might not recover. And what had happened to Leanâlhâm's grandfather, that old healer, Gleann, with his biting sense of humor? What had driven Osha to follow Brot'an, considering the young one no longer looked with blind awe at the shadow-gripper? What had happened to make Brot'an start killing his own kind?

In the bargain he'd just tried to strike, his tale for hers, who would gain the advantage?

They now traveled with the mutual goal of finding the orb of Air and keeping it from falling into the wrong hands at any cost. But whose hands were worse than others by each of their separate judgments?

Magiere glanced again at the scars skipping over Brot'an's right eye. She wasn't ready to make such a deal with him. But she knew she couldn't avoid it much longer—not long at all.